ALSO BY JANN ARDEN

If I Knew Then:
Finding Wisdom in Failure and Power in Aging

Feeding My Mother:
Comfort and Laughter in the Kitchen as
a Daughter Lives with her Mother's Memory Loss

Falling Backwards:
A Memoir

THE BITTLEMORES

a novel

JANN ARDEN

Random House Canada

PUBLISHED BY RANDOM HOUSE CANADA

Copyright © 2023 Jann Arden
Interior art © 2023 Jann Arden

www.penguinrandomhouse.ca

Library and Archives Canada Cataloguing in Publication

Title: The Bittlemores / Jann Arden.
Names: Arden, Jann, author.
Identifiers: Canadiana (print) 20230222137 | Canadiana (ebook) 20230222153
    | ISBN 9781039008717 (hardcover) | ISBN 9781039008724 (EPUB)
Classification: LCC PS8601.R395 B58 2023 | DDC C813/.6—dc23

Lyrics to "You Needed Me" used by permission of Alfred Music. Words and
music by Randy Goodrum ©1975 (renewed) Chappell & Co., Inc. All rights
administered by Chappell & Co., Inc. All rights reserved.

Text design: Terri Nimmo
Jacket design: Terri Nimmo
Image credits: Marcia Jean Harris

Printed in Canada

10 9 8 7 6 5 4 3 2 1

Penguin
Random House
RANDOM HOUSE CANADA

For Nigel and Charlie and Ros and Ann—
and all my darling friends (you know who you are)

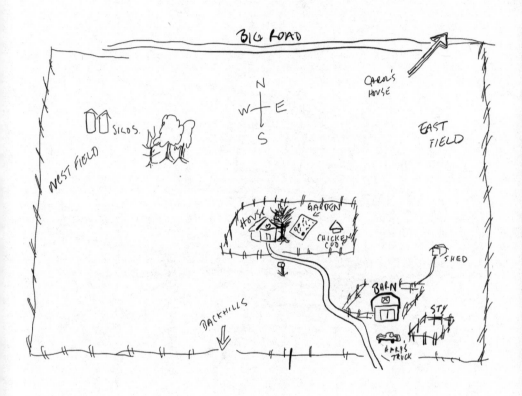

BIG ROAD

CARD'S HOUSE

N
W ┼ E
S

SILOS.

WEST FIELD

EAST FIELD

HOUSE GARDEN

CHICKEN COOP

SHED

BARN

STY

BACKHILLS

ARP'S TRUCK

Life on Bittlemore Farm

A Prologue

Harp Bittlemore is a horrible man, the third generation of Bittlemores to farm a miserable piece of land in the far northern parts of what everybody around here just calls the Backhills.

It wasn't always miserable.

Not so long ago it was lovely and green and full of so much good. Now it's 167 acres of mostly bare dirt and rock and clay and ancient, dead tree stumps that poke out everywhere like tombstones. On the other side of Harp's jagged barbed wire borders, things are still green and lush and teeming with life— at least they are in the middle of a Backhills spring. Ancient blue spruce trees thrust themselves out of the dark, rich earth straight and tall. Flowers bloom and birdsong winds its way around every long blade of grass and butterflies flit and fat black-and-yellow bumblebees hover. But most of what Harp barely manages to husband on his sorry piece of earth is misery.

He and his wife raise some straggly chickens, who at least know how to fend for themselves if given a chance. A man has got to eat, so Harp feeds a few scrawny pigs on very questionable, expired grocery store produce and some scant table scraps through the winter and spring, until he figures they're fat enough to be worth the swift flick of Harp's razor-sharp knife. He chops them into rustic chunks that his Mrs. Bittlemore stuffs into the freezer or to cure in oak barrels full of rock salt and a few sprigs of rosemary. If only his pigs could put on weight as easily as his wife of thirty-two years seems to do.

His dairy herd of twenty-five has dwindled to three worn-out cows, solemnly waiting their turn to be sent to slaughter. Harp often says, "Nothin' is so useless as a spent cow or a barren wife," though every time he does, his wife gives him a searing look that would set the last few strands of hair on his head ablaze if she had her way. His sad old cows have blistered bald patches and fresh burns on their hides from where Harp butts out his cigarettes while he's milking them: he doesn't want to set the barn on fire, after all. He's tugged so hard for so long their teats nearly drag on the ground. Nothing in the world is as sad as a sad cow. Harp catches his reflection in their big brown eyes on occasion. It takes him a moment to realize that the old man floating on that liquid globe is him.

The cows' lives depend on filling Harp's pail with enough milk to keep his wife happy, and to keep butter on the table. And they know it. These cows know a lot of unfortunate things about the Bittlemores.

Harp starts every morning with a hand-rolled cigarette and a mug of coffee that his wife brews thick and black for him. He uses it to wash down a half-dozen fried eggs, most of a pound of streaky bacon, and three thick slices of homemade bread and butter. He stares out the window at the chickens running around the yard, poking at the earth in search of a bug or a bit of forgotten grain, and doesn't think about anything. He doesn't read the paper or turn on the radio or try to make conversation. Or even say good morning to his granddaughter, Willa, when she comes down the stairs to get some breakfast before she heads for school. That useless granddaughter: another creature he's got to feed and about whom his feelings are not what they should be. Harp is never sure about how he should feel about anything. There is a blank in him that gets bigger every year, filled with white noise.

When he grunts and points his bony finger at the brown-stained mug in front of him, his wife waddles over and refills it with scorching hot coffee, then sets a plate of toast slathered in homemade strawberry jam in front of Willa, who nods in thanks, then chews without looking up. Mrs. Bittlemore sometimes thinks it is a thankless task looking after her family, especially that husband of hers. The days of engaging in any sort of cheerful breakfast conversation are long since over, but if she's honest, that suits her just fine.

After Harp finishes his breakfast, he pushes himself out of his exhausted-looking wooden chair, picks up his cigarette pack, and carries his mug and himself out through the screen door towards the barn.

The barn is barely red, the paint beaten away by the rain and the wind. It holds itself together by sheer force of will and a dozen or so two-by-fours Harp hammered into the sides. He keeps a few bottles of homebrew tucked behind some old apple crates stacked in the loneliest, darkest corner of the stable and before he feeds the animals or does the milking, he pours a generous amount of moonshine into his coffee. He tips the mug up and dumps the contents down his throat, enjoying the deep burn of the alcohol, and then he sets his mug on a post outside the barn door. His wife collects that mug without fail every single day.

Depending on how he feels after the animals are dealt with, he may or may not fix a hinge on a gate or straighten a fence post or wind up some stray pieces of barbed wire or move the bales in the haymow a little closer to the chute into the stable below. Sometimes, if he is particularly energetic, he wanders over to the water trough outside the barn and pumps in a few gallons of water. He doesn't bother to scoop the scum and the hundreds of dead beetles and flies off the top of it. Why would he when the cows have learned to push all the crap aside and suck the somewhat decent water up ever so slowly through their teeth? Either that or wait for a hard rain that may or may not fill up the slough in the East Field and quench their thirst there. Neither option is all that great.

As Harp muddles through his chores, he replaces the cigarette constantly dangling from his mouth with a wad of chewing tobacco, which makes him spit constantly, splattering his boots and pant legs. He wipes the brown liquid off his chin with the sleeve of his plaid shirt. He spits onto anything and everything—the side of the tractor or the door of the barn. He'll even shoot a glutinous stream towards a chicken shuffling past. If he is lucky enough to hit one, he'll let out a hoot and slap his knee. There is joy to be found in the misfortune of others—a dark, quivering joy. If Mrs. Bittlemore catches him spitting on her chickens, she cracks him on the head with her wooden spoon. Running that risk also gives

Harp some kind of a pleasure-filled rush, though he's not sure why.

On top of all the kinds of miserable bastard he is, Harp is cheap, though he convinces himself he's simply being "frugal"— a man who knows how to stretch a dollar. He feeds the pigs rotten Spanish onions and other leavings he scrounges from the Dutchman's grocery store in town. Whatever Dutchy throws out back every Wednesday, Harp collects in his truck. Sometimes it's squash or coffee grounds or eggshells. Sometimes it's potatoes or apples or expired boxes of crackers. Sometimes it's old bread or doughnuts or rancid yogurt or mouldy strawberries. Whatever is unfit for the customers, the pigs end up with in their bellies. The pigs don't dare complain, because at least it's something. Though both the pigs and Harp are now wary of the wayward Hutterite cabbages, having experienced the rapid blasts of diarrhea a feed of those once caused. After that, Harp decided that an off cabbage is never worth trying to save. Not even for a pig.

The cows get a half a bale of hay between the three of them. It's not enough, but they're grateful it's hay. Harp tried them on some rotten pig onions once, and they did reluctantly eat them up—the cows are always hungry, even when they are out to pasture, given the pasture is either a giant mud bath or a withered field of clay dust. But his wife said the onions made the milk taste and smell something terrible and threatened to stop baking.

Too lazy to do anything right anymore, Harp only milks the cows every second day, and the cows are also grateful for that mercy, even though their udders get quite achy. Harp seldom resists a cruel urge when it comes to them. On milking days he lingers like foul smoke in the stable after he's done, looking for some new way to torment them. Even if it's just hollering at them or spitting at them or throwing an old piece of shit at their faces, Harp revels in the small bit of power he wields over his cows. When he's had his fill of meanness, he sets the bucket of fresh milk on an old iron bench outside the stable door for his wife to retrieve. Another thing he never carries up to the house himself.

Women's work. Always has been, always will be. The only time a man should be in a kitchen is to be served his meals or to get his hair washed.

⌒

Mrs. Bittlemore, standing at around the five-foot mark, has the look of a barrel with legs sticking out of it. She has not seen her feet in half a dozen years, and it frustrates her no end. She thinks about dieting but gets overwhelmed at the thought of giving up all the things she loves: cakes and pies, and muffins and cookies, chocolate cream–filled Bavarian logs and cinnamon rolls and bread and butter—butter and bread especially. Between meals, that woman can put away a loaf and a half a day. Also, since Harp says he doesn't care if she loses an ounce, why should she?

One summer afternoon, he did call her a fat old bitch in front of Claire, the post lady, but he was drunk and didn't mean it. So Mrs. Bittlemore forgave him (after she cried off and on for three days). She always forgives him because that's what Jesus would do. And also because the two of them are in this life together, for worse (definitely not for better). Marriage isn't for the faint of heart. It's forever even if you're miserable quite a bit of the time.

Anyways, without Harp, who would she cook for? At

thirteen, her waiflike granddaughter hardly touches her food anymore, so the only audience for her tableful of offerings every night is her husband. Mind you, she is a little pissed off and somewhat mystified that the man eats his fill and more, yet he doesn't have an ounce of fat on his body. All that good food just falls out of his arse like it doesn't want to stay inside such a miserable soul—the man could eat non-stop for a month and be thinner at the end of it. But cooking still brings Mrs. Bittlemore a sense of calm and self-worth. It's the one thing she is able to do without Harp telling her how to do it better. It's the only time he minds his own business with no complaining. It's the only time he seems the least bit peaceful.

When his belly is full, he doesn't even seem to notice Mrs. Bittlemore's habit of stepping out the kitchen door to leave a foamy dish of cream on the step for Orange Cat. Mrs. Bittlemore would be in trouble if Harp knew she was feeding that barn cat, good mouser though she is. He doesn't want the flea-ridden beast anywhere near him or his house. He doesn't want any kind of pet. Not a dog or a rabbit or a fish or a bird or a turtle— and most certainly not a filthy barn cat.

Orange Cat has been at the end of Harp's boot enough times to know she should cut a wide swath around him where she can. Over the years he's managed to kill whole litters of her kittens without even a hint of a reprimand from his wife, even though Mrs. Bittlemore is fond of Orange Cat—one of the few creatures she is fond of. She does try to stand up for her. "Don't you be messing around with that cat, Harp Bittlemore," she'll say. "You've got plenty of other things to get rid of around here, like those damn moles in my garden!"

In Harp's mind, it is only going to be a matter of time before he gets that bloody cat, no matter what his wife has to say about it. Someday it will end up skinned and nailed to the side of his barn like the coyotes and the cougars and the badgers and the skunks and the weasels and the sneaky-bastard-of-an-egg-stealing red fox—joining the mosaic of pelts that covers the barnboards like some sort of death quilt. Harp often stands in front of his masterpiece after an evening of good food and drink with his thumbs shoved deeply into his front pockets, staring like he's in a fine upscale art gallery, then spits tobacco juice onto the cracked dirt in satisfaction.

one

ON THE MORNING THE FINAL unravelling of Harp Bittlemore began, the cows peered at their nemesis from the open doors of the stable. It hadn't been a milking day—a blessing. They longed to get out into the faint beams of sunlight in their pasture in the East Field, but they didn't want to risk walking past him.

The cows had hoped he would simply drink his funny drink and stumble back up to the house. But there he stood, right in the middle of the barnyard, staring back at them, puffing away on a cigarette. He blew out a big cloud of smoke, then spat onto the ground and staggered ten steps over to an old blue pickup truck that was sunk into the ground like a coffin, plunked himself in the passenger seat and looked out across the field, where nothing but scraggly bits of spring grass was growing.

The cows were endlessly perplexed by how one rickety old man instilled so much fear in them. They outweighed Harp by thousands of pounds. All they would have to do was lean hard on his skeletal frame—pin him up against a fence or the stable wall and squeeze the air out of his lungs—and that would be the end of all this nonsense. But they couldn't bring themselves to do it. Funny how fear and intimidation work together to form the perfect little bundle of paralyzing terror.

The truck hadn't run for fifteen years, but this skeleton of rusting metal was Harp's second-favourite place in the world. (The first was at the kitchen table, ready to eat, with his white-bone elbows plunked down, fork and knife clenched in respective fists.) He kept a few girlie magazines in the glove compartment, along with another jar of his moonshine, an old buck knife and a faded black-and-white photograph of family he barely remembered from a childhood whose happiness he'd definitely forgotten.

The truck had come to its final resting place right in front of the gate the cows had to pass through in order to get out to pasture. Harp had never thought to move it. Every day, the cows debated as to who was going to try to scoot through that gate first, and this day was no different. (It's hard for cows to draw straws, being that they have no hands. They tend to debate for hours to decide the smallest of things.)

Harp pulled the whisky from the busted-open glove compartment, screwed off the lid and sipped it as quietly as a snake. Soon he floated off into a warm drunk daze in the comfort of the ripped pleather seat. If life had disappointed Harp Bittlemore, you'd never know it. He acted like he held the keys to a kingdom in which he was the supreme ruler of every living thing. The cows watched as his eyes slowly closed. If they ran like hell, they might make it past—they just might.

Berle was the natural leader among Harp's three surviving dairy cows. She was the rebellious one too, never able to accept that this was their lot in life. She was always complaining to the others about how much Harp hurt her every single time he milked her and how Harp's hands were as cold as ice. Even in the still, slow heat of summer, his hands were as frozen as his heart.

Harp didn't believe that any "beast" had a soul, and certainly not one of his useless cows. They were simply property. He kept them fed, watered and housed. What more could a man do? Send 'em on a tropical holiday? He didn't understand why his granddaughter loved the cows (though the answer was simple: the only daily kindness she could rely on were the tender looks bestowed upon her by her fellow sufferers). When Willa stared at him reproachfully after he'd given one of the cows a boot, he'd trot out a few Bible sayings he'd been forced to memorize as a teenager, especially "Men have dominion over the fowl and the hooved things." Which confused Willa no end because Harp never went to church.

Berle dragged a breath into her lungs and let the words sigh out like air from a punctured tire. "I can't take one more day of this. We've got to get out of here. We need to make a run for the Big Road again before he kills us all . . ."

The youngest cow, Dally—calling her young was a stretch, given that she was fifteen—had heard all this many times before, and mildly protested. "We can't r-r-really run, Berle. When's the last time you r-r-r-ran?" Dally was missing part of one of her ears because Harp had cut it off after she lost her balance when she was being milked for the first time. She'd lurched onto Harp's foot and snapped the bone in his big toe.

She certainly didn't do it on purpose, but you couldn't tell Harp that. He'd wrestled her head underneath his arm and sliced a chunk of her ear off as quick as you like. Berle had wanted to kill Harp right then and there, but these types of things take planning.

Now Berle stared at Dally with an eyebrow pulled up as far as a cow's eyebrow can go. In that expression was everything all three of them knew about their situation. The one thing people don't realize about cows is that they know what's happening at any given moment. Their knowledge is deep and detailed. Their memories are long and steady. They've learned over decades from their mothers and grandmothers and great-grandmothers that every couple of years they are bred to have a calf so they'll keep on making milk. On the Bittlemore farm, if cows didn't keep making milk, they disappeared. When they got too old or too tired or too hopeless to be bred, they were sent to slaughter. It was that simple.

You'd think that being pregnant would be a joy-filled time for a cow, but for them it was full of a quiet, dark sorrow. It was no secret after all these years that Harp would only let their newborns stay for two measly days and then he'd hoist them up into his sinewy arms and throw them into the back of his truck and take them away to someplace they never returned from. You could hear the calves bawl for a mile down the road, then came something worse: silence. For months afterwards, the cows would be lost in a grief so heavy that it was hard to put one hoof in front of the other. While they didn't have a way of keeping track of years, Berle, Dally and Crilla, the oldest and scrawniest of them, knew that Harp would likely be bringing the steel canister full of bull semen to them soon. And if he didn't, perhaps that was even worse news.

Dally insisted, "Well, w-w-we can't run! That's a-a-all I am saying. Last time we t-t-tried it, we didn't make it halfway to the f-f-f-far fence."

Of all the cows, persistently anxious and stuttering Dally was the most scared of Harp, and the most worried about bad things happening, because they usually did. "The l-l-last time didn't g-g-go so good, did it?"

No, it hadn't, Berle had to admit. All three of the cows had got caught up in the barbed wire of the East Gate. Berle hadn't really taken into account their size, which became an issue when they tried to squeeze under the fence. The gap had looked bigger to her than it was.

Dally was still going on. "The Big Road is a-a-a mile away. It hasn't g-g-gotten any closer!"

Berle knew that too, from her first attempt after Harp had left the gate open. She'd been young and fit enough that she'd sprinted all the way to the Big Road, no problem. She thought she was in luck when she saw a neighbour's pickup truck parked on the soft shoulder, but when she tried to clamber into the back, she broke the tailgate off. When Harp found her, he stood there scratching his head, clearly dumbfounded that a cow would even consider jumping into the back of a truck.

Looking back at it now, Berle realized she'd been too young and stupid. She'd simply reacted, she hadn't planned. If she'd managed to get herself into the back of that truck, where would she have gone? Nowhere. That's where.

And the consequences of her escape attempt had been harsh. Harp had to pay Leonard Bergen $125 to fix his tailgate. When Harp got Berle home, he'd smashed her half a dozen times with a rake and then locked her up in the Cold House where Mrs. Bittlemore kept the butchered pigs she was curing.

Berle had hated being imprisoned in such a small, gloomy space, especially when it contained three barrels holding three chopped-up pigs she had known personally.

Harp left her there for a week, with no food and very little water, but that wasn't the worst of Berle's problems—he didn't milk her. Her udder stretched like a giant water balloon, causing her so much pain she could barely think about anything else. Thankfully, it hadn't burst, although Berle experienced moments when she wished it had. Dying from an exploded udder wouldn't have been the worst way to go. When Harp finally let her out, his wife insisted he call in the vet to treat the mastitis that was Harp's own damn fault and his wife knew it.

He was sleepless for weeks, thinking of all the things he could have done with the money he had to pay the vet. His ire actually made his temples hurt and planted seeds of revenge in his shrivelling brain. The next time this goddamned disobedient cow wouldn't be so fortunate, and he wouldn't care what his wife thought. Luckily for Berle, it was soon time to breed her again, so Harp decided not to send her to the mythical concrete house. In the few milkless months that followed, things were somewhat peaceful, giving Berle some time to reflect on what had gone wrong and to figure out what she was going to do whenever the right opportunity arose.

Getting all three of them to the Big Road was key. The Big Road was the nearest thing to a highway the Backhills had. It was really only a gravel road that had been coated with thick black tar that everyone assumed was pavement but wasn't, the proof being the way it melted under your sandals in the summer. Despite some setbacks—and the odd cringeworthy recollection of the failed escape—Berle's confidence grew a little bit more as every day passed. In her heart she felt certain that if they got to the Big Road, it would lead them to the Black Diamond Valley, which shimmered in her mind, part dream, part myth. There, sweet grass grew as tall as a horse and crystal-clear brooks raced along in the bright sun and no old monsters tormented your every waking hour.

Mind you, all she really knew about the valley came from the stories that Orange Cat liked to tell. The barn cat insisted that she had seen the promised land briefly as a kitten and she wouldn't stop going on about how peaceful it was.

Orange Cat could talk the leg off the lamb of God. And brag? She could brag like no other fur-covered feline on the planet. Maybe she'd turned out so boastful because of her rough start in life. She and her mother and three brothers had been chucked into the ditch at the side of the Big Road in an old cardboard box that had originally been home to a toaster oven. "We'll just have to make the best of it," Orange Cat's orange-and-black mother had said, and she decided that she would carry her kittens, one by one, to safety in the Black Diamond Valley.

But as in every good tall tale, the night suddenly turned cold and dark, and the valley was much farther away than she'd hoped. It was impossible to move all her kittens without becoming lost in an unforgiving, unknown place. When she caught sight of a faint light over the western ridge, she headed towards it, hoping to find shelter, feed her meowing, hungry babies and get some sleep before they completed their journey.

That faint light off in the distance turned out to be the outside light on the Bittlemore barn. Talk about bad luck. Being dumped in a ditch in a cardboard box was bad enough, but then to seek refuge on the worst farm in the county and fall into the hands of the worst person? That wasn't bad luck, it wasn't any kind of luck at all. It was the start of a nightmare.

One wrong turn in life can change everything. One seemingly insignificant moment can alter the whole game. Soon enough Orange Cat, clever and quick and brave and champion mouser, was the only one of her original family left, and her mother's and brothers' little hides were tacked to the side of Harp Bittlemore's barn.

Every cow knew that you should never trust a feline. But Berle trusted Orange Cat enough that she never bothered to point out that her own story proved she had never seen the Black Diamond Valley. Berle didn't want to hurt Orange Cat's feelings, and besides, Berle needed an ally, someone to believe in. She liked that cat, maybe because the cat wanted Harp punished as much as she did. Orange Cat could have picked up and left the farm a hundred different times over, but she didn't. She wouldn't go, she said, because she didn't want to abandon the cows. What Orange Cat didn't say was that she didn't just want Harp Bittlemore punished, no, she had vowed not to leave the farm until she'd killed the murderer of her mother, her brothers and six litters of her kittens, and she couldn't very well kill Harp on her own. Thinking about killing a human being is a far cry from killing a human being. Harp was sly and heartless and those kinds of people don't go down without a fight.

Berle sometimes dreamed of doing Harp in too, but mostly she fantasized about how, if they just made it to the road, they would be able to hitch a ride with a kind-hearted human who happened to be going by in a vehicle big enough to fit three large dairy cows. And one Orange Cat. When you're desperate, dreams are the only things that keep you from giving up.

To get us all to the Black Diamond Valley! To keep at least one calf or maybe even a set of twins! Oh, what a dream, what a dream!

Berle lifted her head and mooed into the sun-streaked air.

Harp, already drunk as all get-out, cracked an eyelid and glared at them all, crowded together in the stable doorway. He figured he had a year or so left in those old cows, and that would be the end of it.

Too old to breed again. No guarantee any of them would pop a calf.

Too bloody expensive and too much damn trouble keeping dairy cows.

Could buy milk just as good, maybe better, in town.

Swig of 'shine. "Ahhhhhh."

Mother will just have to make do.

Getting too old to be milking cows anyway.

Harp shut his eyes and drifted off again, just as Dally quavered, "Maybe s-s-s-someday he'll let me k-keep a little one, right, Berle? He's gonna need a new milker s-s-s-sooner rather than later. If he let me keep one, it wouldn't be so b-b-b-bad around here." Dally looked up to Berle. If Berle said it was going to be okay, it was going to be okay.

But Berle was through with pretending anything was going to be okay. "Every time I look at your ear, I still feel furious," she said. "I'm not going to hang around here waiting for that man to decide our fate or mutilate another one of us. I have other plans."

"But where can three big b-b-b-black-and-white cows h-h-hide in this world?" Dally wondered. "We wouldn't get as far as the East Gate and he'd sh-sh-shoot us all down. Wouldn't he, Crilla?"

Crilla had kept her silence so far, chewing her cud as best she could as she listened to what seemed to her to be another pointless conversation. Harp had kicked her in the jaw last spring and broken half of her teeth, which now looked like a picket fence that had had a fight with a bowling ball and lost.

He'd kicked her because he was drunk and she was within striking distance: that was all the excuse he needed. Berle was surprised Crilla was still alive at all, given that, as she sometimes joked, she didn't make milk anymore, she made sour cream.

"We've been through this a thousand times," she said at last. "What's the point? This is our life, and we have each other. At least for now."

"He'd ch-ch-chop us up and-and f-feed us to the pigs, wouldn't he, Crilla. I can't think of anything worse than being gobbled up by a p-p-pig."

Crilla let out a long sigh and went back to trying to ignore them both.

Finally, Berle nudged Dally gently on the nose. "I'm not gonna get us killed," she said. "I would never let Harp feed you to the pigs either."

Crilla mumbled something under her breath.

"What was that?" Berle swished her tail back and forth, scattering the flies on her bony hips.

"You heard me, Berle." Crilla chewed her cud a little more, then finished her thought. "You're gonna end up in the out-house pit if you don't cut this nonsense out. That's where he'll put you."

two

MARGARET KNEW THE SECOND ROBERT clambered off her, already panicked and filled with shame, that they'd stepped into a black cloud of misfortune. For three weeks they'd been meeting secretly to exchange kisses in a small grove of barely alive trees between their farms. Tentative pecks at first, trying to figure out each other's mouths like there was treasure buried just beneath their tongues. In the end it wasn't Robert who pushed Margaret into committing a mortal sin, it was Margaret who pushed him. She needed him to tarnish her somehow, ruin her so she could wound her parents. Maintaining her purity seemed to be all they thought about anymore, and Margaret felt smothered with a mountain of rules. At fourteen, she hated the Bittlemores, she couldn't bear to think of them as her parents. Instead, they became something she just had to endure, a fact of her stunted life, and then something she had to escape. Robert was simply an innocent hormonal boy caught in the crossfire.

Thinking about it now, almost fifteen years after that moment with Robert, the old line about swallowing poison and expecting the person you hate to die came to Margaret's mind. We think we're punishing the people who deserve it, but we're really only punishing ourselves.

Poor Robert had been an innocent, blindsided by his affection for her, and she had taken advantage of him, though she'd only realized that long after she herself was safe. Now she also knew how crazy her revenge plot had been. But at the time, she hadn't been able to think of how else to punish her parents for terrorizing her both physically and mentally, along with torturing the animals she loved. On that barren wasteland of a farm, her innocent body was the one small thing in her power. Bringing shame on the Bittlemores by getting pregnant seemed as good as any a place to start. If she ruined herself, she would put an end to them parading her around town like some kind of perfect golden child. She would shame them so deeply they would never want to set foot outside the farm again.

Telling them she was pregnant had been sweet. Margaret knew they'd be angry, but not even she was prepared for the barrage of vitriol that came at her like a derailing train. Harp lurched at her with an explosion of words that would have made a hardened criminal blush, with his bloated wife right by his side, screaming all the nastiness she could think of at the top of her lungs. Spittle sprayed through the air like an acid rain. They chastised her in stereo to the point that the furniture lifted off the floor and the dishes rattled on the shelves.

Margaret let their noise wash over her, and it felt good. The pain of their disappointment made her feel warm inside. She didn't look at their faces, she kept her head down, searching for a crack in the floor she could squeeze herself into. Margaret's parents were ashamed, ruined. Mission accomplished.

~

Even as a toddler, Margaret had never called her mother anything but "Mrs. B." That's what Mrs. B wanted to be called and she drilled it into Margaret's head, pointing to her bloated chest and spelling out the letters one at a time: "M-I-S-S-U-S-B. Missus B." As if a baby could spell.

She told Margaret, over and over again, that a baby girl like her was all she and Papa Bittlemore had ever hoped for in the whole wide world. One day, like a miracle, that little baby girl had just showed up—a living, breathing gift, wrapped up in a blanket in her own little basket. It wasn't until Margaret was seven years old that she asked Mrs. B what the actual real story was.

Margaret, already knowing at that tender age that she had to ask questions carefully for fear of the resulting explosions, carefully inquired, "Where do babies come from?"

"Well, in your case . . . you were, well, you were given to us by an angel."

"An angel? Like from outer space?"

"Of course not from outer space! Listen, you're still too young to know all the silly details, Margaret. When you grow up, you'll understand where babies come from. All you need to know right now is that you were given to us by God."

God must have had a hell of a sense of humour, Margaret thought, or maybe He believed in the sins of the parents being visited upon their children, because nothing ever felt right between her and the Bittlemores. Every day with them was full of an indescribable uneasiness. She remembered how often she would scan their faces for any sign of a resemblance, some tiny glimmer of recognition. There weren't any. Harp was all bones and knuckles and cartilage, his skin as red as a mosquito bite. Mrs. B's cheeks were round, and she had close-set brown eyes, slanted like almonds. She was short and stout and her head was disproportionally small, sparsely covered with greasy strands of what was once maybe auburn hair. She was also as white as a person could be without being translucent.

Margaret was the colour of a freshly dug potato, her hair as thick and black as a starless Backhills night. It was bone straight. Resisting all her efforts to will some curl into it, her hair always looked like she had just dunked her head into a pool of Harp's motor oil.

By the time Margaret was ten years old, she had pretty much concluded that she didn't "belong" to them any more than she belonged to Sophia Loren. By thirteen, she was so miserable that her favourite daydream was them dying in a fantastically violent accident. She replayed one scenario over and over in her head. Margaret pictured Harp falling ass over teakettle into the septic tank, which was filled up with his very own shit. Rather, his shit and her mother's shit and her own shit too. To make it even more thrilling, when Mrs. B tried in vain to rescue her husband, he pulled her down with him. Margaret imagined their mouths gasping for air as their heads sank underneath the crap—the looks on their faces, all contorted and disgusted. And then they disappeared, a few bubbles coming to the surface in helpless surrender. She made sure to conjure up her mother's fat hand rising through the clumps of decomposing toilet paper and human waste in a final attempt to save herself. That was Margaret's favourite part of the whole fantasy and it was as gratifying as anything she'd ever felt in her entire life.

They were horrible people. They were mercilessly cruel to her, mentally and physically, and it became more and more difficult for her to exist even in the small fantasy world she created for herself. They were petty and careless with all the animals on the farm, needlessly mean and inhumane. Every time Margaret managed to get up the nerve to stand up for the cows, or the hens, or the terrified pigs being led to slaughter, Harp would thwack his old leather belt across the backs of her legs until big red welts appeared. It was always for her own good. "The whole damn works of you gotta be kept in line," he'd shout.

When she was little, this just was her world: a hellscape of uncertainty and hardship. The long days and weeks and months on the farm bled into each other, a childhood mired in chaos. And then, one day, something happened—it was as though a light shone down from the heavens above—Margaret was finally old enough to be sent off to school! And on top of that little miracle, she discovered that, contrary to her parents' opinion, she was excellent at many academic things. She was also quick to discover that all kids weren't treated like she was. Some kids' parents were actually nice. In fact, most of the kids' parents were thoughtful and supportive, and most of the teachers were genuinely interested in children and wanted to see them succeed.

Life at home wore away at Margaret's diminishing resolve. Any headway she managed to make at school, any hope that moved into her heart about just maybe being happy, soon moved out. The outcome in her head was always the same: she would be stuck in the same place with the same two people and the same ending until she couldn't face it anymore, and so she was willing to ruin herself to ruin them. Only she didn't really ruin them, she just handed them another hostage—a hostage she created with her own stupidity.

Fifteen years after that moment with the smitten farm boy, lying in the dirt beneath the trees, she still lived with the consequences of that decision to humiliate her parents, if she could even call what she had made for herself a life.

~

Margaret loved school more than anything in the world, except maybe the cows. Having to leave behind her books and her desk and the bustling, conversation-filled hallways was heartbreaking. Her last day in the classroom was spent just before she started to show. She was never able to figure out how her parents pulled the wool over everybody's eyes. Especially given that, as far as she knew, hardly anyone in the Backhills talked to her parents. In fact, people went out of their way to avoid them. But Harp and Mrs. B had worked the rumour mill hard to set the stage for her impending absence from the Backhills school.

Maybe a week earlier, her best friend, Wilhelmina, had told her that she'd overheard some kids whispering that the wife of a close relative of the Bittlemore family had died in a car wreck and that Margaret was going to be sent to stay with the widower to take care of the children. "That can't be true, can it?" she'd asked Margaret as she waited with her for the bus home. "I've never even heard you mention any relatives."

"Of course it isn't true," Margaret replied. "Where do people get this stuff?"

Then another girl, Lilly Swisher, told their mutual English teacher that she'd heard that Margaret had a rare form of cancer and only had a few months to live. Also not true, but in a way Margaret felt that she did indeed have a rare, incurable kind of cancer, considering that Harp and Mrs. B were so malignant. Here she was keeping a real-life secret from the world, hiding the truth from her best friend and the boy who got her pregnant, and all these ridiculous fake stories were flying around. It didn't make any sense. What was happening? She didn't have a clue—until she did have a clue. How could she not have known?

While she was staring mournfully out the window of the bus as it was pulling out of the school parking lot, she saw Harp's old truck turn in and park, and then Mrs. B climbed out and headed into the school. She only found out after the fact that Mrs. B had met with the principal and told him that she and Harp had come into a windfall of sorts, and they could finally afford to give Margaret the life she deserved. They had decided to send her to a fancy private boarding school in France. "It's a real opportunity for her!" she'd said. "Margaret has always wanted to learn French and study—er, fashion and take gourmet cooking lessons."

Mr. Bittlemore had sat beside her silently with his hat in his trembling hand. If he made even the slightest attempt to chime in, Mrs. B kicked him in his bony ankle. She threw him a look that implied further violence should he try to interrupt again.

Why the principal swallowed any of it, Margaret never understood. He must surely have been one of the most gullible people on the planet. But the principal did swallow it, every drop of the lie. After Margaret's bus pulled out of the parking lot, she never went back to school again. That had been her last sort of happy day. If only she could have gone to Paris or Toronto or Las Vegas or even Lloydminster, for God's sake, she gladly would have. Instead, she spent the next five months locked in her tiny bedroom waiting for a baby to be born that she'd only conceived to punish her parents. Cut off from her classmates, from her animal friends and from dear Wilhelmina, she was alone and uncertain of what was to come next. During that first week of imprisonment—it was all a blur—her parents made her write a letter to her best friend, saying that she wasn't dying of cancer or off babysitting unknown cousins, but on her way to school in France. The Bittlemores hovered over their daughter, making sure the letter sounded exactly the way they wanted it to. No secret hidden messages. No codes. No chance for a hidden SOS.

That Saturday a frantic, breathless Wilhelmina showed up at the farmhouse kitchen door, letter in hand. She banged on the rickety frame and cupped her hands over her eyes to peer in through the filthy window. Being spotted, Mrs. Bittlemore reluctantly answered the door. While she blathered on about the glorious opportunity they'd suddenly been able to provide for their daughter and shouldn't Wilhelmina be happy for her friend, Harp sat upstairs on the bed beside Margaret, making sure she stayed put and didn't utter a sound. For the first time, Margaret felt real fear—something in her broke. She could hear her friend's pleading voice but couldn't make out any of the words. She could hear her mother pontificating like someone running to be prime minister. Harp's grizzled hand dug into her thigh just hard enough to keep her from calling out.

⌣

Having a baby was worse than Margaret thought it would be, which meant worse than anything in the world that could possibly happen to a human being.

It was like the pains became a sound, a palpable rumble

that peeled pieces of skin off her body an inch at a time. She'd known labour was going to be bad, but she didn't think she would be lying there wishing she was dead.

In her deluded way, Mrs. B had tried to prepare her for the birth, warning her that at the end she was going to have to bear down like she was about to take the world's biggest crap.

But it was nothing like that. Instead, Margaret felt like she was ripping in two, the pressure on her stomach so intense it was like a cow was sitting on her. Her hip bones felt as though they were about to break in the socket. She heard screams bouncing off the walls of her bedroom and it took a blessed moment of stillness to realize that they were coming from her own mouth. When each wave hit, she felt her eyes roll back in her head and her bowels push up into her lungs. In those moments, she really did want to die. She wanted them all to die—herself, and the baby, and her diabolical parents. Death was a fitting punishment. Margaret had put herself into this terrible situation with her own anger and hatred. No going back now.

The pain made her delirious. The walls moved in and out like they were alive. She pictured herself catching on fire and burning the whole place down—there would only be a scorched piece of earth where the house once stood.

At the first contraction, Mrs. B had made Margaret drink a horrible concoction of herbs and plants and lord knows what else to "help speed things along." Margaret drank down every drop because she wanted it to be over and done with. Her mother kept telling her to breathe, the only advice she seemed to have while her daughter lay there begging her to make it all stop.

At that point, Margaret hadn't been outside her bedroom for nearly half a year. She hadn't had grass between her toes or a ray of sunlight on her face, she'd just paced the floor and counted the hours. For weeks at a time, she couldn't sleep. She couldn't concentrate long enough to read or even think a clear, coherent thought. There was only nothingness followed by waves of anxiety. Even though she was alone, she was never alone. Mrs. B was always there, forcing her to eat tepid porridge and greasy chicken sandwiches and bag after bag of overripe oranges, all of which made her want to gag. Eventually she realized the only way she was going to get out of her prison of a bedroom was to give birth to this thing inside her and start running.

It seemed a straightforward plan: HAVE BABY. RUN.

Margaret hadn't been anticipating the stitches, though. She didn't know which was worse, the pain she endured as the thread wove itself in and out between her torn flesh or the look on Mrs. B's face as she peered between her legs.

She was a grotesque figure: a wobbly tub of fatness, perpetually sweaty, mean and severely unhappy. This was a woman who wanted her daughter to share her misery. As Margaret inched closer and closer to her due date, her mother had started to sleep in a large chair she'd got Harp to haul up and set beside the bed. There was barely enough room for Margaret's bed in the little room, never mind an overstuffed chair.

On her many sleepless nights, Margaret had studied every line on Mrs. B's face and wondered, how could she possibly be this woman's daughter? Maybe every teenager feels that way about their parents. Maybe all the anger and mistrust was normal. But Margaret had nobody to ask. As a very young child, she would wander out to the barn and talk to the cows. The sweet, docile things had always been more like family to her than her parents. They never talked back, of course, but they were very intent listeners. There was something about how those cows tilted their heads and blinked their eyes while she was talking to them that made her feel like they understood her. They'd watched over her from the time she could crawl. Harp would madly shoo them away—arms flailing, hollering, "Get the hell outta here!"—but they always came back, doing their best, she thought, to keep an eye on her.

When she was in labour, she heard them mooing close to the house, long, deep bellows that were the only comforting thing she remembered about any of it. She hated the thought of leaving them behind. She hated that she wouldn't be there anymore to try to keep Harp from acting out one of his spontaneous rampages. Even though she was small and no match for Harp's violence, Margaret tried with all her might to divert his rage, buying the cows some time to get out of harm's way. That's how she realized there was still a tiny little bit of something good inside her.

But she had to run.

So after Margaret had pushed that strange, tiny, innocent being out of her body and endured Mrs. B's brutal stitch-up job, she pretended to collapse in exhaustion—basically playing dead. It didn't feel too far off her actual condition. Margaret's body felt separate from her mind. Everything ached. She waited, and waited, until Mrs. B went downstairs, believing her daughter and granddaughter were both sound asleep.

Listening hard to make sure she wasn't about to turn around and come back, Margaret slowly sat up, and then edged her legs over the side of the bed and stood. Looking down at her baby wrapped in a blanket at the foot of the bed, she bent to pick her up. Stopping herself, she quickly backed away and moved towards the window. She didn't know much, but she knew that she couldn't risk being close to her baby. She was afraid that at any moment she would change her mind—and stay.

She was too young. At going-on fifteen years old, she was still a baby herself, although on this night she felt like she was a hundred. She couldn't stay and fight it out with her parents. She knew she'd sooner die. Running was what she had to do. But she was haunted by that little face. It—she—the baby looked like a little peeled apple. Black eyelashes and heart-shaped lips. No, no, no. She had to make a move. Margaret could hear her parents downstairs, mumbling, arguing, chairs scraping back and forth on the wooden floor. She was running out of time.

She slipped into her clothes—every move hurt. Her mind was racing. Her heart was pounding. She felt nauseous. She rummaged through some of her old school supplies stuffed into her dresser, looking for something to write with. Finding a red felt marker, she wrote one last message to her parents on the wall. Red wouldn't have been Margaret's first choice of pen colour, but it seemed fitting considering what had just gone on in that dingy room. She stole one more tender glance at the baby, then opened the window to a hail of rain and a crash of thunder—it didn't surprise her in the least that a storm was tearing holes in the sky to make everything that much more dramatic. She crawled out of the small, round window, stepped lightly across the porch roof and down the ladder that by some miracle Harp had propped at the side. As she bolted into the night, she felt blood trickling down her legs. It made her faint and breathless to think of how much she might be bleeding. She hoped to God she wouldn't pass out before she got to the Big Road.

Nothing seemed real. This couldn't be her life.

⌒

The trees were like monsters waving their long arms at her, trying to grab her hair and pull her back. Lighting flashed across the sky like giant spider legs, illuminating the barn and the ramshackle picket fence around the house. Rain started to bucket down as she panted across to the gate and into the field. The cows came charging through the yard like they were running interference for her, and then shadowed her all the way across the field, protecting her from being spotted by Harp or Mrs. B.

When she crawled through the barbed wire fence and into the ditch, the cows came to a stop, then stood there in the rain, watching her. She came back for a moment to rub each warm nose. As she turned and made her way up the gravel shoulder and onto the road, they bellowed thick and low into the dark night sky, like they were saying goodbye. She couldn't look at them or she'd start to cry.

That's when she began to run, and she kept running until she couldn't hear them anymore, just the sound of her breath heaving in and out and the rain pounding on her soaking wet jacket. Finally, she had to stagger to a stop at the side of the road, hood pulled up and shoulders hunched over, hands around her knees, panting. It felt like she was crying her head off, but in the rain it was hard to know what was a tear and what was not. Then she thought she heard a baby cry, and straightened to listen, fading in and out of herself. So exhausted and so awake, listening to nothing but rain.

She waited for Harp to come after her. She waited to hear police sirens or her name being shouted or the howling of somebody's hounds. She felt relieved not to hear any of them, but at the same time strangely sad that nobody cared enough to come looking for her. If they'd found her, she might have even gone home again. If she did, maybe they would let her keep the baby. Did she want to keep the baby? Her brain was folding in on itself.

It was an avalanche of confusion.

Margaret crouched down at the side of the road, and stayed there—for how long, she had no idea. Eventually, she stood, took a deep, burning breath and began to move slowly down the Big Road.

~

After a long, strange series of events, Margaret eventually made it to safety. It took a while for her to find her feet, then calm her heart enough to start writing letters to her daughter. That took some doing. Writing to an infant was a lot harder than she thought it would be, and her first letter took her ten months to compose. After countless failed attempts, Margaret decided it would be best if she thought of it like a secret diary she was writing for herself. Then she had to figure out how to send the letter so that her parents wouldn't be able to trace it to her doorstep. She sent the next one only three months later, and then another at the beginning of every month from then on. The letters were always part apology, part promise. She wanted her baby to know that even though she'd left her with those people, she loved her. More than all the stars in the sky, she was loved.

And they always ended with the same vow. "As soon as I can take care of you, darling one, I'm coming to get you. Don't despair."

three

LIFE CAN TURN ON a dime. What seems perfectly peaceful one minute can be turned upside down the next. That's what happened to the Bittlemore family farm when Harp's beloved Pops died, suddenly and unexpectedly.

He was felled by the tiniest, most insignificant thing, a tap on the head, it might just as well have been a feather brushing against his temple. Pops and his two boys—Harp and his little brother, Parker, nicknamed Puck—had been out in the corral separating their bull, Tilt-a-Whirl, from the cows, a routine job they'd done dozens of times. Another day on the farm. As Pops approached, the formidable black bull turned his head ever so slightly to avoid a persistent fly. Such a benign thing, a fly. The horn grazed the left side of Pops's temple where wisps of grey hairs were just beginning to come in. He dropped dead on the spot.

The boys didn't realize what had happened at first. They looked at each other and laughed, thinking that their dad was just fooling around as he often did, playing one of his funny jokes. Puck even kicked his dad playfully in the bum, saying, "Quit messing around, Pops!" When Pops didn't move an inch, the boys ran around screaming, calling for help.

Then Harp dropped to his knees and cradled his father's head on his lap while his little brother ran up to the house to fetch their mother. Tilt-a-Whirl stood placidly by the gate, unaware of what he'd just done. The smallest trickle of blood ran down Pops's temple. It looked like nothing at all, a scratch at best, but just beneath that scratch, the blood was bursting into every corner of Pops Bittlemore's brain. It was one of those freak accidents that shouldn't have happened in a million years, but it did, and it tore the entire family into unrecognizable pieces.

For months afterwards, Harp, who was thirteen going on fourteen and deep in the throes of a very awkward puberty, overheard people in town gossiping about the tragedy. They whispered behind his back when he passed them on the street or whispered right in front of him as though he were invisible when he was in the hardware store or even when he was sitting at his old wooden desk at school. His teachers mumbled two feet away from him like he wasn't even there.

The people of Backhills enjoyed wallowing in the gossip that comes along with any unfortunate tragedy, the way people in small towns tend to do. The way people in any-sized towns tend to do. The rumours became more and more juicy. Like the one about Harp's mother going completely crazy after Pops died, psychotic as all get-out, so grief-stricken she'd washed a fistful of pills down one night with a bottle of whisky but her boys managed to get her to throw them up. (Never happened.) That the farm was already flat broke. (Not yet. Their mother

34

was struggling to survive, but she did her best for months for her sons' sakes.)

The most vicious of the stories claimed that the boys had killed their own father because they wanted the farm for themselves. That one hurt more than any of the others and it was as far from any truth as you could possibly get. After Pops died, Harp learned many bitter lessons, the first one being that people he had known to be good and kind all his life suddenly became meddling, hurtful assholes.

～

Harp fumbled through the rest of the school year. When his mother slowly began neglecting even the smallest of chores, like making them school lunches, Harp took over. Soon, she found buying groceries impossible, just standing in the aisle staring into space. Eventually, she couldn't manage anything. It was heartbreaking to realize that things were never going to be the same.

Harp loved school. He loved it and depended on it even more after Pops's death: the routine, the reassuring sameness—he even looked forward to the homework. School kept his mind busy. "Better a pencil in your fist than a sword," his mother had said one morning at the breakfast table. Having her sons get a good education had been important to her and Pops. But when it became plain that his mother couldn't handle the farm work, he'd walk his little brother to school and most days come right back home again to help. It was the right thing to do. Harp didn't think his mother even realized he'd quit going, and that was for the best.

What finally became his last day at school was marked by a comment from Harp's homeroom teacher. As she stood at the classroom door discussing Harp with the principal, he overheard her whisper, "Go easy on the boy—his mother is floundering." Harp looked up the word in the old dictionary when he got home that afternoon:

Flounder: To struggle or stagger helplessly or clumsily in water or mud.

In the corner of the living room with the giant book on his lap, Harp sobbed his heart out. After that, he vowed never to cry about his father again. His mother, however, started crying and didn't stop. She was floundering and getting worse as the days wore on. Harp tried with all his heart to help, and so did Puck, but eventually she stopped getting dressed in the morning and took to her bed. Soon she wasn't even talking to them. The boys did their best to whip together simple meals, rice and beans or noodle soup with some chunks of old, freezer-burned chicken floating around in it, but their mother refused it all. The rumours that she was going crazy were coming true, and soon enough, concerned neighbours were making calls.

"Something's gotta give, boys." That's what their nearest neighbour said to Harp one day when she caught him out in the yard as she passed by.

Somebody had made it their mission to track down an uncle named Murray whom Harp and Puck barely remembered. All they knew was that he was a priest, and Pops hadn't seen him much because he'd renounced the "bullcrap" of the Catholic Church decades before.

Reluctantly, the priest had said that he was willing to help out "on a temporary basis." Whatever that meant.

It didn't sound good.

The night after they heard that their uncle was coming, Harp and his brother lay in their respective single beds in the little room they shared, whispering quietly about what was happening to them.

"Will we have to leave the farm, Harp?" Puck asked. "Can they make us go live with Uncle Murray?" Puck's round face had become unrecognizable since his dad died. Deep lines had set in around his mouth and forehead, and dark circles had taken up shop under his eyes, as though he was twelve going on fifty.

"Mother won't let anything happen to us," Harp said, but he didn't sound all that convinced.

Little did they know, their mother would be gone soon too, not dead and gone, although she might as well have been. Depression had no intention of leaving her. "It happens sometimes," said the elderly doctor who had paid house calls on their mother on and off over the past several months. "The shock has been too much."

A few days after the idea of the boys going to live with Uncle Murray was suggested, a van showed up at the farm. Two middle-aged women in white coats got out and stood in the muck and weeds in front of the house. They huddled beneath a single umbrella and struggled to keep the various files and papers clutched in their hands dry. Harp and Puck stood in the drizzling rain as their beloved mother walked out of the house and got into the van. She didn't pause to say goodbye or even look at her sons as she passed them.

One of the women climbed the porch steps to where Harp and Puck were standing and told them that someone from the child welfare office would be in touch in the next few days to sort out things with Uncle Murray. She advised both boys to pack a small suitcase and be ready for relocation. When Harp protested that he was old enough to look after the farm and his brother, she patted one of his shoulders. "Oh, my dear boy, I admire you, but no, you are not," she said, and turned on her heel back down the steps.

The van drove off and the boys stood out in the rain, watching it grow smaller and smaller until it finally disappeared over the hill. Harp was happy for the downpour, which was the perfect way to hide the tears he had vowed never to cry again.

That night the phone rang, causing both boys to half jump out of their skin. It was the uncle they didn't know from a rock, calling to "make arrangements."

He sounded flat and small through the telephone. He didn't say anything about being sorry for what had happened to their father or their mother, probably because he wasn't, nor was he the least bit sorry about the way their world had been turned upside down.

With the phone pressed to his ear, Harp stared down at his brother, who was sitting on the floor hugging their beloved dog, Baggs, and asked Uncle Murray if they could bring the dog with them.

"God no!" the priest shouted—the humble apartment the church rented for him was too small for two boys and a dog. "Maybe the people who are going to rent the farm will take him too."

As Harp was struggling to take in the idea that people were about to rent his family farm, Uncle Murray bullied on. "He's an old dog anyway. I suggest you boys be grown-ups about this." The priest was big on religion but not on sentiment.

Puck had heard Uncle Murray's voice bleed through the receiver in Harp's hand. "He's an old dog anyway" rang in his ears. He shut his watering eyes tightly and wrapped his arms around poor Baggs's raggedy neck. Something terrible was coming.

The next morning, Harp stepped over the threshold into a whole new version of himself, one devoid of innocence and with a lot less kindness. No one was going to put his dog down but him. Baggs wouldn't be living with strangers on his own damn farm.

He grabbed his father's twenty-two out of the cabinet—a cabinet he had never dared to open in his whole life—and he marched out into the yard. He whistled for Baggs, who came happily, and then he led the trusting old soul out behind the barn. Just as the sun came up, Harp shot him once behind the ear.

"That's that," he said, and he walked away from the dog he had loved more than any other four-legged being in the world. He and his little brother dug a grave under the giant linden tree beside the house, laid their dog in it with his favourite ball, and never spoke about Baggs again.

For two more days, the boys waited at the kitchen table for Uncle Murray to show up, barely sleeping or eating. Finally, they spotted two cars coming up the driveway trailing clouds of grey dust. Why two cars?

Standing beside his brother, Harp felt perspiration gather in his armpits.

A well-dressed woman wearing a rather ugly blue hat pinned to the side of her head got out of the first car and started walking towards the house.

"You must be the Bittlemore boys?" she said through her tightly pursed lips. "I'm here for . . ." She glanced down at some papers she had clutched in her fist. "Which one of you is Parker?"

It turned out that Puck was being sent to live with some people at the opposite end of the county. Not strangers exactly, but a distant cousin and his wife that he and Harp had only met a handful of times.

The Backhills verdict? The boys should be grateful. It's hard to find anyone who will take in children their age.

Apparently, Uncle Murray, after some thought, had decided he was only willing/able to take in the older boy. Harp was pretty sure that Uncle Murray never intended to take both him and his brother in the first place. Harp listened to this sudden news like he was at the bottom of the farm's well. All the grown-up voices sounded distant and muffled, like they were speaking a foreign language. He needed to keep it together for Puck.

He went to give his brother a hug but thought better of it in case it got them both crying. Instead, the brothers faced each other, looking like little men going off to war, and shook hands. In a way, they were going off to war, they simply didn't know it in that moment.

Harp's life became hard. There's no other way to put it. His uncle was physically and mentally abusive for the entire time Harp lived under his roof. Father Murray, as he insisted on being called (Harp thought it was a better option than "Uncle Father"), pointed his stubby finger at his slippers or his water glass or the dishes in the sink or his dirty station wagon and expected Harp to jump into action, and Harp did.

He didn't mind the chores because it kept his mind off the shitty things that stole his sleep and his appetite. Like the way his uncle liked to pinch his neck or poke him in the middle of his sternum or give a hard twist to his ear, and the special enjoyment he seemed to take from belittling and shaming him. Some nights Harp lay in bed wondering how his Pops and this man grew up in the same family, and thanking whoever there was to thank for the fact that Puck wasn't anywhere near this place.

In the almost four years Harp lived with his uncle, he was only allowed to call Puck at Christmas and on his brother's birthday. Uncle Murray hovered over his shoulder the whole time they were talking, pointing at his watch and hissing, "Wrap it up . . . this is costing me a fortune." Puck never called Harp once—but deep down Harp understood why. Puck had a real chance at a new start and Harp was a hard reminder of a life that didn't exist anymore. Harp hoped that the cousins looking after his little brother weren't as mean as Father Murray, and that the reason his brother never called was just that he was too busy in his happy new life. That's what he was going to keep telling himself, anyway.

Harp fell asleep most nights to flashing visions of slugging Father Murray in the nose. He never did. Instead, on the day of his seventeenth birthday, he walked out the door in the middle of the night.

When Harp didn't come down for breakfast the next morning, the priest climbed the stairs fuming about his nephew's laziness and found his tiny bedroom empty. He stood there for a while, then muttered to himself, "Well, I'll be damned." He didn't call anybody or look for Harp himself, just thanked the Lord that he was finally rid of the boy.

⌒

Harp made it back to the old farm three days later. He'd walked the entire way.

The tenants had only lasted a year, and Father Murray hadn't bothered to rent it out again. The place was boarded up, dried up and completely ramshackle, but it belonged to Harp and his brother, or it would as soon as Harp turned eighteen; their mother had signed it over to them in trust before she was hauled away. Pops had paid it off in full before he died, so not a dime was owing on the land or the house. Harp hadn't really thought about what the back taxes were going to be. He'd cross that bridge when he got to it, but no matter what, he had no intention of ever leaving again.

For three years he did odd jobs for anyone who was willing to hire him. Haying and baling mostly, some garbage pickup and fence repairs. Most of what he earned went towards paying the taxes, and that made him feel good. He didn't always have electricity or running water, but he had a good well and oil lamps, and he felt fortunate to have a roof over his head.

Still, at night, he wandered around the house like a ghost, and he was happy when Puck decided to come home—his little brother had liked his new situation well enough, but the farm where they had all once been happy drew him like a magnet. Slowly the brothers started bringing the land back to life, repairing the coop and getting some hens, acquiring some cattle, planting hay and oats—they even plunked some vegetable seeds into the old garden out beside the kitchen. There was nothing quite like a fresh-dug new potato.

They never talked much about their time away. They swept it under the rug and left it there like a pile of dead flies. And they only brought up their mother once, one night when they were hunkered down at the kitchen table drinking homemade dandelion wine.

Harp told Puck he had somehow managed to persuade

Father Murray to drive him to the home where his mother was. He hated to have to beg for anything from the priest, but Harp would have walked on broken glass to see his mother. Father Murray had told Harp he was a little momma's boy. "You're just making it worse for yourself, but fine, I'll bloody well drive you."

What was left of Harp's mother was unrecognizable. He sat there in her little room, without either of them saying a word. She rocked back and forth in her chair and looked out the window and he looked out the window too. He stared out at the manicured lawn and farther still, into the grove of poplar trees, and imagined Pops out there, cantering by on his favourite horse, waving his hat in the air. It made the back of Harp's eye sockets ache. Harp got up, kissed his mother on the forehead and walked out into the dimly lit hallway. He wanted to get as far away as he could from the smell—part sorrow, part disinfectant. Harp's uncle sat there in his car waiting, a sour expression on his face. "Right," he said. "No point in visiting again, is there, Harper?"

"She's not ever getting better," Harp said to his brother. "She's never coming back."

～

Eventually, Harp and Puck decided they'd saved enough money to start up a small dairy herd. Raising beef to kill didn't sit well with either brother—it didn't feel right to have more things dying. And soon after they got the herd established, Harp married a girl he'd met at the county livestock auction and fairgrounds. She was nothing much to look at, but that didn't matter to Harp. She was over-the-moon crazy about him and that seemed like a good enough reason to marry somebody.

He'd been raised to believe that every man needed a dependable and loyal companion. As a bonus, this one also knew her way around the kitchen.

After Harp brought his bride home, Puck felt more and more awkward. Being around newlyweds prompted him to think hard about his own future, and he decided that the last thing he wanted to do was spend his life being the third wheel on a dairy farm. He told Harp he wanted to move to a big city, he wasn't even sure which one, but that didn't really matter. So that's just what he did, packing one suitcase with the few things he'd collected along the way and heading off to catch the train east. The brothers spoke occasionally after that and eventually found they didn't have much to say on the best of days. After Harp managed to scrape up the money to buy Puck out, they stopped talking altogether. No hard feelings, really. Just nothing left to hold them together.

⌒

Harp had grand visions of the kids he and his wife would have, and how he would become the centre of their universe, like his beloved Pops. He assumed they'd start up a family that same year, but that's not how things turned out.

Although his new wife got pregnant within months of the wedding, it didn't take. Three months in, Mrs. Bittlemore's excitement and anticipation became heartbreak and disappointment, and she sat hunched on the toilet in the small bathroom off the kitchen as the blood pooled in the bowl like a grim watercolour painting. As the tears trickled down her face, she wiped them away with the back of her plump hand. She let out a series of long, slow, mournful sighs.

She lost the next one too, and the one after that.

Harp had supported her after the first miscarriage with a warm embrace and a spattering of consoling words. The second one saw him sulking around the kitchen feeling sorry for himself.

After she miscarried for the third time, five years into their marriage, instead of comforting her, Harp slammed around the house in a rage, kicking over chairs and punching walls. Then he screamed at his wife so hard he got dizzy and had to sit down, muttering that she was a miserable good-for-nothing useless woman as she stared at the floor, her double chin folding onto her chest. She had put on a lot of weight since all this loss moved into her body. Loss weighs heavy, and she felt every single pound of it pushing down on her.

He was drunk, of course. He was drunk most of the time now. That's what made him mean. That's what Mrs. Bittlemore told herself, anyway—that it was only the drink talking and nothing more. He wouldn't have said one cruel word to her otherwise.

But she couldn't prevent herself from feeling shamed. She was useless. She was as barren as an eighty-year-old nun. Even the dim-witted dairy cows could calve, so why couldn't she?

She had always liked her food as much as she liked cooking. But now she ate herself into the only happiness she could find. Whatever she could stuff into her tiny pink mouth, she would: pickles and pies and bread fried in lard and sprinkled with sugar and cinnamon. She ate bars of milk chocolate and buttered popcorn and doughnuts and drank gallons of fresh milk with an inch of thick cream on its top. The cows could barely keep up with her.

She made giant pans of maple fudge and gobbled it all up. She loved to down potatoes drowned in butter and sour cream and laid thick slices of cheddar cheese on top of her pieces of apple pie. Food became what she lived for—and she used it to put a huge layer of fat between her and Harp and the rest of the world.

One last time, like a miracle, she conceived (at this point, Harp could barely bring himself to touch her). She was twenty-seven weeks pregnant when she miscarried and should have gone to the hospital. She should have, but she didn't. Everything happened so fast. When the agonizing cramps came on, she tried to rise from her chair and make her way to the bathroom. It was impossible. She stayed put in the kitchen and delivered the poor little soul right on the plank floor. She stared down between her dimpled, fat legs. So. Much. Blood. It would have been a baby boy.

As soon as her pains started, Harp had headed outside to the yard and lit up a cigarette. He took deep, long drags and scuffed his feet through the dirt. He could hear his wife calling out, making sounds an awful lot like the noises the pigs made when he slaughtered them. But he didn't think to get her any help because . . . well, she'd been through all this before. And besides, he was now certain that he was being punished too, although he wasn't too sure what he was being punished for. Of all the things he could have said to his wife afterwards, Harp told her to clean it up, which she did. He wrapped the tiny thing in a kitchen towel, trying not to look too closely, and carried it out into the fading light. His wife watched him as he disappeared over the ridge, where Harp buried it, never telling her where the grave was. Then he got drunk. Again.

When Harp walked off with the baby in his arms, he walked off with their hopes and dreams. That was the end of it. From then on, they were cursed.

Mrs. Bittlemore was sitting alone at the kitchen table one dreary night a year after she lost the last baby—Harp was dead drunk, slumped in his chair in the living room—when she decided that something had to change. She didn't know what, but she was going to think of something to save herself from her bitterness if it was the last thing she did.

She picked up the newspaper in front of her, the *Backhills Examiner*, and mindlessly flipped through the pages, scanning the sports and the funnies and ads for tractors for sale and the recipes, and then she found herself staring at the birth announcements. Normally she skipped that section because, well, just because it was too hard seeing everyone else having children. This time she stopped to read them.

Lyle and Donna Miller are proud to announce the birth of their son Lyle Miller Junior, at 4:57 a.m. at the Carter Creek Medical Centre, weighing 6 pounds 7 ounces. Lyle is the little brother to Cindy, Carly, Stu, Sarah and Wyatt Miller.

Her eyes moved down.

Kerry and Jacob Ellison are proud to announce the birth of their fourth daughter, Lisa Ann Ellison. Born 10:09 p.m. on Saturday, June 8, weighing 8 pounds even.

And it went on and on. One birth announcement after the other. Here were all these families already burdened with too many children—more babies born to parents who had too many bills to pay and chores to do and not nearly enough hours in the day. *All these other women are having babies like they are going out of style and here I am as barren as an old cave. It isn't fair. It isn't fair at all. Surely no one would miss one itty-bitty baby?*

four

MRS. BITTLEMORE WAS AS STUBBORN as an ox, and as determined as she was fat. Once she got an idea into her head, there was nothing in the world that was going to stop her from getting what she wanted. If she couldn't have a baby of her own, she would damn well get one from somebody else.

She justified the idea to Harp on a nightly basis, prattling on and on. Harp heard his wife's voice as a drone swirling around his head. "Women younger than me have lots of time to have another baby if one of theirs goes missing," she'd say. "It shouldn't be a big deal." And she believed every word was God's truth.

She spent weeks poring over the birth announcements in the various local papers, cutting them out and gluing them into a scrapbook. She noticed that many more babies seemed to be born in the fall than in the summer. She took note of how many more baby girls there were than boys, and how many siblings each happy family had. She was meticulous in the gathering of information. She tracked new parents' names and where they lived and what hospital they'd given birth in.

After several months of collecting and analyzing information, she announced to Harp that the upcoming fall would be a perfect time to "find" a suitable baby. Since Harp still hadn't caught on that he was the one expected to "deliver" the solution to all their problems, she sighed and spelled it out for him.

She expected Harp to waltz into the Manatukken municipal hospital that very next Thursday afternoon, grab a baby out of the nursery and bring that baby home.

No fuss. No acrobatics. Nothing too complicated.

It would all happen right under everybody's noses.

Mrs. Bittlemore had done her homework, under the guise of delivering a bouquet of flowers to a new mother (who looked confused when the nurse placed a bouquet with no card on her bedside table, but loved the flowers anyway). She had scouted the distances between doors, how many paces to the nursery, how many staff on duty, who was where and what was what. She felt like Agatha Christie or Nancy Drew or one of those sleuth-type ladies. After she broke the news to Harp, she sent him to do his own reconnaissance.

Harp was going to enter through the front door during visiting hours, go up to the second floor, walk thirty feet down the well-lit hallway, turn left past the viewing windows and slip into the nursery, where he would pick up the baby girl of her choice—"Remember, check the name and make sure it has a pink bracelet," his wife stressed—and carry that baby back down the stairs and out to the parking lot in plain sight of the whole world.

"I don't want a damn useless girl," Harp protested. "A girl

won't do us any good at all. I need somebody who can work! I need someone who can take over this farm!"

Mrs. Bittlemore reached across and grabbed a tiny bit of skin on his forearm. She pinched it so hard that a red blotch started to bubble up right before his eyes.

"Jesus!" Harp wrenched his arm from her grasp. "Why the jumpin' hell did you do that?"

"We're having a girl, Harp, and that's that!"

Rubbing his already bruising flesh as he stared into his wife's inflamed face, Harp decided it was best not to argue anymore about whether a boy was better than a girl. And by Moses on the mountain, the whole scheme seemed doable. Mrs. Bittlemore told him she didn't think that anybody would pay much attention to a middle-aged man in overalls walking around a hospital during visiting hours with a bunch of other middle-aged men in overalls. Harp would blend right in with all the new fathers gawking through the glass at their brand-new babies. While the Manatukken hospital was small, it was bustling. Chock full of newborns. And since it had never happened before, nobody would be expecting someone to steal one of them.

On the day of, Mrs. Bittlemore took a few minutes to make sure Harp understood that he wasn't just to grab the first baby girl he saw. He was to bring home the white baby girl of her choice, not a Native baby, not a Black baby, not an Asian baby. As soon as he came in the door with it, they were going to have to pass this baby off as their own, so it had to be the right colour. Mrs. Bittlemore was so certain of her plan, she treated this slight issue as if it was truly the only problem they were going to have to sort out.

~

Jon Larkspur was a good man who came from a long line of good men. Men who deeply valued family traditions more than anything else in the world, along with loyalty. He took care and pride in marking special days, and there were a lot of special days in the Larkspur family. Had Jon had his way, every day would have involved some kind of celebration, but he held himself back. Whether it was Easter or Christmas or the winter solstice or Halloween, or his three daughters' "world entry days" (as he called them), he loved the ritual of marking memorable and cherished occasions. And he considered it very important to pass those values on to his three daughters—to involve them in any way he could.

From the food to the drinks to the trimming of the tree or the carving of the pumpkin, Jon masterfully handled all the preparations, and his wife, Connie, was more than happy to sit back and watch her husband's magic unfold. Since Jon didn't want her to lift a finger anyway, they were the perfect match for each other.

From the moment they met, Jon planned every date and Connie found them all unbelievably dreamy. He was happiest when his wife was spinning LPs and singing along to every tune and his daughters were stringing popcorn garlands or baking gingerbread cookies or blowing up balloons or just being silly.

His girls were everything to him. He celebrated the arrival of each new baby girl with his own quirky little tradition, or maybe this one was superstition. Whatever it was, the ritual had to be carried out in just the right way. On the day the baby was born, Jon tucked a treasured old silver dollar his grandfather had passed down to him into the folds of their tiny diaper. He wasn't really sure how the tradition had started, but the same coin had been tucked into his own little nappie after he was born. When Connie got pregnant for the fourth time (this one would be the last, they vowed), Jon knew the silver dollar had one more little girl to bless with good fortune.

And after Baby Larkspur was safely delivered into the world and about to be given the thorough once-over by the doctor in the nursery, he made sure to stop the young nurse in the hallway so he could slip the coin into the tiniest diaper he'd ever seen. "Look after her," he said to the nurse as she turned on her heel.

"I'm not a real nurse yet, sir—I'm still in training! But don't worry, I will."

And the nurse smiled to herself as she walked off with the Larkspurs' newborn. She'd already seen a few odd things in her job, but to think that a silver dollar would soon end up with a lot of poop on it made her chuckle.

⌒

Nurse Betty Rickers had worked maternity at the Manatukken hospital for eleven years. She had seen hundreds of babies come and go, and thanked God that most of the births had been straightforward. The mothers she dealt with were tough farm folk who didn't screw around when it came to pushing kids out into the world, and she respected that. You didn't hear them screaming for more painkillers at the halfway mark, no indeed, and Connie Larkspur was no exception. Betty had been there at the births of Connie's three other girls, and it was no surprise that she delivered the newest addition in textbook fashion and that Baby Larkspur was perfect in every way.

"After the doctor checks her out, why don't we just settle her in the nursery so you can get a good rest before you go home. Maybe even stay another night." Since it was Nurse Betty, it wasn't a suggestion, and Connie and Jon smiled at her gratefully when she whisked the baby out the door.

As soon as she stepped out into the hallway, she was waved down by a frantic nurse who was having trouble getting Mr. Banterman into his wheelchair. She handed the baby over to a young nurse in training and asked her to take the baby to the nursery. As Betty turned away into Mr. Banterman's room, she saw Jon Larkspur booking it down the hall after his baby, a silver coin glinting in his hand, and she laughed out loud. His other three daughters had had that very coin stuffed into their diapers after they were born, for good luck, Jon said. Every family wanted their children to enter the world blessed and protected, and she respected that. The Myers family had the entire hospital smudged with burning sage by an Indigenous elder each time they brought a new baby into the world. The elder walked the hallways wafting the smoke over everyone and chanting a beautiful prayer.

"Where is my head today?" Nurse Betty asked herself as she realized she'd been lost in thought, and rushed to help with the wheelchair transfer. Mr. Banterman was a very big man, just three days out of heart surgery. With a whole lot of hoisting and jostling, they had just settled him in the chair when the fire alarm went off. In all the years she had worked here, it had never gone off, except for the one time they had the drill, but everybody was prepared for that.

This felt different. People were already rushing towards the exits, hollering at the top of their voices. It was complete chaos, panic even. She told the nurse to push Mr. Banterman towards the freight elevator—"Go! Now!"—then grabbed a gurney and raced for the nursery. She could load all three of the babies currently in their care and get out—nobody left behind. Betty hadn't run anywhere in a very long time and was a bit humiliated by how out of shape she was, if she was honest. Puffing, she burst through the double swinging doors with her gurney, but one of the babies had already vanished. She darted around the room, looking everywhere, scanning the floor, the tabletops, the cupboards, the shelves—Connie and Jon's brand-new baby girl was nowhere to be found.

As she told the police during her many interviews over the following weeks and months, she assumed another nurse had taken her outside already. "Everything was so noisy. The alarm made it impossible to think straight. I checked all the bassinets and the incubator. I—I still can't get my head around any of— That poor child was nowhere to be seen."

Every time Nurse Betty told the story of how the hospital lost Baby Larkspur, she wept into a balled-up tissue. Every time, she said, "I feel like it's all my fault . . ."

A lot of lives were ruined that day.

⌒

Nearly fifteen years later, Harp heard his wife scream from the top of the stairs, "She's gone!! God almighty, Harp, Margaret's gone!" He scrambled up the wooden steps as quickly as he could and burst into his daughter's small bedroom. His wife stood in the middle of the floor pointing towards the open window, where the rain was pelting, soaking the curtains and the old plank floorboards.

"She's taken off, Harp! Jesus Murphy! What are we gonna do?"

Harp felt that now he was *truly* being punished for all the sins of his past as he stared at the little bundle his daughter had left on the bed. He pointed his spindly finger at the baby and said, "What in the good goddamn hell are we supposed to do with that? I am gonna find that blasted girl, drag her back here and kill her!"

"You're not going to do any such thing, Harp! You're gonna bloody well sit right down and calm yourself! She will come back. For God's sake, you stupid fool, she just had a baby—I put six stitches into her myself. She won't get far!"

Still, the sight of that sleeping baby rattled Mrs. Bittlemore too, and she stared down at it with disbelief. She and Harp had planned to lock Margaret up just until she'd had the baby and then they were going to deal with the baby somehow, and let her head straight back to school after her semester in "France." No one would be the wiser.

She'd even had it in the back of her mind to have Harp take the new baby to the hospital where they'd gotten Margaret in the first place. That seemed both fair and the Godly thing to do—replace the baby they took, balance the scales. But it suddenly seemed ludicrous. The world had changed since they'd stolen their daughter—maybe because they'd stolen her. There was security everywhere, cameras and the like. They couldn't just drop off Margaret's baby without risking being seen.

"We've got to keep her, Harp. At least until Margaret comes back."

But weeks stretched to agonizing months, and Margaret didn't come back. And so another plot was hatched: the plot of passing off the granddaughter they hadn't wanted to begin with as a daughter, all the time lamenting the loss of the daughter they'd originally stolen. Something that seemed so uncomplicated when they snatched Margaret had turned out to be anything but.

That was a dark turning point for Harp. He felt like his every move was being monitored, his every step traced. Unless he was well and truly pickled, he kept picturing his thoughts floating around his head where everybody could see them. All the lies flitting about like dust motes in a beam of sunlight, illuminated for all to behold.

He would swat them away from his face like a cloud of flies, more real to him than his own hands. He became convinced he was going crazy, and constantly anticipated a uniformed arm grabbing him by the throat and hauling him away. He told his wife that if it got out that their daughter had had a baby out of wedlock and deserted it—run off like some sort of criminal in the night—they would be blackballed and rejected by every single person in Backhills, never mind all the other stuff.

Harp said, "Never mind the other stuff," in a shamed whisper. Shame was so new to him he didn't know what it was at first. Nausea, maybe, or a bad case of constipation, the backed-up crap poisoning his system. He felt this shame everywhere—on his skin and on his tongue and buzzing under the soles of his bony feet. For the first time since he stole that baby, he was scared.

He told his wife that she had better damn well figure out what they were going to do, because that kind of thing wasn't his department. Of course, she came up with the most far-fetched story possible. And there they were, saddled with another child to raise, one who was a painful reminder of their guilt and failures every day she drew breath.

five

THE DAY HAD FINALLY COME. No more planning. No more plotting. No more doubting. Berle had
decided that she was going to kill old man Bittlemore.

While he was around, there was simply no way that anything would change for the better and also no way to escape.
If she killed him, he couldn't very well chase them down the
road and blast them all to kingdom come or lock them in the
Cold House or feed them to the pigs. With Harp gone, Berle
would finally be able to get everybody up to the Big Road.

If making it to the valley of her dreams proved impossible,
maybe she could still find them a good farmer to live with.
There had to be one decent farmer somewhere in the Backhills.
Some nice fellow who appreciated good-natured, mostly well-
behaved cows? Even with Harp out of the picture, there was no
way to stay on. Willa was too young to take over. Though Mrs.
Bittlemore mostly kept her cruelty close to her breast where it
was hard to spot, she was as horrible as her husband. Who

knew what she would be like with her husband dead and gone? Maybe she'd be even worse.

It took every single waking moment for Berle to come up with a viable plan. So many moving parts, so many possible scenarios. The turning point for Berle came when she realized that a good swift kick to Harp's temple while he had his head down yanking away on her teats would do the trick. She didn't know why she hadn't thought of it before. It was so simple: a kick to the skull and it would all be over. Now she prayed for the courage to pull the whole thing off.

⁓

The slow days ate away at Harp's withering body. A heavy paranoia circled him like a murder of crows. Even in his mostly alcohol-medicated state, it was there, sitting on his shoulders. The farm was changing, and the signs of that change were very strange and inexplicable. A couple of days earlier, he had stumbled across the word DIE spelled out in the dirt in the barnyard. He craned his neck around, looking for the culprit who had done it. He yelled out into the empty field. He rubbed the letters out with the toe of his boot, telling himself that he had only imagined it, but a shiver of dread nipped at his ever-shrinking heart.

If he wasn't drunk, he was totally unsettled and anxious. He couldn't hold on to a thought, or string together an idea, or focus on what he was doing, not that he'd really paid much attention to his farm chores for years. Everything was falling apart and he didn't care, or perhaps couldn't care.

First the man he takes the drink and then the drink he takes the man.

He found himself chugging two mugs of homebrew before he could even attempt milking the cows, and as a result he was reckless and negligent, letting the fresh, foamy stuff squirt in every direction. Even Mrs. Bittlemore had complained about how little milk he had been capturing in the milk bucket lately. The booze also made him mean, and he found he took a sinister pleasure in stubbing out his cigarette on the cows' hairy back ends, causing them to crash forward into the stalls, trying to get away from him, and he loved it.

Even so, in a million years, he would never have imagined that his creeping unease had anything to do with the damned old cows he had under his thumb.

~

As Harp sat on his three-legged wooden stool that morning, cigarette dangling from his mouth and a cloud of smoke billowing up around his head, he seemed to be in a world of his own. Berle hesitated and hesitated until he was tugging the last few drops of warm milk out of her. What if she didn't get it right? What if she tried and failed? What would happen to them all then?

No, she had to try, and now, or she'd lose this chance. She drew in a deep, calming breath and turned her head to gaze at the stick-like man to be sure his head was in just the right spot. She roughly measured the distance between her hoof and his forehead, and took aim. Clenching the muscles of her scrawny hind leg, Berle kicked up with every ounce of strength she could muster.

BANG! SWISSSSHHHHHHH! CRACK!!!

~

Harp knocked over the milk bucket as he threw himself awkwardly to one side, just far enough that Berle's jagged hoof only ripped off one of his eyebrows. It sounded like a bomb going off in his head. Blood shot out wildly like water from a sprinkler, or rather thick red paint spraying the three walls of the stall. Harp squealed and jumped to his feet, bolting around the barn like a man on fire, clutching at the gash in his head as he tripped over shovels and into bales of straw and bags of oats and spools of barbed wire.

"GODDAMN YOU TO HELL YOU SON OF A BITCH!"

His veins were bulging from his neck and his eyes were popping out. He wiped his hand across his bleeding forehead in disbelief as the blood kept pouring off his face.

He frantically looked around for something to hit that damn cow with. First he groped at a length of rope that was hanging from the wall and then he changed his mind and grabbed an old truck tire instead. Too soft, he thought, and tossed it in Berle's direction. She was still tied in the stall, her eyes rolling wildly at him, defeat and disappointment stinging her like a pair of murderous wasps. Berle had hoped for a far different outcome than this.

"If only I had a goddamned gun, I would blast the living hell out of that GODDAMN OLD BASTARD COW!" Harp shouted, and he marched up to Berle and kicked her as hard as he could in the ribs with his steel-toed boot.

She was instantly winded and gasping for a breath that would ease the pain. Knowing she'd failed again was worse than the kick itself. At least Crilla and Dally didn't have to witness any of this.

"There you GO, you BITCH!" Harp shrieked, blood dripping off the end of his gin-blossom nose. He kicked her again, this time in her white throat.

Berle staggered against the stall wall and tried to suck in

some small little bit of air. It was all she could do to stay up on all four legs. She watched helplessly as Harp marched over to the far side of the barn and grabbed something off a rusted hook. Berle's eyes grew wide and filled with dread when she saw what he was wielding.

With a single vicious swing of his axe, Harp cut off Berle's tail.

six

COWS CAN SCREAM. AND LOUDLY.

I only know that because I heard such a scream while I was sitting at the kitchen table, and our kitchen was more than a quarter mile up the road from where the barn is. Mrs. B stopped washing the dishes and looked out the window. She clucked her tongue and shook her head from side to side and heaved a sigh. "What has that man gone and done now?"

And then she went back to her dishes like it was nothing to do with her. I, on the other hand, was freaking out.

As I ran out the screen door and down the lane as fast as my two scrawny legs would carry me, she yelled after me, "Where do you think you're going, young lady?" Her voice was thin and irritating. "You need to finish up your breakfast! You better leave all that out there to your papa!" Her voice trailed behind me like a kite string.

I couldn't see Harp anywhere, but bellows were still coming from the barn, sending the birds flying out of the trees and the chickens scattering. I thought I was going to throw up my oatmeal, I was so convinced that one of the cows was dying.

When I kicked the old wooden door of the stable open, I could feel my heart beating in the tips of my fingers, swooshing behind my eyeballs and pounding inside my eardrums (I guess that's why they call them drums). This had Harp written all over it. Who else could be responsible?

Maybe I was about to witness the cruellest thing he'd ever done, and there had been a lot of cruel things. I already had terrible images taking up space in my brain. Like the day I caught him drowning a litter of kittens in the water trough. I could hear Orange Cat wailing in the barn as he plunged the wiggling burlap sack into the water and held it down until he felt good and sure they were all dead. One tiny, drenched marmalade baby escaped from a hole in the bottom of the bag and came up sputtering, its eyes as big as saucers. Harp quickly shoved it back under the water, even though I begged him to stop with tears running down my face and snot pouring out of my nose. "That outta do it," he said when it was dead. And then he pushed me to the ground and yelled at me that I was a fool for caring about these useless, dumb cats.

Another time, he shot the neighbour's golden retriever. He aimed his shotgun and looked down the barrel and pulled the trigger and then he grinned at me, showing off his rotten teeth. He shot the dog just because he had wandered onto our property. All the poor thing was doing was wagging his tail and sniffing the flowers, he hadn't even pooed in the yard. I knew that sweet old Ned. I'd patted him a hundred times as I was waiting for the school bus.

64

After he'd blasted him, the dog dragged himself about a hundred yards out into the field, where he finally collapsed and died.

"I got 'im!" Harp yelled. He lurched across the driveway and out into the tall grass to where the dog was and gave his ribs a poke with the shotgun, just to make sure he was dead.

I didn't know what to do. I just stood there with my hands shoved down into my pockets so hard I ripped holes in them both and could feel my bare legs with my fingertips. It's the first time I remember having a headache.

It got worse. Harp went to the shed and grabbed a jerry can filled with gas. He drenched the dog's golden fur with gasoline and then tossed on a lit match. The smell of burning dog hair is one that you can never forget.

A few days later, Mike Nesbit came by offering a reward of fifty bucks to anyone who found Ned, and I was nearly sick right there on the porch. Mike told Harp that he had put up posters all over the county, but so far no luck. With Ned's burned bones buried next to the scorch mark in the field not a hundred yards from where we stood, Harp told Mr. Nesbit he was sorry to hear poor Ned was lost, shooting me a look that could have stopped a charging gorilla in its tracks. I stood beside my grandmother, choking back the desire to tell Mike Nesbit that Harp had murdered his dog. She grabbed me by the wrist and squeezed. I got the message. Fear made me a coward.

And now here was lovely old Berle, slumped against the stall nearest the back of the stable with blood pouring out of her hind end. I let out such a big gasp it sent the dust motes scrambling through the stale air: her tail was completely cut off, a nub of white bone where it used to be. She looked at me with such pain and longing, tears came to my eyes.

I ran to her and put my hand on her white nose, moaning myself. "Oh, Berle, what has he done?"

Just as I said those words, I realized Harp was standing in the shadows along the far wall, breathing slow and heavy like he'd been in a drunken brawl and lost, an axe dangling from one hand. His eyes were so glazed they seemed to glow like a demon's from one of those zombie movies. A thick, glistening sweat—no, he was bleeding too—wept from his forehead and dripped from the end of his nose like a broken faucet.

Drip. Drip. Drip. I actually heard the drops hit the stone floor.

That bloody axe. I should have grabbed a pitchfork and stabbed him right through his weathered, skinny throat, pinned him to the wall and left him there to die. I hated that I had thoughts like that about my own grandfather, but I did.

"What did you do, Harp?" I yelled. I don't know why I was asking when it was already clear.

Harp stared right past me—right past everything. If he blinked, I didn't see it. He looked like he had been standing in the rain, his shoulders, chest and armpits so sweat-stained I could see streaks of salt starting to create tiny white lines. He tried to say something and just ended up coughing. Mean, and useless.

I looked around for something to bandage Berle's stump. The only thing I could spot was a filthy horse blanket that had been thrown over the ride-on lawn mower in the corner of the barn.

I felt Harp's eyes on me as I headed towards the blanket. I cast one quick glance his way and saw he had a massive gash above his eye where there should have been an eyebrow. It was a terrible sight, but I didn't care one ounce about Harp and his bloody head. Whatever had happened to him, he more than deserved.

"That goddamn cow tried to kill me!" he coughed out at last. "That tail ain't nothing but bone, Willa. It looks worse than it is . . ."

As I carried the blanket back to Berle, he spat some disgusting concoction of saliva and blood from the back of his throat. It landed in a glistening pool in front of my feet, so big I could almost make out my reflection in it, like one of those crazy mirrors in a circus sideshow.

I stopped dead. Intense, itchy heat crawled all over my face in an explosion of hate—the same hate I'd felt when he shot Mr. Nesbit's dog. This time it was worse, because this time he'd attacked one of our kind old cows.

The axe swung from his bony hand like a pendulum. "I know you don't believe me, Willa," he muttered, "but that bloody cow really tried to kill me!"

Berle was moaning in the most pitiful way. It was the saddest sound I'd ever heard in my life. I was worried she might die right then and there.

"He ain't gonna die, if that's what you're thinking."

I shot daggers at him with my eyes, and for once he shut up.

I managed to wrap the blanket around Berle's hind end, but it didn't take very long before it was soaked through. How could I get the bleeding to stop? If I could call Dr. Barabus, the one and only vet in Backhills, he'd know what to do. But that would cost Harp money. He wasn't going to part with one red cent to help a cow, and on top of that, Harp wouldn't want the vet or anybody else to know that he had just chopped her tail off.

"No vet," Harp muttered, reading my mind. He spit again and wiped the back of his mouth on his plaid sleeve.

I would have to figure out how to help Berle on my own. She kept making pathetic sounds and I needed her to shush, worried that Harp would have another go at her. I think Berle was worried about that too.

I didn't believe she'd tried to kill him. No way was he pleading self-defence.

"What in the name of heaven happened here? You can't just chop a cow's tail off and expect anybody to believe that that's normal!"

Harp was getting agitated, scuffling his boots through the straw while swinging the axe back and forth. "He kicked me on purpose! I heard them talking about me!"

Okay, he really was nuts, or drunk, or both.

His face ballooned out and his nostrils flared. "Willa, are YOU the one paying for these CHRIST-on-a-cracker cows! YOU the one feedin' 'em!? YOU puttin' a roof over their GODDAMN heads!" Harp slumped down on a bale of hay and wiped his bloody forehead on the tail of his shirt. "I am lucky to be alive, Willa! You should be feeling sorry for me, not him! I am going to kill that MURDERING COW if he ever goes for me again!"

He pulled himself up to his feet, threw the axe against the wall and marched out into the morning sun.

Berle isn't a HE, she's a SHE, you crazy bastard, I wanted to yell, but didn't. *Coward!*

After he was gone, Crilla and Dally, who had been huddled as far as they could get from the scene of the crime, came over to Berle. She slumped against the wall and let out a huge sigh, then she dropped down on her front knees and laid her head in my lap.

I hate Harp Bittlemore. My own grandfather is a monster.

My actual name is Mayvale, but everybody calls me Willa—the short take on Wilhelmina, my middle name. I found this out during one of those rare times when Mrs. B was willing to talk a little about her daughter, my missing mother. And, of course, after she let it slip that my "sister" was actually my mother. She said that Margaret named me after her best friend at school, a Dutch girl named Wilhelmina deBolt. I guess before she ran away on the night I was born, she wrote my name on her bedroom wall in red felt pen.

I'm amazed that Mrs. B and Harp ended up putting the names my mother gave me on my birth certificate, given that they lied about so much else. They could have called me anything under the sun. Even so, Harp did refuse to call me Mayvale. Apparently, that was the name of my mother's favourite quarter horse. She used to ride Mayvale all the time until Harp sold her off. Didn't matter that she loved that horse more than anything else in the world, Harp had to make ends meet.

Since there was no way that Mrs. B was going to yell after me like I was a horse, she calls me Willa too—though she has to force the *W* out through her lips with an extra blast of air, and it seems like it hurts her teeth. "WHEELAH . . ." Most of the time she doesn't call me anything at all.

The other big thing I know about my mother is that she was only fourteen when she had me. About to turn fifteen, but still. I'm just a hair shy of fourteen myself, and I can't imagine letting a boy anywhere near me, let alone having his baby. Mrs. B keeps going on about how I can't give in to my urges, but I don't have any urges, except the urge to bonk her over the head with her own wooden spoon when she talks that way.

I am always digging for more information about my mother, but Mrs. B keeps most details to herself, unless she's been sipping a little brandy and I ask exactly the right question to set her off. Harp is like a steel trap. Any mention of my mother and he clams up and then he scuttles away like a beetle. And I can't go around asking anyone in town or school who might have known her because, of course, there's the other big secret we're all keeping.

Harp and Mrs. B have told everyone that I'm their daughter—not their granddaughter. Secrets always leak out eventually, but so far I've been too scared of what they would do to me to let this one slip, even to my one and only friend, Carol.

Carol talks my head off most days at school, but I don't mind. She doesn't really talk to anybody else, so all those words and ideas must build up inside her brain. I am pretty sure I am the only person in class who hasn't told her to bugger off at some point. I never had the stomach for that kind of stuff. Kids can be cruel, and Carol makes a perfect target. She is shy and withdrawn and nervous and a weird dresser. In a small school, that's all it takes. I try to keep to myself most of the time—I never wanted to belong to any of the cliques—though I guess Carol is my clique. I was used to being alone at the farm and she was used to being alone in her head.

I remember that on the first day I really paid attention to Carol, she had on a gold knitted beret, an oversized men's suit jacket and green pants, pink rubber boots and a red scarf. All I could think when I saw her was that she looked a lot like Christmas.

She often brings butter sandwiches to school for lunch—yep, just bread and butter. She doesn't even have a measly slice of cheese in her sandwich, no bologna, no lettuce, no jam, just butter. And she loves them so much she always wants to give me half, but I decline every time for obvious reasons. It's become something of a running joke between us.

"Want half of my sandwich?"

"That's not a sandwich, that's a half loaf of bread."

Then we laugh. Carol tries to keep her mouth closed when she laughs. I guess she doesn't want anyone to see her crooked teeth, although she has never told me that herself. It makes her laugh sound a lot like humming.

Hhhmmmmm hmmmmmm, hmmmmmmm–mmmmm.

Sometimes I hum right along with her just to be a jackass.

Though some things about Carol do get on my nerves. She's constantly clearing her throat, for one. But worse, she hardly ever seems to blink, which can get quite creepy if you don't know her at all. She twitches a lot too. I'm guessing it's mostly from nerves, but she did tell me she thought she had some kind of syndrome. She wasn't very specific. Once she grew a lump on her neck as big as an unborn twin. (I read about that in my *Science International* magazine—it *does* happen.) Carol's mother bought her some Preparation H to put on it, which didn't do a thing considering the stuff is for hemorrhoids. I was beyond sure that you couldn't have a hemorrhoid on your neck. It turned out to be a giant infected pimple that I lanced with my X-acto knife in biology class. There it was, looking right at me, and I couldn't help but seize the opportunity to rid Carol of her nemesis.

"There, see? Gone like the wind."

After she stopped screaming, she was really quite grateful. "Thanks, Wills."

"Any time, Carol."

"I hope not. I mean, I hope you never have to do that again."

"It wasn't easy for me either."

"Right . . ." she said.

I guess the other thing I love about Carol is that she might not know my secrets, but she's got my number.

———

I daydream a lot about my mother.

It's hard to wrap your arms around a ghost, but I've made up a thousand stories about conversations we had, and shopping trips we went on, and picnics we took in the hills, just the two of us. It's odd to miss someone you've never met—a feeling that something is just beyond your reach every second of the day.

One other thing I do know: my mother must have had a good reason to leave me behind. I guess she had two good reasons: her parents. Otherwise, she wouldn't have run away without me, right?

I have no idea how she got the nerve to escape. My grandparents let me run around the farm and hang out with the cows, but they keep track of everything I do that involves anyone from the "outside" world. It's like living with the FBI. They spy on me constantly. We have one phone in the house, hanging on the wall of the stairwell, and the cord is just long enough to stretch under my bedroom door. When I have one of my rare after-dinner telephone conversations with Carol, Harp always creeps upstairs to eavesdrop. I know he does because I can hear him breathing outside my door—Harp's whole body rattles when he draws air into his lungs. My grandmother is stealthier, but she farts loudly and often. The two of them create quite a symphony when they're together.

When I hang up, I basically shout "Goodbye" so they have time to shuffle back down the stairs to the kitchen. When I walk in there afterwards, they sit like statues, pretending to be looking at the month-old newspaper and sipping lukewarm coffee, acting like they've been there for a year and not outside my bedroom door listening to me talk about how much I loathe basketball with Carol. I have no idea what they expect to find out. That Carol and I both crave french fries and gravy and are having trouble with math?

Most days, I feel like I am suffocating. If it weren't for school and Carol and the cows—and being outside in the fresh air as much as possible—I would feel like a rat on a sinking ship. The truth is that even though they watch me like cops, neither Harp nor Mrs. B really cares what I get up to, as long as I keep their secrets under wraps and don't cause them embarrassment. They feel a lot of shame about my mother, though I'm not sure they really cared that much about her. One time, after a long day's drinking, Harp started up about Margaret, I don't even know why. He would be off in his own world and then suddenly he would interject some random story. "Some people need to be tied down for their own good," he muttered. "That hell slut of a girl needed a lot of discipline and a whole lot of tying down." That's how I found out that for most of Margaret's pregnancy they kept her under lock and key in her room. I'm pretty sure that isn't even legal.

The words came out of my mouth before I had time to really think them through. "No wonder she ran away. The way you treated her was downright cruel."

"You want cruel? I'll give you cruel!"

Harp is quick with a threat but usually too lazy to get out of his chair, and that night he was drunker than usual. When he went to whack me, I managed to leap out of harm's way. Just like the time he tried to kick at me in the East Field. I zigged and he zagged and he ended up going ass over teakettle down the hill into the stagnant, stinky pond that the geese shit in on their way down to Florida. I didn't dare laugh, but I swear to God the cows did, mooing among themselves as they watched him crawl out of the water. I was out of there before he got to his feet.

My grandparents were ashamed of my mother getting knocked up. They're still ashamed of her, something I feel every time they mention her name. The things Mrs. B admits when sipping brandy are very telling. They didn't want anybody to see her in her "condition." The solution? Lock her upstairs and tell everyone some unbelievable story about sending her to boarding school in France!

After my mother ran away and didn't come back, I don't know why they didn't drop me at the door of an orphanage, or even the fire hall, but they didn't. The more I think about it, the more confusing that is. Also, what would they have done with me if she hadn't run away?

But they kept me, which means I have to keep telling this ridiculous lie, stacked on top of all their other lies. I mean, how hard would it have been to just tell people that I was their grandchild?

Instead, I became the wee little surprise my grandmother never even knew was on the way until she went into labour.

She'd got the idea from the National Tatler, where she'd read about a Russian woman who had given birth at fifty-eight. And here she was, only fifty-four! So she marched me—Mayvale Wilhelmina Bittlemore—into the doctor's office and announced, "Surprise! I had NO idea I was even pregnant!" She was so proud of pulling it off, she eventually described the whole scene for me.

When Dr. Johnson stared at her in disbelief—how could a woman who'd already had a baby not know she was pregnant?—she told him that she had been having indigestion and mild diarrhea, sure. But she'd kept her figure—her very full figure (I can just see her waving towards her ample boobs and belly)—so she didn't think anything of it. Then her water broke and her stomach starting cramping and this dear little baby girl came flying out into the world.

(She'd warned Harp to keep his mouth shut and let her do the talking, and apparently Harp had remained sober enough that he only sat there, twisting his filthy tweed cap between his bony fingers, the whole time she was spinning this tale.)

Taking her at her word, the doctor weighed me and measured me and looked into my tiny ears. He listened to my heart and lungs, tickled the soles of my feet and felt me all over, and then declared me to be quite sound.

But he said he also needed to conduct a quick examination of my grandmother's lady bits. "I need to check you for tears, infection, distended uterus—that sort of thing. All routine, you know. Your husband can wait outside, and my nurse will join us to assist."

My grandmother sputtered and shifted in her chair and thought real hard. "Well, Doctor," she said, "I don't see the need for you and your nurse to go to the trouble. I feel completely fine. This little one"—I'd weighed in at only six pounds—"just slipped out of me like a fish into a waiting net. The labour was easy as pie, much easier than with my first one."

Dr. Johnson looked down at his chart and back up at her. "As you surely know, Mrs. Bittlemore, any woman, let alone a woman of your age, can run into problems after a birth. I wouldn't want anything to happen to you that I would feel responsible for. If you had torn, I guess you'd realize that and want me to fix you right up. So you're probably okay on that score. But how's your bladder? Any leakage?"

"Doctor, honestly, the birth was so smooth I felt completely safe delivering at home, with just my husband to catch the baby. He's almost as expert as you, given he must have delivered a hundred calves in his day. I've been fine ever since. All we need you to do is confirm our daughter is healthy, and we'll do the rest."

"Mrs. Bittlemore, are you really refusing an examination?"

My grandmother said by this point sweat was pouring down her back like a waterfall, and she had to resist grabbing me and running out the door. The fear of being discovered as nothing more than a bold-faced liar almost undid her. But she stood her ground. "I just don't see the point," she insisted.

He stared at her for a long moment. Maybe he was imagining how hard and possibly how very unpleasant it would be to get Mrs. B out of her clothes and onto his exam table.

At last he said, "All right. We'll let it go, given your daughter is healthy and you insist that you're fine. But let me know if you experience any bleeding that seems excessive. Your body has been through a lot, and I think there could be some risk involved for the next couple of weeks. Be sure to get lots of rest . . . and no farm work."

Harp piped up. "No worries on that score. She doesn't do any."

My grandmother gave him a death glare and he shut up again.

"Thank you, Dr. Johnson," she said. "If anything at all bothers me, I promise I'll get my husband to drive me into town to see you."

With me in her arms, she hoisted herself to her feet. They all shook hands and stood awkwardly for a moment or two before Harp finally made a move towards the door, the doctor shouting, "By the way, congratulations!" after them.

~

When my grandmother gets to talking about the past, I wonder if she even remembers I'm sitting there. She probably would keep talking if it were just the walls. But I am all ears. I soak up and store away every tedious story she repeats, hoping she'll let another piece of the puzzle slip. She'll often get going on a rainy Sunday afternoon, with me staring out the window as if I've got nothing better to do than watch the rain slide down the glass, which I actually kind of love: all the crappy old buildings in the yard don't look so bad when they are slightly blurred at the edges. They don't seem real, but like a painting with all the colours running off the paper.

On the afternoon I'm thinking of, my grandmother was feeling very talkative—even somewhat agitated. She sat there at the kitchen table with her hands clenched and resting on the large ledge of her breasts, which were unapologetically plopped on top of the table like loaves of bread. I'd heard her talk about Harp going crazy on my mother a couple of times before. How mad he was that his daughter got pregnant. How he chased her around the kitchen table, cursing her out. How enraged he was that she ran away and stuck them with raising "it"—meaning me.

When Mrs. B got in this mood, it was as if she was trying to convince herself that she bore no responsibility for any of it. But she never forgot to lean towards me at some point or other, smacking a hand on the table to make sure she had my attention, and hiss, "I don't need to remind you that you are not to repeat a single word of what I tell you to *anyone*." Then she'd sit back again, and the words would float out of her mouth like little blackbirds and circle the kitchen in a flock, casting shadows on the walls as they drifted past. I was really tempted to open the door to let them all out.

"When he found out Margaret was pregnant," she began, "I didn't have a bloody doubt in my mind that he was going to do grave harm to that little girl. He was blinded with rage and that's never good with Papa. I really was the only thing standing in the way of Margaret losing her precious life."

That's the other thing about Mrs. B's stories: she always portrays herself as the heroine.

She wrung her hands for a moment like she was going to wear the skin off them and carried on.

Harp never went to church, she reminded me, but his time living in a priest's house after his father died had marked him. To Harp, his daughter was the worst kind of sinner—worse even than a murderer. She'd committed a sin against God Himself by having sex out of wedlock and getting herself pregnant, and he was suddenly crazy with fear that all of Backhills would find out that his daughter was . . . well, not to put too fine a point on it, a scarlet letter whore.

I haven't mentioned that for this dramatic story hour, Harp had remained perched beside us like a magpie on a fence post: it was raining too hard for him to hang out in his old truck. Every few minutes he even added his two cents. Each time, my grandmother's eyes folded into tiny slits as she told him to "Shut your damn trap and let me tell it!"

She moved on to recall how Harp had run after my mother

waving a breadknife, screaming at the top of his lungs, "I am gonna kill you and that devil child in your belly!"

It was like she was seeing it all unfold right there in front of her face again.

He chased after my mother, staggering around on his chicken legs, careening into kitchen chairs and knocking pictures off the walls. "Come here and I'll cut it outta ya!"

Harp winced at that, his face pulling itself into a knot.

Mrs. B carried on. "He yelled, 'When I catch you, ya little bitch, I'm gonna slice yer throat!'"

At that, the knot in Harp's expression loosened and he kind of puffed up with what looked like pride. Maybe he thought this was just what a good father would do. I wanted to punch him in the temple.

"He managed to keep hold of his Mason jar of moonshine *and* the knife," Mrs. B said, now actually smiling at my grandfather. Harp grinned back like a cat at a mouse's birthday party.

I'm sure my eyes were as big as tractor tires. "Keep going!" I said. "Then what?"

"He was just plain crazy, he was!"

Harp let out a cackle and then began coughing violently.

"Well, you were, Harp! You were out of your head!"

"Go on!" So much of this was new to me.

"I had to do something," Mrs. B said, "so I grabbed the kettle I'd just boiled right off the stove, and I smashed it over his head!"

Harp touched the side of his skull like she had just smashed him again, then fingered the burn scar on his cheek.

"BAM! He dropped like a hammer had come down on him from heaven and landed on the floor in a crumpled heap. Margaret ran upstairs and hid."

Harp giggled and my grandmother whacked him across the throat with her tea towel. "You silly old fool. You're a crazy drunk, you are. Drinking is a young man's game, Papa. Now you're old, you need to cut it out."

My grandmother's kettle had left a gash on the top of his head as long as his thumb, and she stitched it up with some nylon fishing line and a darning needle. He'd got a good scalding as well, which explained the somewhat faded scar down the right side of his face he was still fingering.

"I didn't let out a single goddamn sound when she sewed my head shut," Harp said, like he deserved a medal.

"No, you didn't, but you whined about that burn for two months."

"No I never," Harp insisted, and she just looked at him like he was a child.

When I can manage not to be completely grossed out by them, I find it fascinating how they muddle through their days in complete denial of how terrible they both are. I wonder if I will become terrible too. Maybe this type of thing runs in your blood, waiting for the right moment to appear.

Mrs. B wasn't done going down memory lane, though. Without missing a beat, she shifted into the story of the night my mother ran away.

"I had gone down to the kitchen to catch my breath, you know, after the baby came. I'd already stitched her up myself, just like I'd done with your papa's head, and I got her cleaned up, and the baby too"—in these moods, she seems to forget that she is talking about me—"and I needed something to eat. When I came back upstairs afterwards, she was just gone. The bedroom window was wide open. This big thunderstorm was raging and the curtains were already soaked through. The baby was wrapped up on the bed and as quiet as could be, not letting out a sound."

My grandmother seemed sad almost.

She said to Harp, "Remember how loud I yelled for you?"

"I do," he said.

Harp had gone running outside, and that's when he saw that he'd left the ladder up against the side of the porch roof after he'd fixed the TV antenna. He cursed himself out for being so stupid, then rushed around looking for his gun, determined to hunt his daughter down and drag her ass home.

"I begged him to just leave Margaret be and maybe she'd come home on her own."

"Why didn't she take that goddamn kid with her?" Harp mumbled, and spit tobacco juice into an old glass jar he was holding. "That's what I still want to know."

Mrs. B snapped him in the chest with her tea towel. "I'm the one telling the story!" Then she sighed and said that, yes, unfortunately, one problem had gone away and another one had been left in its place. Yep, me again.

I will never understand why my grandparents made the decision to keep my true birth a secret, given that they do nothing but fret and worry that someone will finally catch them in their lies. If only they'd let my mother stay in school—accept whatever the consequences were going to be and get on with life—things would have been so much easier. Way easier than keeping her locked in her bedroom while they pretended she'd gone to France.

None of it makes the least bit of sense. But for some reason—shame, guilt, embarrassment, you name it—they believed their only choice was to live an elaborate lie. Every idiot knows you've gotta keep lies simple. There has to be a reason, a real honest-to-God reason why they can't tell any-body the truth about me. Something that even in between sips of brandy Mrs. B hasn't let slip yet.

But what is it?

seven

IT WAS MY FOURTEENTH BIRTHDAY yesterday. Am I only fourteen? It feels like I'm forty, although I can only speculate how forty might feel. I think our mail lady, Claire, is around forty, and she seems normal enough, I guess. She's still got a good job and that's something.

Anyway, I wasn't feeling very birthday-ish, given Berle. Thank God her hind end seems to be healing okay. I'm no vet, but it looks better every day. And thank God my grandfather is actually behaving halfway decent around the cows—when I'm with them, at least. It's not like we've ever been close, but he cuts a wider swath around me these days too, like I'd caught him with his pants down. (What a disgusting thing to picture.) I caught him at worse, actually.

I wasn't surprised that my birthday came and went without as much as a well wish. I don't have any expectations of either of my grandparents, especially Harp. Still, I did sort of hope that something small would appear—a pair of socks, maybe, or some underwear, even a chocolate bar. Then I felt selfish thinking about my birthday when poor Berle was still suffering so.

On my bus ride to school yesterday I decided to stop feeling sorry for myself and get back to reality. I've been living inside my head for far too long. I need to be there for Berle and help her to get well. I have to figure out what the heck I'm going to do about Harp too. He is so unpredictable. His vicious attacks on the animals are so random and brutal. Nobody is safe. Not the cows or the pigs or the hens or anything else that happens to wander through our yard. My birthday wasn't important. It was just another day on the farm.

But, of course, today turned out to be a completely different story. Why should I be surprised? They must have remembered they forgot.

⌒

"It was somebody's birthday yesterday!" my grandmother trilled when I came into the kitchen for breakfast, thrusting a newspaper-wrapped package in front of my face. When I ripped it open, I realized they had gone out and bought me a book. A used one, but even so, it was a first. So now I had two copies of Nancy Drew's *The Mystery at the Moss-Covered Mansion*.

The card was interesting. It was originally a *Happy Anniversary to my loving husband* card, but my grandmother had scribbled that out and put *Happy Birthday to our loving daughter* instead.

She'd obviously never felt the desire to give that card to Harp: it looked like it was twenty-five years old.

Along with the used book that I've already read three times, Harp gave me his old pocketknife. I've seen him clean his nails with it a thousand times or cut twine or gut trout or open bottles. It's as sharp as a dare and can chop through a fence post. After the incident with Berle, I guess he figured he needed something bigger to protect himself from the killer cows, so he'd bought himself a new one from the hardware store. He shines it with a felt cloth every chance he gets, admiring the blade like it holds the secrets to the universe.

Poor Berle hasn't been the same since Harp attacked her. She only ventures out of the stable on the nicest of days, and then staggers around the field, sandwiched between Dally and Crilla for protection. I wonder what it would be like to have human friends and family who love you so much they never leave your side, who want to protect you and keep you safe. It's as foreign to me as walking on the moon.

I thanked my grandparents for my book and my knife and tried to act as humble and as grateful as I possibly could. It all went pretty smooth, until I blurted, "How do you know she's not dead?"

They both knew exactly who I was talking about.

As the words fell out of my mouth, I realized how harsh it was to be pushing the issue on the anniversary of my mother's disappearance. My grandmother grabbed the pitcher of iced tea off the counter and poured me a giant glass.

"Here, Wheela, you must be thirsty."

For a split second it crossed my mind that she might be poisoning me. Have I mentioned that she fancies her abilities with herbal remedies? (I figure all her medical concoctions are just a way to keep me away from the nosy doctor.) As she set the glass in front of me, her hips bumped into me like they always did. I shook the bad thought out of my head and took a big drink as she waddled back around the table.

Harp acted like he hadn't heard the question. Maybe the two of them really had no idea about what had happened to their daughter.

"That thing's like a razor," Harp said, pointing at his old knife. "Don't be waving it around like a wand."

He was trying to change the subject. I couldn't think of any reason I would have to wave a pocketknife around like a wand. My grandmother added that they had discussed giving me the knife at length and decided it was high time I had some protection out there.

Out there where?

Mostly what I need to be protected from is them.

She poured herself a glass of tea and waved for me to hand over my new old knife so she could cut up the corn cake she'd made that morning.

"See, Wheela, look what you can do with it . . . it cuts like nothing."

"Yes," I said, "it cuts right through cake . . ."

I could have cut that cake with my thumb.

Harp looked like he no more wanted to stay sitting at that kitchen table celebrating my belated birthday than he wanted to be strapped to an electric chair.

I figured I wouldn't get any further that day, pressing them on whether they thought my mother was still alive. But wouldn't they know? Wouldn't police eventually show up at your door? Or you'd hear a Jane Doe report on the news and put two and two together? How could a fourteen-year-old girl just walk off a farm one night and never be heard from again?

While I didn't care much for corn cake—it tasted a little too much like, well, corn—Mrs. B poured saskatoon berry syrup over it and brought the plate over to me, and it was sort of my birthday after all.

"I didn't have a candle," she said. Hands on her hips, she waited for me to take a bite, then leaned closer to watch me chew.

After I swallowed, I said, "I wasn't expecting a candle. Honestly, this is great, thank you." *Why in the world can't I have a normal cake?* I thought. But then I realized this wasn't a birthday cake—this was Harp's lunch I was eating, both of us cramming corn cake into our heads like there would be a test at the end of it. Between bites, Harp chugged a big glass of whisky, doing a very good job of pretending things were hunky-dory.

"Do you want to sing 'Happy Birthday'?" my grandmother asked.

"Like to myself?"

"Papa and I can sing with you."

Harp grunted and shook his head. "I ain't singing anything."

"That's okay," I said, "we can just eat the cake."

My grandmother shrugged, the flesh on her round shoulders jiggling. "Suit yourself."

She began cleaning up the dishes, clanging and banging around like she was mad all of a sudden. As she hurried over to the sink, one of her boobs knocked the jug of iced tea off the counter. It smashed on the kitchen floor.

"For the love of Christmas pudding! Wheela! Get the dustpan and the mop!"

That was the end of my belated party.

Those enormous breasts of my grandmother's get in her way a lot. They are like her own built-in TV dinner tray, with bits of pie crust or a blob of jam or a bit of cheese resting on top of them. She constantly complains about how much her

87

brassiere straps hurt her shoulders. They leave divots that I swear could hold water. My breasts are not all that evident yet, and I'm glad for that. She recently told me that when a girl begins to develop her breasts, she starts to "experience the emergence of her sexual appetite." That statement made me cringe. To say that her little talks about the birds and the bees make me uncomfortable is an understatement. I don't want to talk about sex with anybody, let alone my big-breasted beast of a grandmother.

As I mopped up the floor, I started brooding again about my mother. Was I the only person on the planet that thought the total disappearance of a fourteen-year-old girl was the least bit suspect?

Something nasty has been simmering on the farm these past weeks. Something coming to a boil that I've sensed for as long as I've been alive. I'm a little bit scared about what it might be, to tell you the truth. But truth? Yep, I'd like to know that.

eight

AFTER WILLA AND HARP HEADED out the door, brushing corn cake crumbs off their fronts, Mrs. Bittlemore shuffled around the kitchen, wiping her brow with the back of her fat hand. She had been baking since six in the morning, and by the time the sun was halfway over the barn, it must have been ninety-eight degrees in the kitchen. It was only early May and already some days were sweltering hot, and being a hundred pounds overweight didn't help her in the overheating department.

As she waited for the last pies to bake, Mrs. Bittlemore kept glancing out the window and down the lane that wound to the barn, keeping a lookout for her husband, hoping to spot him if he decided to come home for lunch early. With Willa out of the house at school, she thought she could take a little time for herself, but she didn't want to be caught in the act, as it were. Her treasure was right there above her head in the attic crawl space, calling to her from inside her old tin box. She glanced at the clock and then down the road once more, and then walked over to the wood stove and cracked the oven door to gaze in at the pies. Five more minutes and they'd be perfect.

She hated the feeling of worry that crawled up and down her back like a spider, and wanted to flick it off her dress. Although in all the years they'd been married Harp had never come home early for lunch, she feared that today he just might. Mrs. Bittlemore was expert at creating worst-case scenarios in her head. She had a vivid, wicked imagination. Just her luck, he'd burst into the kitchen early and catch her with her head in the ceiling.

The old, trusty egg timer dinged, and she waddled over to the oven to take the pies out to cool. After one more glance down the lane, she grabbed a kitchen chair and pulled it over under the trap door to the crawl space. Getting up on that chair took every ounce of courage and strength she had. Sweat trickled down her back and between her large breasts as she reached up to push the little door open onto an attic no bigger than the trunk of a car. Stored there was a bag full of old cutlery she didn't know why she was keeping, a few outdated bundles of *Farmers' Almanac*, and the thing she was risking life and limb for—her beloved old cookie tin. Rising onto the tips of her toes, she reached back as far as she could and pulled the box towards her, no bigger than a Bible, but more precious than anything else she owned.

She struggled down from the chair, pushed it over to the table and sat down with a thud. Salty sweat trickled from her brow and stung her eyes, and she wiped it away with the dish towel on her shoulder. Cradling the cookie tin like it was a baby, she pried open the lid.

She glanced out the window. Still no sign of Harp.

As always, the contents of the tin filled her with giddy anxiety. She had become so used to feeling nothing at all that her emotion felt a bit like—was it happiness? She reached in and pulled out the growing bundle of letters she had been hiding from Harp since ten months after their daughter disappeared. They weren't addressed to her, but she felt they were hers all the same.

Mrs. Bittlemore took one of Margaret's letters out of the cookie tin. She held the folded paper up to her face and drew a deep breath into her lungs, as if she could catch her daughter's scent.

She pictured her daughter, pen in hand, writing the neatly aligned words on each delicate page. It made her furious for a hundred reasons, but she did her best to control herself since she surely didn't need to have one of her heart episodes. She was so overweight and out of shape, just getting up on the chair to fetch the tin down made her chest ache. How had she let her body get so out of hand? The nitro pills the doctor prescribed hardly seemed to take the pain away anymore, and she hated taking them at the best of times, since they made her dizzy for hours afterwards. Hard to get your baking done when you have to hang on to the kitchen counter every five minutes until the world stops spinning.

Mrs. Bittlemore caressed the pages, the only proof that Margaret was alive and out there somewhere. It irked her that she never addressed her cryptic messages of love and longing to the woman who had raised her, but always to that bastard child, "Mayvale Wilhelmina." It drove Mrs. Bittlemore mad with jealousy. She didn't sleep for days after each letter arrived. Where was Margaret hiding?

She glanced down the lane again. If Harp found out about

the letters, he'd be on the warpath for sure. Every time she fetched them down, she envisioned Harp ripping each one into tiny bits and lighting them on fire—but she put that risk out of her mind for now. She simply wanted to enjoy these little shards of time with her daughter and once more try to figure out where in the world she might be. How far, after all, could a fourteen-year-old who had just had a baby have gotten?

The maddening thing was how few clues the letters offered. Just when she felt like she had an inkling, another little detail changed her mind. The postmarks were different each time, like they were stamped at random. Red Deer and then Saskatoon; Fargo and then Charlottetown. Smithers and White Rock and Milton, Ontario, and it went on and on. Most of these were places Mrs. Bittlemore had never even heard of. How could Margaret be everywhere and yet nowhere at all?

When she was brooding on the letters, Mrs. Bittlemore sometimes thought of what a terrible baby Margaret had been. She even let herself think that perhaps that little baby had known she was stolen. Maybe she knew she no more belonged on the Bittlemore farm than she did on the moon. She belonged to another set of parents who were in a deep and dark mourning. Parents who, at this very moment, probably looked at every twenty-eight-year-old woman they passed on the street and wondered if this was the baby taken from right under their noses all those years ago.

There'd been headlines in the papers for weeks after it first happened, yelling KIDNAPPED! STOLEN! TRAGEDY!

Two hundred people walked with arms linked together, scanning the fields around Manatukken. Trained cadaver dogs were brought in from Lake Myers to help in the search, with everybody hoping they wouldn't find anything the least bit cadaver-like. Nothing was found, not one clue to where Baby Larkspur had gone.

Time trickled cruelly by. The police chief was heard to mutter, "Well, statistically, after seventy-two hours, it's not good."

Fundraisers were held to support Connie and Jon Larkspur and their three "surviving" children, because Jon was too anxious to go to work. Connie was so full of despair she could hardly lift her head off the kitchen table. Those first few weeks, Connie and Jon were practically comatose. Had it not been for their three other daughters, they might well have died of sadness. They held on to each other like they'd been tossed into an impossibly large, angry ocean with no land in sight.

Flyers continued to be stapled onto every power pole and taped onto every store window for miles in every direction. The police in six counties worked in tandem to solve the most heinous crime to happen in the area in living memory. A kidnapping, of all things—it seemed impossible, but that's exactly what seemed to have happened.

The bearded hippie who ran the café on the edge of town, Gary Moore, told an emergency town hall meeting he thought the baby had been stolen by aliens—he'd seen strange bright-blue lights the night before the baby went missing. He came very close to being punched in the throat by Nurse Betty Rickers.

And then it all just died off like Mrs. Bittlemore had believed it would. Just like she had planned.

"People give up eventually. They always do," she said to her husband.

She and Harp bided their time as the headlines became smaller and smaller. The final one was over a tiny story tucked into the far right-hand bottom corner on the ninth page of the *Manatukken News*:

LARKSPUR BABY FEARED DEAD

Grief-stricken family to hold vigil on Saturday afternoon at the Western United Church. Hot lunch dishes much appreciated.

And that was the end of it. For the Larkspurs, life as they knew it had ended and nothing was the same again. Their three girls did their best to cheer their parents on. They stuck together like they were joined at the hip, worked hard in school and tried to be as happy as possible, given they were being raised by people who were broken and always wondering. But who were always hopeful, because losing hope means giving up. Jon and Connie Larkspur were not about to let their beloved baby girl die in their hearts, even if all the signs pointed to her being dead out in the world, a victim, likely, of some murderous pedophile.

Sighing, Mrs. Bittlemore looked up at the clock. *Best get these letters put away before Harp shows up for lunch.*

She carefully folded the pages and placed them in the cookie tin. Pushing the kitchen chair back into position, she climbed awkwardly onto it and slowly straightened. One of these days she was going to come crashing down, she just knew it.

Stretching as much as she could, she pushed the tin back into the crawl space, shut the trap door and made her careful descent.

Walking over to the window, she looked out across the desolate fields as a familiar rage tingled up her spine. Really, why *were* none of the letters addressed to her? Didn't Margaret feel even the slightest bit of gratitude for the life she had been given? Didn't Margaret care about her and Harp at all? Three square meals a day and a roof over her head for fourteen years! Practically new clothes every single school year. She'd had the run of the entire farm until she got herself knocked up. And they only locked her in her room to preserve her reputation. Any parent would have done the same!

All she and Harp had to show for all their sacrifices was that bloody bastard of a girl, Willa. Mrs. Bittlemore felt a curdling inside her as her resentment turned to something darker. Fourteen years she'd been putting up with that ungrateful little girl. Why did Margaret send Willa the love Mrs. Bittlemore wanted so badly?

That gnawing feeling there in the back of her mind—that worry, that paranoia—Margaret was up to something with all these letters. They were getting longer, and the promises that she was coming for her baby were getting stronger. And every day, Mrs. Bittlemore looked at Willa and saw more and more of Margaret in that beautiful, perfectly smooth-skinned face, that shining hair, those dark eyes, and memories of young Margaret came flooding back like a dam breaking. Willa looked so much like her mother.

Why couldn't Harp have stolen a different baby? One who would have been grateful. One who would have stayed with them and not stuck them with this lemon.

nine

HARP AND MRS. B ARE under the delusion that they keep their business to themselves, but I know from the way people treat me at school that there isn't a single person within forty miles who doesn't know how horrible Harp is.

Some kids walk a wide circle around me because of him, which isn't the end of the world—that's what I tell myself, anyway. If I let that bother me, I would be sunk. Most of them are part of one gang or clique or another, and I don't belong to any obvious category: the jocks or the girlie girls or the brainiacs or the nerds or the headbangers or the pageant-hair cheerleading girls. I don't take it personally when I am chosen second-to-last for baseball (Carol is always last). I really don't mind that there isn't a boy within a twenty-five-mile radius who would ask me to a community hall dance; that's the last thing I want to do anyway. Also, who would I get paired up with? Marky Pyper has a double set of teeth, for God's sake. His baby teeth never fell out and his parents don't seem to think it poses a problem. God forbid they should take him to a dentist. The kids call him Sharky Marky, and Marky seems to LOVE that. Maybe he'll fall in love with Mary Christmas (not kidding, that's her real name). She is more or less an albino. I wouldn't call her that, except that's what Mary calls herself. In fact, it's the first thing she says on the rare occasion she meets anybody new: "I'm Mary and I'm an Albino." Capital *A*.

She is one of the eleven students in my homeroom. She has snow-white skin and snow-white hair and NO eyebrows. Her eyelashes and fingernails look like they've been soaked in bleach, but she has yellow teeth. Or maybe they only look yellow because of her hair. Whenever she smiles, though, I want to hold her down and scrape those teeth with a stick. I realize I am being an A-hole, but there really are some odd kids in Backhills. I'm sure I'm one of them.

Thank the Lord for Carol Stark, my one, true friend. She has auburn hair, and eyebrows too, which I appreciate. Her teeth are white, thank God, although the front ones are far enough apart she can shoot water in a ten-foot stream straight through them. That girl could knock a fly off a fence post, that's how great her aim is, and I am jealous and concerned at the same time.

Carol is as shy as I am forthright, so we make a good team. She is a complicated person, which I also like. She has a lot of tics and idiosyncrasies that could be chalked up to the fact that her mother is an overprotective, super-religious, very hyper person and her father is an alcoholic (I think—Carol never talks about it). But all of that has made Carol very non-judgmental. She is well aware of how terrifying my "parents" can be, but that doesn't deter her from coming over after school once in a while. Even though they are clearly pretty old, she's so unsuspecting a person she's never guessed that they are my grandparents. Carol doesn't even let Harp's spitting or surly cracks get to her. As hard as it is to believe, I think she kind of likes the guy.

Harp ignores her for the most part, which is his way of being nice. Or maybe he doesn't know what to say to her that won't make him sound out of his mind. I once saw him spit at the back of a neighbour kid who dropped by to collect bottles for the 4-H club. He couldn't help himself. Thankfully, the kid never knew he'd been spit on. The glob just hung on to the back of his jacket like a tiny, wet monkey.

The last time she came over, Harp grunted a stream of syllables at her that I thought were completely insulting. She told me it just sounded like he was saying hello.

"Everybody's got some crazy in them, Willa," she said. "Your dad is just like a hurt child. He hurts inside his heart and so he hurts other people and creatures in turn. I don't think he means half the things he says."

Carol's optimism is her dearest, most admirable quality and I love her for it. She is steadfast and loyal and I don't know what I would do without her. One of these days I need to come clean with Carol about my grandparents and put my life into some kind of order. Easier said than done.

⌒

"Lying is an art form mastered by few, attempted by many."

That's what my gym teacher yelled at Carol and me today as we ran around the dirt track at Backhills Junior High. Carol had just tried to get out of gym by telling Ms. Bevan that she thought she was getting her period and shouldn't be running around a field.

Her period? She never told me she had gotten her period. That's a very big thing NOT to tell your best friend. I've seen no sign of mine yet.

"If you had your period, Miss Stark, you'd know it!"

Our gym teacher pointed her painted fingernail at the one-hundred-yard marker, blew the whistle hanging around her neck and yelled, "Let's go, women of tomorrow!!" Whatever the hell that meant.

Carol and I kept right on at a slow jog.

"Do you really think you're getting your period, Carol?" I said, puffing away.

"No, but I thought it would be worth a try."

"You'd tell me, right?"

"Of course, and you'd tell me too, right?"

"I'm never going to get my period." I was very convinced.

"Come on, it's inevitable for girls." Carol could barely get the words out for panting. Neither of us were in peak physical condition.

"Ugh" was the only word I could muster as we rounded the corner of the goalpost for the umpteenth time.

Ms. Bevan always yells quotes at us. I think she means for them to help and inspire, but more often than not they confuse me. She once shouted out, "Failing is the same as winning, only it doesn't feel as good." I'm pretty sure she made that one up.

I like her a lot, though. In my limited experience, most older people don't like kids. But Ms. Bevan genuinely likes us. She always has encouraging words to hand out, even to the most unpopular kids. I often daydream about what it would be like to live with her instead of Harp and Mrs. B. As far as I know, she doesn't have any kids of her own, though she used to be married, according to Carol, whose mother went to church with Ms. Bevan's ex-sister-in-law.

The sister-in-law said her brother got tired of Ms. Bevan because she couldn't "hold up her end of the bargain." That could mean anything. Like I said, this is all according to Carol's mother—who knows everything there is to know about everybody around Backhills.

As Carol and I completed our last lap, Ms. Bevan marched up to us and asked us if we were going to be trying out for the basketball team.

As I squinted into the blazing afternoon sun, I said, "I don't think I'd be much good on a team. Remember, I'm only five foot two. But Carol should try out for sure!"

Carol looked at me like I'd lost my mind.

"There are no height restrictions, Willa." Ms. Bevan wedged her fists into her hips and stared me down. "If you had to be tall, the only person we'd have on the team would be Carol. You girls should come to the tryouts. It'll be fun. I'm bringing cupcakes."

Carol looked at me, betrayed. She no more wanted to participate in sports than pull her thumbnails out.

"Of course, we'll think about it," I said to Ms. Bevan. The cupcake thing was a nice touch. I'd show up just for one of those.

"I'll see you next week. We need enthusiasm, girls!"

"We're very enthusiastic, Ms. Bevan. Carol was just saying the other day that she wanted to get more involved in anything to do with school spirit."

I love teasing Carol, who never fails to take the bait: she was absolutely glaring at me through her greasy bangs. Actually, now that I took her in, she looked like she hadn't showered in days. Carol has her secrets too. Something might be going on at home that leaves her in need of a little TLC.

Ms. Bevan lifted one of her perfectly groomed brows ever so slightly above a big green eye, then blasted her whistle to herd us all back inside the school.

ten

"MISERY LOVES COMPANY"—THAT'S WHAT MY grandmother tells me whenever she gets exasperated with my lack of gratitude for all she thinks she does for me. She has more sayings than Confucius. But that one is never more true than when it comes to her and Harp. Misery does indeed love company—I think it would have been impossible for the two of them to avoid each other in this life. They were attracted to each other like peanut butter and bread.

My grandmother told me one day while we were sitting in the kitchen—our neutral zone, me doing homework while she cooked up the usual storm—that she met Harp at a hog auction. Seems fitting, really. She spotted him sitting on a bale of hay, chewing a big wad of tobacco, spitting the juice into the dirt.

I wouldn't have found one thing about that appealing, but apparently she did.

My grandmother was with her two equally plump cousins, Delva and Sonja, the three of them marching around the fairgrounds with their purses clutched tightly to their bosoms. It must have been a sight to behold: three walking, talking oak barrels, with white stick legs and arms poking out. I've seen a few old photos of my grandmother and her cousins, and all three were as plain as paper. Hair pulled back in tight buns, not a stitch of makeup or a hint of lipstick, dresses as shapeless as flour sacks, fingers like breakfast sausages. Mrs. B insisted that they were the prettiest girls in the county, which I found hard to fathom after seeing the photographs. And Harp didn't back her up, saying that when they got married, Mrs. B was no great beauty, but she made up for it with her sense of humour and her cooking.

Loving her cooking I totally understand. I may not be a fan of cornbread of any kind, but she could turn a bag of nails and a skunk into something delicious. But to think that at some point in her life she had a sense of humour? She has never said a funny thing in my hearing. Not one.

Anyway, Mrs. B said the rotund trio went to each monthly Backhills Agricultural Association auction because it was the closest thing to a dating service in the area. The BAA, as it was fondly known—though that would have been more fitting if they were selling sheep—not only put on a pig and steer auction, it hosted a huge open farmers' market, and people came from all over the place to sell their livestock and set up tables filled with everything they'd been growing in their gardens or baking in their kitchens.

So it wasn't a big secret that Mrs. B and her cousins were on the hunt for suitable husbands. First, they would beeline for the hog barn to see if there were any available young men milling about, which there always were. My grandmother said pigs and men went together like butter and sugar, and marrying a pig farmer would at least keep you in bacon.

The day Mrs. B spotted Harp, Delva and Sonja wanted to sit down and have a coffee and eat the giant cinnamon buns they'd bought from the Hutterite stall at the market. As luck would have it, they found a spot in the direct line of sight of Harp and Puck Bittlemore. Harp might not have been that impressed by three young women stuffing cinnamon buns into their mouths so fast crumbs were flying out of their jaws like mice trying to escape a trap. But he didn't have a lot of options. They were girls, and they were looking back at him, and that was good enough. He sent his little brother to do the reconnaissance.

Delva whacked my grandmother in the arm when she spotted Puck walking towards them, and whispered that she might faint with excitement, which didn't take much. Delva was a big fainter. Mrs. B told me she'd been fainting since she was six years old, tipping over at the sight of anything, pretty much. Blood, for sure, and bats, a burning marshmallow, somebody throwing up—basically, life in general.

My grandmother told Delva to take a deep breath and calm the heck down. "You're gonna scare him off, for crying out loud!"

In the background the hogs were grunting and squealing like they were being murdered, because they probably were. Pigs can be loud when they want to be, a soundtrack perfectly suited to this occasion. When Puck finally arrived at their weathered picnic table, he stood as still as a broomstick for a few seconds, his thumbs wrapped around the red suspenders that were attached to his filthy tweed slacks, and then hollered over the pig squeals, "I don't suppose you'd part with a couple of them sweet buns?"

Sonja and Delva started to giggle, but Mrs. B handed him a half a dozen buns in a paper bag and shushed her cousins.

Puck turned on his heel without so much as a thank you and headed back to where Harp was sitting. He handed his brother a bun and took his own, and the two of them stuffed them into their heads like they were plugging a leak.

Harp couldn't quite believe it. He felt the blood slowly rise into his cheeks like some sort of joy. For whatever reason, he took a bite of his cinnamon bun and threw the rest at my grandmother. She told me she saw it coming like a little dough rocket, thrust her little hand into the air and caught it with hardly a glance. She tore a bite out of it and launched it right back at Harp, and that made him smile.

Delva and Sonja were appalled that the man had thrown one of their own buns at them, but my grandmother was intrigued. She knew right then and there that that was the man for her, and there was nothing on the planet that was going to change her mind. Harp just didn't know it yet. The rest was pretty terrible history.

~

I wish with all my heart that they'd never met, which I guess means in some way that I wish I didn't exist. But the world the two of them made together is truly a blight on this planet, though I guess so far the damage has been limited to the people and animals that call this farm home.

It's been working on me like the yeast in Mrs. B's Parker House rolls ever since Harp attacked Berle with an axe. My mother took off at fourteen going on fifteen, and now that I'm fourteen, maybe I have to get out of here too. I can't beat these two, and I certainly can't join them: I don't want to turn mean, evil and cruel.

But I don't know where to start. You can't do a heck of a lot when you're just fourteen. I can't drive a car, I have no money in the bank. I sure wouldn't be able to get a credit card. I can't hitchhike out of here, when everybody and their dog knows me for fifty miles in any direction. What I've got in my piggy bank wouldn't even buy a one-way bus ticket to Ferintosh. If I knew where my mother was, I would obviously try to get to her, but I don't know where she is. Also, I worry that she wouldn't want to see me. She left me behind, after all, and never came back for me.

I'm sure the story I've made up in my head is probably worse than the actual truth, but that's what I need to find out—the truth.

If I keep letting all this slide, the pressure is going to blow my head off. So I guess I have to become a detective.

I have read enough Nancy Drew books to tip a horse. Her cases always seem to involve a dark and mysterious one-eyed stranger, a parrot and some kind of lost treasure, none of which are much help to me. But someone has to know something about where my mother is and I am thinking that someone has to be my grandmother. No more pussyfooting around and begging for little scraps from her old stories. I've got to figure my whole life out.

eleven

ONE EVENING AFTER DINNER, HARP finally caught his wife while she was staring longingly at the tiny trap door to the crawl space. Mrs. B instantly began taking quick, shallow breaths. Willa had slipped off to do homework in her bedroom after she'd inhaled her dinner, so it was just him and his wife and no annoying kid chatting away. Harp was busy tucking into a third helping of meat loaf and mashed potatoes. He chewed while he spoke.

"What is so interesting on that damn ceiling?"

"What about the ceiling?" (Adrenalin flooded Mrs. Bittlemore's chest.)

"What the heck are you looking at up there? That thing?" He pointed his twisted finger at the trap door.

"I am not looking at anything! I'm taking a moment to think about what I need to get at the grocery store tomorrow, and . . . I'm thinking about our Lord and Saviour, if that's all right with you!"

Any mention of religion always sparked a rant from Harp, which is what Mrs. Bittlemore hoped would happen here. She had been staring at the ceiling without even realizing it. For how long, she wasn't quite sure. Sweat began to trickle down between her generous breasts. She didn't want him getting anywhere near those letters.

"Is the Lord and Saviour in the crawl space?" Harp cackled, and shook his head and went back to eating his meat loaf.

Mrs. Bittlemore let out a little sigh of relief, vowing to be much more careful in the future. It's just that she'd been keeping this secret from everyone for so damn long.

The first letter arrived in the middle of a rainstorm like the one that had raged the night her daughter disappeared, just to make a point, Mrs. Bittlemore supposed.

It was hand-delivered to her front door by Claire, the postwoman. Mrs. Bittlemore never knew Claire's last name and never cared to ask. She thought she was a nosy pain in the ass and had no intention of being the least bit friendly towards her.

Harp was rummaging around in the barn, thank God, and Willa was sound asleep in her drawer when the postwoman knocked. (Willa had been a good baby—that was the one positive thing about the whole situation. She slept through the night and was easily entertained, which meant that so far she hadn't required much more than bottles of fresh cow's milk and diaper changes.)

Mrs. Bittlemore gasped when Claire handed her the envelope, and uttered the words "Thank you" for the first time in a decade. It was ten months since the night Margaret had taken off, and the silence had been loud. Since the police hadn't shown up at the door, Mrs. B assumed she wasn't dead and that she hadn't reported them for locking her in her bedroom, or for kidnapping her in the first place.

Mrs. Bittlemore hated that word. *Kidnapping*. It sounded so—illegal. And, of course, how could she report them for that when she didn't know she had been kidnapped in the first place? Mrs. Bittlemore and Harp had barely spoken a single word about what they had done since Harp carried the baby in the door, and certainly not even a syllable in front of their daughter.

She fanned herself with the envelope, so full of joy or some sort of emotion her heart raced around in her chest like three cats fighting over the same mouse. If Claire was curious about Mrs. B's reaction, she didn't let on. She did, however, ask about the name on the envelope.

"That's your address, Mrs. Bittlemore," she said, "but who's Mayvale?"

Mrs. B stared at the front of the envelope. She'd only clocked that it was Margaret's handwriting, not that she'd addressed the letter to "Mayvale Bittlemore." Her daughter.

No—Willa was Mrs. B's daughter now!

Maybe it was time to tell Claire about their newest addition, given she'd already broken the news to the family doctor. They couldn't keep her hidden away at the farm forever. But she couldn't get those words out of her mouth.

"Mayvale! That's me," she found herself saying instead. "That's what my cousins always call me."

"Okay, Mayvale," Claire said with a snort.

The two women stood there looking at each other for what seemed to be a very long time. Then Claire said, "All right, then, you have a good day, Mrs. B."

Mrs. Bittlemore had that envelope ripped open before Claire had her van door closed.

Dear darling Mayvale, her daughter had written, *my whole heart. Mine.*

Mrs. B read it again and again and again.

Dear darling Mayvale, my whole heart. Mine.

Dear darling Mayvale, my whole heart. Mine.

Mrs. Bittlemore tried to swallow, but it was impossible.

I know you can't read this letter yet. I am so sorry I left you there with them. I didn't know what else to do. I am going to come back and get you. Don't give up on me.

M.

P.S. I know you're reading this, Mrs. B. I'm watching you.

It was suddenly so still. The words on the page seemed otherworldly. A dull pain circled Mrs. Bittlemore's heart. She let the arm holding the letter fall and looked up and all around, sure she would see Margaret standing in the middle of the road with a shotgun aimed right at her.

⌒

Mrs. Bittlemore never intended to keep that first letter a secret from Harp. She meant to tell him. But one day went by, and then two days, and then two weeks. When the second letter came, three months later, it was pure dumb luck that Harp had gone into town for a few things and didn't intercept it, given that this time Claire had stuck the letter right there in the mailbox, with the bills and the *Backhills NEWZ* and all the flyers. Right there in the open for anybody to find!

She considered leaving it unopened, unwilling to face any

new threats that might be coming her way. She sat for a long moment at the kitchen table with the thin white envelope in her hands, then put it up to her nose, seeking a little trace of her daughter, sighed and sliced it open with the breadknife.

My Dear, Darling Mayvale.
I'm sorry I had to leave you.
I'm out here trying to figure out how to get back to you.
I'm going to tell you everything as soon as I know everything.
I love you.
M.
P.S. I'm watching you. No. YOU.

⁓

From that point on, Mrs. Bittlemore nearly killed herself running to the mailbox every day ahead of Harp, to the point of bumping him out of the way with a giant hip check.

He became quite sure his wife was losing her marbles, all the fault of that goddamned baby. If he was honest, he was too. He was going through his moonshine at a hell of a clip, just to get some peace.

After the third letter arrived, Mrs. Bittlemore knew she couldn't keep up the effort of beating Harp to the mailbox. So the next time he was headed to town, she said she wanted to come.

"What about Willa?" Harp asked.

"Well, we can't bring her with us," Mrs. B said. "Nobody but the doctor knows about her yet."

The two of them decided it would probably be safe to leave her in the big steel bathtub for the couple of hours they'd be gone—there was no way she could clamber out of that thing.

When Harp was across the street buying his chewing tobacco at the drugstore, Mrs. Bittlemore snuck into the post office and rented a mailbox, stipulating that all letters addressed to Mayvale Bittlemore would go to that box from now on. Of course, dimwit Claire ran the post office, so it was her who set everything up. Claire only raised an eyebrow, saying, "Whatever blows your skirt up—Mayvale! Here's your key to the city," and handed it over. Mission accomplished. Secret kept.

~

The Bittlemores should have known that Willa would make it out of that bathtub. She had been climbing all over everything for the past couple of weeks, but her efforts had obviously gone unnoticed by Harp or Mrs. B. She was very determined and, apparently, very agile at just barely a year old. She crawled across the bathroom floor into the kitchen and pushed right out the barely latched screen door into the sun.

Willa shuffled merrily on all fours, down the three wooden steps from the porch and onto the grass, and continued across the yard towards the barn, gurgling and laughing the entire way. She stopped to watch a butterfly float past and then started up again to follow it. In another few feet she bumped right into some smooth hooves and furry ankles. She looked up and saw the cows for the first time and laughed her little face off. She pulled herself up by one of Dally's legs. She wanted up.

Dally, Crilla and Berle looked down at the wee human and they were filled with a kind of magical joy—an emotion they hadn't felt since Margaret ran away.

Young Dally, who was barely more than a calf herself back then, exclaimed, "This must be M-m-margaret's little person. W-w-w-where are you going, little person?"

"Yes, she is, indeed," said Berle. "I wish we could keep her with us, but we better put her back in the house."

Berle used her teeth to pick up Willa by the bum of her diaper and started hauling her back up the dirt path, the other cows trailing her. The baby thought the whole procession was hilarious and chortled the whole way.

"This one is going to be more trouble than Margaret ever was," Crilla said. "She's brave. Look how far she got!"

"I miss M-m-m-margaret," Dally whispered.

"We all do. But we haven't seen the last of her, Dally," Berle said. "She'll come back for this one, I'm sure she will. In the meantime, we'll keep a close eye on her. A very close eye."

When they reached the front yard, Berle pushed the broken gate open with very little effort and plopped Willa onto the front porch, Crilla planting a big lick on the top of the baby's head. "You stay put, you," she said, and all three of the cows reluctantly retreated back to the barn. God forbid Harp found them anywhere near the house or there would be hell to pay. Berle kept looking over her shoulder to make sure the little bugger wasn't following them back down the road.

When Harp and Mrs. Bittlemore drove into the yard, there was the baby, sitting on the front step, looking like she'd just had the best day of her life.

twelve

GIVEN HOW RETICENT THEY WERE to share the news of me, Mrs. B's miraculous menopause baby, with the people of Backhills, I find it really surprising she and Harp didn't insist that I be home-schooled. But I did have a birth certificate. Mrs. B had talked the doctor into issuing her one, even without the physical exam, because I'm sure he never had anybody lie to him before about having a baby. So, thankfully, when it was time to start grade one, they registered me, and off I went, with Harp's warning ringing in my ears—"Don't you say nothing about anything to nobody." Like I would want to tell a single soul about my life on the farm.

These days, if Harp talks to me at all, it's always short and sweet. For instance, "Don't do anything stupid." Anything stupid like what? Chopping the tail off a cow or shooting a dog or making up some crazy story about where your own daughter has been for the past fourteen years?

I think if I'm ever going to figure out what I need to figure out, at some point I am going to have to spill the beans about who they really are to me, and start trusting people a little bit, especially Carol. Every day I'm starting to ask myself why I just don't tell Carol they aren't my parents, but my grandparents. I know she thinks they're kind of old-looking, because she said so on a few occasions, and once she did say, "You sure don't look like either of your folks."

Maybe I could trust Ms. Bevan? If I'm honest, she's the one I'd tell. She's like nobody else I know.

One of her sayings from the other day was "There is no staving off womanhood." But she sure has "staved" off most of it, because she's not at all curvy or busty or ladylike. She's as thin as a piece of twine, with short, bleached hair that sticks up like she's been electrocuted. And she's always in a track suit, even at the school dances she chaperones. But she always has these brightly coloured nails that are at least an inch long—a complete contrast to the rest of her tomboyish look. And she fusses with them, even painting them according to the season: little Christmas trees at Christmas, pumpkins and ghosts at Halloween, bunnies and eggs at Easter, turkeys at Thanksgiving. (She does it all herself, so her turkeys look a bit like brown turds, though I'd never say that to anyone.) How she manages to bounce a ball or swing a bat without busting them all off is beyond me, but she does. During tests in health class, she sits at her desk and admires them endlessly. Or she spreads topcoat after topcoat on them, always starting with her thumbs, leaving our classroom smelling like we refinished a ten-piece dining room set in there.

She makes sure to remind us girls that we can talk to her any time about anything. I really should take her up on that, but I know what she means—boys and sex and bullying and our periods, not runaway mothers and grandparents who have lied to an entire town. But I do daydream about walking up to Ms. Bevan's desk and spouting out every detail of my crazy life, every little thing that has been weighing me down. In my mind the classroom bursts into flame at my first words and I hang on to Ms. Bevan's arm like it's the only lifeline keeping me from tumbling into the molten lava that is now spewing from my mouth. As she listens intently to my story, she nods in deep concern and blinks away the diamond tears streaming down her deeply concerned face. Ms. Bevan pushes a bucket of Kramer's fried chicken towards me and it's all wings and I am repulsed (it's my fantasy). Then she calls the police, telling me they are on their way to the farm to arrest my grandparents and that I will be going to live with Carly Simon and James Taylor.

When I snap out of it, Carol is waving her arms to get my attention. "Willa, what the heck? You're doing it again!"

I daydream a lot, apparently.

I probably won't tell Ms. Bevan about Harp and my grandmother quite yet—I need to figure out a lot more things before I spill the beans, like where my mother ended up, if she ended up anywhere at all, that is. Once I tell her, there'll be no going back. Also, I don't want to seem like I'm off my tree. It's hard to get people to believe you if they think you're bonkers.

But I have considered talking to her about acquiring a bra, even though she may not be the right person to ask for advice, since she most definitely doesn't need one. I would prefer not to have breasts myself, but given my grandmother, I doubt it will be avoidable, genetics being what they are. Please, God, just don't give me boobs as gigantic as hers. I won't be able to stand up straight!

I do need a bra, though, and I have no idea how to broach the topic with Mrs. B. She'd probably want to make me one from an old flour sack and some chicken bones, because "Homemade is always better in the long run, Wheela . . ."

My grandmother is indeed crafty. She fixed the rabbit ears we had on our television a few years ago by using a coat hanger and some duct tape. God forbid we should spend twenty bucks for a store-bought brassiere.

I should just talk to Carol. She has been wearing a bra for months, which in my books makes her an expert. Unfortunately, I am not the only one at school who has noticed Carol's new developments. A few of the boys have been very verbal about it. Boys are much meaner when they hang out in groups. When they started to pick on Carol, I wanted to punch them all in the balls. She was mortified by all the weird commentary.

An over-the-shoulder boulder-holder? That's the kind of thing they think is hilarious.

If there were an invisible cloak that existed in the world, Carol would sell her soul to have it so she could throw it over her head when she walks past these morons in the hall.

The other day Ms. Bevan caught some of the boys having a go at her, and blasted her whistle hard enough to rattle the trophy case. "Back to class, you imbeciles!"

She doesn't take any crap from anybody. (I hope I grow up to be just like her.)

She told Carol to simply let it go, reminding her that the boys were going through puberty too, and were most likely going to be bizarre and objectionable for at least the next few years. (Ms. Bevan teaches "puberty" in health class, and every time she raises the subject, all the boys snicker and us girls blush like watermelons. I personally don't want to learn about hair growing in armpits, or anywhere else for that matter. I certainly don't want to learn about menstrual cycles in school.)

After she blew her whistle at them, the boys skulked down the hallway back to their homeroom and Carol and I made a pit stop at the bathroom. She didn't want to talk about what had happened, she wanted to pee, she said. But I could see that she couldn't let the boys' cracks go. It's like she absorbs all the taunting into her body. Her shoulders pull together like they have strings attached to them and her chin tilts down until it looks like it's glued onto her neck. Shame can make a person physically sick if it's not put someplace other than inside your rib cage.

I know that from experience. If I took every single awful thing Harp and my grandmother say to me (or about my mother) to heart, I would be in a padded room by now.

Everybody has their own stuff to deal with in life, that's for sure.

⌒

This afternoon Carol came over after school so we could work on our English project together. I had to beg my grandparents to behave themselves and not hover around us like thunderclouds, and for once they did manage to leave us alone in my room. Not even any eavesdropping.

We were supposed to choose a famous writer who was no longer with us, and explain the lasting effect of their work on modern society. I, of course, chose Walt Whitman, and Carol said that was fine because she didn't give a crap who we did the project on.

All my mother left behind when she took off was a battered book of Walt Whitman poetry and a badly tarnished 1794

silver dollar coin that was tucked inside it. Other than the tarnish, the coin is in pretty good condition. You can make out
every detail of some guy with long, flowing hair—not sure who
he is.

I keep Walt and the coin stuffed behind my Nancy Drew
books. From my eyeballing of it, the silver dollar is a little too
big for the pop machine in front of the drugstore. Not that I
would use it anyway. I cherish it. There is no other trace of my
mother anywhere else in the house, not even a photograph.
Why don't my grandparents have at least a few pictures of their
own daughter—somebody they claim to love—set out on a shelf
or hung on a wall?

Carol had never heard of Walt Whitman, which wasn't surprising. I don't recall seeing a single book in Carol's house—
lots of ceramic owls, hundreds actually, but no books.

"What is this, Willa?" Carol asked when I handed Walt to
her.

"It's a book, Carol."

"Ha, ha, very funny. I know it's a book! So—what?—you
want us to read it and explain it to people, I guess?"

She grabbed a piece of her red hair and pulled it off to one
side of her face, then opened the book to a random page and
started to read like she was a newscaster. That didn't last
long . . .

Nor any more youth or age than there is now;
And will never be any more perfection than there is now,
Nor any more heaven or hell than there is now.

The look on her face said it all. Complete confusion.

"I don't always understand it either, Carol."

"I guess it means life is what it is, right?"

"And it's all there is, I think. It was my m—" Almost let the big secret slip. "I just think it's just a really cool book of poems. I thought we could make a model of Walt's house in Camden, New Jersey, too. They turned it into a museum. And maybe a Walt Whitman puppet."

"We could use one of my brother's GI Joes and put a beard on him. That's a wild beard Walt has there." She'd flipped the book over and was staring at the illustration of the poet.

Suddenly we heard a fart and then my grandmother's gas crawled underneath the door like poison. Carol and I laughed our heads off as Mrs. B and Harp scurried away down the stairs.

thirteen

HARP CREPT INTO THE BARN the next morning, as stealthy as a coyote, after making sure that his wife was busy in the kitchen and that Willa's school bus had loaded her up and driven away over the hill.

Berle was hunched in the farthest stall from the door, and she didn't notice him right away when he slid in. Since the tail incident, she preferred the stillness and lack of light in that part of the barn. It had been two weeks since she'd lost her tail and she still hadn't eaten much of anything. Willa tried to tempt her with apples and pails of oats, whatever she could find for treats when she came home from school, but Berle was too depressed—depressed and defeated, the weight of failure and its consequences sitting on her heart like a stone.

But then she caught a glimpse of movement over her left shoulder and her big heart began to race. She knew it was him. Berle could see his breath rising up above her head now, like ominous smoke signals. Maybe he was coming to finish her off.

Harp wasn't sure what he was going to do. First, he just wanted to get a good look at the goddamned cow that had nearly killed him. He'd made Willa do the milking since the cow tried to kill him. He didn't like to admit it, especially to himself, but he was afraid of Berle, and the other two. The morning of Berle's attack felt like a blur. One minute he was sitting on his milking stool and the next minute he was struck by a blinding pain.

But goddammit, he did remember how good it felt when he chopped off Berle's tail. When he replayed the scene over in his mind, he experienced a pure joy. It made him so giddy to think about it, the throbbing pain in his forehead took a back seat for a moment. The gash above his eye had got infected, and stayed that way, getting worse as the days went past. His wife told him he should get to the doctor and get it looked at, but he refused.

("You're gonna lose that eye," she'd said matter-of-factly.

"I got two of 'em," he'd replied, and washed away the pain with a little more whisky.)

He didn't really want to tangle with that cow again. Now he'd experienced first-hand just how vicious a cow could be, he thought the wisest course was to send Berle and the other two to the concrete house to be slaughtered.

But his wife was having none of that. "We don't have much time left with these cows, and I want to get all the milk and cream we can," she'd said. "Crilla's too old to breed, and I'm not sure about the other two either. If they can't get with calf, that'll be the end of them. Then you can start talking about the damn concrete house."

Harp had chewed on her words with disdain. He didn't like

to be told anything, but he also didn't like what happened when he really riled his wife.

And Willa was always checking on Berle too, making sure her tail was healing okay. That made him furious: she never asked one single damn time how his head was coming along. He was determined to punish the bastardy cow, but he didn't want to attract Willa's attention. And cruelty was as much of an addiction for him as moonshine. Maybe he could just do something small that Willa wouldn't notice—a tiny cigarette burn or a couple of punches to the neck.

Harp inched his way towards the back of the barn. "There, there," he whispered through his thin lips. "I just wanna see how that old tail is coming along—or lack thereof!" He laughed at his own joke so hard that he choked on his spit. He stopped to gather his wits about him, then grabbed a pitchfork off the wall and advanced on the cow, holding it in front of him.

Berle tried hard not to be terrified, but Harp clearly had the advantage. Since she couldn't get around him and his fork, she started to bellow as loud as she could, a sound that shook the walls of the barn and carried out over the fields. Dally and Crilla heard their friend's familiar cry and came running from the East Pasture as fast as their hooves would carry them.

When they burst through the open stable doors, Harp was clearly shook: the bloody cows were talking to each other! Not possible! He needed to get the hell outta there.

"This ain't over," he mumbled, backing up to slide along the wall, then past them and out the barn door. One cow he could handle, but three cows posed a problem.

~

Dally and Crilla had always listened to Berle's escape plans, and dreams of revenge on Harp, because that's what friends do. But mostly they'd humoured her, and just put up with what the old man dished out. What else could they do?

Even after Harp attacked Berle with the axe, they thought that had to be the worst of it. But the sight of that pitchfork in Harp's hands made it perfectly clear that if they didn't end Harp's reign of terror, he was going to kill them all.

The cows talked all through that long day and deep into the night about how three old cows with no way to escape and no access to weapons of self-defence could strike back. At last, they realized that if they were going to rid themselves of Harp Bittlemore, they'd have to recruit a human being to their cause. Willa, to be specific.

And to do that, they were going to have to call on Crilla's special talent. It just so happened that Crilla was one of the few cows on the planet who knew how to spell. Not really big words, just little words, easy words, simple words—but enough that she could make their intentions understood. As risky as it was to attempt communicating with a person, they had to deliver their message before things got any worse.

fourteen

CAROL AND I WERE SITTING outside on the school swings after we'd polished off our mediocre lunches, and I thought, *This has got to be it—this is the moment I unburden myself.* I knew I needed to somehow get the words outta my head and reveal my terrible secret. But where to start?

"How's your little brother, Carol?"

"My brother is the same, Wills, although he's still down about losing his ear." She spoke the words like it was the most normal sentence in the world.

"I'm sorry to hear that." The ear thing, right—I forgot about that. Her brother had snagged the side of his head on a random strand of barbed wire while trying to catch his horse and tore his left ear right off. Makes me wince to think about it.

Then I asked how her dad was—"Still drinking too much," she said—and how he was doing with work—"He doesn't say much about it"—and how her mom was—"Holding up"—and then I ran out of ideas. I closed my eyes and took a breath so deep it made me dizzy.

"Carol, my sister is my mother and the Bittlemores have pretended to be my parents but they're really my grandparents, and I think they might have killed her!"

I thought I said this out loud, I really did, until I heard Carol, almost shouting. "Willa . . . Wills . . . hello? Are you in there?"

I blinked at her.

"You do that a lot, ya know."

"Did I say something?"

She shook her head, tucking a long strand of red hair behind her ear. It fell back out immediately.

I suddenly felt relieved that I hadn't accused Harp and my grandmother of murdering my mother while sitting on a schoolyard swing set. I don't really believe they murdered her. But I'm pretty sure they did something bad, like burying her in a bunker somewhere on the farm, with a small breathing tube sticking up out of the dirt. I decided to make a point of keeping my head down to try to spot that tube when I walk around doing my chores. Like that will be a problem—my head has been hanging down a lot lately. Maybe they sold her into slavery, or maybe she had amnesia. Okay, enough already. I was being selfish. Carol seemed like she could use my support and friendship, and here I was trying to make it all about me.

As if to prove my point, she sighed and said, "Willa, I wish I had your life. You're one of the most well-adjusted people I know. Your parents seem like a team. I wish my parents had a little bit of that team spirit. All they do is disagree."

I couldn't believe what I was hearing. "Um, team spirit? Carol, Harp and Mrs. B don't get along all the time. They hardly talk to each other."

"Well, they sure seem to stick together."

She was right about that much. They stick together purely because they don't have another single soul on the planet to rely on, and for good reason.

Carol swayed slowly back and forth on a swing that was clearly a few sizes too small for her. Her stringy red hair hung down over her face while her sneakers dragged back and forth in the dirt, the ends of her toes making deep grooves. I didn't say anything because I didn't really know what to say. Why can't Carol see through their crap?

"I think you were going to tell me something, Wills. But you drifted off, as per usual. What's going on?"

"Nothing, really. I was just thinking about stupid stuff. Everything is a-okay in my world."

Then I did the old switcheroo, turning it back on her. "Seriously, Carol. It sounds like your parents are going through a hard time. Are you all right?"

Carol's face pulled in on itself as her lips pursed and her brows joined together on the bridge of her nose. I immediately felt like a creep for pushing the issue.

"I don't want to talk about it. Is that okay?"

"Of course it's okay! We don't have to talk about anything. We can just do sign language or charades. See?" I jumped off the swing and started pretending that I was a mime going up and down a staircase. That made Carol smile.

I know what it feels like to have people whispering about you. I know what it feels like to have strangers try to pry information out of you. People are always biting their tongues around me, dying to ask about my sister and her whereabouts. I'm not daft. The weird, reclusive Bittlemores always top the gossip list in Backhills.

The wind picked up Carol's long hair and flung a hank of it into the corner of her mouth. She is forever dragging hair out from between her teeth. I don't think I've ever seen her entire face exposed because her hand is always in front of it. She pulled the strands out with her pinky finger and squinted at me like one eye was suddenly glued shut.

"Wills, I guess it's just life, but I don't even know where to start. Everything feels so weird."

She hesitated a moment longer, and then the proverbial dam broke, and she began blurting out a hundred things all at once. Her unmanageable hair and her big, dark freckles kept her up at night worrying that she'd never be pretty and then, on top of that, she was supposed to feel sorry for her little one-eared brother, Fleck (his real name is Fletcher, but Fleck is what everybody calls him), but he was constantly telling her that her real dad was the Devil, whose sperm was flaming red, hence her hair.

When I could get a word in, I told Carol that she should stop worrying about the stupid things her mutilated brother said. I doubted very much that the Devil was anybody's dad. I doubted the Devil even had a penis. I said that I, for one, loved her red hair and, in fact, that I once had a beautiful dog with hair exactly that same colour.

She dug her sneakers into the dirt to stop the swing and stared at me. "You never had a dog. Did you have a dog?"

I couldn't believe she was asking me about the dog, not the Devil's penis. Carol was right—I'd never had a dog, never mind one with red hair. Harp would have shot it or drowned it within the first week of its life.

"You got me there," I said. "But if I'd had a dog, I would have wanted one with your colour red fur, for sure."

Carol chuckled a little at that and wiped her nose with her sleeve. "We should go back in," she said, jumping off the swing set. "I don't want to be late for Social Studies. And then we have those basketball tryouts after school."

I watched her long legs pull themselves past each other like they were stilts as she headed towards the school. She looked back at me through her tangled strands of hair and waved for me to hurry up, then paused to wait for me. When I reached her, she placed her hands gently on my shoulders so she could look me in the eye, and that's when she told me what I sort of already knew. In a small town, bad news travels like a brush fire.

"My dad got fired because they think he stole stuff from work. Mom says we might have to move."

I felt sick, the thought of my only friend moving away twisting my heart into a knot.

Carol made me realize that I wasn't the only one with troubles at home. I wondered if I would ever be able to tell her about my grandparents. I had been living in my own little world. "Whatdya say we forget about those dumb basketball tryouts. Surely we can find something a bit more fun to do."

"No way. The least I can do is make sure you get one of Ms. Bevan's cupcakes. Don't worry about me—I'll never make the team."

⌒

Carol stood in the middle of the gym clutching the ball like it had been glued to her fingers. All she had to do was pass it to one of the other girls and then run beneath the basket and wait for the ball to be thrown back to her. Simple, right?

But all the kids were yelling "PASS! PASS!" and Carol was frozen to the floor.

"YOU STUPID TROLL! PASS THE BALL!"

Nola Stucker spat the words at Carol like the brat she is, glancing for approval at her posse of yes-girls and laughing like a maniac, her toothy mouth falling open and shut like a puppet's. She tossed her long blond ponytail from side to side, then yelled, "WHAT ARE YOU WAITING FOR—YOUR THIEVING DADDY TO COME DO IT FOR YA?" Nola took another quick glance around to see who was watching her performance.

Carol's lip started to tremble and then tears made a beeline for her chin. She remained frozen.

I sprang up from the bench and rushed to her side. It took a bit of coaxing, but I finally got her to hand me the basketball.

The kids were now booing me for trying to rescue Carol, so Nola figured she would up her game: "Waaa Waaa Waaa! You crybaby! YOU AND YOUR DYKE LOSER FRIEND ARE SO LAME!"

Nola Stucker is the worst kind of bully, the kind that gets even crueler with an audience. At that moment she was everything I hated in this world. Sure, she's pretty and popular, a cheerleader—blond, blue-eyed, already curvy—but she's mean. You can't change mean. Mean lives in people like a disease.

Telling Carol to stay put, I marched up to Nola and the band of brats surrounding her like a swarm of bees. These four girls have been the bane of our existence these past two years in junior high. Nola, Martina, Janice and Paula—they love making our lives miserable, like they are the four horses of our personal apocalypse. They go to the bathroom together, walk the hallways together, change in gym class together, eat lunch together—they are never apart if they don't absolutely have to be.

Nola, the biggest, blackest horse of them all, started in on me while I was still ten feet away from them.

"What do you want, Bittlemore? Is your beanstalk friend crying? Did I hurt her feelings? Boo hoo hoo . . ." Nola's face reminded me of a sphincter, at least that's what I pictured as she talked her shite. The whole pack of them tossed their heads in more fits of laughter.

Ms. Bevan was by now blowing her whistle hard, but I didn't stop. I didn't think about what I was going to do either—I just threw the ball as hard as I could at Nola's smug face and took off for the gym's big double doors, and looked back over my shoulder to see Carol racing after me.

"YOU HIT MY FACE, YOU BITCH! MY FACE!! YOU'RE GONNA GET IT, BITTLEMORE!"

We had never run that fast in our lives. I didn't know Carol had it in her. Maybe I should have talked her into trying out for track and field instead. We came to a stop at the far end of the parking lot and stood there gasping for breath. And that's where Ms. Bevan found us.

The ball had snapped the bridge on the straightest, most perfect part of Nola's nose.

I did feel bad. I did feel guilty. I knew I deserved to spend weeks in detention, but I didn't care. It was worth it.

But no way was Nola going to let me get away with breaking her nose. Carol and I would have to be on the lookout.

fifteen

MARGARET REMEMBERED HOW, SOAKED to the bone, she'd stood on the side of the highway in the rain and wondered what the hell she was doing. She'd run without any sort of plan, which had proved to be a really bad idea. Now she was simply waiting to see what would happen and sobbing her head off. How could she have left her baby with Harp and Mrs. B, the two people she loathed more than anybody else in the world. The poor little soul would be totally at their mercy. They wouldn't dare hurt her, would they? She didn't know the answer, just that she couldn't go back. Not yet. Maybe not ever.

When headlights appeared over the hill, she'd managed to stop crying and stick her thumb out. People hitchhiked all the time back then, sometimes just as far as the next farm. So she wasn't surprised when the transport truck started to brake.

Margaret hadn't cared what direction it was going, only that it was heading away from the farm. She'd felt she also didn't have the luxury to be choosy about the person driving. A nasty old trucker? She'd take her chances with him if that would get her out of here.

The eighteen-wheeler rolled about a hundred yards past her and then stopped. Margaret took one last look back in the direction of the farm and then she ran towards the truck. When she got there, the door swung open. She hauled herself up onto the running board and leaned into the cab.

"Thanks so much for pulling over," she said, waiting for a reply before she climbed into the passenger seat. She was so, so sore. Her torso ached, her legs, her feet, her head, her back. Her stitches were throbbing too.

Did I just have a baby?

Was any of that real?

What am I doing here?

The driver leaned into the dashboard lights, and Margaret was surprised to see the crumpled face of a middle-aged, grey-haired woman, puffing away on a cigarette.

"Well, hello there, darling. Climb on in. I'm Tizzy Holt. I can take you as far as Schellenberg, if that suits you."

Margaret almost started sobbing again, but she didn't, she just scrambled into the passenger seat and set her damp bag at her feet. She didn't even know what she had thrown into it. She'd remembered to grab a wad of money she'd managed to squirrel away, though it wasn't much. She hoped she'd at least shoved in a pair of clean pants and a toothbrush.

Tizzy put the big beast in gear and headed back onto the road.

"What's your name, dear?"

Margaret blurted out, "Margo"—and guessed from then on she'd be Margo. "I'm headed for Schellenberg too."

"What a lovely coincidence!" Tizzy took a long drag on her cigarette and blew the smoke out a sliver of open window.

Margaret was pretty sure Tizzy could tell she was a runaway, but Tizzy only said, "Get comfortable, Margo, we have nineteen hours to go."

Nineteen hours? Margaret had never heard of Schellenberg, but she was grateful that her very first hitched ride was going to take her such a long way from the Bittlemore farm.

And she was grateful that Tizzy Holt didn't ask her anything but her name, not even how old she was. Instead of grilling her, she made glorious small talk and told her far-fetched stories that flew right over Margaret's tired head. When it finally sunk in that Tizzy knew she was in trouble and was willing to help, no questions asked, Margaret fell into an exhausted sleep to the soothing sound of Tizzy's voice. At some point it started to sound like waves rushing up to the shore, not that Margaret had ever heard a real wave in her life.

She woke up four hours and 250 miles later, near a town called Waverly.

"I need to eat," said Tizzy, when she noticed her passenger was awake, "and I bet you do too." Tizzy was right.

They pulled off the highway into a truck stop where everybody knew everyone. Tizzy introduced her young sidekick as "my pal Marg."

Margaret's name was getting shorter by the hour.

She wolfed down a cheeseburger and french fries and a large slice of coconut cream pie. *This pie isn't as good as the ones Mrs. B makes*, Margaret thought, and then felt insane for thinking that, and bolted for the bathroom, where she threw everything up. Afterwards, she sat on the toilet as waves of fear and shame rolled over her. She didn't have a clue what she was doing. What if she had broken the law somehow? A person couldn't just abandon her baby.

Smarten up, she told herself. *You didn't leave her in a box in the ditch. Surely to God they'll take her to the hospital to get checked out?*

But still she felt really alone. She couldn't think of a single person she could call for help. Her best friend, Wilhelmina, thought she was in France, and even if she called her, she was only fourteen and her parents would send Margaret right back to Harp and Mrs. B.

Not Robert either. Once she got pregnant, she didn't have the guts to let him know, afraid her parents would kill him, even though she'd gotten pregnant in the first place to punish them! It was all a mess.

She only had herself, and a lady truck driver who, thank God, had turned out to be a decent human being.

Margaret got up from where she sat and splashed water on her face. She took the one pair of clean pants she had managed to remember out of her still-damp backpack and started to get changed. Blood had soaked through the pad she'd stuck in her underpants, and also through the underpants. When she rummaged around in her backpack, she realized she had forgotten to bring any extras, so she pulled the bloody ones back on, then used most of a roll of toilet paper to fashion a new pad. As she headed back into the truck stop diner, she tried to walk as normally as she could, but it hurt to stand up straight and she felt like she was a little too hunched over.

When the check came, Tizzy wouldn't take her money. "Keep that, honey. You're going to need it," she said. Margaret stared at her tiny roll of ones and fives, wrapped up in a hair elastic, and realized that they looked pathetic.

When they got back to the truck, Margaret started to climb back up into the cab, and Tizzy gently grabbed her elbow. "You don't need to sleep in the passenger seat. You can bunk out in my hotel on wheels!" And she boosted Margaret up into a mini bedroom in the back of the cab that looked as inviting as anything she'd ever seen in her life. It featured a fluffy duvet with two equally fluffy pillows, and dozens of glossy pictures of Sophia Loren stuck on the walls and ceiling.

"You got a thing for Sophia Loren?" Margaret said, giving her what felt like her first smile in months.

"I do," Tizzy said, and grinned back. She piled the duvet on top of Margaret, making a nest that smelled like cigarette smoke and maple syrup, and told her to get some rest. Before she closed the little door, she leaned close and said, "It's not always going to be so hard, Marg."

Which was good to know, because if it got any harder, Margaret didn't think she would survive it.

"Shut your eyes now, young lady, and leave the driving to Tizzy Holt. Next stop, Schellenberg!"

sixteen

CRILLA LOVED TO REMEMBER THE DAY, a long time ago now, when her mother taught her to spell. She was a heifer, and still living, by some miracle, with her mother at another dairy farm. It was a much bigger dairy farm than Harp's, but that didn't mean there hadn't been cruelty there too. After Crilla was born, she'd been taken away from her mother and moved to a separate stable with some other equally confused and desperate calves and forced to drink from big bottles with rubber nipples. Then one day, when she was able to eat hay and oats, the farmer said something about her being "weaned" and she got turned out into a field with her mother. Crilla didn't recognize her right away, but her mother sure knew who she was.

While she wasn't able to answer Crilla's question about why or when certain cows learned how to spell, her mother soon set about teaching Crilla all the necessary survival skills, including her alphabet. When Crilla wondered what use spelling was to a cow, her mother just said, "You never know when there is going to be an emergency."

Crilla asked, "How will I know it's an emergency?"

"Believe me, you'll know beyond any shadow of any doubt."

Her mother had found that using her right front hoof was the fastest way for her to sketch out letters in the dirt, but she said that Crilla's grandmother had preferred the back left. "Try all of them," she told her daughter. "Each of us spellers has our own style."

Crilla, who turned out to be most adept with the left front hoof, was dazzled by the alphabet her mother had carved out in the middle of the field that summer day—all twenty-six human letters lined up for twenty yards, each one more beautiful than the last. Her mother spent the next stretch of quiet afternoons teaching her daughter dozens of words that could come in handy: WHERE, WHEN, S.O.S., HER, HIM, BAD, OW, HURT, CAR, RUN, BAD, GOOD, LOVE, YES, NO, MAD, HOW, WHY, WHO, EAT, FOOD, CAT, DOG, MAN, BOY, PIG, HEN, HAY, HOME, BARN and, of course, HELP.

"That's the word you'll need most in an emergency." And she encouraged Crilla to practise that one until she could scratch it out in mere seconds.

She also taught her the four words she herself had used in an emergency.

Years earlier, Crilla's mom had come across the boss farmer with his hands on one of his own daughters out behind the barn. The next day she wrote YOU. SIN. GIRL. SEX. in the dust of the farmhouse's driveway, and then hid behind the shed to see what would happen. The farmer spotted them first, and looked around, horrified, wondering who in the hell had seen him. Who had done this? He wiped the words out as quickly as he could with his big boots. And, as far as Crilla's mother could tell, he never looked sideways at his daughter again.

Crilla was in awe of what a few well-placed words could do, and was so proud of her mother.

The last lesson?

"Crilla, you have to make sure that no human ever sees you spelling out their words," her mother said. "It's always got to be our secret, do you understand?"

seventeen

I WAS LYING IN BED on Saturday morning, on the phone with Carol, strategizing as to how we were going to avoid Nola and her gaggle going forward, when Harp yelled from the bottom of the stairs, "YOU UP THERE! Get your butt down here and do your bloody chores!"

Harp's voice always sounds like an alarm going off. But there is something about me trying to laze around a little on a weekend that ticks all his boxes, which is extra aggravating because he barely does his own chores anymore. I wish he would just leave me alone, but as Harp says, "Hold a wish in one hand and a shit in the other and see which one comes true first." I don't know what that means, but the shit part seems about right when it comes to my grandfather. He also tells me that dreams are for sleepers. (He has a lot of sayings.) But he wasn't going to quit hollering, I knew that much. I could barely hear Carol on the other end of the phone.

"Harp's yelling at me to get going," I said to Carol. "See you later?"

We'd been plotting for ages to somehow get our butts into town, and today we really had to go to the library to work on a project. But then we planned to hit the matinee of *Starglider 3: The Last Star* at the Orpheum Theatre. Carol is a huge fan of Gareth Garner, who plays the handsome and brave hero, and she's dying to find out if he and the series' tomboyish but beautiful and intrepid girl-pilot will finally team up and save the Master Flyer Fleet. I'm hoping they won't have to kiss, but I suppose those things are inevitable.

I'm going to spring for the tickets, of course, not just because money is tight at Carol's house, with her dad being unemployed and all that, but also because I want to make up somehow for making such a mess of the whole Nola situation. Breaking a bully's nose? Not good.

I don't care what she and her gang of imbeciles do to me, but I sure don't want anything to happen to Carol. She is having weird little panic attacks about what kind of revenge Nola is dreaming up and she doesn't deserve any of it. I know it's coming, whatever it is. Even Ms. Bevan warned me that I need to be on the lookout for retaliation, saying, "That girl is as malicious as she is good-looking." She got the first part right. Nola isn't the least bit pretty to me. It's all mascara and hairspray. She probably even stuffs her bra. To my mind, Carol is destined to be way better-looking than Nola can ever hope to be, she just has to suffer through a period of looking not so good to get there.

Carol said, "Okay—my mom and I will pick you up at the end of your road at one."

"Great. Gotta go," I said, and hopped out of bed to sneak

the receiver back on the hook, then beat it up the stairs for just a little more lying around, since Harp had stopped yelling for a moment.

Flopping right back down on my bed, I ruffled the pages of the Walt Whitman, thinking I might try another poem or two. But I wasn't in the mood. As I picked it up to put it back on the nightstand, the old coin fell out from between the pages and onto my chest. *Hmnn.* After I got dressed, I stuck it in my jeans pocket and made a mental note to find somebody who would know if it's worth anything. If it turns out to be valuable, maybe I should sell it and add it to my shoebox stash. I figure my mom would understand if I use the money to get away from here, just like she did. If she ever finds out, that is, which is looking pretty unlikely.

Harp yelled up the stairs again. "Move that lazy behind of yours, Missy!"

I sighed like I was hard done by, but I really don't mind doing my chores. In fact, I looked forward to getting outside and checking in on the cows—Berle's stump is almost healed—and the pigs and Orange Cat, who is looking very pregnant these days. I really don't know how she keeps getting knocked up, given that Harp traps or shoots any stray male who comes near, but she does. It's gut-wrenching to think about him murdering this next batch of fuzzballs. I'm not going to let that happen. This time I will try to make sure Orange Cat is nowhere near Harp when she gives birth.

Maybe I can ask Carol whether the cat can come live with her for the summer? I'm pretty sure her parents will say no, but it doesn't hurt to ask.

After lunch, I ran up to my room to put on a clean top. When I came downstairs again, Mrs. B asked, "Why are you going to town anyways? What do you need to do there?"

"I told you already. We have to go to the library to work on a project for history class."

And this wasn't a complete lie. Though the movie is our top priority, we still haven't begun the assignment Mr. Stoneman gave us, designed to shine a light on the community—God help us. We're supposed to help "discover the past and unravel the unique history of Backhills." Carol and I picked Backhills's most famous bank robbery as our topic, and we're sure we can quickly find what we need, given that Backhills has a pretty good library for a small town. Mrs. Ivy has been the librarian for as long as I've been alive, and for many years before that.

Actually, on one of my infrequent visits a few years ago, she mentioned that she had known my sister, Margaret, and asked me how she liked living in France. Good lord, my heart just about jumped out of my rib cage. Mrs. Ivy didn't pry or pursue some aggressive line of questioning, which I appreciated. When I responded that she was fine, she left it at that. Still, the conversation just about made my head blow off. Did she really think my sister was living in France? Even the cows seem like they know Harp and Mrs. B are liars, but everyone else seems to give them a pass.

~

When we waltzed into the library that Saturday afternoon, it was so damn quiet, and spotless and sanitary, it felt like walking into a morgue, although I had never been in a morgue. As predicted, when Carol and I appeared at Mrs. Ivy's desk and told her we were looking for anything about the Baldwin brothers and the notorious bank robbery of 1919, she didn't hesitate for a second.

"Follow me, ladies," she said as she glided through a maze of tall, dark walnut shelves. "I think you'll find everything we have here in section 114 B. Dale and Cleaver Baldwin. That's them. You may also find these helpful." Mrs. Ivy pulled a stack of books at least a foot high off a couple of shelves and turned on her brown kitten heels to go back to her desk. "Call me if you need anything further, but do it discreetly—actually, just come to my desk. We don't want to bother the other patrons."

I nodded, even though I didn't see a single other soul in the entire library.

"Oh, and you should also consult the microfiche files from the newspapers—it's the very latest thing, you know, for compiling information." She pointed at a big filing cabinet sitting by a machine with a large screen. "You'll be surprised at the amount of information you can find in there if you take the time to really look."

Carol and I immediately plopped the books down on a table and beelined for the micro-thingy station. It took us a minute or two to find the right reel and get a grip on how to move the articles around, but when I finally got it centred in the viewer, I couldn't believe how amazing it was to stare into the past.

Carol was delighted too. "Oh my lord, Wills—look at these old photos! It's so cool!"

When we found photos of the Baldwin boys, we discovered that they were not the best-looking fellows we'd ever seen, but they had nice eyes and thick black hair that didn't even look real. As we scrolled around to find all the stories about the old bank robbery, I was kind of shocked that so much crime had happened in our sleepy, boring, mostly quiet town: rum-runners and moonshiners, tractor jackings, rustling, illegal moose hunts, blackmail schemes, pyramid schemes—even a story about a group of prostitutes who were caught working out of the Hembroff Hotel. The Hembroff Hotel? Where they have bingo and bratwurst every Thursday night for the old farmers? Who knew?

Carol madly took notes as I worked the microfiche machine like I had invented it, narrowing down to the articles about the bank robbers.

After about five minutes' reading, it was clear that the Baldwin brothers were not the smartest pair of thieves in the world. Cleaver, the younger one, was supposed to be a dynamite expert because he worked for the Blackwood Railroad Company blowing up stuff to clear the way for the tracks. His job was to dynamite the safe.

But first he had to blast open the bank's steel-reinforced front door. Cleaver blew up the entire three-storey building instead, burying himself and his brother Dale in the process. How could the guy not know how much explosive to use to blow open a door? I think even I could have figured that out.

When Cleaver was done, all that was left of the building was a pile of rubble. The $22,000 they were trying to steal was still intact inside the safe—it's why they call it a safe, right? But the one gold brick the bank had on display in a glass case just inside the front door was blasted right across town and crashed through the window of the bakery. After they got the window repaired, the owners renamed their place the Goldbar Bakery and started selling a specialty banana bread with actual gold leaf plunked onto either end. It was a big hit.

The Baldwin brothers were kept under guard at the local hospital until they healed from their injuries, and then were transferred to the lock-up to await trial. The night before they were to appear before the judge to enter their pleas, they shimmied down the side of the Backhills jailhouse on a rope of tied-together bedsheets. We found an article with pictures of the sheets dangling: the brothers sure had a long damn drop once the bedsheets came to an end—like at least twenty feet.

Dale was found drowned a few days later in a slough in a field not a mile away. (Our local sloughs can suck the boots off an astronaut.) Cleaver was never seen again. A rumour went around for years that he had broken both ankles in the drop, but he still managed to escape even with bones poking out of his skin. They made 'em tough as nails back then. Or they liked to make up a good story.

Carol's eyes lit up as we scrolled past pictures of Dale's drowned body, laid out on the back of a wagon and surrounded by stern-looking men holding shotguns. "I can't believe they took pictures of a dead guy," she said. "I didn't even know they had cameras back then. I think it's cool that Cleaver escaped. I bet he's still alive somewhere."

"Cleaver would be super-old by now, Carol, too-old-to-be-alive old—and don't forget, he's a bad guy. Bad guys aren't supposed to get away."

"He didn't kill anybody, Wills, he just blew up a building." She looked at me through sheets of dangling hair. "I think it's romantic."

I rolled my eyeballs at her and kept scrolling. But I must have hopped too far to the left because suddenly I'd jumped ahead about fifty years to something labelled "Manatukken Crime Line." Manatukken is a town about a hundred miles from here. Definitely not part of the project we were working on. Scrolling quickly, I hit a group of colour photographs showing a stoic-looking couple sitting on a plaid couch. These were a lot more recent than the ones of the Baldwin brothers. One image made my heart skip a beat as I scrolled past. For a split second I thought it was a picture of Margaret!

I must have gasped, because Carol punched my arm and said, "What? What is it?"

I scrolled back frantically. "I'm trying to find it, Carol, hang on a second. Damn, I went past it—no, here it is."

As I stared at the photo, Carol began to read the attached news article out loud.

MISSING LARKSPUR BABY STILL NOT FOUND

Jon and Connie Larkspur desperately seeking any information about their newborn daughter, Rose, abducted from the Manatukken hospital last Thursday afternoon . . .

I asked Carol to please stop reading since I wasn't really taking in what she was saying. I fiddled around, trying to make the photo larger. The woman's name was Connie Larkspur. She and her husband, Jon, were sitting on a floral sofa. Maybe in their house? There was a clock on the wall and a shelf filled with framed photos of little girls. Jon was staring straight out at me, while Connie had her head turned towards her husband. Her resemblance to my mother was uncanny. I mean, I've only seen two pictures of Margaret in my entire life, and briefly—I don't know where Mrs. B even keeps them—so I didn't have a lot to go on. I was probably making things up in my head. Was I seeing my mother everywhere because I was that desperate? Most likely.

"What's the matter, Willa? Do you know these people? What a horrible story. Someone stole their baby! Can you imagine someone doing that? I wish someone would steal my little brother. I'm kidding."

Carol wouldn't shut up, so I held up a hand, palm towards her.

"It's nothing, Carol. Just for a second there, I thought it was a photo of my—my sister, the one who went to France. But of course it can't be."

I started packing up. "We better get going, or we're going to miss the movie."

"Whoa," Carol said, scrambling to gather up her notes. "No way can we miss it!"

As we headed for the door, I remembered my other mission, and stopped to ask Mrs. Ivy if she had any books on old coins I could take out. She disappeared into the stacks for a moment and came back with *The Book of American Coin Collectibles*.

"It's the only book on rare coins we have," she said. "It needs to be back two weeks Wednesday."

"Thanks, Mrs. Ivy."

By this point, Carol was holding the door open and yelling at me to get a move on. I couldn't wait to drown my troubles in a giant vat of popcorn at the movie theatre. I wished I could have stayed and looked for more photos, but I knew for sure that I was coming back here way sooner than two weeks from Wednesday.

⁓

When I got home, my grandmother was shuffling around the kitchen, humming as she put the final touches on dinner. I don't think she realizes when she's humming, even though it drives Harp nuts. He must tell her to "shut that noise the hell off" at least three times a day. The tea towel she had draped over her round shoulder kept slipping off every time she bent down to check the cheddar biscuits she had in the oven to go with what smelled like lamb stew.

Grunting as she bent to retrieve the towel from the floor, she straightened and stared me down. "You look like you've got ants in your pants, Missy, so sit your behind in that chair. You're late. I hope you all got your work done with what's her name. You better have, because don't think you're gonna be traipsing into town every ten minutes."

She always acts like she can't be bothered to remember Carol's name, practically my only friend in the world, which usually gets a big rise out of me. But tonight I was too focused on what I'd seen at the library to care about my grandmother's nonsense. A photo of a complete stranger that troubled me so much I made the mistake of asking Mrs. B, yet again, about Margaret.

"Do you think Margaret will ever come back here? Do you think she's got amnesia? Otherwise, why wouldn't she want to at least meet me?"

She didn't answer me, just kept sucking air through her teeth and humming a wordless and annoying tune as she paced back and forth between the stewpot and the table. Her expression was completely blank. She didn't look in my direction once. It was like my questions had fallen onto the floor at her fat feet and she was making sure she ground them into the floorboards. Everybody thinks this lump of a woman is my mother—what a joke.

I am the only person on the planet who knows she isn't. Well, my mother does, but she's gone. And Harp, but he's an even worse liar.

What could possibly be so terrible? My darkest thought was that my mother hadn't come back for me because she was dead. No—my darkest thought was that they had done something to her.

God forbid that I bring up anything about the photograph I just saw. That's something I need to keep to myself until I figure out what it means. Still, I was severely tempted to blurt out, *I SAW A PHOTOGRAPH OF SOMEONE WHO LOOKED EXACTLY LIKE YOUR DAUGHTER*, just to see the look on Mrs. B's face. Maybe that look would tell me all I need to know. Instead, what I yelled was "Why won't you tell me about my mother!"

That stopped her pacing and humming, but all she said was, "How about you have a cherry Popsicle and tell me about your afternoon at the library?"

"What? I don't want a Popsicle. It's almost suppertime! I want you to answer my questions for once."

"Wheela, you're still sad about that old cow. You need to get over yourself. Nothing died. Nothing in the long run was harmed. You seem to think life should be light as feathers? It's not. It's heavy from the moment you come into the world. You think it should be easy and pain-free? Well, Papa has a business to run—the farm doesn't run itself."

It kinda does. A business to run? This farm is the farthest thing from a business. Was she delusional?

"I want to know about my mother!" I could feel my cheeks turning red.

"You watch your sassy mouth! You think you're so smart, but you don't have a clue about—"

A honk from the post lady's van interrupted our confrontation just as my grandmother was about to launch into some kind of tirade. I heard the squeak of the mailbox door and both of us turned to the window to watch Claire stuff some envelopes into the rusty old lopsided thing.

On Saturday, we are always Claire's last stop, following a logic only she knows. She has delivered our mail for as long as I can remember, though she doesn't have a single wrinkle on her face. She always wears her brown hair scraped back in a ponytail so tight it pulls her eyes into the shape of almonds, and I never see her in anything but navy shorts and a light-blue government mail shirt. It doesn't matter if it's the dead of winter or the middle of summer, that's what she has on.

She waved at my grandmother as she jumped back into her truck and hollered, "Same old, same old, Mrs. B!" and it was like she broke a spell. Claire floored the gas and drove off with a spit of dirt flying into the air.

"Eat your Popsicle first or your stew—I don't care in the least." My grandmother rushed out the kitchen door and down to the mailbox. She snatched the handful of letters out and shuffled through them like she was dealing cards at a high-stakes poker game. She glanced towards the barn and then up towards me watching her from the kitchen window, and then she shoved the letters down the front of her dress and patted them to make sure they were safely tucked away.

In that moment, I snapped: I can't live like this anymore. Carol and I are going to be having a conversation about the fact that my so-called sister is my mother and my so-called parents are my grandparents. I don't care if she faints or barfs or hates me for lying to her all this time, but I am going to tell her about Margaret. And then my best friend is going to help me get to the bottom of all these lies and secrets.

eighteen

BEV OLDMAN HAD JUST GRADUATED from the police academy when she landed her first job in Black Diamond. Rookies almost always served for at least a year in a small town, where they could sharpen their teeth on petty crime and traffic violations. Nothing big ever happened in Black Diamond, and Bev was kind of counting on that.

It was a miracle that she had graduated at all. Her instructors would look at each other during her physical training and shake their heads. Bev was consistently at the bottom of that class, but they put up with her because of her cheerful, can-do attitude. While she aced the academic part of the training with almost perfect written exams, her gun skills were average. By "average," the police academy had noted that she had managed to shoot another trainee in the hand. Luckily, the trainee she shot admitted that he had come up behind her unexpectedly and argued that the loss of his thumb was a justifiable punishment for his lame attempt at humour, which had involved him wearing a gorilla mask and shouting "Gotcha!" at a woman with a gun in her hand. So they didn't kick Bev out. Still, the incident left her devastated. She only went back to the gun range because her instructors insisted she "get back on the horse." They were big on that kind of attitude.

And now here she was, pulling up to the unassuming Black Diamond police station in her aging car for the very first shift of what she hoped would be an uneventful year or so of policing. And she was as nervous as she'd ever been in her life.

Taking a deep breath, she walked in through the front door as confidently as she could and introduced herself to the desk clerk.

"Hi, I'm Beverley Oldman, the new girl on the beat."

"On the beat?" the clerk said dryly. "Good to know somebody is."

Bev couldn't believe she'd actually said "on the beat," never mind "new girl." Clearing her throat, she tried again. "I am looking for Captain Tripp. Could you point me in the right direction, um—I'm sorry, I didn't get your name."

"That's fine. I never said my name. It's Kerry Wheeler. Call me Wheeler—everybody else does. See that guy right there, sitting at the big desk over by the wall? That's Randy Tripp, captain extraordinaire."

Bev was not sure if Kerry was being sarcastic or not. Or maybe she really thought the captain was extraordinary, which sure would be nice.

"Thanks so much, Kerry—I mean Wheeler. Much appreciated."

Bev rounded the counter and headed towards Captain Tripp. His desk was big, one of those wooden monsters that weighed five hundred pounds, with the three drawers down the side that never opened properly. It looked like it had been sitting in that very spot since the First World War.

"You must be the new kid in town!" Randy Tripp got up, came around his desk and extended his rather small hand to Bev and waited for her to shake it. "Go on, it's just a damn hand!"

She grabbed on and tried her best to squeeze the captain's hand evenly—and not too hard or too soft.

Her new boss was a short fellow, at a stretch maybe five foot six. (His height had always bothered him, but he tried to make up for it with his sense of humour and higher-than-average intelligence—according to him.)

"Welcome to the Black Diamond police force," Captain Tripp said. "Shall we get down to it?"

Bev was thrilled to be cutting to the chase. She was there to work hard for the community and then get the hell out of there and back to civilization. "Yes, sir, let's get down to it. You can count on me. I'll get the job done, sir, no matter how big or small. I am here to serve." Bev winced and made a mental note to dial down her eager-rookie talk a little.

"I wasn't kidding, Constable Oldfield. Let's cut the pleasantries completely and simply get to your caseload."

Now Bev felt too intimidated to correct him for screwing up her name.

Tripp removed a giant pile of files from the corner of his desk and dropped them on what was apparently her new workstation, in the darkest part of the office. It looked so small compared with his giant desk. Dust exploded into the air when the files hit the metal desktop and hung suspended in the slim beam of sunlight coming down from the only window in the entire building.

"These are the Black Diamond and surrounding area open cases. Go through them and figure out which ones are going to take priority. Don't get too excited, Oldberg—they're mostly concerning a bunch of local knuckleheads who have long-overdue fines—speeding, parking, spitting, fighting, adultery."

"Adultery?"

"That was a joke, Oldham."

"It's Oldman," Bev said, her cheeks flushing.

The captain barrelled on as if he hadn't heard. Maybe he hadn't. "Wheeler can help you track down addresses and phone numbers. You shouldn't have a lot of trouble with any of them, but don't let them pay you with bloody chickens or kittens or cabbages. We want cash money. The department is barely squeaking by this year, and we can use every dollar we can get."

Bev hoped Captain Tripp would say he was kidding again, but he didn't. Instead, he turned on his heel and walked over to a small kitchen area, where he removed something smelly from the microwave, then carried it back to his desk.

Bev stuck her purse in a drawer and pulled a stray orange plastic chair up to her new desk. There had to be well over a hundred folders stacked up, so she figured she had better get at it.

The first file Bev opened was for one Mrs. Sheila Stevens. Shoplifting. Never finished her community service, nor did she pay her $350 fine. Bev read a little further and discovered that Mrs. Stevens had been caught repeatedly shoplifting brassieres.

It was going to be a long year.

nineteen

I LIKE MY ROOM, for the most part. It has a slanted ceiling covered in faded floral wallpaper that was put up before I was born. On the south wall, facing the front of the house, there is a little round window that opens and looks out across the field. When summer nights get unbearably hot and muggy, I squeeze through the opening and go out onto the porch roof for some cool air. It always takes my breath away—being out there under all those stars. They look like pieces of broken glass on a black tar road. I don't ever get tired of staring up at them. There never fail to be too many things to think about, and there never fails to be something shooting across the sky.

Still, every summer, I'm finding it harder to squeeze myself through the opening, which used to be so big I never touched the sides. It's my measurement window, I guess, simple proof that one day I will outgrow this whole house.

Carol was sprawled across my floor, flipping through an old

Sears catalogue we must have looked at a thousand times—we had the thing memorized. I was perched on the edge of the chair that sort of goes with the little oak desk set against the wall across from her. I was working up the courage to tell her the truth. I flipped on the green plastic desk lamp because it lends such a cozy light. It was an actual present from Harp that he got from the Salvation Army store and brought home for me. I will never figure him out. Except for this lamp, everything else in the house is old and has a story attached to it. Like the wooden rocking chair on the porch that once belonged to Harp's great-aunt, Cuppy Hartford-Bittlemore. Harp told me on several occasions how her family dragged it across the country in 1897. He insisted it was worth a lot of money because President Lincoln had once sat in it. I told him that Lincoln had been long since dead when that chair was still a tree and he told me to bugger off.

Our kitchen bench used to be a pew from Pastor Simon Westerfield's Church of the Nazarene. Mrs. B says the pastor is her third cousin once removed. I have no idea what the "removed" part means, but she makes sure to tell me that every time she tells the story. The silver spoon collection hanging in the kitchen belonged to Harp's mother. Harp is very touchy when it comes to his mother, and Mrs. B repeatedly warns me never to bring up the spoons or Harp's mother in front of him. I think when I finally get out of here, I'll take the green plastic lamp and those spoons, just to spite him.

Speaking of old things, when I'd flipped through the antique coin book I borrowed from the library, I found my mother's silver dollar on page 115. At least it looks like the same one, and the date matches: 1794! It's called the "flowing hair dollar." I have no idea why, except maybe because the guy on the coin has long hair. The book said it's worth forty to fifty thousand dollars, which seems impossible to believe. That would buy me a dozen bus tickets out of here for sure. I'm so perplexed about how such a valuable coin ended up stuffed in Margaret's old book. If it's worth so much, wouldn't Harp have already sold it? Harp would sell his soul to the Devil if it made him a twenty.

When Carol started laughing her fool head off, I looked up and, lo and behold, she was eyeballing the boys' underwear section (no surprise). She and I have looked through that Sears catalogue so many times, the ink is worn off the corners from us licking our fingers to turn the pages. She thinks the boys in their tighty-whitey underpants are hilariously funny, but they are definitely not for me—I love looking at all the hunting knives and the fishing tackle and, yes, the bras. I still hadn't got one.

Carol said I should make up my damn mind. "Just order yourself a bra, for Pete's sake!"

"Well, if I do, I'm having it sent to your house. There's no way my grandmother will let me have something store-bought. She keeps threatening to make me one."

"Would that be so bad?"

"Are you kidding me? She'd have to measure me, and that is not gonna happen."

"Here's one here by Warner. It's only nine ninety-nine. Let's order you that one. Sears delivers things to the post office now, you know. You just have to go pick it up."

"Ten bucks? Is the thing made of gold thread?"

I got up and flopped down beside her in the middle of the tiny bedroom floor, and together we flipped through the catalogue, looking at all the people who seemed so happy to be wearing just underpants and bras, their smiles big and easy. I wondered if wearing a bra was going to make me smile like that.

I pulled the coin out of my pocket and held it up.

"Carol, I looked this up in that book I borrowed from the library. If it's really what the book says it is, I could cash it in and buy all the bras in the world."

"Oh brother, it looks like some old penny, if you ask me."

"Old penny, my eye! Ya, I get it, but I mean, what if it's rare?" I handed her the coin. I pulled the library book from underneath my bed and found the flowing hair coin page. "Look at that."

Carol held the coin up to the light and looked back and forth from it to the book, squinting hard. "Well, it does say 1794, I'll give you that—so maybe it *is* super-old. We could ask that nosy lady at the post office. They have special coins in there for sale, or at least they used to. My parents bought me a set of wild geese coins when I was ten."

"Lucky you." I was a little bit jealous.

"It wouldn't hurt to ask her." Carol smacked my crossed knee.

"Not in a million years am I asking her. She'd tell the whole town. That's all I don't need. I need to find out for myself."

I shoved the book back underneath my bed and hid the coin under the green lamp on my desk. I was pretty sure Mrs. B wouldn't find it there. She never messes with much of anything when she comes into my room. She doesn't care, or she isn't interested in what I have, which isn't much. My next challenge? Figuring out how to find a coin expert somewhere around here that I can get to either on foot or by bus. Such are the challenges of being fourteen and not able to drive yet.

"Your call, Wills." Carol heaved a big sigh, and it was my turn to be a mind reader, which wasn't too hard in this case.

"Nola has been suspiciously quiet since I broke her nose," I said. "I wonder what she's cooking up for us. Has she even looked at you?"

Carol closed the catalogue and shrugged. "If she has, I wouldn't know, because I try never to look at her. She's not a good person. She scares me, Wills. Now she's so mad, she might actually try and kill us both—or even worse."

"What's worse than being killed?"

"Living every day in fear of being killed, that's what!" Carol started chewing on a piece of her stringy hair.

"I'm sorry about the stupid basketball thing. I honestly don't know what I was thinking. We shouldn't have even gone to the tryouts. You hate sports. I mean, *I* hate sports. I made us both even more of a target."

Now or never, I thought, and leaped in. "I'm going to make it up to you by telling you a very big secret."

"I'm not sure I wanna know." Carol laughed, and when I crossed my eyes at her, she said, "No, I'm serious, I don't think I want to know. The last time you told me a secret, I couldn't look at Ms. Bevan for a week."

I had got my hands on a very blurry Polaroid that was making the rounds at school and it basically showed Ms. Bevan kissing Mr. Toews, the principal. Carol hadn't been impressed, not one little bit. It did kind of make us both want to barf.

She gave me a poke. "I know you're gonna tell me anyways, so go ahead—what?"

My heart started going a million miles an hour, and I felt like I needed to run to the bathroom. I took a deep breath. "Carol, you're not going to believe what I'm about to tell you, but I swear to you it's the truth. Harp and Mrs. B are NOT my parents."

"I think I need to lie down," she said, and flopped back on my bed.

The words were coming out of my mouth like bullets now, unstoppable. "They're my grandparents. Margaret—you know, the one I told you was my sister. Well, she's not my sister. She's my real mother, not that I ever met her, because she went missing the day I was born and Harp was so mad about the whole thing I wouldn't be surprised if he killed her. There—I said it."

Carol was gobsmacked. She went as white as a sheet and moaned. "I think I'm going to be sick."

"Throw up in this if you have to," I said, handing her one of my white cowboy boots. "I hate these stupid things."

"Wills, I can't believe you've been carrying this around your whole life. Honestly, I don't know whether to pop you one right square in the chops or . . . or . . ." She hugged me like I was one of the underpants boys from the Sears catalogue.

"You're not gonna throw up on me, are ya?"

She shook her head from side to side.

"So you believe me?"

"Of course I believe you. I always thought something was kind of weird with your folks. I've never minded them as much as you do, but I don't have to live with them—plus, aren't they like eighty-five?"

"More like sixty-five."

Carol retched into my boot and then kept right on talking. "You really think she could be dead? Your sister—I mean your mother?"

"I have no idea. Remember me getting so flustered that day at the library? In that old newspaper microfiche, I saw someone who looks *exactly* like my mother. I haven't stopped thinking about it, but it doesn't make any sense. The picture is really old, which means the lady is way older than my mom. I don't know what the heck is going on, but I want to see if I can find out."

Carol grabbed the boot and threw up in it again. She wiped her mouth with one of the shirts I had on the floor and then lay back down. Catching my unimpressed expression, she said, "Geez, Wills, it's not your secret that's making me sick. I ate a pan of praline fudge this morning."

Who eats a whole pan of anything?

Burping, she said, "This is a lot to get my head around."

"I guess the first thing we should do is get back to that library as soon as we can and take another look at that photograph."

~

I didn't sleep much that night. Telling Carol set everything tossing and turning inside me. The next morning, I got up and headed outside to milk the cows without stopping in the kitchen. The less time I could spend with my grandparents the better.

As usual, Dally and Berle were lined up in their stalls waiting for me. Crilla, who was long past needing milking, was hanging around too. She didn't like to miss out on our visits.

The milking stool was off its hook, which was weird because I distinctly remembered hanging it up the day before. Also, the metal bucket was already sitting underneath Dally. Had Harp snuck out here early to play some kind of practical joke on me? It had to be. My grandmother wouldn't help me darn a sock, never mind set out a milking bucket.

"What are you three up to?" I asked, and Berle let out a big moo. Before I started on Dally, I took a look at Berle's tail. The tape was off and it had healed well, but it was reduced to the size of a pot handle. Still, she flicked it back and forth at me like a dog wagging her tail. It was comical, but incredibly adorable.

I gave Berle's haunch a thump, and said, "Looking good. But hold your horses a minute. I have to do your friend first."

It had taken me years to figure out how to milk a cow so that I really got the milk flowing. I am sure that it hadn't been pleasant for any of them to put up with an eight-year-old pulling on their thingies—it certainly wasn't pleasant for me. Milking looks easy, but it's not. Until I got the hang of it, my wrists would ache something fierce. I even got blisters!

I sat down on the stool by Dally's side and pulled my hat over my ears to protect my hair, which she likes to lick. She usually licks the hat right off my head, but at least it isn't my hair.

I always talk to them when I'm doing the milking. They seem to understand every word. I tell them everything Mrs. B says about my mother, and I tell them about all the cruel things Harp has done—they've experienced more than their fair share of those. I also tell them about my hopes and dreams. They are my confidantes and friends, and while I'm with them, I always feel understood and I never feel alone.

After I finished up with Dally, I moved on to Berle. By this point in the morning routine, Orange Cat has usually made an appearance. She likes a few squirts of fresh milk and a scratch on the head. Pausing the pulling and squirting for a moment, I called her and waited to hear a meow. Nothing. Come to think on it, I hadn't seen her yesterday either. I was pretty sure Harp hadn't got rid of her, or he would have said something. Or maybe he wouldn't, given that Mrs. B would chase him off the farm with her broom if he touched a hair on Orange Cat's behind. It always strikes me as strange that she protects the cat but tolerates Harp mercilessly killing litter after litter of kittens—"Do what you have to do, old man. We can't have dozens of cats running around the place." No one has ever said either of them makes sense.

After I finished milking Berle, I hung the stool back on the hook, tugging hard to make sure it wouldn't fall off.

On the way back out of the stable with the bucket of milk, I happened to look down at the barn floor. The early-morning light pouring through the open half-door shone like a spot-light—and there, as plain as day and written in the dirt, were the letters *S. O. S.*

I stared at the message for a full minute, wondering what the heck was going on. Then I turned around, and all three big black-and-white cows were staring back at me.

"Okay, you guys. I promise. I'm going to figure out what Harp and Mrs. B did to my mother. Then I'm going to find her. And when I do, I am—we are—going to make sure they don't hurt you or anyone ever again." My heart was beating three times its normal speed by the time I finished that speech, but I meant every word of it. Even though I had no idea how to make it come true.

twenty

MARGARET SAT AT THE COUNTER of the café and sipped on the worst black coffee she had ever tasted. She was tired after her twelve-hour shift at the John Deere factory in Dearborn, Michigan. She had been working on the tractor assembly line for eighteen months now, which was nothing short of a small miracle. Most of her other jobs had lasted six, tops. She rubbed her temples with the heels of her hands and could think of nothing more tempting than heading home and falling into her bed, but tonight was the night she wrote her monthly letter to Mayvale. She was pretty sure Mrs. B destroyed each one of them the second they arrived, but Margaret wrote anyway. Even if it was an exercise in futility, it helped her keep going.

It was that thread of connection she craved. Every day, she straddled the bittersweet worlds of guilt and desire: she wanted her daughter back, but she was afraid that if she went to get her, Mayvale would reject her. Why would she want to have anything to do with the person who abandoned her? Countless times, Margaret had found herself behind the wheel of her decrepit old car, ready to drive hundreds and hundreds of miles to get her kid back. But then doubt and despair would creep up through her rib cage and lodge themselves in the back of her throat, choking off any attempt she made to be brave.

What was she supposed to do? Just show up on the Bittlemores' doorstep and announce, "Well, Mayvale, here I am—your real mother—the one who left you with those two losers. Come with me to your new and wonderful life"?

That also couldn't have been further from the truth. Margaret didn't have a wonderful life. She worked paycheque to paycheque and didn't have a single dollar saved up for anything. Certainly not for a cross-country trip, and certainly not enough to take care of a fourteen-year-old girl. That didn't stop her from playing the same fantasy over and over in her head, the one where Mayvale would show up just as Margaret was coming off shift at the factory and run into her open arms, yelling, "HEY, ARE YOU MARGARET? I AM YOUR DAUGHTER! I've been looking for you my entire life!" Even though she doubted very much that her daughter even knew she existed. Why would her parents have told her a thing?

In every letter or postcard, whether it got to Mayvale or not, she vowed she was coming back for her baby as soon as she was able. But here she was about to turn twenty-nine years old in three weeks. Most days she felt more like she was sixty.

The few friends she'd managed to make since landing in Dearborn didn't know a thing about her being a mother. All she'd told her pals from the factory, Louise and Darren, was that she'd once lived in Canada and had got out of there after a bad divorce. They'd occasionally hang out and have a beer after work—certainly not close friends. Margaret was relieved neither of them had dug any further. They told her she was probably better off having left. They had no idea how true that was.

"Most bad marriages don't end in divorce—they don't end!" Darren said, and laughed his head off, then offered to buy the girls another round.

Margaret said, "Not for me, Darren. One is my limit—you know how wild I am." Louise passed as well, saying she needed to get home to her kids. Margaret winced a little. How great would that be?

Sitting alone in the café, she rummaged in her old bag and pulled out paper and pen.

The letters allowed her to imagine a world where she and her daughter were together and blissfully happy. A world where they lived on a little farm with cows and a cat and a garden and fresh air. A world where there were no crazy parents and no secrets and no heartache.

Margaret didn't even have to think about what she was going to write.

Dear Mayvale,

I thought I'd write you a quick letter before I headed home from that little café I told you about a few months ago . . . the coffee is still terrible but I drink it anyway. Are you happy you'll soon be finished school for the year?

I can't believe you're already 14. You must be getting so tall, although I'm not all that tall, to be honest! Rob (your father) was already 6 feet. I bet he grew for another 5 years!

I wish I could see you. Maybe someday, darling girl. Your absent mother has dropped the ball so many times, she can't even find it anymore.

Sorry, I'm just terrible at being funny. I bet you're funny, Mayvale—I have a feeling you're a real character!

I think about you every day and hope that these letters will find you eventually.

I know I'm not brave.

I know I've been gone a long time.

I feel like I've grown up at the same time as you have.

Someday I'll tell you everything, but I want to do that while I look into your eyes. I hope we get to do that.

Love you always,
Mom (Margaret)

She licked the envelope and sealed it up tight. She wrote the address to the Bittlemore farm on the front for what felt like the millionth time and tucked it into her bag. She'd get one of her trucker pals to drop it into a mailbox somewhere far from Dearborn. Enlisting Tizzy Holt to help her out with the letter drops felt like the only clever thing she'd ever done. Until she was ready to face her daughter, the Bittlemores would never be able to figure out where Margaret was.

twenty-one

BEV OLDMAN HAD BEEN ON the job nearly two weeks and, like the eager new cop she was, she had managed to rip through almost half of the 148 files that Captain Randy Tripp had dropped on her desk. No case was too small, no fine too insignificant. She'd resolved a variety of minor outstanding violations: unpaid speeding tickets, stunting charges (Mark Reynolds doing doughnuts in the middle of the grocery store lot in his pickup truck), expired licence plates, even fifteen-dollar parking fines. Bev had also managed to track down the McMullen brothers and get them to their court date. (She wasn't sure who was charged with assaulting whom, because the brothers had beat each other up on more than one occasion.) None of these tasks were the least bit challenging, but Bev was determined to impress the captain with her enthusiasm and effectiveness. No amount of wishing she was working in a big city was going to change anything. She needed to put in her time, and keeping busy made the days go by quicker until she could get out of here.

Near the end of another very long shift of fighting crime, Bev thought she'd stay at her desk just one more hour and move another little stack of files into the Solved pile. She took a gulp of her freezing-cold black coffee and let out an audible sigh.

Randy touched the top of her head as he headed past her on his way to the tiny precinct kitchen to refill his thermos with hot water. "Catch any bad guys today, Oldham?"

*Old*man! *What's so hard about remembering* Oldman? The thought flapped inside her head like a flag in the wind.

When he came back, he stopped and pointed a finger at the two piles on her desk. "You're making a dent, kid, and that's saying something."

"And I'm meeting some fascinating people too. Even the McMullen boys were very co-operative, all things considered."

"They're as crazy as a shithouse door. Two shithouse doors!" Tripp seemed very pleased with himself for the word-picture. He touched the top of Bev's head one more time and headed for his desk.

Stop touching my goddamned head!

She couldn't seem to bring herself to utter the words. She hoped maybe the touch was affection, or his weird acknowledgement of a job well done. Whatever it was, she wished he would quit doing it. One of the things she needed to work on was standing up for herself and speaking her mind. Next week for sure, she'd say something about it to him.

It took Constable Oldman (Bev loved thinking of herself as "Constable Oldman") another two and a half months to meticulously make her way through the remaining case folders. She completed jobs that nobody else had bothered to tackle—or wanted to tackle, more like—and now she was in the home stretch.

Only seven measly folders left. That night she took home the last few files to read in bed so she could get a jump on what she needed to do the next day. She didn't know what she was going to do with herself after she resolved these last cases, but she could hardly contain her excitement. Well, actually, yes, she could—Bev had never been good at feeling proud or celebrating what she accomplished. But when she got this done, she was going to start believing in herself, dammit!

She pushed her tortoiseshell glasses up her nose and opened an especially thick and ragged-looking folder. It was coffee-stained and ripped in various places, with pieces of tape stuck around its spine to hold it together. She opened it to a cover page that read *Case A7150, Missing Baby Larkspur* over an *Unsolved* stamp.

Finally, Bev thought, *something that isn't a traffic fine or drunk brothers breaking bottles over each other's heads.* This was real. Innocent victims. Real tragedy. Real crime.

Scanning quickly, she realized that the Larkspur baby had gone missing almost twenty-nine years ago from the Manatukken hospital and no one had ever figured out what had happened. Black Diamond was over a hundred miles away from Manatukken, but it made sense that multiple counties had been involved. Solving crime was a heck of a lot different almost thirty years ago—so many things had changed. Intrigued, Bev poured herself a glass of Buckshot Chardonnay from the bottle on her nightstand and took a big gulp. It tasted terrible, but the town of Black Diamond had a tiny liquor store with only two kinds of wine—red and white. This particular bottle may well have actual buckshot in it, but it would have to do.

Bev took another big slug and set the glass back down. It really was unbearably sweet, or tart, or who knew—it was that hard to tell.

Anyway, all that time ago, someone had walked into the small hospital in Manatukken and stolen a newborn baby girl. From the mountain of dog-eared paper in the folder, officers from three different counties joined in on a door-to-door, farm-to-farm investigation. They took out ads in seven or eight different newspapers begging for information, organized volunteers to conduct shoulder-to-shoulder searches of fields and woodlands, plastered hundreds of *Missing* posters in every store, school, gas station, truck stop, and campground within five hundred miles, had the parents appeal to the kidnapper or kidnappers live on TV. They even tapped into the national police database looking for similar crimes.

What a tragedy for this family—what absolute hell for them.

Bev felt the hair stand up on her arms. This folder was the very first of the batch that could turn into an actual big-time cold-case investigation. She took another swig to steady her excitement—immediately regretting it. There wasn't enough oak-barrel aging in the world to make this wine drinkable. No matter, Bev still felt the hope swelling in her heart. She wanted desperately to be the officer to solve this cold case.

But had her training prepared her for something this major? Was she really capable of putting all the pieces together? Almost twenty-nine years is a heck of a long time, and a lot of the players—the witnesses—might be pretty old or pretty dead.

"That's enough of that," she said, screwing the top back

onto the Buckshot bottle as she pushed her doubts away. "Gotta keep a clear head. Gotta get an early start."

Bev took off her glasses and pinched the bridge of her nose and then gave her eyes a deep and satisfying rub. A real, honest-to-God case. Tomorrow morning, she would drive to Manatukken and interview whoever was still around to interview about Baby Larkspur, including the parents, if she could find them. Perhaps this was the beginning of a whole new chapter in her little life.

~

At her desk first thing the next morning, Bev called and left a message for the hospital administrator, Charlie Rutherford, telling him to expect a visit from her later that day to talk about the Larkspur cold case. He called back in less than thirty seconds to make it very clear that he hadn't been around when the only kidnapping in Manatukken history had taken place.

"It was a very long time ago, Ms. Oldman—"

"Constable Oldman," Bev interrupted.

"Yes, Constable. I was about to say that we do have a nurse still working here who was junior at that time and I will make sure she is available to you. I look forward to seeing you and being of any assistance possible."

~

Bev pulled into Manatukken around 1 p.m. It was a tidy town, laid out like a Monopoly board, looking very peaceful and unassuming. She rolled down her window and asked the first person she saw where the hospital was, and the elderly woman gave her a big smile and pointed straight down the street she was already on.

She parked her car in a spot for visitors near the hospital entrance and walked in through the sliding doors.

The hospital appeared to be from another time entirely, with its linoleum floors, Arborite countertops, and stainless steel edging around everything, but it was as clean as a whistle and charmingly bright with the sun coming in through the lobby windows. Bev removed her uniform hat and tucked it underneath her arm as she approached the desk.

"I am here to speak to Charlie Rutherford."

The brown-haired woman at the desk, whose name tag read *Sharon*, was chewing what appeared to be the world's biggest wad of gum. Looking Bev up and down, from her shiny police hat under her arm to her equally shiny black shoes, she shoved the wad into one cheek and said, "Who should I tell him is here?"

"Constable Oldman." Announcing her police rank was always satisfying.

"Um, you can take a seat while I page him or, well, you can just keep standing." The woman burst out with a shrill, high-pitched, unbearably loud laugh. "No, seriously, though, you might as well sit down, because Charlie is the slowest guy on the planet."

Instead, Bev took the opportunity to walk around the lobby, peering down the hallway that led to the hospital emergency department. She looked at the size of the windows, where the fire alarms were, the position of the pop machine, even peeked into the main-floor bathrooms. She scribbled away in her notepad and tried to picture the place as it would have been twenty-nine years earlier, filled with bodies and movement and, eventually, chaos.

After about ten minutes, a youngish man in a bad suit

turned up at reception, and Bev walked over to him.

"You must be Miss—er, sorry, my bad—Constable Oldman. I'm Charlie, the boss around here! Actually, I have a few fellas above me, so I guess I'm the, um, the glorified but very important admin guy. If something goes wrong, I get all the credit!" He smiled awkwardly and wiped his brow with a hanky he pulled out of his jacket pocket. He glanced over at Sharon and said, "Hold my calls."

Sharon looked confused, which made Bev doubt he got any calls she would have to hold.

"Shall we?" Charlie, still sweating a lot, waved at her to follow him. *Nerves*, thought Bev. She wrote that down.

He led her through the double doors to the small triage area and then into the heart of the emergency department. There were only a few people propped up in beds with IVs dangling or heart monitors beeping—it was a quiet afternoon.

"Come this way, Ms. Oldman. We may not be the big city, but we are quite modern, we manage, although a bit more funding would sure go a long way." Bev nodded and, again, scribbled in her notepad. "Believe it or not, Deb is still working in maternity after all these years!" Charlie led them up a small stairwell to the second floor, stopping once to run his hanky across his forehead. Two flights, no windows. Twelve steps each flight. A fire alarm to the right of the door at the top of the second flight. Bev jotted it all down.

"Do you have fire drills here, Mr. Rutherford?"

He nodded. "Quarterly. We all converge in the parking lot and do a head count. Never an issue."

"Do you bring out all the patients?" That seemed to Bev like an impossible thing to manage. "I mean, the ones on oxygen or hooked up to whatever? Do they get brought out too?"

Charlie looked like he was starting to feel more anxious—maybe he hadn't expected to be asked these types of questions. "No, not for the drills," he said at last. "But staff do practise for potential patient evacuation."

Bev wrote another couple of lines, closed her notepad and shoved it into her coat pocket.

The maternity ward was in the same place it had been when Baby Larkspur went missing, at the end of the hall on the second floor. Bev counted steps in her head as she followed Charlie down the narrow but well-lit hallway. To her it looked as though the hospital hadn't changed in forty years, but she knew never to assume. So she asked him if, as far as he knew, anything was different now.

"With the exception of a new lockbox system for the pain-killers, we haven't changed a thing," Charlie said. "We were having some thefts . . ."

He seemed grateful when they reached the nurses' station before he had to explain about the missing pain meds. Deb—Deborah Almond—was waiting for them. Short, blond, with huge green eyes, a great manicure, pink lipstick, and a cardigan sweater over her pale-blue uniform. She shook Bev's hand, then said, "I'm a little nervous. I haven't had any reason to speak to a police officer since, well, you know what happened all those years ago. I was just a kid back then."

Bev had already done some digging and found out that the older nurse on the ward that tragic day had died of breast cancer only seven months earlier, which Bev thought was not only unfortunate timing but unfortunate in general—just a shitty disease.

"You have absolutely nothing to worry about." Bev pulled out her notepad again. She wasn't sure why she'd even put it away in the first place. "I'm new, so I've been asked to take a fresh look at the Larkspur case, which, as you know, is still unsolved. I just want to chat about anything you might remember about the incident. Sometimes, later, people remember little things they don't even think are important, but then they turn out to be crucial. So don't hesitate to tell me even the most benign, boring details. You'd be surprised at what's rolling around in your brain."

Deborah took a big swig out of her plaid thermos.

"I could use a coffee myself," Bev said, and she looked around for a machine.

"Oh, this is soup."

That was a new one. "Ah, well then."

Deborah cleared her throat and cautiously launched into her story.

"It was a normal day, I mean—I was in training, so everything back then seemed awkward and sort of hard. I wasn't really in charge of anything, you know?"

"Okay—go on."

"We had three babies in the nursery, I do remember that—and then the fire alarm went off! And we had to take it seriously because we didn't know if it was a drill or what. Everybody was running around and then the Larkspur baby was, POOF, gone! But we didn't actually realize she was missing until, like, a half-hour later. All the patients, including Mrs. Larkspur, had been taken out to the muster point and I remember people telling me she was freaking out." Deborah took another swig of her soup. "I thought my supervisor, Betty—God rest her soul—had got the other two babies out and she assumed that I had the Larkspur baby with me, but I'd already dropped her off in the nursery. It still makes me so sad to think about it."

"Do you recall anything out of the ordinary from before the fire alarm went off?"

"Not really. The father, Mr. Larkspur, was a really nice man. I knew him from around town—everybody knows everybody here. Well, back then we did. Anyway, he came up to us in the hallway before the alarm was pulled. I was taking his baby for some little tests, like normal stuff that you do with babies. Nothing was wrong—with the baby, I mean. The baby was normal." Deborah was getting agitated and was starting to talk more quickly.

Charlie, leaning at the end of the counter, cleared his throat and rolled his eyes in Deb's general direction. "She's looking for details, Deborah. Details! Out-of-the-ordinary things—like a unicorn eating an ice cream cone or a tall dark stranger running away with a baby in a briefcase." Charlie seemed to think he was being clever, but Bev thought he was basically just a bully.

"That's all right, Mrs. Almond," she said. "You're doing fine, so just carry on." She looked over at Charlie and gave him a little smile, although she wanted to punch the sweaty little weasel in the temple.

"I've gone over it all in my head so many times. That poor, poor family, I went to the same school as their girls, a few years earlier mind you. But I remember them. They seemed like a tight-knit bunch. I was standing in the hall with their dad one minute and then . . ."

"So, you were standing in the hall with Mr. Larkspur before the alarm went off?"

"Yes. He tucked a little souvenir—a talisman—in his daughter's—"

"What do you mean?"

"He put a silver dollar or something in her diaper.

Apparently, he did that with all his girls. I thought it was so funny and cute."

"Are you sure it was a silver dollar?" Bev was intrigued. She hadn't read a single word about any type of coin in the file.

"I didn't look at it that closely, but yeah, it was a silver dollar. He said it was for luck, but I guess it wasn't all that lucky."

Deborah was starting to sound upset again and glanced at Charlie. "I didn't see anyone strange or anyone who didn't belong there. It was just a lot of noise and rushing around. After Mr. Larkspur tucked the coin in the baby's diaper, I took her to the nursery and put her in her bassinet, ready for the doctor, and I left. A few minutes later, the alarm went off. I followed protocol and went back to the nursery and grabbed the baby closest to me and carried it to the muster point. Later, of course, I wished I'd grabbed the Larkspur baby. But then somebody else's baby would have been the unlucky one, right?"

"Where was Mr. Larkspur when the alarm went off?"

"He'd already left, I guess."

"Mrs. Almond, you've been really helpful. I know these cold cases can dredge up a lot of not-so-good memories. But I appreciate you making the effort."

Bev closed her notebook and stuffed it back into her coat pocket, and awkwardly shook the nurse's hand. What she really wanted to do was hug her, but that wasn't really the thing to do in a situation like this where she had to remain totally professional. Turning to the annoying admin guy, she said, "Do you mind if I wander around a bit more, Charlie? Maybe I can get a sense of what the kidnapper might have seen and where they might have gone."

"Knock yourself out. If there's anything else I can help you with . . ."

"There is one thing. Does the hospital have a number for the Larkspurs? I need to check in with the parents."

"Sharon can probably help you out or, you know, they'd just be in the phone book—which, believe it or not, is still a thing in Manatukken."

"Thanks." She stuck out her hand towards him reluctantly, and just as she had anticipated, his hand was somewhat moist. She nodded again at Deborah, and then strolled away, discreetly wiping her palm on her pant leg. She needed to talk to Jon Larkspur about that coin. Why hadn't anybody made any mention of it? It could be a big step forward in the case. Pushing through the door into the lobby, Bev had to hide a grin: she was feeling like an honest-to-goodness police officer.

When she stopped in front of Sharon, the receptionist was eating Cheerios out of a Tupperware container. She offered some to Bev.

"Oh, I couldn't—I'm still full from lunch—but thank you. Charlie said you might know how to reach the Larkspurs?"

Sharon seemed relieved to not have to share her little stash of snacks. She shoved the Tupperware back into her purse. "As far as I know, they still live in the same old place!" Consulting her phone book, Sharon wrote down the number, ripped the piece of paper off her little pad and handed it to Bev. "There ya go."

And out the sliding doors Bev went. Next stop, the Larkspurs'.

twenty-two

CAROL AND I MET at the library on Tuesday, but we couldn't spend any time chasing down the photo of the woman who looked like Margaret because we had to finish our actual school project about the old bank being blasted into smithereens. Neither of us needed to get a big fat fail. Our new plan was to meet up again on Thursday night after my chores were done and comb through as much stuff as we could.

It's nearly impossible to go to town more than one time a week without having an entire panel of investigative experts (ha!) grilling me for information. When I was getting ready, Harp was in his practically decomposing chair in the living room, and he'd been drinking, no big surprise. He'd been typically quiet while Mrs. B gave me a lecture about how I was never around anymore and everything was falling to shite and I needed to hike up my trousers and start pulling my weight around here—but thankfully she'd disappeared back to the kitchen, where we could hear her incoherently muttering as she crashed pots and pans. Once he was sure Mrs. B wasn't going to be hovering over his shoulder, Harp, like the great conversationalist he is, began his tirade right smack dab in the middle of whatever he'd been thinking.

"She left you high and dry. She didn't give a shit about you. Why do you care about somebody who didn't give two shits about you?"

I soon figured out that he was talking about Margaret. Could the man suddenly know how to read minds? Did he know that I was going to the library? How was that possible?

Then, to my utter horror, he lurched forward and grabbed my face and turned it towards his. His bony fingers were like a Vise-Grip around my jawbone. "You need to quit wishing and hoping that she's gonna come back and fetch you."

That furrowed brow—I mean that ONE furrowed brow—made him look like he'd had a stroke. His whole head looked lopsided. He may have cut off her tail, but Berle had very much left her mark on him. The red, infected gash, the exact shape of her back hoof, was still seeping a glutinous slime.

It was hard to speak with his hand clamped around my head, but I managed to get out, "I have no idea what you're talking about. I'm going to meet Carol to work on our school project—we need to have it finished next week." I am a terrible liar, and a coward too, since I wanted to shout at the top of my lungs that I was working on a huge exposé on how he murdered his daughter and passed me off as his own kid all these years. But obviously I didn't.

"That bitch screwed us over! It was never part of the plan to bloody leave you here with us!"

Plan? What plan? Neither he nor Mrs. B had ever said

anything about a plan. Maybe it was the booze rattling off a lot of nonsense, but, as my grandmother had told me on many occasions, "A drunk man's words are a sober man's desires."

I was relieved when he finally let go of my face. I steadied myself and took a deep breath. "What plan, Harp?"

"The GODDAMN plan! ARE YOU LISTENING? You were gonna be put back in that place. And you were supposed to be a boy! You, you don't listen—neither of you listen. It was never supposed to be you sitting here like a queen bee. What a mess you've made of my goddamn life!"

What an uplifting thing for someone to yell into your face. That you'd made a mess by simply being born.

This time when he lunged, Harp managed to grab my arm, squeezing his fingers into my flesh. His eyes were bloodshot slots, the perfect size to jam a nickel into. I refused to utter an audible OUCH because I knew it would fill him with delight. He liked hurting things—that was no big secret.

I grabbed his hand and pulled his fingers away, one by one. "I need to get to the library now."

I was halfway out the door when he hollered, "Hey you! Come back here! I mean it!"

From experience, I knew it would be worse if I didn't do what I was told, so, reluctantly, I trudged back, stopping just out of his reach. Harp looked exhausted—his head propped on one skinny wrist as he swigged from his Mason jar.

"What now?" I was trying to stay calm.

"She's been up in that ceiling again."

"Why would anybody be up in the ceiling? Maybe you heard a squirrel?"

He blinked at me very slowly and motioned with his head in

the direction of the attic crawl space. "No, it's not a GODDAMN squirrel."

I could hear my grandmother breathing on the other side of the kitchen door, that distinct wheeze of hers causing my arm hairs to stand on end. She'd been listening, but not interfering. That really made me curious. There were three people living in this house and two of us were not going up into the crawl space. That left one.

⌣

Carol was waiting for me outside the library. When she saw me jogging towards her, she started waving like a maniac. I felt like I was about to cross the finish line of a marathon and Carol was my cheering section. I was exhausted because it nearly was a darn marathon—three miles from the farm into town. I only sort of walked/ran it, but I was still completely out of breath. Ms. Bevan would not have been impressed with my fitness level.

When I stopped in front of her, Carol said, "You're all red." Like she'd uncovered another secret.

"Carol, I ran all the way here because I was trying very hard NOT to be late! Did you think I was going to arrive in a taxi? Or on the back of a cow, maybe?"

"I was just making an observation. I guess I thought Mr. or Mrs. B—or whoever they are—might drive you for once."

"Are you kidding me for real? My grandmother doesn't have a licence and Harp is only capable of driving me crazy."

Carol shrugged and sort of laughed through her nostrils, which sounded like she was tooting a small trumpet.

Inside, after Mrs. Ivy handed over the same pile of stuff we'd asked for on our very first research trip, we beelined for the microfiche machine. As I examined the flimsy sheets, one after the other, Carol hovered over my shoulder eating a giant dill pickle. I couldn't decide whether it was the sound or the smell that distracted me the most. "Could you not do that, please?"

"Sorry."

"Thank you. A pickle? Really? Oh my God!" Carol begrudgingly chucked the remaining piece of pickle into the nearest garbage can.

And there was the photo! I turned the little black knob on the side of the machine until I got it into focus. "Carol, that's the lady. It says here that her name is Connie Larkspur."

"What does she have to do with the bank being blown up?"

"Carol, we have moved on, remember? We can check off the blown-up-bank project and should get at least a B-plus for it. This is what I was telling you about the other day, the lady . . . this lady! She looks exactly like Margaret."

Carol just looked confused.

"Don't you remember me telling you my parents are actually my grandparents because their daughter, who I thought was my sister, is actually my mother?"

"I guess I lost track of all the details. I was too busy throwing up into your cowboy boot."

"You said you believed me."

"I do believe you, Wills. I'm just trying to get my head around it. It's like a bad movie."

"Margaret had me when she was fourteen years old and then she ran away the night I was born, probably because my grandparents are crazy or whatever. Or maybe they did something horrible to her. That's the mystery I need to solve."

Carol's brows stitched themselves together like two black crows—she was thinking hard, too hard. "Wait a minute. So your sister in Paris is your mother? Or did your sister—your mother, I mean—ever really go to Paris? Holy God Almighty, Willa!"

Of course the first time I hear my friend Carol raise her voice, it has to be in a library, with Mrs. Ivy peering over her glasses at us from behind her counter.

"Carol, keep your voice down," I whispered.

"But Jesus Christmas cookie, Wills, let me get this straight. Your sister—I mean, your mother—she ran away after she had you and, obviously, she didn't take you with her. So Mr. and Mrs. Bittlemore really are your grandparents, which is probably why they look kind of old?"

"Honest to God, Carol, you've got to at least try to keep up."

I was shaking now, and my eyes were watering so hard I could barely make out what was on the microfiche. I would start crying, for sure, if I let myself take the whole mess in even just a crack further. I had to push it all away from my heart.

But I wanted Carol to see the photograph, so I pushed my chair off to the side and pulled her over to the microfiche machine. "Look down through this goggle thing at the lady on the far right. She's the one—she looks a heck of a lot like my real mother. Like Margaret."

"So your mother's name is still Margaret?"

"Yes."

"And your sister, uh, I mean your mother, had sex with somebody and had you."

"Yes, that's what she did."

"And then she ran away."

"According to my grandparents. I guess I'm hoping that she had a really good reason to abandon me and nothing worse happened to her."

"Wills, your life is so exciting! It's like you're living right in the middle of an adventure. I think it's cool that your sister is your mother. It would be like—well—if my brother were my father!"

"No, it wouldn't. That would be totally impossible—your brother is younger than you are, Carol."

"Oh yeah, you're right. Still, though. How weird would that be?"

Carol leaned over and peered into the machine again. "Holy moly, I remember this now, Wills. This is the woman whose baby was stolen!"

I'd been so focused on Connie Larkspur's face, I hadn't even registered the headline. I nudged Carol out of the way and looked through the eyepiece again. No wonder she was staring so blankly back at us from somewhere lost in time. Someone had stolen her baby and the police hadn't been able to find her! Had she ever gotten the baby back? I had so many questions swarming around in my head.

It felt like the universe was sending me clues, finally pushing me in the direction of truth. The resemblance might not mean anything at all, but I knew I had to dig a little deeper. I didn't know if this Connie woman was even alive.

Carol must have noticed me drifting off into my own little world again. "Willa! Wills! We have to pack up for the night. Mrs. Ivy is giving us the evil eye because the library's about to close." She added, "And I've gotta get home, and you better get going too or you'll be in a heap of trouble."

On our way past Mrs. Ivy's desk, I asked the librarian how I could find out whether someone was still living in Manatukken. She said if I had the name, it would be easy enough to look them up in the phone book, except this library didn't have a

Manatukken phone book because the town was a hundred miles away.

Okay, so I needed to get my hands on one of those phone books. Then I needed to find an expert to tell me if my mother's coin was worth anything and keep Carol away from dill pickles for the rest of time, if I could manage it. My to-do list was getting longer by the minute.

twenty-three

MY GRANDMOTHER WAS SITTING at the kitchen table when I got back. Harp was nowhere to be seen—likely passed out somewhere. She had picked up where he left off and was drinking the ruby-coloured brandy the two of them made from the fruit of a few scraggly cherry trees in the yard. She seemed annoyed with me when I came flying through the side door, likely mad that I'd been somewhere where I'd had a scrap of interaction with the outside world—somewhere other than this stupid farm.

She took a big slug of her cherry brandy and smacked her thin, wrinkly lips. "You suddenly decided you like school now?"

"I've always liked school." *It's the only time I can get the hell away from you two*—but I didn't say that out loud. "We're working on a special assignment and all the stuff we need is at the library. Why don't you go there sometime? They've got lots of books about pigs." I was pushing it just a bit.

"I know all I need to know about pigs. I know all I need to know about everything. I know you're a know-it-all, that's what I know."

She was for sure tipsy, so I figured I'd just let all the bombs fly.

"I want to write a letter to my mother. Do you know where a person would send something like that?"

My grandmother immediately glanced at the attic hatch, like a string attached to her chin had pulled it up when I said the word *letter*. I took a mental note. As soon as I had a minute to myself, I was going to get up into that crawl space and see what was so interesting.

I said, "I think it's time I reintroduced myself to her somehow, don't you? I'm sure she was under a lot of duress before she ran away. But come on—by now she's gotta be wondering how I'm doing."

"Duress? What *duress*? She was a spoiled rotten brat who didn't appreciate anything she had. Nothing was good enough for her. She put Papa and me in a very sticky situation and all we did was try to save her reputation so she could hold her head up in life."

She took another gulp of her liquid fire and started choking. "It went—down—the—wrong—tube—" she spluttered.

It took a few moments for her to recover herself. I didn't make any effort to help her, not that she would have noticed if I had. Would it be murder to not help a choking person? All joking aside . . .

When she finally got herself sorted out, she pointed a gnarly finger at me. "You need to stop all this bullshit. I'm sick of you going on about Margaret, Margaret, Margaret." She skipped right over the letter part.

And right then, just like a dam breaking, she went on about Margaret, Margaret, Margaret, telling me the same old horrible story about Harp chasing her around with the knife, and how they locked her up for five whole months for her own good, and how kind and caring my grandmother had been towards the ungrateful girl. I'm not sure why she kept retelling this story. Maybe she thought if she told it enough times, the ending would be a happy one. One thing was very obvious: my grandmother didn't think she had done anything wrong—she was trying to make herself into the tortured, forgotten victim in all of this. I hadn't bought into that crap when I was eight, and I was certainly not buying into it at the ripe old age of fourteen.

She went on and on, hardly stopping for a breath of air, wearing herself out. Finally, she went silent for a moment, staring at the floor like she was replaying that night's events in her head. "It was very awful, Wheela," she said. "It was an awful time. Papa was in a bad place. I never got all the blood out of my rug . . . look there, see?" She pointed to the old braided rug in front of the door. I could barely make out the rusty old stain.

My mother must have been so scared that night. Being chased around with a knife and thinking she was going to die, at the hand of her own father, of all people.

I needed to get that image out of my head, and blurted out the first thing I could think of.

"What about my real dad? Do you know where he is?"

She looked up at me. "Oh, Wheela, Robert and his family moved away before you were born. I told you that before! They don't know a single, solitary thing about you. People say they ended up in the Yukon somewhere. I think his father was a miner of some sort . . . And they didn't move because he got

Margaret pregnant, if that's what you're thinking. Not even that silly boy knew she was knocked up."

She took a little sip this time, and a bit of liquid trickled out of the corner of her mouth. She wiped it off with her tea towel.

"But Robert *is* my dad, right?"

My grandmother thought about this for quite some time, turning her cup around in her hands. Finally, she gave an exasperated sigh. "Harp is your daddy. He's the one that raised you."

"But do I look like him—like Robert, I mean?"

My grandmother pondered the question carefully. She seemed to be getting a bit anxious. She glanced at the clock and said something about it getting late.

I asked again. "Do you *think* I look like him?"

She took one last swallow of her brandy and let herself drift. "Yes, I suppose—at least a bit." Her eyes seemed to glisten for a moment. "He was a strong, healthy boy—tall, with green eyes like a cat. Eyes like yours. He was lean. Not a bit of fat on him. He had that same gap you have in your front teeth." She closed her eyes for a moment, her mouth turned down. "He wasn't a terrible person, just stupid. He and Margaret were both so stupid. And you—I know you think I'm terrible, but I'm not! Sometimes a parent is forced to do things to save face and make everybody else happy. You just wait until you have kids of your own!"

My grandmother seemed surprised by her outburst, and I sure didn't know what to say to that. We sat there quietly, not looking at each other for what seemed to be the longest time, and then she started talking about my dad again.

"That boy didn't talk much, so you're nothing like him in that department. You never know when to shut up, like now— now would be a good time to shut up." A very slight smile spread across her face. I had to rub my eyes to make sure I wasn't seeing things. For a second, I thought she might be enjoying herself.

She drained the dregs in her teacup. "We need to go to bed, little girl," she said. "You've got chores in the morning, and school. Five a.m. comes around in the blink of an eye."

Mrs. B was finally at the end of her information highway, probably already thinking that she had told me too much. I went to refill her cup with what was now lukewarm water from the kettle—she waved me off.

"Do you want some more cherry brandy in there instead?"

"Lord Jesus NO! One drunk in this family is enough."

My grandmother hoisted herself up and shuffled over to set her teacup in the sink. She started putting some cheddar biscuits she'd left on the counter into a big Tupperware container and popped one into her mouth and started chewing on it like she'd not eaten in a month. She licked off every single one of her fingers and then reopened the Tupperware and grabbed another one.

I didn't like watching her eat—to me, it seemed like she was punishing herself somehow.

I pointed at the clock and got out of my chair. "You're right, Mrs. B. We should get to bed. We have to be up in five hours! I've got school and you've got the . . . well, Harp's breakfast to get."

I took the Tupperware out of her hands and put it away. She pointed at Harp's tobacco spit jar, meaning that she wanted me to empty it and rinse it out. I hated dumping that thing. I went out the screen door and poured the contents into the old metal barrel where we burned all our garbage. When I came back into the house, Mrs. B was frantic—agitated, rambling on about stuff that didn't make much sense to me. Maybe all that brandy had soaked into her bloodstream.

"Everything is falling apart. Lord, it was just a matter of time, I should have known. Just look at this ramshackle house! Some days I wish I could just disappear!" She blew her nose into the tissue she had stuffed into her bra strap. After looking at what she'd blown into it, she slipped it back neatly under the strap. I didn't feel like hanging around for whatever this was. I felt uneasy.

I had headed for the stairs, where her voice stopped me.

"Margaret had other plans for her life and those plans obviously didn't include you or me. Lord, no, no, no—I guess she figured there were far greener pastures elsewhere, out there, wherever. None of this was good enough." She spread her arms as wide as they would go and gestured around the room. She was clearly quite drunk, or sad, or both.

"Elsewhere? Like where?"

"Oh, you never mind. Off to bed you go, girl." She was perspiring around her hairline, and I could see streaks of sweat showing through her cotton dress beneath her breasts.

"Nowhere. Nothing. I didn't mean anything."

My grandmother knew that she had slipped up and now she needed to completely take the attention off herself, so she went with her famous "shock and distract" strategy. "She didn't love you, Wheela. That's all there is to it. How could she, when she didn't know you for more than a minute?"

I was shocked. It was a really hard thing to hear. My grandmother fell silent and turned to stare out the kitchen window into the blackness. She was probably trying to figure out how she could backpedal. When she faced me again, I could almost see the words buzzing wildly around her head.

"How could you possibly love her! Babies don't remember anything, Wheela! You love a ghost, you hear me? A ghost."

That really made my chest hurt. She was right. I love a ghost. But then again, a ghost is a better option than these two idiotic people.

"Believe me, Wheela, we don't know where she is," my grandmother said. "We don't know nothing. She could be dead for all we know. You're better off believing she's dead."

No, I'm not better off. I'm going to find her. I'm going to figure out what those two wicked people did to their daughter. And I'm going to find out why Connie Larkspur looks so much like my mother.

twenty-four

AFTER WILLA WENT OFF TO SCHOOL the next morning, and Harp stumbled out the kitchen door, mumbling that he was going to fix a fence, Mrs. Bittlemore, feeling a little hungover from all the cherry brandy she'd drunk the night before, retrieved the precious tin from the crawl space and sat at the kitchen table with all the letters spread out in front of her. There were well over a hundred of them, from the very first one, thirteen and a bit years ago, to the one that had arrived just last week. She mopped the sweat from her brow and glanced out the kitchen window for the umpteenth time. Her husband was probably flopped out in his old blue truck getting plastered. Harp hadn't fixed anything in a decade.

The handwriting was as careful and tidy as you like. All the Ws were like little works of art—calligraphy. That's what they called it. No return address on any of them, and every single one of the letters had a different postmark! They wove a mysterious trail through the prairies of Canada and down through the midwestern United States. There were a few from the Maritimes and from as far away as Florida. It made no sense at all. Mrs. Bittlemore rested her head on her folded arms and tried to think. *Where is she? Why doesn't she just come and knock on our front door and get it over with? Is somebody else writing these letters?* Was this some kind of cruel joke? Always the *I love you* at the end and *I'll be back for you someday.*

"JUST BLOODY COME BACK IF YOU'RE GOING TO AND STOP FUCKING US AROUND!"

A dog barked in the distance and it snapped Mrs. Bittlemore back to reality. Had she really just yelled so many curse words? Had somebody heard her?

Nervously, she glanced out the kitchen window, and God Almighty if Harp wasn't staggering up the lane, drunk as you like, stopping to bend over and catch his breath every twenty steps. He looked old and haggard and miserable. What had happened to them both? Harp had turned into a mean drunk and she was trying to stuff all her sorrows down her throat, smothered in jam and butter. She had let herself get so fat it seemed beyond fixing. With all the baking she did, she certainly didn't need more snacks, and yet she had goodies hidden all over the house. Chocolate bars and cream-filled jelly rolls and potato chips stuffed in behind the extra sheets in the linen cupboard. Homemade caramels in her sewing box, pecan squares under the bed. Harp didn't seem to notice. He didn't sleep with her anymore anyways. Some nights he passed out in his chair in the living room and other nights he slept on an old cot in the shed behind the barn.

Willa's questions about Margaret were exhausting. The girl was becoming a real problem. She was growing like a weed, and weeds are persistent, to say the least.

Mrs. Bittlemore tried to keep her secrets all straight, but she knew she had been letting too many little things slip out. My God, if Willa were to find these letters, there'd be hell to pay.

Perhaps it was time to burn them all. That bitch Margaret had made it perfectly clear they weren't meant for her anyway.

And besides, she was long gone . . .

Well, maybe it was time for Willa to go too. There was no end to the things that could happen to a person on a farm. She imagined Willa splayed on the ground, staring blankly into the vast grey sky. The thought made her shudder slightly.

But drunken old Harp wouldn't need to know anything. He hardly knew what day it was anymore. And it didn't have to be gruesome: Willa did love an ice-cold glass of lemonade . . .

Mrs. Bittlemore's mind started whirling with a thousand diabolical ideas. She knew a lot about plants and what they could do to a body—and with such a small, young body, you wouldn't need much.

No! NO! She caught herself mid-thought. This was insane.

She shook her head and stuffed the letters back into the tin box, then glanced out the window. Help! Harp was so close to the house she didn't have time to put the tin back up into the crawl space.

Her eyes darted around the room, desperately in search of some place to stash the tin. Maybe under the table, behind the stove, in the broom closet, in the pantry, under the couch—but she was frozen. When Harp opened the kitchen door, she stood there like a deer caught in a gun scope, the tin clenched in her puffy hands. Her heart was exploding. Could this be the actual end?

Mrs. Bittlemore grabbed on to the edge of the table and steadied herself, sweat pouring down the sides of her fat neck.

"Mint?" she said, holding out the tin.

"Jesus, woman—no! You know I hate mints."

Mrs. Bittlemore's nerves and her pounding heart had tied her intestines in such a great knot it pushed a pocket of air towards the exit, and she let out a great fart.

"You piggy pig!" Harp said, laughing so hard it bent him over. "Just an old, fat, worthless pig."

It was right then and there that Mrs. Bittlemore decided: she would be much better off without either of them.

twenty-five

AT HOMEROOM, I COULD FEEL Nola Stucker's eyes burning two holes into the back of my head. She'd looked like a raccoon for a couple of weeks after the head-bonking incident, and I'd heard that her mother was so worried about whether her nose would heal straight that she'd driven her to a plastic surgeon in a town two hours away from Backhills for a consultation. The doctor said that Nola's nose would have to be "rebroken" at some point down the road, which did not sound the least bit pleasant.

(I should have told them that I was totally available to break her nose again, for free, if need be.)

Carol and I stayed together as much as possible, just to be on the safe side. I told her under no circumstances was she to head down the hallway without me. We were mostly together anyway; we ate lunch together, we walked to classes together, we studied together, but revenge was in the air—and it would be coming from Backhills's own "Duchess of

Darkness." So far all that had happened was that at least one of us had to remove a spitball from her hair at some point during the lunch hour. Spitballs were so immature and disgusting—more spit than balls. Still, if I said I wasn't a little bit nervous about what was coming for us, I'd be lying.

And now, at lunchtime, it came.

As Carol and I quietly ate our sandwiches in the corner of the cafeteria, Nola rose up out of her orange plastic chair and started walking our way, her girl gang flanking her as closely as flies on shit.

"So here are the little ugly bitches," she said when she got to our table. She kicked Carol's chair, which made Carol drop her butter sandwich on the floor. I bent down immediately to pick it up. Carol was as white as a bowl of rice.

"You're a mean person, Nola," I said.

"I'm the mean one? Pretty sure it was YOU who broke MY nose, you stupid lez." Nola popped a big bubble. The girl is never NOT chewing gum.

I got to my feet, trying to be as bold as possible considering I was outnumbered and Nola is six inches taller than me. "Ya, your nose isn't looking too good these days. I'm guessing your pageant days are over."

"Are you done standing up, lezbo?" she said, and fake laughed.

"Is that supposed to be a short joke?"

One of Nola's gang called out, "No, it's supposed to be a gay joke, you fag."

Nola turned around and told her to shut the fuck up. "I'll deal with this, Janice! Who even asked for your opinion. Jesus!"

Humiliated, Janice slunk to the back of the pack. I kept looking up at Nola. I wasn't even sure if I was breathing.

"Doesn't your freaky friend talk, Bittlemore? Or is she even more stupid than you?" Nola dodged around me and leaned over Carol, hissing, "I hear your daddy lost his job and you're gonna lose your house and every ugly, second-hand thing in it. Maybe that's for the best. A house filled with a bunch of used furniture and idiots is no loss at all."

Carol didn't move. She didn't look up. She just sat there, her auburn hair dangling in front of her face.

I wedged myself between Nola and Carol. "I may be short," I said, "but according to science, I'm still growing."

That's what I came up with? *According to science?* I couldn't believe it.

Nola looked confused. "Whatever," she finally said flatly. "I'd keep my back to the wall if I were you girls. Or do you even call yourself girls, you weirdos?"

As her gang laughed in unison, Nola pushed Carol's lunch tray off the table with a crash. Ms. Bevan turned up just as I gave Nola herself a hard push. I was very relieved to see her and very ashamed all at once.

"Willa Bittlemore! What are you doing!"

Of course she'd only seen me pushing Nola and not Nola pushing Carol's tray.

"Remember to keep your back to the wall, loser," Nola said, and stalked past Ms. Bevan and out the door, her bevy of bots in tow.

Carol was on her hands and knees cleaning up the mess. I got down there to help too. I felt like running after Nola and beating the living crap out of her, not that it would help.

Ms. Bevan hovered over us with her hands on her hips.

"What was that all about?"

"Nola and I were having a friendly chat."

"I'm not sure why you keep antagonizing that girl, but you seem to want to stoke that fire. I thought you were smarter than that."

With a sigh, Ms. Bevan got down on her hands and knees too and began wiping up the Coke that had pooled under the radiator with some serviettes.

I said, "Nola's not very nice to Carol. I was just sticking up for my friend."

"How did your lunch tray end up on the floor, Carol?"

"I'm just clumsy," she whispered.

Ms. Bevan got to her feet, balled up the soaked paper towel and tossed it in the wastebasket. "How do you two think this is going to end?"

"In an all-out war and the school going up in a ball of flames." By now I was smiling.

She wasn't, though she might have been slightly smirking. "All right. Well, I better make sure our insurance is up to date." She caught my eyes, and the smile dropped from my face. "Willa, why don't you just apologize for breaking the girl's nose and save yourself some grief?"

"Because it wouldn't make any difference at all if I said I was sorry, and besides, I'm not sorry."

"Willa, you're a smart person, so start playing it smart. You won't win if you keep exchanging punches with the most entitled, self-righteous student in the entire school."

"You mean me?" Carol popped out from underneath the table covered in pudding.

Ms. Bevan leaned down to pull her up off the floor. "No! Not you, Carol."

Just then the bell rang to end the lunch hour.

"Off to class, you two. And resolve this issue with Nola before it gets out of hand."

I was pretty sure it was too late for that.

twenty-six

ON MONDAY MORNING, HARP'S WIFE, who seemed to Harp to be getting ornerier and more obese by the day, flicked her tea towel in the air over her husband's head and told him to get outside and deal with the pigs. It was slaughter day.

Mrs. Bittlemore was eager to refill her coffers with ham and bacon and big thick chops. She'd kill the pigs herself if she wasn't already too busy looking after that spoiled little girl and her damned husband. Did she have to do everything around here? But, of course, Harp would get it done. Ever since he was forced to shoot his dog, he'd had no problem killing things—his heart had never been the same.

Willa cringed thinking about what was about to happen.

The sound of the frightened pigs was the most terrible thing of all, so high-pitched and, well, there was no other way of putting it—their squeals sounded like children trapped at the bottom of a well.

When she was little, Harp used to make her sit at the dinner table, sometimes until three in the morning, staring at a piece of ham she wouldn't eat. When the two of them finally realized that she didn't care if she sat there three days—she was never going to put a bite of one of her "friends" anywhere near her lips—they stopped trying to make her.

Willa grabbed her school bag and made for the door, as Mrs. B clucked her tongue and rolled her eyes. She didn't think her granddaughter was much of a farmer—she was too much like her mother. Life would be a lot easier without having to deal with her ridiculous antics.

After Willa was gone, Harp snatched his filthy checkered jacket off one of the hooks at the back door, pulled on his rubber boots, grabbed his perfectly sharpened knife and headed for the pigsty.

⌒

Dally just happened to be standing in the perfect spot by the water trough to catch sight of Harp staggering into the pig enclosure, a knife clutched in his hand. The three terrified pigs, cowering in a corner as if a storm was coming, started to squeal.

"Crilla! Berle! It's h-h-h-h-happening—he's gonna chop up the pinklets! We've gotta d-d-d-do something!"

Berle turned herself around and felt her heart drop—Harp, head down, arms outstretched, was herding the pigs up against the fence. "I have had it with that horrible man!" she cried. "We're gonna break down the gate and then we're gonna—well, we're gonna save the pigs! Let's go!"

Dally and Berle started trotting towards the pigpen. Harp, off in his own little world, too busy trying to decide who he was going to chop up first, didn't seem to see them coming.

"What are we going to d-d-d-do—like j-j-j-just smash into the f-f-f-fence thing?"

Berle just kept barrelling towards their objective, not at all like a cow who'd recently had one foot in the grave. Dally glanced back at Crilla, who threw her head into the air and hollered, "Yes, just put your head down and smash the damn gate!" Crilla was too old and too tired to help with the smashing, but she could still yell orders. "We've gotta save those pigs!"

At last, Harp caught one of the pigs by its back leg and flipped it upside down in the muck. His knife was raised, and he was about to plunge it into the screaming pig's neck when he looked up and saw one of his black-and-white milk cows rushing the pigsty, head low. Harp didn't have time to call out before both Dally and bits of the broken gate ploughed into him, sending his scrawny body flying into the side of the flimsy lean-to that sheltered the pigs from the sun. Berle crashed through the rickety fence on the other side and cornered him.

"YOU GODDAMN BASTARDS!" he shouted, pinned in the mud under the rubble. "I'M GONNA KILL EACH AND EVERY GODDAMN ONE OF YA!"

But Dally had already turned on her heel and rushed back out the gate, the pigs racing after her, all of them headed for the barn.

Berle yelled, "No, the barn's not safe! Head for the North Field and hide in the trees. RUN!"

As she watched them race into the field, she wasn't too sure what she was going to do next. For now, the pigs were safe. But as soon as Harp gathered himself up and got back on his feet, there would be hell to pay.

Crilla creaked over to her, one eye on Harp, who was still lying under a shattered fence post in the mud, swearing a blue streak.

"Now or never," Berle said.

Crilla had doubts, as always, but she nodded. This time she was going to be part of whatever it was that Berle needed to do. All for one and one for all. As quickly as she could manage, she headed for the lane.

Harp struggled to get himself upright, still in shock from what had just happened. His left boot had come off in the scramble, and he reached for it and pulled it back on. He wasn't imagining it this time—the cows were definitely trying to kill him. No one would ever believe him, but he wasn't crazy.

Crilla found a good spot and scratched out DEAD MAN in the dirt of the lane. Then she and Berle made a hasty retreat, both of them smiling like they hadn't smiled in years. No way would Harp miss it.

Harp didn't miss it. When he finally dragged himself out from underneath the fence and staggered up towards the house, he saw those words like an omen. He spun in a circle trying to find who had done this. And then he threw up his breakfast.

When he finally made it back home, he flung the kitchen door open and tried to call out to his wife. Not a word would come out. He smelled like pig shit and barf and felt like he was going to throw up again. When Mrs. Bittlemore spotted him, she put a hand on each of her ample hips and surveyed him, top to bottom.

"Judging by how you look, I'm assuming things didn't go so well."

Harp wanted to tell her what had happened, but he couldn't

seem to bring himself to say a single word. All he managed was to shake his head.

She sighed, and said, "There's always tomorrow. If you're not up to it, old man, I'll just have to do it myself."

twenty-seven

EVERY SINGLE DAY, CAROL IS already at our lockers when I get to school. Today, no Carol. I stuffed my lunch bag onto my shelf and went to homeroom. No Carol. She and I had a spare first thing, so after homeroom I checked the gym, then popped my head into the science lab—Carol was nowhere. I headed back to the lockers, hoping she was just running late. And there she was, scuttling around the corner where the main corridors met, holding tight to her pile of textbooks. Stalking her were Nola and her cronies, all yelling variations of how Carol was going to get what was coming to her.

Where was Ms. Bevan when you needed her?

When Nola saw me, she flipped me the bird and then her and her idiot squad shot past us down the hallway, laughing.

Carol looked mortified.

"What did they say to you, Carol?"

"Oh, just the same old, same old." She pulled the hair out

from the side of her mouth, tucked it behind her ear and tried to smile at me. That broke my heart.

"Come on, Carol. What did Nola say?"

"I told you, just the usual stuff. You and me are losers and lezzies, and I'm not going to make it out of the school year alive—and that we, I mean me, that I'm going to get what's coming to me. Honestly, I wish she'd kill me and get it over with."

"Somebody's gonna die, but it's not going to be you!"

She still looked so down I rooted around for something to distract her. I was about to mention that Harp was going after the pigs today, but I stopped myself just in time: that wouldn't cheer up anyone.

"Carol, you're not going to believe this. I think the cows can spell. After I milked them the other morning, I found a big S.O.S. spelled out on the barn floor."

"What the heck are you talking about, Willa? Have you lost your marbles? Cows can't spell. And even if they could, you'd think they'd write MORE FOOD or MOO or something simple. How would they even know what S.O.S. means?"

Shaking her head at me, she dialed the combination to her locker, opened it and carefully placed her books inside. I always marvel at Carol's locker: it is the neatest, tidiest inside of a locker I've ever seen.

Carol grabbed her sweater and pulled it over her head and slammed the locker door. Suddenly she seemed to be in a hurry. As she hustled down the corridor, I trailed along and kept talking. "Seriously, Carol, who else would have spelled out S.O.S.? It had to be one of the cows. I swear they know exactly what I'm saying." I stopped dead. "Or maybe . . . maybe it's my mother back from wherever and she's trying to communicate with me? Is that possible?"

Carol stopped too, turning around. "Don't you think your mother would just come up to you and tap you on the shoulder and say, 'Hey, it's me, your mother'? That's what I would do. Maybe tomorrow I can come over and check it out. Today I've got to get out of here. I've got some—um, some issues happening."

"You can't see the letters because they're gone! I didn't dare leave them there in the dirt. Harp already thinks the cows are out to get him. I wiped them away with my boot before I went up to the house. But I'm telling you they were there, as sure as I have pants on."

Carol was now booking it towards the door that led out to the parking lot.

I called after her, "Maybe I could come over to yours after school? I really don't want to go home. Harp and Mrs. B are slaughtering the pigs today."

She stopped again. "I'm sorry, Willa, I feel terrible, but . . . my mom—well, she's not doing that great—she just left a message with the principal that I'm supposed to meet her at the hospital."

I was struck dumb. Here I'd been blathering on and on. "Carol! Why wasn't that the first thing that came out of your mouth?"

"Nola sort of threw me."

"But what happened, for crying out loud?"

"They think my dad has had a heart attack."

Carol started to cry right there in the hallway. Her hair fell out from behind her ear as she sobbed, and landed back in front of her eyes. "Wills, I gotta go . . ."

"Okay, well, don't worry until you have something to worry about, that's what my—Mrs. Bittlemore always tells me."

"You're calling her Mrs. Bittlemore now?" Carol looked at me as though I'd lost my mind. She gave a last shudder and snot bubbled out of her nose. I offered her the sleeve of my sweatshirt, but she shook her head and turned once more for the doors.

"Do you want me to go with you to the hospital?" I called after her.

She stopped, her hand on the double doors. "But you'll miss class."

"Like I care."

She nodded, wiping the snot off her face with the end of her scarf. "Yes, I do want you to come."

"You could have used my sleeve, ya know." I grabbed Carol's arm and pushed the doors open. "I'll never figure you out. Jesus in a jockstrap, of course I'll go to the hospital with you—you're my best friend."

I spun around and scanned the parking lot. "There's gotta be somebody we can hitch a ride with!"

Nobody anywhere.

I looked back at the school and spotted Ms. Bevan through the window. I started flailing my arms around. "Help me get her attention, Carol—wave your arms! I bet Ms. Bevan will take us!"

And then she spotted me and Carol, looking like we were trying to take flight, and she came running.

⌒

Ms. Bevan drove her Toyota Celica like a bat outta hell. I swear we flew around corners on two wheels half the time. An Anne Murray cassette was blasting so hard out of the speakers I could barely hear myself think. *You put me high upon a pedestal / So high that I could almost see eternity.* The way Ms. Bevan was taking the corners, we were going to see eternity before Anne did.

We barely paused at the four-way stop near the hospital entrance. At least if she slammed us into a pole we'd have help close at hand. We took a hard right into the parking lot with Carol looking like she was going to throw up. She was so tall and the back seat of that car was so small, her head had been hitting the roof with every bump we launched over. We screeched to a stop at the curb right in front of Mrs. Stark, who was standing there waiting for her daughter with her arms folded tightly across her chest. I could tell she had been crying. I didn't know if that was a good sign or not.

Carol and I scrambled out. Mrs. Stark threw her arms around Carol and burst into hysterics. I thought the two of them were going to crumple to the ground, but they managed to prop each other up and make it to the front doors by hanging on to each other. In that moment I realized that I'd never hugged an adult in my life, or been hugged by one. It made me feel hollow.

Carol glanced back over her shoulder then, nodding for me to follow them in.

"You going to stay?" Ms. Bevan asked me.

"If that's all right with you."

She nodded.

"Thanks for the ride."

"You're welcome. Take good care of Carol," she said, and climbed back in the Toyota. She peeled out of the parking lot with the dulcet tones of Anne Murray trailing behind the car like a bouquet of heart-shaped kites.

—

Mr. Stark had been taken directly into intensive care and the doctor hadn't come out to give Mrs. Stark the update on his condition yet. She told us what had happened once we got seated in the waiting area.

"He was just sitting in his chair, watching the morning news on TV, and he started to make this moaning sound and clutching his chest. I thought he was choking, so I tried to give him the Heimlich manoeuvre, which wasn't such a great idea considering they think he had a heart attack. I could have killed him!"

I said, "But he could have been choking, Mrs. Stark. I mean, you didn't know! I would have done the exact same thing."

She moaned in distress and Carol leaned into her, whispering, "Where's Fletcher?"

"I haven't told him yet. I don't think he'd be okay waiting around here all day and I didn't want him to worry . . ." Her mother was getting weepy again. "But I needed you. I'm glad you're here too, Willa."

We sat in three of the rigid plastic chairs lined up neatly along one of the salmon-coloured walls and we waited for someone to come and talk to us. It was taking so long, I got up to inspect the assortment of ancient magazines displayed on a bench on the other side of the room. They were so filthy, I was reluctant to pick one up, picturing snotty, sweaty fingers flipping pages and little heads coughing uncontrollably into the paper folds. An ancient TV in the corner was fixed on a fishing program with the volume off. Carol and her mother were staring at the tiny screen like they'd never seen a television before in their lives—or maybe they'd never seen a fish? And a giant fish it was, being hauled over the side of a boat with its mouth agape and its body twisting madly as it tried to free itself, which

I could more than relate to. The fisherman took a large stick with a hook on the end of it and bashed the fish over the head with it, again and again and again. At that point, I went over and turned it off, over the angry objection of the one other person in the waiting room.

"Hey," he complained, "I was watching that!"

I ignored him.

I hauled Carol with me over to the vending machine, where we got some BBQ chips, a Mars bar and some corn nuts to share. I eyed the cream soda, but we'd used up all our change. My grandmother never lets me have pop of any kind. She says soft drinks cause emotional instability and hair loss, among other things. I do not know where she gets her ideas.

Mrs. Stark began rummaging through her purse looking for her house keys. "I've lost them somewhere! How will we get into the house?"

"Did you check your coat pocket?" I asked. In my short experience, that's where keys always end up.

Mrs. Stark rifled all her pockets and pulled out a five-dollar bill, which to my mind was even better than finding her house keys, especially when she handed it to Carol, saying, "Here— you girls get yourself a pop." Her hair was standing straight up on one side, like she had gone to bed with wet hair.

The keys were in the last compartment she checked. "Oh, thank God! Here they are!"

Finally, the doctor showed up. Staring at his clipboard, he told us that Mr. Stark was very lucky to be alive, because he'd had a major "myocardial infarction." That sounded a lot like a gas attack to me—"Excuse me, I just let rip a pretty smelly infarction." But no, it was a heart attack.

"Eventually, your husband is going to be fine," the doctor

continued. "But he needs rest, lots of it, and he's going to have to quit drinking and smoking, change his diet, and eliminate anything that triggers stress."

Like losing his job? What doesn't trigger stress?

"Mrs. Stark, he'll need all the help you can give him, but if he makes all these changes, he should recover nicely."

The doctor shook Mrs. Stark's slender hand and retreated to the nurses' station to rifle through a stack of charts.

Carol hugged her mother so tightly, the two of them looking so relieved, I felt a pang of something I couldn't even describe in my chest.

Actually, I could describe it. I wanted a mother of my own. I wanted to be wrapped around her so tightly that not even water could come between us. Not even air.

Then Carol stuck an arm out and waved me in, and she and Mrs. Stark hugged me too, and it made me realize even more what I'd been missing all my life.

twenty-eight

HARP WAS A COMPLETE WRECK when I got home from the hospital. Mrs. B said he didn't want to talk about it, but that, through an unfortunate series of events, he'd lost the pigs.

Lost the pigs? That was good news!

But Harp did want to talk about it. The cows had tried to kill him again, he muttered, and had made a hell of a mess of the pigpen, and somebody was going to have to bloody fix the goddamn thing. And not only had all three pigs escaped, but so had one of the dang cows, and Harp couldn't find a single one of them, and everything was going to goddamn hell.

Me, on the other hand—I was so happy, I felt like I'd swallowed a rainbow. At least somebody had managed to get the hell out of here. But I also had to wonder where the pigs had gone. And which cow?

I threw my school bag onto the kitchen table and hurried out the door to do my chores. I found Crilla and Berle standing shoulder to shoulder in the stable, looking pleased with themselves and kicking at the dirt like they were covering up a secret.

"I hear a lot went on today! What are you two up to? Where's Dally?"

Of course they didn't answer me, but I got a sense they knew.

I made sure they had some hay, and a little extra pile of oats, and loaded up a bucket with some feed for the chickens.

Then, just as I was leaving the barn, Orange Cat showed up. She wrapped herself around my legs like an enchanted rope and purred like there was no tomorrow.

"Where have you been, Lady Orange? And what are you going on about?"

She headed over to some bales of hay stacked in the corner and started to meow as loud as I've ever heard her. I put down the bucket of chicken feed. Just as I reached her, she squeezed between an old wooden crate and a pile of tarps. I poked my head down between the bales to see where she had gone, and that's when I saw them—three little orange kittens with their eyes still pinched closed. I gasped with pure joy!

Orange Cat was pleased with herself, and who could blame her. So far, she'd managed to keep these little darlings away from Harp—and I was determined that it was going to stay that way. He was so certain the cows were trying to kill him that he wouldn't come anywhere near them—he'd been making me do all the stable chores. I reached my hand down and pulled out a little bundle of fur, maybe eight or nine days old. The cows wanted to see the kitten up close too—they sniffed the little orange creature with their big pink noses and we all just stood there revelling in a rare moment of happiness.

I hadn't forgotten about the impressive S.O.S. written in the dirt. I didn't know how they'd done it, but they had. I looked first at Berle and then at Crilla and said, "You guys have got to help me protect these kittens!"

I swear they both nodded.

"Okay, for now we're going to leave these babies where they are," I said. "You cows have got Harp fearing for his life! He won't dare come into the stable with you around."

I returned the baby to Orange Cat, and she let me give her a little pat. I knew the kittens were going to be zipping around like frogs in a fire in the next couple of weeks, and that meant I'd have to figure out someplace else for them to stay.

"I'll be back—I'll bring some treats," I said to Orange Cat, and she started to purr again.

Carol didn't come back to school all week. I missed her, but I talked to her every night on the phone to get the update on her father. I hadn't mentioned a word about Mr. Stark to my grandparents, given that I didn't think either of them knew who he was, let alone cared if he lived or died. But he was improving, which was good.

In the mornings, I milked the cows—Dally showed up just as I got there, and then booked it out of the stable and into the East Field as soon as I was done—and I made sure that Orange Cat had enough to eat.

In fact, I took over all the animal-related chores. Harp wouldn't go anywhere near the barn, not even to sit in his old blue truck. He was still recovering both physically and mentally from the pig escape. He hadn't found any of them—I wasn't sure he'd even looked, no matter how hard Mrs. B nagged him—and he seemed embarrassed to even mention it. As for Mrs. B, no way was she fit enough to walk the farm looking for some runaway pigs.

On Saturday afternoon Harp and Mrs. B had another chore lined up for me. All three of us were outside in the yard trying to straighten the fence around the garden.

Harp yelled, "Don't just stand there, you stupid girl, grab that wire!"

I actually couldn't believe that the two of them were working together to mend the fence. But Mrs. B was about to plant the garden vegetables that could stand the still-lingering cold nights. Harp said he didn't want the deer or the chickens wandering in there and getting at all the new sprouts that would soon be poking up.

I was leaning on my shovel catching my breath when I saw Carol come running over the hill waving something madly in the air. Surely to God nothing else had happened to her dad?

She bolted up to where we were standing and handed a postcard to me.

"This came to our house!" she said, hardly able to squeak out the sentence. She caught her breath for a moment, then said, "It's addressed to Mayvale Wilhelmina Bittlemore! That's gotta be you, right?"

Before she'd finished the last sentence, Mrs. B snatched it out of my hands, and then Harp snatched it from hers, turning his back so none of us could see anything. My grandmother looked like she wanted to kill him where he stood, but she had to maintain some sort of decorum in front of Carol—who was staring at us all like we were nuts.

"But that was addressed to you," she said, as Harp walked away from us, glancing over his shoulder to make sure nobody was following him. He paused to unleash a loud fart and then kept on moving. Carol started to giggle. I just smiled awkwardly and shrugged.

Harp was probably wondering how in the world a postcard addressed to me ended up at the Stark place—hell, I was wondering too. He kept flipping the card over and back. I didn't have a clue who would be sending me a postcard. (*Please let it be from my mother* was all I kept thinking.) Was he searching for a return address? If it really was from my mother, that's what I was hoping for.

Carol looked so pleased with herself, she seemed about ready to lift off the ground. Winking at me, she blurted, "Gee whiz, Mrs. Bittlemore! I think the card is from your—um, your daughter in Paris? I didn't read it. I mean, maybe just a couple of words, but—"

"It's none of your damn business who it's from!"

Carol turned beet red—my grandmother had pinched her feelings.

As hard as it is to believe, I could see that Mrs. B instantly regretted being so snippy. She clearly wanted to get this encounter back on track. "Now, Carol, never you mind what I said—it was good of you to bring it over to us—you're such a good friend to Wheela."

I must have been in shock. Finally my feet came unstuck and I ran up behind Harp and tried to get a look at the card over his shoulder. This could be a piece of mail for *me*, from *my mother*.

"C'mon, Harp, let me see it!"

"Just leave well enough alone," Harp growled, and headed for the house. When I went to go after him, my grandmother grabbed me by the shoulder and told me to mind myself.

Stunned, I stood there with Carol and watched them both go into the house, my grandmother's generous bottom end swishing from side to side. Soon they were arguing—we could hear their raised voices, but not what they were saying.

"Wills, the card was from Prince Edward Island, not Paris—or at least that's what the postmark said," Carol said. "With Dad still in hospital, and Mom staying by his side most of the day, I've been so busy with Fleck I forgot to pick the mail up yesterday. And then today, when I went to the mailbox, there it was! I brought it over as soon as Mom got back and I wasn't stuck babysitting. I thought you'd be so excited to see it."

And I was excited to see it—well, what little I did see. I'd only had it in my hands for a split second.

"Why did your parents get so mad?"

"Those people are not my parents, remember? I think they're scared . . ."

Carol was looking at me with so much affection it made me feel almost dizzy. "That didn't seem so much like fear as guilt—like they're hiding something. Why do they want to hide a postcard to you from Margaret? They know you've figured out she's your mother."

My grandmother had never looked so freaked out. If this card was actually from my mother, nothing would ever be the same again. I felt so weird. I kept hearing Carol's voice repeating over and over—*a postcard to you from Margaret*—like an echo in my head.

Carol's voice floated away.

I slumped down into the grass, and the last thing I remember is feeling like the clouds were stuffing themselves into my mouth. I couldn't swallow. I couldn't breathe. Everything went white. Everything was blank.

Taste of burning eggs . . .

Humming lips . . .

Skin prickling . . .

My grandmother must have seen me from the kitchen window, because when I opened my eyes, she and Carol were standing over me like a couple of old trees.

"Carol, I think Wheela has had enough excitement for one day. You should get on home." Crankily, she said, "Come on now, Wheela, you need to help me get you up."

"But, Mrs. Bittlemore, shouldn't we call a doctor?" Carol crouched down and started to pull me up by my belt loops.

"Wheela doesn't need a doctor. She needs to rest and to eat, that's all. She never bothers with breakfast. You head home now, and I'll take care of her."

Carol let go of my belt loops, and I lay back down. "I'll call you later, Wills," she said, and then trudged off for the gate, her head hanging so low it was almost bumping into her knees. Here she thought she'd be the hero, bringing us good news.

My grandmother hollered after her, "Did your folks see the postcard?"

Carol turned around and shook her head. She must have thought we were all a bunch of weirdos.

My grandmother kept yelling. "Don't you say anything to them about this, Carol Stark. You'll only cause Wheela trouble, and you don't want to cause her trouble, do you?"

Thank God Mrs. B had zero clue that I had told Carol my secret. I didn't want to think about what she would have done if she knew. Maybe send Carol to Paris . . .

I tried to sit up, but my limbs were still tingling, and my eyes wouldn't fully open.

I felt my grandmother's fingers dig in underneath my arm-pits—she was breathing like she'd been in a boxing match. I didn't protest, I just let her hoist me onto my feet—it was mostly me doing the hoisting. She smelled sickly sweet, like rancid cream. It was sad to think that this was one of the few times she'd ever touched me.

But this was a time to find the positive, not dwell on her despicable character.

My mother sent me a postcard! She was reaching out to me! Why now?

Prince Edward Island?

twenty-nine

BEV OLDMAN PULLED HER CAR into the gravel turnaround that she hoped belonged to the Larkspur family. Yesterday, after she got the address from the receptionist, she had meandered around several back roads in search of the house, which she found oddly peaceful and calming. But she was still a city girl at heart, and finally had to admit that she was lost. In the end she had back-tracked to town and stayed the night in a motel. This morning she'd asked for a map at the desk and got the clerk to put an *X* on her destination, and had got here after making only one wrong turn.

The Larkspur house was modest. It had an inviting red front door and lots of windows. The pale-brown siding on the exterior made it almost disappear into the surrounding trees. From a very weathered mailbox on a post, shrubs stationed every foot or so down both sides led the way up a little stone walkway, until nothing was left for Bev to do but climb the front steps and ring the bell. Only, when she got to the front door, the bell was a knocker. Who has a knocker? Bev clanged the metal lion's head two or three times, listening for any sign of life from inside. Finally, she spotted a figure coming towards her through the frosted sidelight.

The small middle-aged woman who answered the door seemed perplexed to find a police officer. "Can I help you?"

"Hello, Mrs. Larkspur?" Bev held up her badge so the woman could see it clearly.

"Yes, that's me. Connie Larkspur."

"I'm Constable Bev Oldman. I'm from—um, Black Diamond, a few counties over from you guys, as you probably already know." Bev knew she was already talking too much. "I'm new to the general area and I've been working on some cold cases—your cold case, actually. Anyway, my chief asked me to take a fresh look at the disappearance of your daughter Rose. I'm hoping to ask you a few questions that you've probably been asked five million times over the years, but I was thinking that, quite possibly, some little thing was missed."

Connie looked at her skeptically. "It's been nearly thirty years."

"I know, but I still feel like we could turn a few stones over and maybe get a little closer to figuring out what happened?"

Connie sighed softly, but she opened the door and motioned for Bev to follow her inside. In the kitchen, she showed her to a chair at the table and went over to the stove to put on a kettle to boil for tea. When she came back and sat down across from her, Bev pulled her notebook out of her jacket pocket and started flipping through the pages.

"I guess we should start at the beginning—the day you went into the Manatukken hospital. Everything went off without a hitch, according to hospital records—healthy baby, no complications. A nurse says she took Rose for the usual newborn checkup stuff and then the fire alarm went off."

"The sound of that fire alarm has been in my dreams for all the years since," Connie said. "There's not a day goes by where I don't think, if I had just done this or done that, Rose would be with us today. Jon and I have spent decades looking at every little girl and then every woman we walk past—*could it be her*? We still gawk at every stranger, wondering whether they were the one who took her. Losing Rose took over our lives, and our other three girls suffered because of it. Constable . . ."

"Oldman."

"Constable Oldman, we're at the point where we want to get on with our lives. I mean, the statistics are very clearly working against a happy outcome."

"I can understand that, but—"

"No, you can't. To have a child taken from you and to never see that child again is like a slow, steady death. I still have days when I don't want to be here."

"But, Mrs. Larkspur, what if we could find her? If nothing else, maybe we could at least answer the big questions. Where did she go? Who took her?"

Connie started tearing up. "What if she *is* out there? She won't have a clue who we are. If she was lucky, and I pray she has been, she'll have a family and a life and she won't know us from a rock."

Bev sighed. This wasn't going the way she had imagined it. At the very least, she needed to ask her about the coin her husband had tucked into their baby's diaper. "Somebody took your daughter, Mrs. Larkspur. Somebody out there knows what happened. People make mistakes. They overlook little things and they leave a trail behind them. I believe that. Maybe I'm naive, but I honestly think I can figure this out."

Connie got up and made the tea, then stood by her kitchen sink to stare out into the backyard. There was an old swing set and a couple of bikes leaned up against the fence.

"I have two grandchildren now, Constable. Can you believe that? Two. When I look at them, I see Rose. I think we all do. I'd like to think that she's alive. A mother is supposed to be able to feel that in her bones. But me? I just don't know."

"Can I ask you about the coin Mr. Larkspur put into Rose's diaper?"

She turned around, looking a little startled. "None of the other officers asked me about the coin. It was Jon's grandfather's. It started out as kind of a silly joke. When our first little girl was born, we took a photo of her hand with the coin beside it—you know, to show how small her little hand was. I don't know why Jon started putting it in the girls' diapers. Especially since he always ended up having to clean the poop off it. It was just a thing he did."

"The coin was never found at the hospital or on the grounds—we know that, right?"

"As far as I know, yes, you're right, it was never found. I assumed it went with Rose."

"You wouldn't still happen to have the photo with the coin, would you? It would be helpful to have a picture of it. Maybe it ended up in a pawnshop or something and I could track it backwards. It really is the tiniest things, Mrs. Larkspur, that hang people up."

"All right," Connie said. "Let me go look. It might be a bit of a wait, though, as our photos are all tossed into boxes. We are terrible at putting things in actual albums."

"Nobody puts photos in albums, do they?" Bev smiled and took a glug of her Earl Grey. "I'll happily wait, and finish this lovely cup of tea, thank you."

By the time Connie came back, Bev had poured herself another cup. Connie handed her two photos: one that showed the coin and one taken of Rose's pink "Baby Larkspur" ID bracelet. "They found that in the parking lot, after whoever took her cut it off." Connie blew her nose and tucked the tissue up her sleeve.

"Thank you for this. It's all so helpful. A crime like this isn't just a spur-of-the-moment act, Mrs. Larkspur. It was thought out. The fire alarm was pulled to distract everyone, and that gave whoever it was a chance to move about without attracting anyone's attention. If the bracelet was found in the parking lot, they likely cut it off as soon as they reached their vehicle, which means they did have a vehicle. They couldn't have made a get-away on foot, because there was nowhere to walk unnoticed with a baby in Manatukken."

"Jon and I have always wondered if they stole the baby for themselves or to sell to someone halfway round the world."

"I read the file, and to me this doesn't seem like the work of some child trafficking ring," Bev said. "This was someone who knew about this community—not a local, but not someone from far away either. They knew where the nursery was, even that there were new babies in it. To me that says somewhat local. I've started checking all the old motel records on or around that date. Some owners kept their ledgers and some didn't. Still, you never know—I might find something."

Bev stood and tucked her notebook back in her pocket. "Thanks for taking time for me, Mrs. Larkspur."

"Please just—well, you can call me Connie."

"I'll be in touch as soon as I find the smallest little thing, or even if I don't find the smallest little thing. People make mistakes, Connie. The smartest people make the dumbest ones."

~

Connie Larkspur waved as Bev got into her car and drove off in the wrong direction. A few minutes later she went past again, going the right way back to town. It made Connie crack the very faintest little smile. She liked Bev Oldman. She liked her very much.

She didn't like what the visit had brought vividly back to life.

The police had swept through the hospital, looking behind every curtain, every cranny, storage room, basement cupboard, nurse's locker, ceiling panel, every drawer. Every inch of the place was ripped apart. They had bombarded Connie and Jon with the usual questions—which weren't usual at all, because they'd never dealt with a kidnapping before. Every step in the investigation was completely new territory for the small police force at Manatukken.

The questions had been excruciating.

Did the Larkspurs have any enemies?

Did they owe anybody any money?

Did they associate with anyone who had a criminal record?

Did they know of anybody who could have done this?

She and Jon had just kept saying no no no no no.

The police alerted the surrounding counties, and the other forces began cross-referencing for possible suspects. Drifters, pedophiles, burglars—any unknown persons who might have been in the area. Everyone waited for days to see if a ransom note would appear. It never did.

Every effort was futile. Their baby had disappeared into thin air. The one suspect that looked promising was literally a dead end—it turned out he had been run over by a train several weeks before Rose was taken.

Connie and Jon spent months in shock and disbelief. Most days, Connie sobbed until she literally threw up. She couldn't eat. She couldn't sleep. She couldn't think or talk or focus on anything except her missing Rose. Everyone was worried sick about her, especially her other three children. Her young daughters felt completely helpless to console her. The happy and vibrant mother they'd known had slipped into a void, and nobody seemed to be able to follow, not even Jon, who was in his own hell. Grief is like a sea of tar holding down your arms and legs. Breathing requires so much strength.

It wasn't only the police who were looking. Friends and neighbours scoured the entire area night and day for months. Posters were put up in every store window for a hundred miles. Connie only found out later, but at a certain point cadaver dogs had been brought in. The only other time that cadaver dogs had been used around these parts was when the Baldwin cousins fell into an old septic tank. When the dogs finally discovered them, they weren't dead yet, thank God, just completely exhausted and covered in shit. The dog handler said the shit had made the dogs' job extra hard, because it masked the boys' own scents.

All that effort, but no one found a single trace of her baby girl. Not a hair. Not a sound. Not a glimmer. Not a sliver. Only the cut bracelet in the parking lot.

Rose was gone.

Something random and evil had entered the Larkspurs' lives, and it crushed their souls. But not a single person in the whole county wasn't grief-stricken. It was a big thing for a small town.

Months went by.

Years went by.

Connie and Jon had the other three kids to keep them going, but even so, it was hard to keep breathing. They would fall asleep holding hands and wake up in the morning still hanging on, each of them hoping that it was only a bad dream.

She was grateful for one thing: her marriage was able to bear the weight. Their love grew out of the abyss into a fortress of strength and solidarity. They remained steadfast, indivisible, and managed to keep on raising the daughters they had with some joy and laughter and, most of all, security.

Connie didn't know about Jon at this point—he was so in love with the grandchildren, it had been a while since they'd talked about Rose—but no matter what she had said to Constable Oldman, she still clung to the faint hope that her lost child would be found someday.

That whoever had taken her had at least wanted to keep her alive.

thirty

MRS. B HAULED ME STRAIGHT up the stairs and put me to bed. Despite myself, I fell asleep and slept all the way through until morning.

I woke up immediately thinking about how to get my hands on that postcard, which I had every intention of seeing with my own eyes. When I got downstairs, my grandmother and Harp were already at the kitchen table shoving pancakes down their throats.

"You slept late," Harp growled. "Those goddamn bastard cows need milking."

I said, "I'd like to see my postcard, please." I thought the "please" was a nice touch.

"I burned the damned thing. That woman is just trying to stir up a whole lotta trouble. She had her chance, and she blew it." As he spit this out, Harp literally had pieces of pancake falling out of his mouth.

Mrs. B got up and began throwing more batter into the

frying pan. "You better not have burned that card, Harp Bittlemore, or I'll kick your ass all the way to next Sunday."

Sighing, Harp dug into his back pocket and threw the folded postcard at my grandmother's face. She sat her fat bottom down on a chair that, miraculously, didn't break apart under all that weight, flipped the card over and read it. Then she handed it to me.

I couldn't believe it.

She folded her arms over her ample chest. "See for yourself. Your runaway, useless, selfish mother seems to think she has the right to disrupt our happy lives."

First I checked the address. I'm not sure how the card ended up in the Stark mailbox, given it was our address all right, but I'm sure glad it did. I stared down at lines of neat handwriting: proof that my mother was still alive.

> *Dear Mayvale,*
> *I don't know if you see these notes and letters. I'll*
> *keep on writing them, no matter what, so you know*
> *how important you are to me.*
> *I know they've told you lies about me.*
> *Someday we will both know the truth.*
> *I know I failed you, but I'm a different person*
> *now.*
> *I'm going to come back for you someday, I promise.*
> *Love, M*

Mrs. B burst out, "You see! She admits it herself! 'I KNOW I FAILED YOU!' She has failed you! Papa and I have given you everything, and you're as ungrateful as she was—it must be genetics!"

"Well, they're your genetics, so I guess Margaret and I come by our selfishness and lack of gratitude honestly."

Mrs. B's cheeks were now flaming red, and Harp was staring hard at his pancakes, smoking furiously.

I was on a roll. "She says 'these' notes—that she'll keep writing 'these notes and letters' no matter what. Does that mean there are more of them? Where are they?"

"Ya," Harp spit at his wife, "where the hell are the rest of 'em?"

"SHUT UP, you imbecile!" My grandmother grabbed the cigarette out of his mouth and threw it into the garbage can.

Things got very quiet. We three sat there alone with our racing thoughts. The postcard was from Prince Edward Island— at least that's where it was postmarked, which didn't necessarily mean anything. My mother could be anywhere.

It was clear that neither of my grandparents was the least bit happy to hear from their daughter—in fact, it was the opposite. They were annoyed and agitated.

And then the garbage went up in flames.

Harp didn't miss a beat, just spun around and threw his half-empty cup of coffee on top of it. Smoke circled the kitchen table like miniature storm clouds.

It struck me then that my grandparents were right for once. If my mother had cared about me even one tiny bit, she would have called by now, tried to explain herself at least, or at best, come back to get me. My grandparents were not great people, that was no secret, but they hadn't abandoned me at the side of a road. I always had food on the table and I wasn't chained to a post.

The hardest part to get through my head was the fact that my grandparents lied to everyone about Margaret having a baby. Sure, it would have been a tad scandalous that their fourteen-year-old daughter got knocked up, but people always get past that stuff and move on to new scandals. That big lie was the wall I couldn't climb over. They lied to me, they lied to the town, they lied to Margaret's teachers—well, to her whole school and her best friend, who all thought she had moved to Paris. It was all so exhausting.

I said, "I'm going to get some fresh air. The smoke I can handle, but you people are wearing me out."

thirty-one

BEV OLDMAN SAT AT THE SMALL metal desk in her motel room, staring at the not-so-great Polaroid photo of the coin that had been crapped on by three different children before it disappeared with Baby Rose. She pulled the desk lamp down to get a better look.

"Jesus . . . I think that says 1794? Could it really say 1794?"

Bev rummaged around the desk and pulled her notepad from underneath a mountain of loose papers, then unburied the phone. She picked up the receiver and called the front desk.

"Hello, it's the Front Desk—thank you for staying at the DeLux Motor Inn, Delores speaking, how can I help you?"

The longest greeting in the world was finally over.

"I'm wondering if you could recommend a pawnshop around here? I have something I'd like to have appraised."

"What were you looking to have appraised, if you don't mind me asking?"

"A photograph of an old coin."

"Did you want the photograph appraised or the coin in the photograph, ma'am?"

"Um, the coin. It's an old one and I was hoping to talk to someone who might know something about it."

Delores snort-laughed, then yelled, "BRIAN! BRI!!!! Hang on a second, ma'am, would you believe that my boyfriend just happens to collect coins? Ain't this your lucky day!" She laughed again, which started her coughing. After some strenuous throat clearing, she handed over the phone.

"Hello, DeLux Motor Inn, Brian speaking, how may I help you?"

⌐⌐

After Bev knocked at the office door, Brian opened it and thrust his hand out before she was even inside.

"Let's see it," he said, and she handed the photo to him.

But with his bare eyes, he couldn't make out the details in it any better than Bev had, which made her feel slightly better. He said, "I'm gonna need my magnifying glass. It's just in the office." He scooted through the inner door, photo in hand.

Delores was sitting at the desk smoking a hand-rolled cigarette. She gave Bev a wink. "You must be 107."

"That's me."

Brian came back on the run. "Hey lady, don't freak out, but I think this is a photo of a 1794 flowing hair silver dollar. This thing is worth a lot of money!"

"What the heck is a flowing hair silver dollar?"

"There was only a few thousand of these coins made, and not a whole hell of a lot of them are still around. I bet you get as much as fifty grand for this. Do you have it with you?"

"Sadly, no. It got, um—lost through a series of unfortunate events."

"Geez, lady! Seriously, I hope you find that sweet little bitch. If I had a coin like that, I'd sell it and get the hell outta this place, you can bet your ass I would."

Delores looked at Brian with big sad eyes.

"So it's really that rare?" Bev wondered whether the Larkspurs knew what they had been sticking into their kids' diapers all those years ago. Jon had to have known. How could he have not known?

"Yep, it really is." Brian handed the photo back to Bev. "I'd sure like to see that coin if you find it. Hope you do."

"Me too. Thanks for your help."

If the kidnapper or kidnappers knew what the coin was, they must have tried to sell it at some point. Bev went back to her room and searched the Yellow Pages. Then she got on the horn, starting with the pawnshops, then moving on to jewellery and antique stores, asking if anyone remembered someone in the last three decades inquiring about or trying to sell a 1794 flowing hair coin. Or even an old silver dollar. Of course, it was ridiculous to think anyone would remember all these years later, which they didn't, but it was worth a try.

Climbing into bed that night, totally wiped, Bev resolved that she would start fresh in the morning, moving on to canvass the same kinds of places in Morton, Highoaks, Turner Valley, Backhills, Derritt and Trinity Cove. Maybe she'd get lucky.

～

She didn't. By 3 p.m. the next afternoon, Bev had exhausted all lines of inquiry offered by the phone book, and was sitting, cross-legged, on her motel bed, a big bottle of ginger ale and a bag of popcorn twists on the side table—her dinner. (The motel room came with a coffee machine and a microwave, but she couldn't bring herself to eat one more Hungry Man meal.)

If she was going to find the coin, she realized, her own dogged efforts were not going to be enough—she needed an army of eyes and ears. As far as she knew, any time the police department offered even a small monetary reward, people came out of the woodwork with a whole lot of useless tips. But you never knew—this was a very valuable item, so a reward was worth a try.

She knew she should get on the phone to Captain Tripp and explain the lead she was chasing, and ask him if the police budget—recently improved by all the unpaid fines she'd persuaded people to cough up—would extend to her placing a small ad in the personal column of the local papers offering a reward. But, if she was honest, she didn't want to risk him saying no—or worse, telling her to stop everything she was doing.

So she dug in her purse and pulled out her bank book. She had four hundred dollars in her savings account, so she could afford to spend some of it. Also, if she looked at it another way, this was an investment in her future as a police officer.

By four o'clock, Bev had phoned in her ad:

$100 REWARD!
Seeking a 1794 silver dollar with sentimental value last seen at Manatukken Hospital 29 years ago. If you have information leading to the recovery of this rare coin, please leave a message, and a callback number, at 717-469-6167.

And then she thought, what the heck, in for a penny, in for a pound. She consulted the trusty Yellow Pages again and found a local print shop that said it would turn around a job in twenty-four hours. She hustled over there, squeaking in the door just before closing, and the next day at noon she picked up two hundred posters with the reward information and the photo of the coin, and spent the rest of the day driving the whole district, sticking them up everywhere.

thirty-two

IN THE AFTERNOON, I HEADED for the library, which was extra quiet on a Sunday. Carol was supposed to meet me here, but she was nowhere to be seen. Once again, I asked Mrs. Ivy for a pile of the local newspapers on microfiche. She must have been getting sick of me asking for the same old stuff—she had her arms folded in front of her chest like an army general, and her expression, when she handed the sheets over, didn't seem too thrilled.

After saying a big warm thank you to try to smooth the waters, I plunked myself down at the machine and began scanning for anything I could find out about Connie Larkspur and her family. I was still reeling from the postcard—something my mother had actually touched. Knowing my mother was still out there was very conflicting. I was overjoyed, sure, but I was bitterly disappointed too. Now I was sure Margaret knew where I was, so why hadn't she come to get me, or at least meet me?

I was getting a handle on how to work the film machine, it seemed, because pretty soon there they were—a bunch of photos of Connie and Jon sitting with their kids in the living room.

Connie and Jon standing in front of their house.

Connie and Jon at a tractor pull.

The Larkspur kids at a sack race.

Jon getting an award for community service.

An announcement that their first grandchild had arrived.

In some of the pictures, Connie looked like my mom and in some of them she didn't. Carol told me one time that it was normal to trick yourself into seeing what you wanted to see.

Maybe I was only willing my brain to make some kind of a connection.

Another grandchild announcement.

I didn't know what I was looking for. I guess I thought something would just jump out at me, like clues are supposed to do.

At last, Carol came up behind me and flopped herself down on the edge of my chair.

"I think you're gonna need your own chair."

"I'm okay here, Wills."

"Ya, no—get your own chair."

Sighing, she got up and dragged a chair as close to me as she could get and sat down again. "I was so worried when you fainted. Maybe your iron is low. My mom has low iron and when it really dips, she's always sleepy and has zero energy."

"I think maybe I forgot to eat, but mostly, if I'm honest—I was just so shocked the postcard was from my mom, I couldn't seem to—I felt kind of . . . I guess I really did just pass out."

Carol leaned past me and started scrolling through the microfiche. "Good lord, these papers print everything you ever wanted to know about everybody. Here's a two-headed cow. Oh my God, it was born ten miles from here! I can't believe all this stuff. So sad about the baby."

"What baby? The two-headed cow had a baby?"

"Not the two-headed cow, silly. The Larkspurs' baby! Remember? I read you the headline about them making a plea to the person who took their baby." Carol pointed at the photo. "He was stolen right out of the hospital in broad daylight. How horrible is that? Oh wait, he was a she."

"Geez, how did I not remember that? I must have been too excited that Mrs. Larkspur looked so much like Margaret."

"Everybody has a doppelgänger, Wills. It likely doesn't mean a thing."

"I bet I don't. And you sure don't."

"Sure I do. On the other side of the world, in Latvia or somewhere like that, there are a couple people walking around who look exactly like us."

"Weird. It would be so crazy coming face to face with yourself." We stopped and stared at each other until it was uncomfortable.

"Okay, Wills—I'm pretty much over sitting in this library, looking at pictures of old people," Carol said. "And now that you got a postcard from your mom, you should be too. You've got a real, honest-to-God clue that your mom is alive and maybe living in PEI and she knows about you and she wants to be with you at some point. WOW is all I can say about that!" Carol laughed like she really was delighted for me, which was so nice to hear for a change.

"So whattaya say, Willa Bittlemore—let's get out of here and go and eat a chocolate sundae at Murt's!"

And that's what we did.

thirty-three

MRS. BITTLEMORE MOVED AROUND the kitchen silently. She had little jars lined up on the kitchen counter—filled with mysterious powders, crushed berries and mashed roots—along with bunches of dried herbs tied up in neat little bundles and tinctures she had brewed and carefully poured into glass vials. Her heart was pounding. Was she really going to do this?

The postcard from Margaret had hit her like an electric shock, leaving behind a fog of doubt and anxiety. Yes, she had intercepted many other letters and cards from all over the damn continent. But this one was the first that broke through all the safeguards she'd established. All these years of keeping secrets and telling lies had slowly built up in her body like an all-you-can-eat buffet—it was all unravelling.

Mrs. Bittlemore couldn't sleep anymore, let alone think or be rational. Margaret was getting closer and was bloody well out to get her. And Willa had to be dealt with, right here and right now.

All her stupid questions.

All her nosy bullshit.

It was preying on her nerves, keeping her up at night. Yes, something needed to be done. But it needed to look completely natural.

Mrs. Bittlemore had killed enough mice and rabbits and hogs and cows and gophers and coyotes and cats in her life. She knew how to kill things.

Frantically, she dumped bits and pieces of roots and herbs into her big white mortar, and began smashing them with the pestle, pounding and mixing with all her strength. She was clearly out of control, bumping around the kitchen like she'd never been in one before. Turning to fetch another of her little jars, she knocked the mortar and pestle off the counter.

That stopped her in her tracks. Was she really thinking of killing Willa?

Yes, it turned out she was. Willa would be home from the library any minute now.

She bent and scooped up what she could salvage and she put it back in the mortar and gave it one last grinding. Then she dipped a teaspoon in, filled it and poured its contents into one of her mother's china teacups. She poured in hot black tea, added lemon and honey, and stirred.

The cup stood on the counter in front of her, steam rising towards the ceiling.

She caught herself again. What was she thinking! No! She dumped the cup out into the sink.

She felt dizzy and disoriented, and her heart was pounding. She needed to sit. But she came down hard on her kitchen chair and it broke beneath her with a crack. She rolled onto the floor like a walrus and she floundered there, unable to right herself. Could. Not. Get. Up.

"I am a pig," she whispered solemnly, and then she cried like she was eight years old again.

When the tears had passed, she lay there whimpering for a minute or two. Rolling back and forth, she finally managed to sit up. All she had to do was grab the table and she could pull herself to standing. But she was afraid the table would collapse too, so she inched over to the door frame. At some point while she was hoisting herself to her feet, she decided once and for all that she was going to do away with Willa. This was all that girl's fault, after all.

She'd wanted a baby of her own. Leave it to Harp to bring home the one asshole baby in the nursery, and not the one she wanted at all!

All Mrs. Bittlemore had wanted out of life was a baby of her own, not some other whore's brat. No, she only wanted someone who would love her without question. Someone who would gaze at her adoringly and run to her when she needed comfort. Someone she could dress up and parade around town. All those failed pregnancies that had rotted away in her uterus, all the babies she'd lost—they'd torn away at anything decent in her heart.

She clung to the countertop with one hand to steady herself. With the other, she once again put together a mixture of things that would stop all the thunderous noise in her head. She crushed hemlock and nightshade and tobacco and snakeroot and snippets of this and that in her stone bowl. She'd make the tea so sweet not even a snake would know it had been poisoned.

Mrs. Bittlemore had a passing thought that she could do it

all a lot quicker with rat poison, but she shut that one down. She had to try to make it look like natural causes, or at least like an accidental poisoning . . . or maybe she could make people believe that Harp did it.

Maybe she should just fucking drink the poison herself. No one would give a shit if she died. Hell, maybe she should take all three of them out to the barn and burn the place to the ground with them in it.

No. It was Willa who had to go.

But first, Mrs. Bittlemore realized, she should deal with Margaret's letters. After Harp had nearly caught her red-handed, she'd decided she needed to keep the tin close, so she'd ripped a hole in the lining under the couch and shoved it up in there. The crawl space was too high to get to easily—and considering what had just happened with the wooden chair, she very well could have broken her neck the next time she went to retrieve them.

As much as Mrs. Bittlemore loved to pore over the letters, she couldn't stand guard over a pile of envelopes twenty-four hours a day. The house was too small. And Harp would kill her if he found them, simple as that.

She got herself down far enough to reach under the couch, grabbed the tin and stood, breathing heavily, clutching it to her heart. "I have to burn them all," she moaned, but it was an agonizing decision.

She carried them over to the wood stove, opened the lid and dumped them in, one after the other—dozens of notes from her daughter, going up in flames in a matter of seconds. Willa would be home soon, and she could never find out that Margaret had been writing to her. As the flames crackled, though, she realized that now that Willa wasn't going to be around much longer, she could have hung on to them. But it was too late: the letters were ashes.

All these years of thinking things would be okay, that things could be normal. She and Harp should never have kept Margaret's baby. That girl had poisoned what was left of their marriage, replacing it with lies, suspicion and deceit. They should have left her on the steps of the church or the fire hall or . . .

If only the kid had been more grateful, none of this would be happening.

⌐

Orange Cat snuck into the house through a hole in the screen door. The whole farm was in disrepair, so every door and window and fence and building and barn needed to be painted or repaired or bulldozed into the ground. With Harp passed out in his truck, Orange Cat just walked right into the kitchen and hopped up onto the counter.

Mrs. Bittlemore was so distracted she didn't notice her there.

The back door burst open as Willa got back from the library.

"Is that you, Wheela?" Mrs. Bittlemore's heart was pounding so hard it was practically exploding beneath her floral dress. Who else would it be? It was either her ungrateful granddaughter or her miserable husband. It was now or never. No turning back. She wouldn't be changing her mind again. She turned to grab the cup of poisoned tea and her mother's antique plate stacked with Rice Krispie squares off the counter, only to find Orange Cat blocking her way.

"Get away! Scat!" Mrs. Bittlemore hollered.

Orange Cat looked Mrs. Bittlemore straight in the eye,

stretched out her left front paw and pushed the teacup onto the floor.

As it smashed into pieces, Mrs. Bittlemore let out a great gasp and lunged for her. "Jesus Christ, you stupid, stupid cat! Get outta here!"

Orange Cat jumped down and shot towards Willa, where she stopped to wrap her fluffy tail around Willa's legs, purring.

Mrs. Bittlemore grabbed the broom, shouting, "Out, out out out out with you!!"

The cat swirled one last time around Willa's legs and then darted back out the hole in the screen door, as Mrs. Bittlemore tried to whack her, only managing to send half of the broken teacup underneath the stove.

Willa grabbed a Rice Krispie square and headed towards the stairs, calling over her shoulder, "Sorry about your tea. I can make you another cup if you want."

"It was for you! I was trying to do something nice!"

Willa stopped and turned around. "Thank you, Mrs. B. Seriously, that was very nice of you." She took a moment to look around the room and noticed her grandmother's usual chair was collapsed in the corner like an accordion. "What happened in here?"

"Never you mind."

Willa shrugged and climbed the stairs, with no idea how close she had come to something very terrible.

Just then, Harp stumbled through the back door. He looked around at the mess in his wife's usually orderly kitchen.

"What the hell is all of this?"

"I fell," she muttered.

"You sure as hell did, and you managed to make a goddamn shambles of the place." Harp didn't bother taking his boots off at the door, he just marched past the broken chair and kicked part of the busted cup off into the corner.

"Clean this up, woman! What are you good for anymore? NOTHING!"

Normally Mrs. Bittlemore would have cracked him across the jaw, but today she'd lost a bit of her snap. Harp's words filled her up with rage that set her to sobbing uncontrollably.

"SHUT UP SHUT UP SHUT UP!" she howled.

"YOU SHUT UP!" Harp kicked another piece of the cup towards her. "Where the hell is my dinner, woman?"

Harp poured himself a big mug of moonshine right in front of her, then stomped away and flung himself into his chair in the living room to wait for his wife to feed him.

thirty-four

HARP HAD NEVER FELT ANGRIER at his idiot of a wife. She knew he was a nervous wreck about every weird thing that had been going on, but when he tried to tell her that the bastard cow kicking his head was an attempt to murder him, or that he was finding messages spelled out in the dirt, or that the cows had pushed the pigsty down on top of him and helped the pigs escape, she didn't believe him. He wasn't sure how it was possible that such big, dumb animals could be plotting to destroy him, but that's what was happening.

Instead of supporting him like a wife should, she was off in her own little world, more useless every single day. Sitting drinking in his blue truck, he'd get to wondering why in hell he ever married her in the first place. Delva or that other one, Sonja, would have been a far better choice. Hindsight is twenty-twenty.

Harp's mother crossed his mind for a split second. He could picture her standing out in front of the house in the sun, waving at him and his little brother. Her garden was so tall with tomato and pea vines, they poured over the wire fence. It was like a lovely mirage.

And then, here he was, slumped inside that very same house, except it was now decrepit and unkempt. He shook his mother out of his brain and took a big gulp of his moonshine.

He should never have let his stupid wife talk him into taking that baby. The goddamned postcard had been a painful reminder of how easily the whole thing could still come crashing down. Margaret was out there alive somewhere, and taunting them, threatening them, maybe from the neighbours' place right next door. She could be watching him right now. He took a slug from his mug and staggered up to go peer out the window, searching for her face in the brush. Maybe it was even worse: maybe she'd come back because she knew she'd never belonged to them. Maybe that's why she was writing to Willa.

If Margaret finally found out she'd been stolen right from underneath her real parents' noses, the cops would be down on them like an avalanche.

How would she know, though?

Harp replayed the hospital scene over in his mind—pulling the fire alarm, walking out the front door like a ghost, nobody noticing him or the baby he had tightly wrapped up in his arms. He still couldn't believe how easy it was. He felt the old rush of power pull through his chest, fainter now, of course. But there had been so few times in his life where he'd felt in control, and that, definitely, was one of them.

He had practised the route three times. Walked the whole thing through while his wife waited outside in the truck with a stopwatch: four and a half minutes from start to finish.

On the chosen day, he strolled through the reception area and the emergency department, past dozens of people perched on plastic chairs waiting to see the doctor about their cuts and fevers and broken wrists and food poisoning.

He climbed the stairs and then stopped in the hall by the nursery viewing window, pretending to stare in fondly, like a relative on a visit. When the coast was clear, he backed up along the corridor, then pulled the red handle of the fire alarm.

He only messed up one thing. He grabbed the wrong baby. The one his wife wanted had been born two days earlier—she'd read the birth announcement aloud to Harp and made him memorize the name. But the alarm was louder than he thought it would be and he hadn't counted on all the people running around like chickens off the chopping block. He didn't stop to check the chart, he just grabbed little Rose in her pink blanket and took the stairs and exited out the side door of the hospital, right along with two dozen other people.

He walked calmly to his truck and put the baby in an apple box his wife had saved especially for this—she'd stuffed it with a brand-new baby blanket she'd bought in Red Deer. Nobody knew them there, so she picked up a few other things while she was at it—some little clothes and shoes, and even a couple of toys. Harp got into the driver's seat, feeling mighty powerful, even though his hands were shaking like he was trying to hang on to a lightning bolt. He glanced around to check on the baby—she was so quiet! But she seemed to be okay.

A few minutes later, Harp was driving down the highway, radio blasting, cigarette dangling from his lips. When the baby finally started to cry, he cracked the window and turned the radio up, a little at first and then as loud as it would go. Gordon Lightfoot was singing about the wreck of the *Edmund Fitzgerald*.

Harp loved that song. He hummed along, trying to slow his heart, which was beating like a rabbit's. He kept checking the rear-view mirror to make sure no one was following him. Not one other car was even on the road. He passed a tractor pulling a hay wagon, but that was it. He felt like he was flying in a jet, not driving a red pickup truck. The song played on, and the baby screamed, and the wind blew Harp's thinning hair straight up into a set of devil's horns.

When he got home and carried that baby inside, he felt happy for the first time since before his father had died. His wife lit up like a Halloween pumpkin and came rushing towards him as he came through the door. He even got a kiss planted square onto his lips and a big thank-you hug. He'd finally given her a baby.

She'd had bottles ready to go and the little outfits and a drawer filled with diapers. The baby, who had stopped crying at last and was only shuddering with little hiccupy sighs, had a dirty diaper, and Harp stood by his wife's shoulder as she changed her first diaper. As she picked up the used one, a coin rolled out onto the floor. It was covered in poo, but she rinsed it off and laughed at how silly it was to find a coin stuffed into a diaper. She'd saved it in a tin box and then she gave it to Margaret on her tenth birthday, telling her it was a family heirloom.

Harp took another slug of moonshine and wondered for a moment what had become of that coin.

If he was honest, that was one of the few really sweet memories of raising that baby. Margaret was always like a stranger to them both. Once her diaper was changed, she started to scream again. For six months there was hardly a pause in the screaming, and there wasn't a damn thing his wife could do to stop it.

Morning, noon and night, the wailing went through the house like a pack of howling wolves.

It preyed on their sanity.

His wife had thought that having a baby to call her own would bring her the happiness she'd always dreamed of, the warmth and the love and the softness—it brought her none of those things. Margaret looked through them both with what could only be described as disdain.

There was no connection, no affection whatsoever, between them, and worse, the Bittlemores also had to live with what they'd done.

After a couple of months, Harp tried to talk his wife into taking the baby back to Manatukken. "We could dump her at the fire hall."

"It's too late for that. We'd get caught. I know it. We'd both end up in jail. All the police in the whole province are still on red alert looking for the kidnappers. *We* are the kidnappers!"

"We could say we found it on the side of the road. We would be the good guys here!"

His wife would have none of it. But they did think about killing her.

One freezing-cold night they even left her outside, plunking her down like a box of apples by the barn.

After they went back to the house, his wife sat for an hour or so at the kitchen table slamming back the rhubarb wine, her knee going up and down like a jackhammer. Then she full-on panicked and raced back down the lane, but the baby was gone, basket and all. She screamed and ran back to the house, where Harp tried his best to calm her. Maybe, he told her, the coyotes or the cougars had taken care of their problem for them. That caused her to scream even louder.

The two of them sat up all night waiting for the police to show up, or sirens to sound off in the distance because some poor soul had found a tiny chewed-off arm or leg on the road. After she stopped screaming, Mrs. Bittlemore didn't cry a single solitary tear. She only worried about what she would do in jail. Kidnapping was one thing, but murder was another.

But they got lucky, if you could call it that. When Harp staggered into the barn the next morning, there was Margaret, as right as rain, cooing away in one of the stalls, surrounded by the cows. It was the damnedest thing.

Mrs. Bittlemore convinced herself that they must have left her there themselves, and they never talked about it again.

They raised Margaret like she was a mannequin. They dressed her up and made sure she was fed. They put up a little tree at Christmas, gave her some chores, sent her to school when she was old enough and hoped for the best. They all led separate lives. Nobody thought about the past and nobody dared think about the future.

⁓

Harp sighed heavily and drained his mug. He was sick of his wife, sick of Willa always asking questions, sick of all the nonsense around here.

He needed to get away from this goddamn useless farm and sort a few things out. His old fishing cabin would be just the place for a man to do some thinking. It was only a few miles away, and it was fitted out with a cot and a little wood stove—it would be perfect.

He would head out there in the morning, without telling his useless wife he was going. She'd have to grin and bear it.

There he would have some peace and quiet—no bastard cows or lost pigs to deal with—and he could drink whatever he wanted without anybody hovering over him. He was a grown man and he was tired of being told how to behave. NO MORE. He needed to show everybody who was boss around here.

thirty-five

THOUGH HARP HADN'T COME NEAR the cows since the great pig rescue, all the animals knew the cease-fire wouldn't last. The pigs were still hiding in the trees in the North Field, afraid to come back to the barnyard. Dally was quite happy to be looking after the pinklets. It felt good to be wanted and in charge, which she seldom was with anything. It was also lovely to sort of feel like a mom. Dally knew these pigs were old enough they didn't really need a mother, but she could, at the very least, be some kind of a fun aunt.

She spent most of her time with them, only coming back so Willa could milk her, and that was where she was now.

Berle and Crilla were standing in the lee of the barn, swishing the flies off their backs, trying to decide what to do next. Eventually, Harp was going to snap out of his funk. And he'd come for them and the pigs—and they had kittens to deal with too, on top of everything else.

Orange Cat had thought about moving them somewhere else, but she couldn't figure out anywhere safer for the moment than the crate behind the bales in the barn, surrounded by the cows. When Dally wasn't checking on the pigs, she was thrilled to be standing watch over the kittens. For the first time in her life, she felt like she had a real purpose. Berle and Crilla were happy for her, even though the circumstances surrounding Dally's new responsibilities were quite terrifying. The air was thick with uncertainty—or maybe with the certainty that Harp would come for his revenge and they had to either be ready to deal with him or be gone.

Over the years, Crilla had poked a lot of holes in Berle's escape plans, but at last she was willing to get on board with whatever Berle thought they should or could do to protect themselves. She was even willing to be the instigator. After all, what did an old cow like her have to lose?

"It's time to end all of this nonsense, Berle," she said, as they stood there ruminating. "I know I'm ready to fight, and so are you and Dally and the girl and Orange Cat and the pigs—maybe even the kittens!" Crilla blew a great waft of warm air out of her nostrils.

Berle felt a little teary. Having Crilla's support meant everything.

"I have a few ideas," she said, "and we need to get in motion right away. First, I'm going to call upon you to write some of your words."

Crilla nodded.

"While you do that, I'm going to figure out how to round up some gasoline. I think the Missus still keeps a tank of it by the garbage cans. Good thing for us she loves to burn garbage almost as much as she loves to eat biscuits."

Berle turned and started up towards the Bittlemore house to scout the gasoline situation, passing Orange Cat on the way back.

The cat called over her shoulder, "Don't get too close to those crazy people. I was just at the house and Fatty is up to no good. She's mixing up some bad things, some very bad things. I think she's planning to feed them to all of us or one of us or some of us. I knocked a cup off the counter that smelled not right just as the girl was coming in from her day. I'm gonna move the kitties tonight—maybe to the old well or a silo."

"Good idea. And then I need you to help me with a few things. We've got to put an end to their meanness, once and for all. Harp and the Missus have no business having a farm. No business hurting the lot of us. We're going to stop that from ever happening again!"

thirty-six

MARGARET RUSHED AROUND HER CRUMMY studio
apartment, throwing jeans and T-shirts and a few
toiletries into a canvas bag.

Tizzy had called her to say that the PEI postcard drop had
gone off without a hitch, as usual. "Your daughter will be getting
that card right about now, I figure. I gotta tell ya, Margo, you have
been a real darn interesting part of my life all these years."

Tizzy had become such a dear friend. Tizzy had helped her
get on her feet and stay there. She never pressed Margaret for
more than she was willing to give. She knew all about the
Bittlemores and the farm and the baby that she'd left behind.
She always told Margaret, "Nobody is perfect—not you or your
parents, not anybody." For years, she'd dropped in on her every
time she was close, helped find her new places to hang her hat,
alerted her to new jobs, and hosted her on Christmases and
birthdays. Tizzy had become more of a parent to Margaret
than the Bittlemores had ever been.

She was also the one who encouraged her to send the letters in the first place, saying, "It doesn't matter if you don't hear back—you have to let that child know you're thinking about her and that you love her."

Sending those letters had been a lifeline.

Margaret had never really been able to believe that her parents hadn't tried to find her. Would it have been that hard? And what had they told people when she disappeared? She'd never doubted that in her crazy way Mrs. B had loved her, and even Harp had had his moments. But they let her vanish and, as far as she knew, never reported her missing. She guessed, as far as people in Backhills were concerned, the Bittlemores' daughter had gone to Paris and never come back.

For years, she checked the personals section of the national papers, thinking they'd leave her a cryptic message of some sort. If they had, she'd missed it.

Tizzy told her they probably didn't have the brains to do something like that. Tizzy was right.

Still, Margaret was a mess of conflicting emotions. She didn't want to be found, and yet she was consumed with the idea of the Bittlemores wanting her back.

Month after month, Tizzy would pick some random mailbox far from Michigan and drop Margaret's cards and letters into it. The different postmarks had been Margaret's idea. She'd done everything she could to prevent her parents from finding out where she was, she knew, because something wasn't right with those two—they were mean, yes, but also secretive and so isolated. Margaret hadn't belonged on that farm. But neither did her daughter.

She had left Mayvale with them for too long while she waited for her life to be perfect. She'd finally realized it was never going to be perfect, which was why she was packing her bag.

Tizzy knew all the stories about how they'd locked Margaret up when she got pregnant, but she still thought her friend was being overdramatic, paranoid even. "You just wait—one of these days you're gonna hear back from your little girl, and she'll tell you she's been just fine. Lots of kids are raised by their grandparents—hell, I spent every summer with my grandpa, and I loved it!"

"You don't know these people, Tiz. They made my life a living hell, and they've most likely made Mayvale's life a living hell too. Maybe you're right when you say that people change. We can only hope. But even if they've treated her better than they treated me, I'm sure they've turned her against me. I need her to know that I didn't run away because I didn't love her. And that's going to take more than sending her a letter once a month."

"You gotta stop thinking the worst. Thoughts are *things*. You're not helping yourself with that kind of attitude."

But Margaret couldn't take one more day of guilt and remorse and regret. She had to know what had happened to Mayvale. She had to see her daughter and somehow make it right. Even if Mayvale spat in her face and told her to leave and never come back again, Margaret was willing to take that chance.

Tizzy had offered to drive her back to where this had all started, and the irony of this trip was not lost on either of them. Tizzy had picked her up in the rain that night fourteen years ago, and now she was going to take her back, like a book-end on this whole episode.

Margaret looked around her little apartment, the emptiness of it, the absence of a real life, happiness, joy, fulfillment. It was nothing but a box she hid in, waiting for the end to come. She was almost thirty and she was tired of feeling like she didn't belong anywhere.

It was still dark as she turned the key to lock the apartment door behind her. Tizzy and her big rig were waiting for her on the street in front of the building. Margaret opened the passenger door to hop in and then said, "Tizzy, hang on a moment—I forgot something."

She ran back to her apartment, unlocked the door, grabbed the little African violet she kept on her tiny kitchen table, relocked the door and ran back to the truck.

"There, that's what I needed," she said, a little out of breath as she settled in her seat. "I can't very well leave Marilyn behind, can I?"

Both women were laughing as they started the long drive back to Backhills.

thirty-seven

CAROL WAS ALONE IN THE GIRLS' bathroom on Monday, brushing her teeth after lunch, when Nola's crew came in, armed with cans of red paint—the kind that doesn't come off with anything but turpentine.

Carol didn't even have a chance to move before they started spraying her. She pinched her eyes tightly shut and bent over so it wouldn't get in her face. Nola and her zombie squad emptied their cans all over Carol's hair and clothes and shoes and legs and bookbag. They never stopped laughing, taunting, jabbing, insulting.

By the time I got there (one of the kids I passed in the hall had pointed to the bathroom door and told me Nola was in there with Carol), I knew it was going to be bad, but I didn't know how bad. It looked like a bloodbath. I'm not the bravest person in the world, but I managed to push Nola and her henchwomen away from my friend, paint be damned.

Carol looked like she'd been at a serial killers' support group. So much red paint! I told her to run, which she didn't even attempt to do. "I'm not going anywhere—I . . . I'm staying right here with you!"

But it was all she could do not to cry, I could hear it in her voice. I grabbed the spray can away from Nola, while the other two imbeciles darted out to the hallway.

"You stupid idiot, Bittlemore! She's getting what she deserves!"

"Carol didn't do anything to you! Jesus, Nola, you can't just go around spray-painting innocent people!"

"You two started this!" Nola shoved me back towards the toilets, which were also red.

"I'm the one who threw the basketball at you, because you were being HORRIBLE to Carol. Why are you so mean ALL the time? Still, I'm sorry I hit you in the head. I didn't know my aim was that good."

She was coming at me again when Ms. Bevan burst into the bathroom and blew her whistle as loud as that whistle would blow. She looked around at the red paint covering pretty much every surface—stalls, sinks, toilets, windows—and Carol.

"You three to my office—now!"

⌒

I thought Ms. Bevan would be at least a little on our side, but she wasn't. She suspended all three of us, effective immediately. I guessed that was more or less fair—until I learned that I was about to be stuck in the girls' bathroom with Nola, restoring it to its original glory, and not at home, hanging around and maybe doing some sort of extra homework.

Ms. Bevan was on a tear. "If whatever this is doesn't stop

right here and now," she said, "I am going to expel you, Willa. I mean it. And Nola, shame on you—you bring so much of this stuff onto yourself. I have to say that you're not the greatest version of yourself right now, and you do *not* want to peak in high school, trust me. And Carol—since you clearly got the worst of this deal, I won't make you repaint the bathroom. Instead, you're going to be the new assistant coach of the basketball team. You can work alongside me for the rest of the season and . . . well, you'll probably even have some fun. Maybe think of it as a career opportunity."

Carol looked like she'd rather paint the bathroom.

I, on the other hand, was going to be stuck with Nola in a small space filled with toilets.

While we all stood there wondering what was coming next, I could hear someone crying, and it wasn't me and it wasn't Carol.

Nola's crusty exterior had cracked open and out came the tears. "Please don't tell my mother, Ms. Bevan. I'll paint whatever, but I don't want my mom to know I'm suspended." Nola started to sob so hard she flopped down on the floor.

It was very disturbing and weird. Suddenly Nola's behaviour started to make a lot more sense to me. We judge people without knowing their backstory. We make assumptions without really asking ourselves why a person is the way they are. Why are they mean or angry or violent? Why are they bullies?

I mean, I broke the poor girl's nose. Who was the bully now? Me!

Ms. Bevan decided to show us just a little mercy. "None of your parents need to know anything. But you two, get yourselves back to that bathroom. The janitor will set you up with paint and coveralls, and everything else you need. The harder you work, the sooner you'll be done."

thirty-eight

TIZZY DROVE FOR THIRTEEN straight hours, only stopping so they could fuel up and use the bathroom. Another seventeen hours on the road, and they'd be in Backhills. But Margaret hadn't been able to sleep a wink in the truck for all those hours—not for a lack of trying— and Tizzy needed a break, so she pulled into a motel parking lot, announcing she was going to buy them a damn room for the night.

"Margo, we need to get some shut-eye. The last thing we want to do is drive off the road somewhere because I fell asleep at the damn wheel. We have to lay our heads down on an actual bed."

Margaret couldn't argue that some quiet and the absence of rocking back and forth in a truck cab would be welcome. "I hate that I can't pay my own way," she said, but Tizzy just brushed her off and headed for the motel office.

When she turned the motel room key and pushed the door open, she announced, "Nothing but the best for you, my darling, there's even cable TV! You've waited this long to see your daughter, and a few extra hours and a little comfort isn't going to make much difference."

And Margaret knew that was true. But now that she was on the way back, she was so sick with nerves she wanted to get it over with. Her whole body seemed to be vibrating with way too many what-ifs.

What if Mayvale didn't want to see her?

What if Mayvale hated her?

What if the Bittlemores had made up a terrible story about how Margaret was a terrible person?

Not that they needed to make that up, because Margaret had pretty much convinced herself that she WAS a terrible person. Once she'd gotten pregnant, she really hadn't wanted the baby. Who could possibly want a baby before she'd even made it to fifteen? Margaret certainly didn't. She thought of the old adage of drinking poison and wanting the other person to die. She'd wanted to punish her parents, and it had backfired.

What if this whole trip was a bad idea?

Before she even had a chance to open her mouth, Tizzy cut in.

"I know what you're thinkin', and you can stop right there. This is *not* a bad idea. You need to do this, girl. You need to either close a door or open a window, because this is no way to live a life. Not for you and not for your dear sweet baby."

Margaret blew out a long sigh and pulled the blankets up around her neck. A tear rolled down the side of her head and found its way into her left ear, making a muffled, watery sound as it settled there. And that was the last thing she remembered until she woke up the next morning with Tizzy Holt pushing a bag filled with doughnuts towards her head.

"Time to giddy up!"

The women smiled at each other.

They ate their doughnuts, slammed back two cups of luke-warm black coffee each and hit the road.

thirty-nine

MRS. BITTLEMORE DIDN'T KNOW WHETHER she was more shaken up by her failed plan to poison Willa or by the fact that Harp had packed a bag and taken off in his truck, telling her he didn't know when he would be back.

Well, she did, actually. "If only that goddamned cat . . ."

Perhaps the universe was telling her something, and that something was DON'T KILL PEOPLE.

No, she didn't believe in all that hooey. The universe no more cared about her than a shit cared about a fly.

And there was no harm done. Willa hadn't suspected a thing, so Mrs. Bittlemore just needed to try again. She'd make a big pot of soup and some cheesy bread rolls. Surely a cat couldn't knock a huge pot of soup off the stove.

She buzzed around the kitchen like a fat bumblebee, chopping and dicing. Her mind was mostly blank, except when it wasn't. She had never attempted to kill anyone before, and that was stirring up some unforeseen emotions and suppressed thoughts. Like the fact that she didn't have a clue what love felt like. That realization punched through her head in between slices of the knife as she cut up onions and carrots and celery and potatoes to make the broth.

A big loneliness crept in. She'd spent all these years hoping for the feeling of love to wrap itself around her so that she would experience even a faint hint of joy. That hint was there when she was chewing and swallowing food, but that was it. Eating was the closest thing to love she could imagine, as her ever-expanding waistline showed.

All the years of living with Harp and trying to come to terms with the things they'd done, the failing farm, the failed pregnancies and the complicated web of lies that was unravelling—all of it had smeared sadness on every moment of her life. Instead of making her happy, stealing Margaret had only increased her misery. Keeping Margaret's baby had quadrupled it.

Mrs. Bittlemore threw the vegetables into a giant pot, along with three heads of garlic and a whack of dried thyme and oregano and a glug of Worcestershire sauce. She'd make the broth pungent and spicy in order to hide all the other things she was planning on putting in there later. She dumped in a gallon of cold tap water and two fistfuls of salt. She was pleased with herself. She could dump in kerosene at this point and nobody would taste it.

After slamming a heavy lid onto the pot, she marched out the screen door into the yard. Rage made her bloated body as agile as an athlete's. She raced after a large brown hen that had been poking its beak into the dirt looking for bugs, snatched it up—the bird squawking as though it knew exactly what was coming—and snapped its neck with one smooth, swift twist. Within minutes it was plucked and gutted and floating in the pot of gently simmering vegetables.

forty

WHEN BEV GOT BACK to the motel after an afternoon spent putting up more posters in yet another little town a couple of hours away, she found a stack of messages about the silver dollar shoved under her door. In hindsight, it might not have been the greatest idea in the world to put up so many posters and take out quite so many ads. So far nothing useful had come from anybody who had got back to her, and she couldn't help but let loose a big sigh as she picked up and flipped through these new responses.

She wasn't completely over the moon about her rustic "headquarters" at the motel, but it was cheap and more or less central to all the little towns she was canvassing. It made much more sense to stay put rather than go all the way back to Black Diamond every night. Her boss had been more than generous in his support of what he believed was a wild goose chase, even telling her he would reimburse her for gas and mileage if she kept her receipts.

Oh well, she thought, staring at the slips of paper. She had nothing else to do tonight. Bev threw her jacket onto the only chair in the room and then rummaged in her purse, looking for her glasses.

"Bingo!" she said, and stuck them on her head. Then she unscrewed the lid on a three-day-old bottle of red she had in the little motel fridge and poured herself a glass.

Slumped on the edge of the bed, sipping her very terrible wine, she found herself once again thinking about what kind of person could have pulled off so brazen a daylight kidnapping. You'd have to be desperate, but you'd also have to blend in. You'd have to be someone that nobody would look at twice. Someone who was not too old, not too young, plain as a local farmer maybe. Manatukken was a farm town. Folks came to the ER with dog bites or because they'd had a combine run over their leg or they'd stepped on a nail or had fallen off a barn roof. Mundane injuries. Mundane people.

It was not a hospital that did open-heart surgeries or treated cancer. It dealt with the simple injuries and ailments of simple people. So it stood to reason that somebody simple had waltzed in there, pulled the fire alarm and grabbed the first baby they saw. This person—and Bev was sure that it was a single person—walked in planning to take a baby and walked out with a baby. They didn't want revenge on the Larkspurs. The crime hadn't been some kind of vendetta. They didn't want money. They probably didn't even know that the baby's name was Rose Larkspur, or that she was the daughter of Connie and Jon—it was just a baby.

Next, this person likely carried the baby back to wherever they had come from, and when they changed that first diaper, they found the silver dollar. Certainly, none of the pawnshop owners she'd talked to had ever seen such a valuable coin. So it was likely the kidnapper didn't know it was rare. Maybe the coin simply became a souvenir marking that fateful day. Or maybe this person put it in their pocket and never thought about it again. Or it fell out of Rose's diaper and rolled into the ditch.

God only knew. Only God knew.

Or maybe that coin was still with Rose, wherever she was— in a drawer or in an old Crown Royal bag along with a bunch of Rummoli pennies (world's best-ever card game, as far as Bev was concerned).

But it was somewhere, and Bev was going to find it. Taking a big sip of the worst wine she'd ever drunk in her life, and that was saying something, she started calling people back.

forty-one

SOME THINGS ARE NOT SO easy for a cow to pull off, no matter how determined she is. It took Berle a couple days and several trips back and forth to figure out how to collect a little gasoline. Hooves and jerry can lids were not that compatible, though she was easily able to handle the spigot with her tongue. Yuck.

Now, as Berle nosed the jerry can of gasoline back towards the barn, she heard Mrs. Bittlemore rushing in and out of the screen door like there was a storm coming. Berle had heard a hen squeal on one of her trips the day before and had made a mental apology for being too late for that little friend.

There was barely enough gas in the can to wet a matchstick, but she didn't need much. The plan was very straightforward. When Harp got back from wherever he'd gone, she was going to lure him into the barn, lock the doors from the outside and burn the place down.

As to the luring, she'd suggested that Crilla write GO GET HARP on the stable floor before Willa came down to milk them in the morning, and that would surely get him to come and see it for himself. But Crilla had objected.

"I don't want the girl anywhere near here when the barn goes up. No no no. Not good. Let's leave her out of it. Let her do her chores and go off to where she goes. We need to get Harp down here on his own." She'd thought for a minute, then said, "I know what I'm gonna write."

"What?"

"NOT YOUR BABY. Berle, when he sees that, he will crap his pants. Mrs. B was *never* pregnant with Margaret. We all know that. That baby just appeared."

"You're right—that's a mystery for sure."

"So where did she come from? That baby belonged to someone else. Maybe some deranged people gave her to them?"

That didn't seem credible to the cows. Who would willingly give those two horrible people a baby—or even let them adopt one?

"She had to have been taken," Crilla whispered. "Yes, they took her, but from who?"

But Berle had stopped thinking about Margaret, and was staring off into the distance, haunted by second thoughts about frying the old man alive.

And once she'd got the gasoline back to the barn and hidden it behind a bale, she told everybody as much. "Maybe all we need to do is to set the barn on fire," she said. "It'll burn fast and there'll be lots of smoke. Everybody will see it, and the fire department and the police and the whole damn town will show up to put it out, and we'll be rescued."

Berle was a lot of things, but despite her one attempt on

Harp's life, she was no murderer. If she killed him now, she would be just as horrible as he was. It was the farm that needed to be destroyed, so that an animal would never be treated cruelly by Harp Bittlemore again.

It was the farm that needed to end.

That would be the end of Harp.

There was no Harp without the farm.

No Mrs. B without Harp.

These points were pretty hard to argue against, and soon all the farm animals agreed to Berle's plan.

To pull it off, everybody needed to be out of the barn and waiting behind the silos. The silos were four hundred yards northwest of the barn. They were steel and had no chance of catching on fire even if the wind was up and sparks flew.

Berle hesitated for a moment when she recalled that years ago Harp had stored coal in one of them. Had that coal been burned? She wasn't sure. If it was still there, it might be a problem. The land was so dry. The whole place was a tinder keg, except the yard, oddly enough, which was permanently riddled with mud puddles.

Berle surveyed her co-conspirators: Dally and Crilla, Orange Cat and her kittens, the remaining chickens, and the pigs, whom Dally had decided to bring back to the barn after Harp had headed out in the truck.

"No matter what happens when it all starts to go down, you don't move," Berle said, very stern and businesslike. "You'll be safe until I come and get you."

Dally got the part where they all hid behind the old silos and stayed quiet while the barn burned down—but she was confused about the logic of burning down their home. "What's going t-t-t-to hap-p-p-pen to us afterwards? Wh-where will we live?"

"Dally, you leave that to me and Crilla. There are good people out there in the world and we have to keep believing that. And Willa will help us. I have faith in her because every bone in that girl is good. She is going to figure out how to help us."

Berle told them all to get a good night's sleep because tomorrow their lives were going to change for the better. She truly was the most optimistic cow of them all, despite the loss of her tail and the years of cruelty at the old man's hands.

Orange Cat had one more question. "How are you going to start the fire?"

"Harp is going to light the match."

forty-two

TIZZY AND MARGARET WERE SEVEN hours out from Backhills when Tizzy noticed she needed to fill up again.

Margaret had been staring silently out her window for hours, watching the blur of the road go past. She turned to Tizzy and carefully took in her rugged profile.

"Tiz—are we really doing this?"

"We aren't, but YOU are! No matter what happens, it's time for you to face this head-on. No more wondering or wishing or doubting. It's the not knowing that steals your damn joy every day."

"What if she—"

"What if? Would meeting her at last be any worse than what's already been going on? You're miserable and I'm personally fed up with it. You've gotta move forward, kid."

Margaret gnawed a piece of loose skin off one of her cuticles. She knew that everything Tizzy said was true.

"Okay, Margo, we're gonna fill up at the gas station about ten minutes from here. After that, there's not much on this road until we get to Backhills. So whatdaya say—one more bathroom break? Then order me the biggest, blackest coffee they have." Tizzy smiled at her, pushing her top denture forward and wagging it up and down. It was a thing she did that was pretty much guaranteed to crack Margaret up.

And it did. "That shouldn't be legal," Margaret said, giggling.

In ten minutes exactly, Tizzy turned her eighteen-wheeler into Pat's Big T and came to a stop in front of the diesel pump.

As Tizzy fuelled up, Margaret ran inside to use the bathroom and grab their coffees. She loved a good truck stop, the endless rows of chips and candy and fish tackle hats with built-in joke hair for the bald guys who liked to wear them. So much crap in one place! Maybe it would be good if she brought something to her daughter. One of the hats? No, that would be stupid. Candy? Of course, she had no idea what kind of candy her daughter liked, or even if she liked candy at all. Air freshener? Key chain? Energy drink?

Then Margaret spotted a shelf filled with fireworks and, against her better judgment, grabbed an armful of zingers and blaster balls. Every kid liked fireworks, didn't they?

On her way out the door, a coffee in each hand and the bag of fireworks between her teeth, she glanced at the posters plastered on the window. One caught her eye, asking for information about a missing coin.

Without even realizing it, she started to read it out loud, and the bag of fireworks dropped to the ground.

"Lost . . . Rare silver dollar coin . . . Manatukken . . . Reward."

She knew that coin. But Manatukken?

1794.

She'd had a coin like that a long time ago.

The photo on the poster was a bad photocopy, probably from a bad photograph, but the memory of it was instant and visceral.

FLASH to her bedroom.

FLASH to her bedroom nightstand.

FLASH to her Nancy Drew book.

Being pregnant. FLASH FLASH FLASH.

FLASH! Looking out her little window.

Rain coming down.

Cows in the field.

Harp. Mrs. B.

Was that her silver dollar in the photo?

No. There are millions of silver dollars. MILLIONS.

Margaret tore down the poster anyway and stuffed it into her jeans pocket. She picked up the bag of fireworks and headed back to the truck.

When she hoisted herself into the passenger seat, Tizzy reached for her coffee. "Looks like you bought out the store."

"I just got some fireworks for Mayvale. Probably a bad idea, but I wanted to bring her something. Then I saw this poster for a lost coin." She pulled it out and unfolded it for Tizzy. "I used to have a 1794 silver dollar myself that I left behind when I took off. Looks like I should have taken it with me— maybe I gave up a small fortune!" Margaret laughed. "But it's just so weird—the closer we get, the more these memories are coming back."

"A silver dollar from 1794? Damn, woman! At least there's something out there older than me. And you're right, you should have taken it with you!"

Tizzy hit the gas and they lurched back onto the highway,

causing Margaret to bounce into her door and almost land in Tizzy's lap, laughing some more.

After the truck steadied out and Tizzy hit cruising speed, Margaret reread the poster, then stared hard at the photo of the coin.

"I might call this Constable Oldman—I don't know. I'm curious, that's all."

She snuggled back into her seat and took a big sip of her coffee, burning her tongue. "Ouch. Shit. Watch out, Tizzy, the coffee's stupid hot!"

She pinched the coffee between her knees to let it cool down some and gazed out the window at the open fields and the fir trees dotted along the horizon. Nothing looked familiar yet, but why would it? She'd never been this far from the farm. The night she ran away was the first time she'd ever been anywhere.

She could picture her parents as plain as day: Harp with his bony, chalk-thin frame, sucking on his chaw, and her mother waddling around the kitchen stuffing biscuits into her mouth. She wondered how much they'd changed or not changed.

Then she wondered whether she should be scared of them. They obviously hadn't cared that their only kid had left in the middle of the night and had never come back. Maybe they'd been happy to see the back of her. It was all SO weird. Completely, unbelievably strange.

And she started to feel anxious again. What if Mayvale wasn't even at the farm? What if she'd died or they'd killed her and they'd buried her the night she was born? It was possible. After all, not one other single soul knew Margaret was even pregnant.

Shit! Best not to think about any of that stuff. It was going to be what it was going to be. The whole point of this trip was to find some sort of peace.

But Margaret suddenly felt like she was going to throw up. It was just there, at the back of her throat, and then she had to grab the bag filled with fireworks and let it fly, all the worry and all the uncertainty, along with the contents of her stomach.

Tizzy reached over and put her hand on Margaret's shoulder. "I guess your kid will have to live without small explosions."

"Ya, some of them are in wrappers, though, so I could wash 'em off. These cost me forty bucks, for fuck sakes." Margaret carefully set the plastic bag on the floor by her feet. "Sorry about that. God, this is all so nerve-racking." The truck cab smelled like maple syrup and wet socks.

"Crack your window a bit, darling, and keep your eyes on the horizon: that should settle your stomach. Six and three-quarter hours to touchdown."

After a minute, they both realized it was going to take more than a cracked window to get the horrible stench out of the cab.

"Jesus," Tizzy said, "we need to pull over for a sec—we're not gonna make it ten minutes with that smell in here."

forty-three

IT HAD TAKEN ME AND NOLA the rest of Monday, all day Tuesday and part of Wednesday to complete our bathroom repainting job. Red is not an easy colour to cover up. It took three coats of Cotton White #34 before the place looked like nothing bad had ever happened in it.

On the first day, Nola was quiet, but after that you couldn't shut her up.

I nodded a lot and listened to some very tall tales. Nola's mother had been married *five* times. She was one of those women who could not live her life without a man falling all over her. Every time her mother took up with a new fella, Nola, her only child, was kicked to the curb—sent to her room after school to entertain herself while her mother was very clearly entertaining herself. Nola ate dinner alone in her room, night after night. It's no wonder the girl was the way she was. She talked and I listened and painted.

I wouldn't say that we were friends by the end of it, but we reached a truce of sorts.

"I'm sorry I threw a basketball at your head, Nola." This time I meant it.

"I'm sorry too." She laughed a bit and stuck out her hand towards me, like an olive branch, I guess. We shook messy, sticky, white paint hands.

"I'd pick you for my team any day, Bittlemore," she said, then asked, "What kind of a name is Bittlemore, anyway? It sounds like peanut brittle. Butter dish. Butt kisser. Boat builder. I could go on."

"I'm sure you could, but please don't."

Ms. Bevan swooshed in just then and stood there taking a long look around with her hands on her hips. After she inspected every stall and every corner, she turned to us, looking very pleased with herself, and told us it was a job well done.

"I may have to hire you two to paint my garage!"

I don't know what happened to me then. Only, what with Nola's tale of woe and Carol's dad having had a heart attack and the postcard arriving that proved my mom was alive and the rain that began streaming down the bathroom windows, I felt like the world had finally cracked me open and I couldn't hold any of it in one second longer.

And so I blurted out my secret to them both like a long-held burp: "You're probably not going to believe me, but my parents are actually my grandparents."

Ms. Bevan looked startled. "What do you mean, Willa? How do you figure that?"

"Their daughter, their REAL daughter, is my mother! She ran away when I was born and I've been, well—*they've* been—lying. Passing me off as their kid. People have always thought that Margaret was my older sister, because that's what my grandmother told them. But Margaret is my mom. It's all so confusing."

I slumped down onto the floor by one of the sinks. Out of the corner of my eye I could see Nola running around like a headless chicken.

"Holy shit, Bittlemore!" she finally burst out. She sounded like she'd won the lottery. "HOLY ACTUAL SHIT!"

Ms. Bevan shouted, "Nola—I don't want to hear another word from you! Have a little respect." She sat down on the floor beside me, and she took a deep breath—then didn't say anything for what seemed like an eternity. Maybe she was in shock. Maybe she didn't believe me.

She ran her hands through her short hair a few times, like she was buying herself time. Then she said, "I want you to take a few deep breaths, Willa. You know, this kind of thing happens more than you think. It most definitely isn't the end of the world." She reached over and patted me on the kneecap. Ms. Bevan wasn't a touchy-feely kind of person, so it seemed kind of awkward, but nice just the same.

Nola had sat herself down on one of the toilets and was staring at us like we were a circus attraction, loving all the drama.

Ms. Bevan continued with her pep talk, like she was trying to establish a baseline of credibility here. "I thought your sister went off to a boarding school years ago. I mean your mother, excuse me—but I remember hearing about Margaret or reading something in an old file. Are you really sure she's your mother? Did your parents—rather, your grandparents—did they tell you this? Have they got proof? To register for school, you must have had a birth certificate, no? There has to be some sort of paper trail, Willa."

I shrugged. It wasn't the reaction I was hoping to get from Ms. Bevan.

"And if it's true, this isn't the end of the world, Willa. People tell fibs all the time . . . Well, in this case, it was a pretty big lie, but I don't think it's illegal to lie about something like this. A lot of young girls have babies who are raised as their own by another member of their family—like I said, it's more common than you think."

"But she never came back! Margaret ran away or disappeared or maybe something worse. She never went to a boarding school. I think she's been writing to me and they've been hiding her letters. Just last weekend, Carol brought me a postcard from her that went to the Stark place by mistake. That's the only reason I got it. Something has never felt right. How can someone disappear?"

"You'd be surprised how easy it is to disappear. People do it all the time. They owe money, or they want out of a bad marriage, or they want to start over. Look at me—I'm teaching in Backhills, so that's gotta tell you something." She smiled and got to her feet, then stuck her hand out to help me up off the floor. "Shame can make people do unimaginable things. Do your parents have family somewhere, like an aunt she may have gone to live with? I'm sure there's an explanation."

"My grandparents acted like that postcard was a grenade. I'm telling you, there's something not right about what happened to her. She was a fourteen-year-old who had just had a baby and ran off into the night and hasn't been seen since. I think that's wrong and weird, don't you?"

"They never tried to find her? You know that for sure?" Ms. Bevan folded her slim arms neatly in front of her chest.

"I've asked them a million times where she is, but they never answer me. Is it legal to let a minor slip off into the night and leave her baby behind? Why would they lie to me and everyone else all these years, claiming to be my parents? Sure, they told me the truth eventually, but they probably felt like they had to, to distract me from the real story." I was starting to get a headache behind my left eye.

"Willa, this must be a lot for you. Leave it with me for a few days and I'll make some inquiries. I'm glad you told me, but I'm sure there's an explanation for all of this. How about I drive out and have a talk with your grandmother? You know, she and your—your grandfather probably wanted to do what was best for you, which probably doesn't make sense to you at your age."

I found that hard to believe. I don't think Harp or my grandmother had done one single thing in their lives that was in my best interest. And I didn't really want my teacher driving out to the farm. Harp would be furious and I don't know what my grandmother would do.

I said, "Maybe for now you could just check the school records. I know for a fact they pulled her out of classes five months before she had me."

Both of us had pretty much forgotten about Nola sitting there listening to everything we were saying. Then Ms. Bevan pointed her whistle at the middle of Nola's chest and warned her, "Not ONE WORD about any of this leaves this bathroom, or you'll be painting this entire school until you're forty years old."

Nola nodded, the expression on her face solemn. She crossed her heart and mimed turning a key in front of her little pink mouth.

forty-four

MS. BEVAN DIDN'T WASTE ANY time. After she left the girls to finish up in the bathroom, she marched up to the office and asked Pepper Strang, school secretary and busybody, where the school kept old registration records and transfer documents.

"Everything is in boxes in the basement. There's no system because I wasn't working here yet. Lord God only knows what you will find. Mice, most likely, and a penetrating darkness."

Pepper handed Ms. Bevan a very big set of keys. "I have no clue which one fits that old door. I'd just kick it in," she said, and had a good laugh at her own joke.

The basement was just as dark as Pepper had said it would be. It took Ms. Bevan five tries to find the right key for the storage room door. When she got it open, just enough light filtered in that she could spot a long string dangling in the centre of the room, which she hoped was attached to the sixty-watt light bulb high on the ceiling. Thankfully, when she pulled the string, the bulb came on.

She rifled through box after dusty box until, after an hour of searching, she found what she was looking for—*A* through *F* registrations and transfers going back fifteen years. "For Pete's sake, everything's all clumped together—not the greatest organization I've ever seen," Ms. Bevan muttered as she opened it up, waving some kind of bug away from her left ear. It looked like the box was from 1912, it was so water-stained, and it seemed to have been nibbled on over the years. She pulled out a stack of files and started reading out names, surprised that they seemed to be more or less in alphabetical order:

- Allen
- Ackhurt
- Ashard
- Amesfurth
- Appton
- Banton
- Beadley
- Beard

Aha! BITTLEMORE.

Ms. Bevan pulled the manila file out and held it up in the faint light. *Margaret Bittlemore.* All her report cards from the first to ninth grade: average marks. Volleyball and baseball team photos, attendance sheets (in grades eight and nine she'd skipped a fair bit), but no real disciplinary problems. Margaret hadn't burned the gym down or shown up to class drunk or broken another student's nose. She seemed like an ordinary student until the paper trail stopped dead in the middle of the ninth grade.

That alone didn't mean she'd had a baby. There would have to be a record of a baby, wouldn't there? Surely there would be a hospital involved, or a family doctor at the very least?

Was Willa really this girl's daughter?

Anything was possible, she supposed, but why did people make their lives so darn complicated?

Ms. Bevan couldn't find any trace of transfer documents indicating that Margaret had been sent to a school of any description in Paris. There *was* a letter from Mrs. Bittlemore informing the principal that Margaret was leaving the school, so that was something. Maybe the Bittlemores changed their minds and sent her to live with an aunt? But where did she go after the baby was born? If there was a baby . . .

Maybe Willa just had a very active imagination?

But all of this was a bit odd. If Margaret was an older sister, there was quite a big gap between them. Also, Willa wasn't a kid who made things up. Ms. Bevan had never known her to be a liar. And fourteen years is a long time not to hear from a daughter, a sister, and especially a mother. The Bittlemores were still there on their farm, but their oldest daughter didn't seem to be anywhere, and it was all feeling a little nefarious somehow.

If she was honest, Ms. Bevan had a soft spot for Willa, and she was intrigued by this little mystery. The only sensible thing to do was to take this old file with her on a visit to Harp Bittlemore and his wife. She'd just ask them straight out where their older daughter was.

forty-five

JUST AS MS. BEVAN WAS deciding to drive out to the farm to ask the Bittlemores some pointed questions, Harp burst in through the kitchen door, half-drunk and hollering for his wife.

He had managed to stay away from home for two extremely whisky-sodden nights, and now he was on a mission, toting the shotgun he'd used to kill Mike Nesbit's dog—it was far and away his favourite gun, and he and it had shot a heck of a lot of pain-in-the-ass, unwanted critters over the years. Harp had sat up until dawn at his fishing cabin, drinking whisky and licking his wounds. His own goddamn cows had attacked him again and he had decided it was time to even the score.

"Those murdering bastards!" he yelled as he crashed through the kitchen. "MOTHER! Where the hell are you?"

There was no answering yell, no sign of her at all except for a pot of soup simmering on the stove, one of his wife's slow-cooking marvels. If he hadn't been so hungover, he would have eaten the lot of it, and a couple of the fresh cheese buns right out of the oven too. But no, he couldn't stop to eat anything: he had things to do, things to kill. Those cows were conspiring to murder him, and he was going to beat them to the punch.

"MOTHER!" he screamed up the staircase. Still no answer.

He had the gun, but he needed the shells if he was going to get the job done. He stumbled into the living room, bashing his bony shin on the edge of the coffee table. "Jesus, fucker!" he yelped, hopping on one foot until the pain died down. Then he lurched to the cabinet, where the box was usually kept, but they were gone. The one measly shell he'd found in a tin in the shed and crammed into the barrel wasn't nearly enough to kill all those bastard cows. And those pigs were gonna get theirs too, if he could find them!

"MOTHER! Where the hell are you?"

"I am right here, you old fool." Mrs. Bittlemore came through the back door with a bucket filled with wood for the stove. They'd had electricity on the farm since 1951, but she loved her black cast-iron monstrosity. Everything tasted better when she cooked on that stove, and nothing or nobody would ever change her mind. "What the hell are you doing with that gun?"

"I'm going to kill the cows before they kill me!"

"You've lost your godforsaken mind. Those cows aren't trying to kill you." She stuffed a few sticks of wood into the stove and closed the lid with a clang as flames started to shoot up.

"I can't find the shells! I had them in the cabinet and now they're gone."

Mrs. Bittlemore smirked a little. She was the one who had hidden the box after Harp had gotten drunk one night and threatened to shoot Orange Cat, certain she was pregnant again. After he passed out, Mrs. Bittlemore shoved the shells behind the clawfoot bathtub. Mrs. Bittlemore didn't love much of anything in this world, but she did feel some affection for that cat, even after the stunt with the teacup.

"I haven't seen them. You said you needed to buy some more next time you're in town. Did you forget?"

"I had a whole bloody box of shells!"

Just then they heard tires cutting through the loose gravel of the lane. Mrs. Bittlemore glanced out the open kitchen window and spotted a strange little foreign car stopping by the side door. Quickly, she scuttled to the stove to put the lid on her poisoned pot of soup. It was going to be Willa's dinner—her last dinner. She had to get it done before that little shit figured out that Margaret wasn't really a Bittlemore. That Harp had stolen her.

No way was *she* going to jail, leaving Willa free as a bird. The girl wasn't even her kin. If she was going down, Mrs. Bittlemore was going to take everyone with her.

—

Ms. Bevan sat in her car in the driveway of what she hoped was the Bittlemore farm.

When she'd gone back to the bathroom to tell Willa that she was headed for the farm to talk to her parents, Willa had wanted to come. Maybe she should have let her, given that she wasn't really sure she was in the right place. But she'd said no, thinking that the Bittlemores might be more honest if their conversation happened without the girl listening. When Willa protested, Ms. Bevan told her to head over to Carol's after school, and she would call Willa to tell her what she found out before she came home.

She sighed loudly, and double-checked the map that she'd folded out into what looked like a kite ready to take flight. It was the biggest map she'd ever seen, but it was the only map of the area at the library. She'd had to beg the librarian to let her borrow it, as it was a not-for-lending item. Whatever.

She ran her finger along the route she had taken and then looked up at the house. It had to be the place. It looked weathered, to say the least. Every building, the barn, the shed, the fences—they all needed a coat of paint and a whole lot of TLC. She thought about Willa living there in such disrepair and it broke her heart a little.

She stepped out of her car into a puddle of mud. *Great, trust me to wear my white sneakers.* She gave up on the map folding and stuffed it into the back seat. Right now there were more important things to deal with.

Looking up from her one muddy foot, she noticed a sad-looking dairy cow standing at the door of the barn staring at her. She felt like she should say something to her, so she called, "Hello there, cow!"

The cow nodded like it was saying hello back. Well, okay. That was a funny coincidence.

Harp was bent over, staring out the window. "Jesus H. Christ! Who is that? She looks like some kinda saleslady."

When he straightened up, Mrs. Bittlemore pushed her hand into the middle of her husband's back and shoved him towards the half-open door. "You go out there and get rid of her. I've got things to do. Willa will be home soon."

"I've got things to do myself! Did you forget I was about to shoot the goddamned cows?"

"Harp, get the hell out there."

Grimacing, he obeyed. At first Harp was going to take the gun with him to make a point, but then he thought better of it and leaned it just inside the door. Once he was outside, he stopped at the top of the wooden steps. "Can I help you, lady?" he called.

"Mr. Bittlemore, I presume?" Ms. Bevan realized she was smiling a little too hard because she was suddenly nervous. Somehow she was feeling chilly in the middle of a warm spring day.

"What if I am?" Harp came down the steps and spit on the ground very close to Ms. Bevan's one clean shoe. She stood her ground. Without having asked a single question, she understood why Willa was trepidatious about ruffling this man's feathers. She needed to play this as cool as possible.

"I'm Dawn Bevan, Willa's teacher—well, one of Willa's teachers. I like to meet all my students' parents at some point during the year, and I have not had the pleasure of seeing either you or Mrs. Bittlemore at any of the parent–teacher evenings. So— here I am."

Standing to one side of the window, where she could keep an eye on things, Mrs. Bittlemore had started sweating profusely. Her soup concoction was bubbling away, but nothing was going the way she wanted it to. She strained to hear what her husband was saying to this little pint of a woman. She had short hair like a city lady, and it was *so* blond. Was that a whistle hanging around her neck?

Taking a deep breath, she stepped out onto the porch herself and folded her fat arms over her breasts. She could feel her heart pounding.

"Well, hello to you, Mrs. Bittlemore! I was just saying to your husband that I am one of your daughter's teachers." Or was it "granddaughter," like Willa said? These two were easily in their late sixties, or more. Mrs. Bittlemore would have been seriously pushing it to have had a child fourteen years ago.

"Is Willa in some sort of trouble?" Mrs. Bittlemore more or less yelled from the porch. "What did she do this time?"

"She didn't do anything! I was just in the area, and decided to stop by . . ."

Ms. Bevan was trying to figure out how to ask the question about Margaret. Should she just blurt it out?

She said, "I think you had another daughter who went to our school, right? That was before my time."

Mrs. Bittlemore felt so nauseous she had to lean against the railing.

"She left us in the ninth grade, didn't she?"

Mrs. Bittlemore was so rattled by the questions, she stood there with a blank look on her face. Even half-drunk, Harp realized he needed to step in.

"Yes, that was our oldest, Margaret. She went away to another school years ago. Overseas. Right, Mother?" He glared over his shoulder at his wife, whose mouth was still shut tight. "We get letters once in a while, don't we?"

Mrs. Bittlemore managed to nod.

Harp moved a little closer to Dawn Bevan, his hands clenched behind his back. This was turning into a bad dream.

Ms. Bevan said, "Yes, Willa told me her big sister had gone to Paris. How exciting! And that was right about the time Willa came along, wasn't it? Such a crazy time for you both. A new baby and your oldest girl—"

Harp swung his fist as hard as he could, smashing the teacher in the face. Her body slammed to the ground, blood streaming from her nose.

He'd panicked, plain and simple. Nobody in all these years had asked one question about Margaret. Everything had been manageable. Nobody bothered with them or cared enough to test their outlandish stories. That's how bad people get away with bad things. People turn a blind eye.

Crouching close to her, he realized she was completely out. But she wouldn't stay out for long.

"Mother!" Harp yelled. "Get your ass down here and help me. We need to move her into the barn."

His wife hobbled down the steps and came to stand beside the tiny woman lying in a heap on the ground. It was difficult for Mrs. Bittlemore to bend over, but she managed to grab a foot and Harp got the other, and the two of them started dragging their unwanted guest down to the barn. The teacher didn't let out a sound.

Is this what a dead body felt like? It was so heavy. But no— Mrs. Bittlemore could see the blood bubble out of the little lady's nose.

Harp puffed. "She's not dead, if that's what yer thinkin'. But she knows something. I know she knows something. I don't know what, but we gotta fix it."

⌐

Berle saw Harp knock the lady who had gotten out of the car right off her feet. Now he and the Missus were dragging her limp body towards the barn. Berle not only felt terrible, but she was at a loss as to what she should do. The whole plan was going to go right out the window. She couldn't very well burn the barn down with a strange lady lying unconscious inside it. She needed to figure out how to help her. She needed Willa. Where was Willa?

In the meantime, she and Crilla had to get out of there. After checking that the jerry can was well hidden, the two cows trotted towards the silos. Harp and Mrs. Bittlemore were so focused on the poor lady, they didn't even notice them.

⌒

The Bittlemores managed to haul Ms. Bevan into one of the stalls and drop her on a pile of filthy straw. They stood over her like scarecrows, completely out of breath. Harp gave her a kick to see if she'd move—she didn't. As he stood there looking down at the pale, unconscious face of Willa's teacher, Mrs. Bittlemore swatted him hard on the arm.

"JESUS MARY MOTHER OF GOD! What's that?!"

She pointed at some letters drawn into the dirt of the stable floor.

NOT YOUR BABY

"I've been telling you, you old bitch—those cows are leaving messages for me. They're too smart for their own good, and they're up to something. Now they know we—"

"No, they know *you* took that baby. YOU! I didn't have anything to do with that. You coulda said no. And for God's sake, Harp, the cows did *not* spell this out. A cow can't write, let alone spell. You are out of your head nuts about those cows."

Mrs. Bittlemore felt her heart racing and a dull pain starting to form into a wad in the middle of her chest.

Harp was having none of it. "You're wrong, old woman. I've been trying to tell you for months that the cows are out to get me. I'm going to get my bloody gun. This is the goddamn end." He wiped spit from the corner of his mouth and realized his knuckles were bleeding where the teacher's teeth had caught them. "And then we'll get ridda this thing." He kicked Ms. Bevan again, and she still didn't stir.

His wife said, "We need to get rid of that girl."

"That's what I just said. We'll get rid of her right after I shoot the damn cows."

She pointed at Ms. Bevan in the straw. "Not her, Harp, but, well, yes, her. But we also have to get rid of Willa. She is a big problem. We need to clean the slate. And don't you eat any of that soup I made."

She sounded so matter-of-fact it took Harp a moment to take in what she meant. Then he said, "Get rid of Willa? My God, woman. That's going too far. And why the hell can't I eat the soup?"

"It's laced with so many medicinal herbs and such, it'd knock a horse off its feet in about twenty seconds, that's why."

Harp looked at his wife as though he was seeing her in an entirely new light, maybe even feeling some sort of attraction. "All right, I won't touch it. But I got to go up to the house and get my gun."

"The shells are behind the bathtub," Mrs. Bittlemore called after him, and Harp threw his bloody fist in the air and gave his wife a thumbs-up. He was feeling light-headed and strange. After a moment or two, he realized that he was happy.

forty-six

CAROL CAME TO FIND ME in the girls' bathroom when the final bell rang. I didn't think my
punishment detail would ever end. I nodded
goodbye to Nola and got out of the girls'
bathroom, glad to see the back of it. I think the fumes had been
giving me an even bigger headache than my family dilemma.

It was a sunny afternoon, even warm. On the way to Carol's
place, we made a detour to the hardware store because they
had one of those glass-bottle pop machines. Pulling a bottle of
root beer out of those ice-cold steel grippers is always so satisfying. Carol, as usual, got herself a grape Crush, a drink I think
is disgusting.

Soon we were sitting on the floor of her bedroom, wondering what we should do next. It felt like days since Ms. Bevan
had told me she was heading out to the farm. I was hoping
she'd have called the Stark place by now, but I needed to be
more patient. Harp was most likely showing her around the

farm. Just as long as neither of them were being total A-holes.

Laughter kept floating up the stairs from the living room. Mr. Stark was finally home from the hospital, still taking it easy, and he and Mrs. Stark were watching *I Love Lucy* reruns from yesteryear and laughing their heads off. It was nice to hear somebody having a good time. When I came into the house, I could see how much weight he'd lost, and I told him he looked like Tab Hunter, which made him smile.

Carol checked her Timex watch. "Ms. Bevan has been there for three hours, Wills. What could be taking so long?"

"I have no idea, but she told me to stay put until she called."

"But that was at two. It's now ten past five."

Carol was right. This wasn't feeling good.

"Maybe your grandparents invited her to stay for dinner?"

"Ya, right. Like that would ever happen," I said, trying to picture my grandmother sitting at her kitchen table with her fat, folded arms squished in front of her, watching Ms. Bevan eat her famous garlic mashed potatoes. Never. Neither Harp nor my grandmother would have let her step foot inside the house, let alone feed her dinner. They would have hustled her out of there just as fast as they were able.

"I think I better head home and see what's going on."

"Maybe she left already and just forgot to call. She's a busy lady."

"I don't think she would have forgotten. She knew how upset I was, and it was her idea to go over there and try to find out the truth."

As I got to my feet, Carol said, "I'll come with you, but I'm sure you'll find that they're all just having a very constructive, friendly conversation."

It's amazing to me that, despite everything that has

happened to her, Carol always thinks the best of everyone, even Harp and my grandmother. I don't think I'll ever be able to be even half that optimistic.

"I'm just going to walk Willa home," Carol called as we headed past her parents and out the door. The two waved merrily at us, like they were on a parade float.

⌐⌐

Tizzy and Margaret were about ten minutes away from the farm and Margaret's heart felt like it was skipping around.

"Tizzy, I need to get some air. Can we just pull over for a minute or two? I'll take a short walk and get myself together. Or maybe we could stop in Backhills instead, and I'll phone the house? Jesus, I'm kinda freaking out."

"You still know the number?" Tizzy said, shifting into low and parking.

"Believe me, it'll be the same damn number!" Margaret jumped out of the cab of the truck and sat down on a big rock in the ditch.

Tizzy followed her out of the cab, stopping for a big stretch when her boots hit the pavement. "So what are you gonna do when they pick up? 'Hello, is Mayvale there, please? It's her mother and I'd like to have a quick catch-up.'"

"No, I'll hang up as soon as someone picks up. I just want to see if they're home."

Tizzy looked down at Margaret, sitting on a rock, fists clenched and both her legs bouncing up and down. She felt for her, she really did, but now was not the time to chicken out.

"You can do this, Margo. You can. I'll be right beside you the whole way. I will not leave your side, my darling girl. Come on, now, look at me."

Margaret glanced up, then put her hand over her brow to shade her eyes from the sun.

Tizzy said, "I would never in a thousand Sundays let you do this on your own."

"I know. It's just that while I knew this would be hard, it's more than hard—it's super fucking difficult. I'm giving it a ten outta ten on the difficulty scale."

Tizzy lit a cigarette, then came down to stand in the grass beside Margaret. "Look, just say hello to the kid and say you're sorry and take what's coming to you, whatever that is, and we're outta there."

Margaret pulled the poster out of her pocket and stared at it. "I had a coin just like this one, Tizzy, and the coincidence just seems too much. I want to call this number too, and get hold of that police officer, Constable Oldman. So can we drive to a phone booth first? Please? What's another hour when we've come this far?"

Tizzy just stared at her, and Margaret added, "Yes, I'm putting it off, but I don't care. Also, I think I need a beer."

"Okay, let's find a beer and a pay phone in Backhills and you can call your police lady. Jesus, you're a piece of work." Tizzy leaned down and stubbed out her cigarette on the rock between Margaret's legs.

forty-seven

BERLE AND CRILLA WATCHED the barn from beside one of the silos, trying to figure out what to do about the lady Harp had knocked out.

"We need a tarp, Crilla. You and I have to get that lady onto a tarp and pull her out of there."

"But we need the Bittlemores to leave first," Crilla said, ever the rational one. "Once they're out of there, I know where to find a perfectly good tarp, and you do too, if you'd only stop to think. It's in the barn already, covering up his crate of moonshine."

"It's our lucky day," Berle said, with a good dose of sarcasm. "If it wasn't for bad luck, we wouldn't have no luck at all." She wasn't completely sure what that meant, but felt it was true.

Leaving Dally in charge of the other animals, they hustled across the field to the barn right after they saw the Bittlemores lurch up the road to the house.

Berle nudged the barn door open, and there the poor thing was, lying on the filthy straw in the last stall. She had blood all over her face and on her shirt, and she was still out cold.

"He really hit her hard," Berle said as she tried to pull away some of the dirty straw. "I kind of hoped she'd be waking up and she could walk out of here."

Crilla was studying her handiwork in the dirt of the stable floor. "I see somebody tried to brush away our little message. Not all that well." NO Y UR B BY was still visible. "Wish I could have been a fly on the wall when they saw that."

Berle pulled the big blue tarp off the whisky jars and dragged it close to the stall. All they had to do now was somehow get the lady onto it. It wasn't the first time they'd wished they had hands.

"You keep a lookout for Harp and the Missus while I see what I can do," Berle said, and she grabbed the lady's sleeve in her teeth and started to gently pull.

Crilla went to stand by the door. But soon Berle called, "I can't shift her by myself. Come here and grab her pant leg."

When Crilla bit down on the woman's ankle by mistake, they heard a faint moan.

Berle said, "Was that you or her?"

"Good grief, I think she's waking up. I didn't mean to bite her, it's just her pants are tight."

"Make sure you only get the pant leg this time, and keep pulling. We've almost got her there."

Once the cows had finally wiggled the unknown lady onto the tarp, they set off to drag her out of the barn and across the field towards the silos.

Harp was vibrating between murderous and rattled. "What should we do now, Mother?"

As Mrs. Bittlemore madly stirred her soup, it crossed her mind that she and her husband should throw back a couple of bowls and call it a bloody day. *But no! Never surrender!* If she was going down, she really did intend to take everybody with her.

"Get out there and move that woman's little car into the shed! Now!" Mrs. Bittlemore threw a set of car keys at her husband's head, and he managed to catch them. "I'm not stupid, but you are," she said. "I took them out of her pants pocket just now, thank you very much."

Harp was dazzled by his wife's quick thinking. He nodded and went to hide the car while Mrs. Bittlemore stared up at the clock in the kitchen, wondering why, today of all days, Willa was late getting home from school.

forty-eight

AS THEY DROVE INTO BACKHILLS, Margaret was
startled by how unchanged everything looked.
Maybe a few new little shops had popped up here
and there, but mostly time had left the town the way
it had been the last time she set foot in it. Tizzy parked the
truck on the far edge of the FOOD R US parking lot at the end
of the street. It was empty, save for three or four cars parked as
close as possible to the front door.

Margaret said, "FOOD R US? This is new. Were they drunk
when they named it, do you think?"

Tizzy shook her head as she turned the engine off. The two
women jumped out of the cab and started walking towards the
diner across the street. Fir trees lined both sides of the main
drag. They were maybe seven feet tall the last time Margaret had
walked down the sidewalk, and now they were twice that size.

They sat down at a booth near the bathrooms and, conve-
niently, the pay phone. "I remember eating here when I was

little. My parents brought me to town on a couple of rare occasions for a hot dog and a sundae, if you can believe that. God, this is so weird."

"You remember me picking you up in the rain and the dark? Nearly fifteen years ago now, kid. Your life really changed that night, and soon it's going to change again."

An elderly waitress with thinning hair came up to the table and asked what they wanted.

"Two beers," Tizzy said. "Buds, if you please and thank you—in the bottle."

The waitress nodded. "Draft gives me a headache and the runs." She didn't seem to mind doling out personal information. "Luckily, bottles is all we got. Just gonna write that down so I don't forget." She took a pencil out of her hair and licked the lead tip, and they watched her write down *2 buds*.

Tizzy looked at her kindly. "You got it right."

"My brain isn't what it used to be," the waitress said, "and it wasn't much then either!" She laughed at her own joke and trundled off.

Margaret stood up and headed towards the pay phone. Partway there, she called, "Tizzy, do you have a quarter?"

Her friend flipped a coin through the air and Margaret missed it completely. It fell on the floor and slid underneath a chair. "You did that on purpose, Holt."

Margaret got down on her knees and retrieved it, stuffed it in the slot, then waited for the dial tone. She made the call, and the phone rang seven times until some guy at a motel switchboard finally answered.

Margaret said, "I must have the wrong number."

"If you're calling for Constable Oldman, you've got it right. The constable is a guest here and we've been taking messages for her. You calling about the coin too? We've been getting lots of calls, which is no surprise when the coin is worth so much money. Do you want to leave a message? She's usually back by suppertime."

"Yep, I'm calling about the coin. Did she find it?"

"I'd rather not say, but no, she didn't. Would you like to leave your name?"

Margaret wasn't sure she should, but then decided she was beyond worrying at this point. "Tell her that Margaret Bittlemore called and that she may have some information about a similar coin. I'm not sure if it's the one she's looking for, but . . ."

"Is there a number where she could reach you?"

"No. Tell her I'll call back later."

"All right, Mrs. Brittlemire, I will slip your message under her door."

⌐

Tizzy was already halfway through her beer when Margaret got back. "The constable wasn't there. I'll call later. Shall we go?"

"What about your beer?"

"I'll take it with me. Hey, ma'am!" The waitress spun around from eating a piece of pie at the counter. "Is it okay if I take a road pop?" Margaret pointed at the Budweiser.

"It's your life, lady. Be sure to recycle."

Tizzy saluted the waitress. "That woman is a real trip." Then she smacked Margaret on the arm. "Next stop, your reunion!"

forty-nine

I HUSTLED DOWN THE OLD dirt road to that wretched farm as fast as I could go. Carol wasn't interested in running, so we kept it to a very brisk walk. She kept telling me that if she ran, her knees might dislocate without warning. Good grief.

I was worried about Ms. Bevan, but Carol kept reminding me that I was a dramatic person who really needed to check myself back into a place called reality.

"She probably went home hours ago." Carol was adamant, and for Carol that was something.

We came over the top of the hill just after dinnertime. No car in the drive, so I guess Carol was right—Ms. Bevan had been and gone. But everything looked so still. There was no birdsong. No rustling of leaves. No cows bellowing or chickens clucking. It was like a ghost town.

I opened the screen door to the kitchen, with Carol right on my heels—I mean, so close she kept running into the back of my legs. My intuition was screaming that we should turn around and run. No Harp and no Mrs. B, but they had been here recently, because a giant pot of soup was gently simmering on the stove. It smelled delicious, no surprise. I almost called out, but something told me not to.

"Carol, I'm going to look around the house and see if I can figure out where they are. Why don't you head to the barn and see who you can spot? I don't even know where the cows are. I'll come and find you."

"This is kind of cool," she said. "It's like we're Nancy and Kathy Drew."

"There is no Kathy Drew."

"I know, but if there was, right?" Carol grinned at me, then turned around and sauntered towards the barn. She looked like she was off to buy new shoes.

⌒

Carol pushed open the barn door and caught the Bittlemores standing there like a couple of old trees in the beam of sunlight she'd allowed in.

"Oh! Hi there! Willa is up at the house looking for you. What are you guys doing?"

They stared back at her as if shocked that Carol Stark had appeared before them like a lost fawn.

"Is everything okay?" Carol, as usual, was immediately concerned about them.

Harp looked over at his wife with white-hot panic shooting from his eyes, silently saying, *Now what do we do?*

After Harp had hidden Ms. Bevan's car, the two of them had hustled back to the barn to finish her off, then bury her, or at least hide her a little better until they could sort everything out. But when they got there, she was gone. Vanished!

Mrs. Bittlemore had waddled around searching every pile of straw, behind every barrel, under every saddle and blanket and crate of whisky. Somehow, the woman had come to consciousness and managed to escape! This was a disaster!

They were just about to head out the door to start searching the fields—they had to prevent that woman from getting to town—when Carol walked in.

Mrs. Bittlemore gave herself a mental shake and walked up to Carol like she was leading a parade—seemingly confident and sure. "Willa finally got home, did she? Well, we were just headed up to the house. Came down to feed the cows, didn't we, Harp, since the girl missed her chores. Let's all go see what I've made for dinner. Would you like to stay for dinner, young lady?"

Mrs. Bittlemore grabbed hold of Carol's arm so hard she winced.

"That kind of hurts, ma'am."

"I'm sorry, dear. You're so darn slim and I forgot my own strength." She let up a bit on Carol's arm but hung on to it just the same.

Out of Carol's eyeline, Harp was shrugging wildly and tipping his head towards the fields. Trying to communicate that their first priority was finding the teacher he'd slugged.

She shot him a stern look and said, "Come along, Harp. Let's go for dinner, shall we? I've got that nice chicken soup and some fresh baked cheese rolls."

Obediently, Harp followed the two of them out the stable door. Willa's teacher couldn't have gotten far, but though he looked in every direction, he couldn't see her anywhere. As a matter of fact, he couldn't see anything else either. No cows, no cat, no chickens. And the pigs had never been found.

He stopped dead, feeling more out of control by the minute.

"Don't make me tell you again, Harp. It's dinnertime!"

"But what about that—"

"First things first, Father," his wife interrupted. "First things first."

fifty

BEV OLDMAN HAD FELT A BIT hungover that morning. She'd only had two, maybe three glasses tops, but the wine wasn't the best vintage, which she already knew before pouring that third glass. She'd called people about the silver dollar until midnight, reaching a mishmash of weirdos and collectors who offered to buy the coin if and when she found it. They were giddy at the prospect.

After she'd had a shower, thrown back two cups of the world's worst coffee and a couple of Aspirins, and chugged a big glass of water, she'd bitten the bullet and called Randy Tripp. She'd been worried that he was going to order her back to HQ and tell her to work from there. But he hadn't.

"I honestly think I'm inches away from a big break, Captain," Bev said, as she watched some more notes being slipped under her motel room door. "I've literally got tips coming in as we speak."

He said, "You're doing a good job, Constable Orman. Persistence, resilience and repeat."

That didn't sound like the greatest slogan she'd ever heard.

"And I gotta tell ya," her captain continued, "we sure appreciate you paying for your own motel room."

"I am—?"

"It shows what a dedicated go-getter you are. Anyway, I'm sure it's all going to pay off. Oh, and Wheeler reminded me to tell you to keep your gas receipts. We'll kick in for a tank of unleaded. Least we can do."

"Yes, it is, sir."

"Thanks for calling, Ordham. Keep me in the loop. I'm here if you need me."

She hung up, sighing. Then retrieved the new messages, and went through them and a few more still strewn across her bed. None of them seemed all that credible, mostly nerds wanting to see the coin in person, which she didn't have. Then she dumped out her wallet and searched for a recent gas receipt. *It must be in the glovebox*, she thought. Bev flopped back onto a stack of pillows and closed her eyes—but just for twenty minutes.

Bev bolted upright two and a half hours later to a rapid knocking at the door. There was a bit of drool on one of the pillows, which she immediately flipped over in embarrassment. "Hello? I'm coming! Hang on a second . . ."

There was no one at the door, but there were six more messages scattered across the floor. Bev picked them up, not expecting much. Two of them looked like more of the same, but there was one that seemed interesting, from a Margaret Bittlemore. She hadn't left a number, just said she'd call back.

Bev rifled through her notes to see if she'd come across a Bittlemore anywhere. Surely she'd have remembered a name like that, but she had a lot on her mind. Nothing. Shrugging, Bev tromped over to reception and borrowed the phone book from the front desk. It covered fourteen counties, so she thought she'd simply look the woman up. If she'd seen the poster, she was likely from somewhere around here.

And there was indeed a Bittlemore in the listings for Backhills.

Bittlemore, H.R., 117 Rural Route 34

It wasn't Margaret Bittlemore, but with that last name they'd most likely be related. Wanting to get at least one thing accomplished today, she threw her weathered-looking file, a sad apple and a thermos half-filled with the remnants of her morning coffee into her bag. Backhills was only a forty-five-minute drive away. Surely she could ask somebody random where the address was once she got into town. Didn't everybody know everybody in these places?

Bev headed for her car, talking to herself. "No stone unturned. No lead unchecked." She threw everything into the passenger seat, turned the key and sped out of the motel parking lot, gravel flying and the apple rolling out of the bag onto the floor. She stopped the car and leaned over to grab the apple, honking the horn with her boob as she did. When she sat up, she saw the motel manager waving at her like an old friend. She must have assumed the honk was for her.

fifty-one

DAWN BEVAN HAD NO CLUE what had happened to her. One of her eyes was completely sealed shut. Her entire head, but especially her jaw, felt like it had been crushed in a vise. There was blood all down the front of her yellow short-sleeved shirt and on the whistle still hanging around her neck. She was lying on the ground and she could smell—dung? Dirt? Animals? Aching everywhere, she closed her eye again.

Something licked her hand and she bolted upright, then felt like she was going to be sick.

"What—where—what is going on?" She was in a daze, head pounding, nausea coming in waves, barely able to make out three large shapes looming over her.

Crilla stopped licking the lady's hand and told the others to stand back to give her some space, which they did. They all looked at each other with relief.

Orange Cat had been hunkering on the roof of the small

lean-to beside the silo that sheltered some bales of straw, and chose that moment to jump down, giving Ms. Bevan a start.

"God sakes! What is happening? Where am I?"

The cat wrapped her fluffy tail around her wrist, purring wildly.

"Nice kitty, there, there—be a nice kitty." Ms. Bevan wasn't really an animal lover, but the purring, she had to admit, was soothing . . . and were those kittens? Several balls of fluff were nosing out of a basket tucked between a couple of bales.

Little flashes of the day started crawling back to her in bits and pieces . . .

Willa and Nola in the bathroom—wait a minute. Willa had blurted something about her sister being her mother? Then Ms. Bevan was parking by a house. The Bittlemore house. That old man coming out onto the stoop, followed by his wife. Did they have a conversation? Did someone actually punch her?

And why was she now sitting on a blue tarp surrounded by kittens, cows and—were those pigs?

That was the moment Orange Cat spotted Harp and the Missus leaving the barn with Carol. Harp had his shotgun, and Mrs. Bittlemore seemed to be pulling Carol along.

"LOOK! They've got Carol! I bet they were surprised to see this lady gone, and they'll be mad, mad, mad. I need to get up there to see what they're doing." She took off, startling Ms. Bevan all over again.

Berle called, "We'll be right behind you."

"Hold on," Dally said, "w-w-we need t-t-t-to get this l-l-lady up and o-on her feet."

"I'm on it!" Crilla was already spelling GET UP in the dirt in front of the lady.

Ms. Bevan couldn't believe what she was seeing. *What in the actual hell is going on? Am I dead? Did I die? Is that cow actually spelling?*

Still, she obeyed orders, leaning heavily on Dally, who'd come close and offered her a shoulder.

Then all of them—the beat-up lady, the cows, the pigs and the kittens—started through the field towards the house. When Crilla saw Ms. Bevan looking back at GET UP spelled out in the dirt, she nodded at her, and the teacher, floating out of her body on a wave of disbelief, let out a moan and threw up.

~

Mrs. Bittlemore hauled Carol in through the screen door, hollering for Willa.

She'd get these two pains in the ass to eat some of her special soup and be done with them. And then she'd find that teacher lady and deal with her once and for all. Her useless husband couldn't even knock somebody out properly. Mrs. Bittlemore would deal with him later.

"Willa, I found your parents!" Even with Mrs. Bittlemore clamped onto her arm, Carol was so pleased with herself, she managed a smile.

Mrs. Bittlemore finally let go, leaving Carol to rub the place where she'd been latched on.

"There you are, Wills! What took you so long?" Carol was still rubbing her arm when Willa bounded down the stairs and came to a stop in the middle of the kitchen, both hands resting on her slim hips.

"Where were you guys? I was worried about you." Willa was more suspicious than she was worried, but she knew she needed to play it cool.

Carol seemed quite chuffed about locating her grandparents, but the two of them looked sweaty and dirty and were acting even weirder than usual. Willa turned wide eyes on Carol, trying to get a sense of what had been going on before she came down the stairs. But Carol didn't really seem to pick up on her friend's inquisitive expression.

Had Ms. Bevan actually come to the farm and asked her grandparents questions?

Well, there was only one way to find out.

"Hey, was my teacher here this afternoon? She told me she was coming to talk to you guys about Margaret. She wants to help us find her. Wouldn't that be nice?"

Both of her grandparents remained silent.

"Did you hear what I said?"

After a few more seconds of silence, Mrs. Bittlemore pointed at Willa's chair.

"You sit down there, Missy. I'm gonna dish up some of my special chicken and dumpling soup for you and your friend. You got home so late, you're lucky you didn't miss dinner."

She started filling up two big bowls, her chest feeling a bit tight. All this bloody stress. She cleared her throat, finding it difficult to pull a deep breath into her lungs. *Just nerves*, she thought.

"No thanks, Mrs. B," the dratted girl said. "It smells great, but Carol and I aren't hungry."

⌒

Harp, in the meantime, was rummaging around in the bathroom. He had found the shotgun shells behind the old clawfooted bathtub, exactly where his wife had told him they would be. He loaded up his gun and shoved another handful

325

of shells into his coat pocket. Blood was still dripping from his cut knuckles. He grabbed a white hand towel and wiped the blood off, then hung the towel back on the bar. "Fucker—what a mess," he muttered. The towel was probably ruined. His wife would be adding him to her shit list again.

⁓

Harp suddenly reappeared in the kitchen. He leaned the gun on the door frame—close enough for him to get to fast if need be.

"I'll have some of that soup," he said, forgetting himself. His wife glared at him until he got it. Sitting down in his chair, he said, "Oh, ya—maybe I'll just wait until you girls have had your fill."

Willa was completely perplexed by this polite new version of her grandfather and looked at him like he'd grown horns: Harp never practised restraint when it came to food. Clearing her throat, she said, "So my teacher, Ms. Bevan, didn't come to see you today?"

"Nope," Harp said flatly. "Just been us all day. Right, Mother?"

"I won't take no for an answer!" Mrs. Bittlemore pounded the tabletop so hard the bowls popped up and spilled a little. "You girls sit down and eat your soup!"

Willa and Carol were both so startled they sat right down, picked up their spoons and filled them with the hot soup. They were about to shove them into their mouths when Orange Cat came flying through the air.

fifty-two

BEV OLDMAN PULLED INTO A DIAGONAL parking spot in front of the post office. Given that
all she had was the rural route address, she
figured the post office was the best place to
find out where it was and how to get there. Even though it was
kind of late in the day, a woman was behind the counter sort-
ing through some parcels.

"Can I see whoever's in charge, please?" Bev was being stern
yet friendly. "I'm trying to locate the Bittlemore place. I have
the rural route it's on, if that helps."

Straightening up, the woman took in Bev's uniform and
nodded. "I can tell you exactly where that is. It's twenty minutes from here—I can even take you if you want! Did something happen? Does this have anything to do with them using
purple gas in their truck? 'Cause I could tell you a few stories
about that!"

"Uh, that won't be necessary, Miss—what's your name?"

"Claire. I'm the postmistress here, and have been forever."

"Just point me in the right direction, Claire. Thanks."

━

Claire watched the police officer peel rubber big time as she backed her car up onto the main drag and took off towards the Bittlemore place. *That is a very spunky lady,* she thought, and this was definitely one of the most exciting days the post office had seen in years. What in the hell was going on at the Bittlemore place?

fifty-three

ORANGE CAT HAD SNUCK into the kitchen via the giant hole in the screen door just in time to see Mrs. Bittlemore yelling at Willa and Carol to eat her chicken soup. The cat smelled a rat: Had the old lady spiked the soup, just like she'd spiked the tea?

Just as the girls were about to shove big spoonfuls into their mouths, Orange Cat went into combat mode—springing through the air like an acrobat, her front legs stretched out like arrows, claws out like swords, and landed on the kitchen table.

Harp fell back against the wall, scared out of his wits. "GOD DAMN THAT CAT!" he shouted. He grabbed his shotgun and spun around, trying to take aim.

Orange Cat knocked the spoons out of the girls' hands, then leaped towards the stove to take out the big pot of soup as Mrs. Bittlemore wildly whipped her tea towel through the air, trying to keep her away. She was screaming too, and Harp was yelling, and Willa and Carol hit the floor and crawled under the table through a maze of chair legs, and then the shotgun went off. *BLAM!* Chunks of ceiling came down, old drywall and splinters of wooden beams. Harp let off another round, aiming at the cat, but instead he blasted a hole through the wall into the living room, releasing more debris and dust and the sulphurous smell of gun smoke.

"Carol, we gotta get outside!" Willa pushed the words out through her teeth, trying to whisper, but also to somehow be heard through the mayhem. The girls started crawling for the door, pushing the chairs aside. Orange Cat let out a piercing howl as she jumped at the pot of soup, and it hit the floor, the splatter barely missing Willa's legs. Harp had managed to reload and now he fired towards the stove. Instead of hitting the cat, the shotgun blast went wide, and dozens of the little black pellets ripped through Mrs. Bittlemore's right thigh. She squealed in terror, pain rushing through every nerve in her body.

⌇

Shots rang out across the field. First one, followed in a few seconds by another, and then another. Berle and Crilla could feel the weight and the whoosh of Harp's gun—on the farm it was a familiar sound.

"What the fuck is going on?" Ms. Bevan was still hanging on to Dally's shoulder as their strange procession moved across the pasture. She was surely in some sort of dream, except constant pain reminded her that she was indeed very much awake and wandering through a field with some tiny kittens rolling by her feet like tennis balls. "My God, what is all this shooting?" Moving her jaw to speak was agony.

Bad things were happening in that farmhouse, and she

needed to get there as fast as she could. Which wasn't very fast: even with Dally's help, snails moved quicker. She tried to shout "HELP," but her jaw hurt so much when she tried to open wide, she was sure that both it and her nose were broken.

A scream cut through the air. Was it Willa? Ms. Bevan's heart was racing.

Then they all spotted Willa and Carol come spilling out the door and onto the porch like someone had tipped them out of a wheelbarrow.

Ms. Bevan tried to call out Willa's name, but now she couldn't make her mouth work at all. Urgently, she pushed off from the cow and stumbled towards her students. The girls were coming towards her now too, in a full-on gallop, their hair whipping straight back. She madly waved one arm in the air, which tragically made her nose start to bleed again.

"Ms. Bevan! Holy crap!" Willa called out her teacher's name and both she and Carol flapped their arms in response.

But Ms. Bevan had spent the very last of any energy she had. She sank down in a heap on the grass, surrounded by a bunch of her newly found four-legged pals.

⌒

A big cloud of dust followed Bev down the old gravel roads on the way (she hoped) to the Bittlemore farm. She hated the dust, and was glad she wasn't stuck driving behind anybody, but she loved the crunching sound of tires on the crushed rocks. It reminded her of being a kid and going on car rides with her grandparents.

Still, it felt like she had been in the car for an eternity—the Bittlemore farm had to be getting close. She kept her eye peeled for a small yellow house with a crippled barn and maybe a couple of black-and-white cows in a field. Claire said it would be hard to miss, but also said, "If you do miss it, you'll know because you'll see the Stark place—a red-brick rancher with an old motorhome parked in the field. If that happens, just turn yourself around."

~

Mrs. Bittlemore stood there stunned at having just been shot in the thigh by her own husband—the gall. There was a fair amount of blood trickling down her leg and seeping through her dress, but she was more concerned about the girls, who, in all the noise and confusion, had escaped out the door. The soup had been a complete waste of time and effort.

Harp was in a right state—he was digging more shells out of his coat pocket and jamming them into the gun.

"Forget about shooting the bloody cat, you dumb ass!" she shouted. "We need to find that woman you hit and get those girls back." Glancing down at the pool of blood now gathering on the floor by her foot, she added, "And give me your belt!"

Harp was reluctant, but when she glared at him and pointed to the damage he'd done to her thigh, he pulled the old brown belt through his pants' loops and handed it to his wife. After all, he still had his suspenders on.

"Get over here and help wrap this around my leg!"

Harp obeyed, even though he really didn't like being so close to his wife. He hated the pungent smell of her sweat, and worse still was catching a glimpse of her naked leg.

Once the belt was cinched, Mrs. Bittlemore hissed, "This is all your fault! Now get outside and fix things!"

Harp nodded and clomped out onto the porch. His gun was loaded and ready, and he had two pocketfuls of shells. Yeah, he had to deal with that lady, but first he would blast Orange Cat to smithereens and then he would shoot the cows and the pigs until they were good and dead.

As Mrs. Bittlemore limped out behind him, they saw Willa and Carol running towards a parade of animals that looked as though they had just stepped off Noah's ark. The three cows, and that woman. The pigs! And were those kittens? Harp would kill them all, and she would make sure of it.

fifty-four

WHEN ME AND CAROL GOT outside, we ran towards the road. My grandparents had both lost their minds. I think Harp was trying to kill the cat. I don't think he came close, but he blew some holes in the house.

I glanced towards the pasture, and there were the cows coming towards us—and Ms. Bevan! She was waving her arm in the air and trying to yell, leaning on Dally. She looked sick and scared and very bloody. Grabbing Carol's arm, I pointed, and we headed for them instead, confused as hell about what was going on. By the time we got there, Ms. Bevan was sitting on the ground, looking like she'd been hit by a truck.

"Willa," she gasped, wincing. She put a hand to her jaw and managed to croak out, "Thank God you're alive!"

"Thank God I'm alive? Thank God *you're* alive! What the hell happened to you?"

Instead of answering me, Ms. Bevan just whispered, "Oh no!" And she pointed towards the house in utter terror.

We turned, and there was Harp shuffling towards us with his gun, my grandmother limping along behind him in a bloodied dress.

None of us knew what to do. There wasn't much we could do. We didn't even have a stick to fight Harp off with.

They were maybe fifty yards from us, and Harp was lifting his gun, when we heard the roar of some kind of big vehicle coming down our little road—it sounded like a thunderstorm. Harp and Mrs. B stopped in their tracks, and Harp tucked the gun in behind him. I risked craning my head around to see what was coming just as an eighteen-wheeler roared over the hill like a runaway train and screeched to a halt not far from where my grandparents were standing. Dust swirled around the cab for a moment or two and then the passenger door slowly opened.

A young woman hopped down from the cab.

"Hello?" she called to my grandparents, who just stood there staring at her.

Everything suddenly seemed so quiet. Maybe it was because there had been so much noise, the yelling and screaming and the gunshots. One thing about an open prairie field and a calm breeze, you could hear a nickel drop on a chicken.

The truck driver stayed put, but I could see her looking over at me and Carol and the cows and Ms. Bevan. So I stuck my hand in the air and waved, trying to indicate, *Yes, two fourteen-year-old girls are standing out here in a field with some cows and our severely injured gym teacher while a crazy old man and his wife are coming for us with a shotgun.*

Had it not been for Tizzy cheering her on, Margaret would have turned around and gone back home—or wherever there was to go back to. But now here they were, pulling up to the farm that held such warped memories of her lost childhood. Nothing much had changed. The trees by the road were a little bigger, the barn was a little more faded, and the house looked smaller, if that was possible. And those two people standing there in the yard, staring at the truck as though it were an apparition, were her parents.

"Looks like they knew you were comin'." Tizzy was trying to keep things light. "Is that them?"

"That's them. Jesus give me strength."

Margaret climbed out of the cab and took a few tentative steps towards her parents, calling out a hello.

⌒

Harp had no idea who it was, but his wife recognized her immediately. Margaret. Mrs. Bittlemore's chest tightened up and she could feel her lips trembling.

⌒

Margaret was having a hard time looking at her parents, so she glanced over into the field where a motley crew of people and animals had gathered. One of them was waving, but the angle of the sun made it impossible to make out who it was. She and Tizzy seemed to have interrupted some kind of get-together.

She turned back to her parents. *Better get this over with.*

"Remember me? It's your—it's Margaret." She couldn't quite get herself to say that she was their daughter. "I came here to—I came here to . . ." Margaret could hardly take a breath. She looked back at Tizzy and Tizzy nodded at her. *Get on with it, girl.*

Margaret turned back to her parents, finally taking in the fact that her mother's leg was tied with a belt, blood dripping into the dirt, and that Harp had his shotgun tucked along his side.

The group standing out in the field looked like ghosts. They were moving forward so slowly that they might not have been moving at all. There were cows—was that Berle? And Crilla? And the youngest one—could that be Dally? There were pigs too, and kittens, and three women huddled together. *What the hell is going on?*

Mrs. Bittlemore finally spoke. "Well, look who the cat dragged in."

The reference to the cat was not lost on Harp, who grimaced.

"Do you know who this is, Father? This is the little bitch that brought the whole world down—this is the whore that ruined our lives."

⌒

Voices carry a good distance on a calm, practically windless prairie day, and Willa could hear every single word her grandmother said. And she was so shocked, she sat down beside Ms. Bevan on the ground. It felt like millions of pieces were all coming together in her head in a series of little flashes. Well, maybe not in flashes, but giant bolts of lightning.

⌒

"This is the girl who thought she was better than all of us, too good for this place, too damn good for everybody—even her own kid," Mrs. Bittlemore said.

It still wasn't getting through to Harp. It was all too much. He needed a drink.

"Who is it, Mother? Another goddamn school lady?"

"You're the biggest idiot on the planet, Harp," his wife said, and she limped closer to Margaret, who stood her ground.

"This is your daughter, Harp. This is the goddamn baby you took, the baby I didn't want. I told you I wanted the other one. Was it so hard to get it right? You only had ONE THING TO DO! But you took the wrong baby."

Margaret was trying to process what she was hearing. The baby Harp *took*? The *baby* he took? From where? From who?

Tizzy opened her door and jumped down to the ground. The man standing in front of Margaret had a shotgun, and the old, fat woman was all bloody, with a tourniquet around her thigh. That was not even close to normal. None of this felt right. She and Margaret had walked into some big trouble and they needed to figure out how to get out of it in one piece.

Harp's eyes widened. Margaret. After all these years, she'd come back to—what? Take her revenge? Ask for money?

He flew into a rage. "What the hell do you want? We don't need this shit! Go back to where you came from, you slut!"

Tizzy stepped forward with her fist raised, but Margaret grabbed on to her and shook her head, whispering for her not to do anything that would set the guy off. Now she remembered exactly why she had run away from this place.

Harp felt panic rise up into his chest as the two women stared at him. He lifted his shotgun and pointed it at them.

"Now wait a minute." Tizzy stepped in front of her friend with her arms wide open. "What are you going to do here, sir, shoot everybody? Last time I checked, a shotgun only has two barrels. Yup, there's only two of us, but there's a whole bunch of them." She gestured to Willa and Carol and Ms. Bevan and the cows and the pigs, all of whom were now standing at the fence. Not that any of them looked like they could put up much of a fight.

One of the girls was holding up an older lady, who obviously had been beaten up. The other girl was staring at Margaret with giant tears rolling down her face and wrapping themselves underneath her chin. Those eyes! This was Margaret's daughter! She had to be.

Margaret was now staring back at that girl, taking in every curve and every freckle on her darling face—completely at a loss about what to do next. She did have a shotgun pointing at her. She took a chance and called out her child's name.

"Mayvale? It's you, Mayvale. I know it's you."

"Mom?" Willa started to climb the fence. "Momma!"

"Don't you fucking move, Willa," Harp yelled. "I've got two shells and I'll kill two of ya. I don't care which!"

Willa stopped moving. This was something out of Harp's mouth that she believed.

Just then the cows started mooing and groaning and moaning. Just cows making noise, right? No one ever said that humans were the brightest bulbs in the universe.

—

"He's got two shells and there's three of us, Berle." Crilla sounded like she'd already made up her mind and was ready to die for the cause.

Berle was thinking hard. "He's had fourteen years to grow the hate he has for Margaret. If we rush him, he may shoot one of us and not shoot Willa, but I don't think he's gonna let Margaret walk out of here alive."

She made up her mind. "I've got an idea that just might work. You wait here and protect the girls while I walk around to the back of the house. Trust me, he's so fixed on Margaret and Willa, he's not gonna notice. We've got to try, right?"

Dally had witnessed many of Berle's well-intended plans go south. Her heart filled with trepidation. "B-b-be careful, B-b-b-Berle, y-y-ou don't want to go and d-do something stupid."

Berle gave her a stern look. "Dally, I know some of the things I've dreamed up haven't exactly turned out, but I've never been stupid." And she turned on her heel and slowly ambled away from the group. As she predicted, Harp didn't even look up.

~

Like Margaret, Willa was repeating *took the wrong baby* over and over in her head. So Margaret had been taken from someone. If that was true, then Margaret wasn't the Bittlemores' daughter. If her mother wasn't their daughter, that meant Willa wasn't their granddaughter! No wonder she felt like she'd never belonged with these people!

~

Mrs. Bittlemore couldn't believe what was happening. This was turning into a circus with too many clowns. First the nosy teacher, then Willa and Carol screw up her plan, and now Margaret and her witchy friend show up. "Well, Harp," she said, "we are sure in a pickle here, aren't we?"

The tourniquet must not have been tight enough, because the blood was constantly dripping down her leg. She was feeling weaker, woozier and unclear. She wanted to sit down, right on the ground where she stood, but that wasn't going to happen. It was all finally coming to an end. All the years of lying—all the layers upon layers of secrets that weighed her down.

She looked around her, at the old house and the crooked fences and the slumped-over shed—everything was in ruins. She found that she was glad it was over—relieved, even. Happy.

Tizzy had been watching her sway from side to side. "You need to find yourself a chair, ma'am."

"And you, whoever you are, need to shut up."

Mrs. Bittlemore turned to her daughter. Well, no, not her daughter anymore. "Where have you been all these years, Margaret? Where did you go? All the letters you sent, month after month after month, always from a different place. You must think you're so clever."

"That was me." Tizzy smiled proudly. "Us truckers—we cover a lot of ground."

Mrs. Bittlemore would not be distracted. "You were taunting me all these years—toying with my heart. You're a sick and ungrateful girl, you hear me? You have no idea what we went through for you! What Father and I sacrificed so that you could have a better life. Your real mother had so many kids— she had *so* many kids. I just wanted ONE! Was that so much to ask, that Jesus give me one child to be my own? One child to love? But you wouldn't let me love you! And your stupid father, he couldn't get one single thing right." Mrs. Bittlemore aimed a kick at him, but it hurt too much, so she spat at him instead. "This is all your fault! You're nothing! You're nobody!"

She limped a little closer to Margaret. "He's the one who walked right in the front door of the hospital in the middle of the day and took you! Nobody cared that you went missing. Maybe they looked for you for ten lousy minutes at most! Your mother already had enough kids. She didn't care that you got taken."

"Just shut your damn mouth!" Harp yelled. "This is your fault, not mine. You told me to do it!" Harp was shaking, and the gun was shaking too, just a few feet from Margaret's face.

Calmly, Margaret said to Harp, "Shoot me and get it over with, or put that gun down."

Harp stopped shaking and looked Margaret square in the eye. First his lips began to quiver and then his eyes filled with tears. In a minute he was crying uncontrollably. Laying the gun on the ground, he slumped down beside it, still sobbing. Tizzy walked over and picked it up, snapped it open and took out the shells.

"You made the right choice, Mister," she said.

But Mrs. Bittlemore was not done. "You weren't even ours, and then you got yourself pregnant because you're a slut and whore and a sinner."

That was the last straw for Willa, who shouted, "Please STOP IT! Don't talk to her like that!"

Mrs. Bittlemore glared at the girl and then plunked herself on the ground beside her husband. Harp kept weeping, but his wife didn't comfort him, just sat like a toad clutching her chest.

It felt as though a tornado had passed over the Bittlemore farm. Everyone—Willa, Carol, Ms. Bevan, even the cows—was trying to take in what had just been confessed. In the sudden calm, Willa bent and slipped through the barbed wire fence. She hesitated for a moment, but then she ran towards Margaret.

Margaret didn't have a clue what to do. Her arms, hanging by her sides, felt heavy and awkward. Should she hug her daughter? Shake her hand?

When the girl skidded to a stop in front of her, all she could manage was, "Hi there, Mayvale. Though I'm guessing you don't go by Mayvale, right?"

"I'm Willa. Short for Wilhelmina. My mom named—well, you named me that too."

"Yes, I did. After my best friend."

The two of them stood there staring at each other.

They looked more like twins than mother and daughter. Dark hair and olive skin, full mouths with pink lips. Same cherub face with a strong jaw.

In the presence of her mother, Willa felt her whole body blush, like a swarm of big, fuzzy bumblebees had found their way into her heart. It was a strange yet wonderful sensation.

Then Carol and Ms. Bevan came staggering up, followed by the cows, the pigs, Orange Cat and the kittens. Ms. Bevan cleared her throat and whispered carefully through her broken jaw, "I hate to break this up, but I'm pretty sure I need to get to a hospital. I did have a car here, but I don't know where it's gone. And even if I found it, I don't think I can drive."

"I can drive you," Carol piped up. After she offered, nobody told her she couldn't—so . . . "Willa, okay if I take Ms. Bevan to the hospital?"

Willa nodded, coming over to give Carol a hug. "Of course! Carol, you're the best." Turning to her teacher, she said, "And thank you for believing me, Ms. Bevan. I'm just so sorry you got hurt."

Ms. Bevan tried to nod at Willa, which made her turn even paler.

Harp stopped crying long enough to croak out, "The lady's car is in the shed. Keys are still in it."

Ms. Bevan couldn't even look at Harp, never mind attempt to speak to him. For a scrawny old guy, he sure had packed a wallop.

As Carol and Ms. Bevan set off for the shed, Tizzy patted Margaret on the shoulder, winked at Willa and headed for the house. As she pulled open the flimsy screen door to go inside, Mrs. Bittlemore mustered enough energy to yell, "What the hell do you think you're doing, going into my house?"

"I'm going to call the police to report a kidnapping, among other things. I'm assuming you have a working telephone?"

⌣

Just as the screen door banged shut behind Tizzy, Bev Oldman drove into the yard. She pulled her car up beside the giant eighteen-wheeler and popped out of the driver's side like a bunny from a magician's hat.

The group just stared at this woman in a police uniform who had appeared as if Tizzy had conjured her.

"Bittlemore farm, am I right? Yay, I found it. The post lady, Claire, gave me not-so-great directions, but I made it anyway. I'm Constable Oldman."

At that moment, Bev realized she was staring at something resembling a crime scene. A couple of cows and three pigs seemed to be standing guard over a weepy old guy sitting on the ground beside a shotgun. The rather large woman plunked beside him was bleeding through her housedress.

Harp was so shocked by the sudden arrival of a cop he stopped snivelling and blurted, "Jesus H. Christ! That didn't take long! Now what? Are you here to arrest us?"

"Did you say Constable Oldman? The one from the coin poster?" The question came from a dark-haired woman standing next to a girl who was her spitting image.

"Yes, that's me. By any chance are you Margaret Bittlemore? If so, your message is why I'm here. I decided I wouldn't wait for you to call me again, I'd just track you down."

But now Bev's first aid training course kicked in. "Hang on a minute, Ms. Bittlemore—I need to check on that old lady over there."

Bev went over to Mrs. Bittlemore and crouched down to examine her wound. "Ma'am, that doesn't look too great. I'm gonna call this in and get an ambulance here ASAP. Looks like a fair amount of buckshot hit ya? An accident, I hope."

Mrs. Bittlemore rolled her eyes and struggled to get to her feet. "You're not taking me anywhere."

"Stay down, ma'am," Bev said.

"It was an accident," Harp whined, giving his face a wipe with a dirty handkerchief and getting up off the dirt. "I was trying to kill that fucking Orange Cat." He didn't offer his wife his hand—didn't even look at her.

Bev stared at the two old people, trying to evaluate the situation. "Must be a really evil cat for you to want to shoot it," she said.

Tizzy came out the kitchen door and looked surprised to see a police officer standing in the driveway. "Damn, you people are fast."

"You people?" Bev lifted an eyebrow.

"Yes, you—the police. I just called to report the goings-on here and ask for help. You're going to want to have a long conversation with those two beauties. I don't even know where to begin."

"Do I still need to call an ambulance?"

Tizzy shook her head. "Negative. One is on its way, along with most of the Backhills police department."

"Before they get here, maybe one of you fine people could tell me what's been going on here." Constable Oldman took her notepad out of her jacket pocket. "Let's start with everybody's names."

Willa was the first to pipe up. "I'm Willa, er, Mayvale, and I'm her daughter." She pointed at Margaret. "She had me when she was fourteen years old while she was living here with those people." Willa pointed at Mrs. B, who had given up and was still sitting on the ground, and to Harp on the porch. "We just found out that Harp Bittlemore, that man over there, kidnapped my mother from somewhere and brought her here and locked her in her room. I don't blame her for running away."

"Slow down there, Willa Mayvale," Bev said, scribbling in her notepad. "I'm having a hard time keeping up."

"Harp hurts everything and everyone—they both do. See these cows? He cut the tail off one of them and the ear off the other. The pigs? They'd all be dead except they knew enough to hide from him. And don't get me started on all the kittens he's drowned over the years."

Bev, who was writing as fast as she could, put up a hand again. "Hang on just a minute."

But Willa was on a roll now and couldn't stop. "Today he punched my gym teacher, Ms. Bevan, in the head. She had blood all over her shirt and—and my friend, Carol, who doesn't even have a driver's licence, just drove her to the hospital."

That was when Margaret hugged her daughter to her. Willa let out a big sigh that ended in a sob and let her head rest on her mother's shoulder.

It was Margaret's turn now. "Tizzy and I—Tizzy drives that eighteen-wheeler there—we arrived a little late to the party. Most of the damage had already been done, I'm afraid. I ran away from this place when I was fourteen, leaving this one—my baby—behind. It took me all this time to get up the nerve to come back for her. My whole life I thought these people were my parents, but they've just confessed that they stole me from somewhere when I was a baby! I think they can tell you a lot more about that than I can."

⁓

Tizzy had painted quite the picture when she called 911 for assistance. In under ten minutes, two police cars pulled into the yard, sirens blaring and lights flashing. The ambulance wasn't more than a minute behind. Three officers got out of their vehicles and started towards them, hands on their guns. The yard did look like a war zone, Margaret thought, but then again it always had.

Bev intercepted the officers, showed them her badge and started to fill them in on what she knew about what was going on.

The paramedics had hopped out and grabbed their stretcher, then ran to where Mrs. Bittlemore now lay on the ground. They soon hoisted her onto the gurney and loaded her into the ambulance, with her moaning and complaining the entire time. She also kept insisting that she wanted her lawyer and her goddamn phone call.

Harp was handcuffed and then more or less dragged across the yard by the armpits. He stunk so badly from cigarettes and booze that the officers hauling him along looked at each other with are-you-smelling-what-I'm-smelling expressions. They pushed him, with some relief, into the back seat of one of the patrol cars, where he slumped like a bag of old potatoes. He hadn't said a single word.

"What are we arresting him for, Constable Oldman?" one of the cops asked.

"I don't know yet," Bev said. "There's a lot to unpack here. Can one of you ride along with the wife to the hospital?"

The largest cop nodded.

"And take him down to the station for questioning. I don't want to talk to them together, ya know?"

"Oh, and Constable Oldman," the big cop said. "You might want to poke your head around the corner of the house and check out something sort of weird back there. I don't know what to make of it."

Bev nodded at him and made her way across the yard. When she got around the back of the house, she quickly scanned the area, not seeing anything but a messy, unkempt space filled with junk. Then she happened to look down at the bare soil of what must have been a vegetable garden. Spelled out in big childlike letters in the dirt were the words BAD MAN TOOK BABY. She noticed a cow peering at her from around the side of a nearby coop. When she met her eye, the cow seemed to nod at her.

Bev knelt down by the foot-high letters and shook her head. "What the hell?"

The cow was still staring at her, pawing the dirt with her hoof.

"Bad man took baby, eh? Yes, a bad man did take a baby. I guess that says it all." She got to her feet, half laughing and half freaked out. Had she really just solved a major cold case?

⌒

Willa was gathering the kittens and putting them into an old box when Bev came over to her.

"They're cute little things, aren't they?" Bev said.

"They sure are. My grand—I mean, Mr. Bittlemore used to get rid of all Orange Cat's litters. I was never able to find them in time . . ." She held one of the kittens up to her chin. "I'm going to name them. I was thinking Nancy and Drew and Enid."

"Those are perfect names."

Bev looked past the girl to where Margaret was leading the three cows towards a ramshackle paddock by the barn, with the pigs tagging along behind. Could that woman actually be Baby Larkspur?

⁓

Crilla, Berle and even Dally, who was barely born when she ran away, were ecstatic to see Margaret, live and in person, after all these years. And even happier that the Bittlemores were gone and likely wouldn't be coming back. The cows could feel the sadness lifting off their shoulders—the farm itself felt like it was taking deep breaths. Margaret kept patting their heads and kissing their noses, and the pigs got in on the action too, swirling around Margaret's feet like they were on a merry-go-round. Everybody was gladder than glad. Still, nobody was used to good things happening and it felt mighty strange to be surrounded with all this pleasantness.

⁓

"You silly pigs . . ." Margaret said aloud, as she finally shooed them in and shut the gate behind her. "What a weird damn day. What a completely insane, bizarre day."

She turned around and headed back to find her daughter. Her daughter! And there she was, not a dream, not a ghost, not a lost memory, but a strong and determined young lady. Margaret stopped for a moment to watch her talking with the constable as she carefully lowered the orange-and-black kittens into an apple crate.

This was certainly not the reunion she had been picturing in her mind, but maybe it was better. *My daughter*—she kept repeating it in her head. *Daughter.* She was so fierce, a little warrior! For her to have survived Harp and Mrs. B was no small feat. In fact, it was a miracle.

The two of them had so much lost time to make up for—so many things to talk about. Margaret still didn't know how she would ever be able to explain why she left her own flesh and blood behind that dreary night. But she could hear Tizzy's voice in her head, telling her again and again that she had been a kid herself, that she couldn't blame herself. Tizzy was usually right.

Bev came up to Margaret just then, interrupting her train of thought.

"So you called and left me a message about the coin? Geez, I almost forgot what the heck I drove out here for in the first place." She let loose a high-pitched giggle that took them all a bit by surprise. Margaret and Willa exchanged a look, silently communicating that this police officer had one heck of a crazy laugh.

When Bev stopped giggling, Margaret said, "That's right, I did. I had a coin just like the one on the poster—a 1794 silver dollar. I left it here in the house when I ran away. My parents gave it to me for one of my birthdays, if you can believe that."

And then Willa piped up. "I have a coin—a silver dollar. I mean, I have your silver dollar." She tilted her chin at her mom. "I have it tucked inside my Nancy Drew book right this minute."

Bev let out a great whoop. She quickly unfolded the flyer she had in her coat pocket and showed it to Willa. "Is this the coin?"

After peering closely at the photo, Willa said, "I think so. I can go and get it if you want?"

"Yes! Good grief, yes! God, I'm getting chills. Margaret, this is going to come as a shock, but if this turns out to be the coin I think it is, I may know who your real parents are."

Margaret's legs went out from under her, just as Tizzy flipped an old washtub upside down and helped her sit. "I'm sorry, but I feel like I'm going to pass out!" She put her head between her knees and tried to take deep breaths.

⌒

Willa ran for the house. She bolted up the stairs into her little room with the round window, the old saggy bed and the green lamp. She sat on the edge of the bed and pulled open the crooked drawer of the nightstand. There she was on the cover, Nancy Drew, shining a flashlight, eyes focused and steady. Nancy Drew, the intrepid young woman who never backed down, who never gave up, who always righted wrongs.

Willa took a deep breath, opened the book—and it wasn't there!

Her heart sank. And then she remembered! She'd tucked it inside the rare coin book she'd borrowed from the library. She leaped up and rushed around the room, searching. Nothing. Finally, she stuck her head under the bed—there it was! She pulled it out and shook the book back and forth, and the coin rolled out onto the floor and very nearly disappeared down a space between the floorboards. Willa slammed her hand down on it just in time, then picked it up. Clutching it and the rare coin book, she ran back down the stairs just as the phone started ringing. She stopped and turned around to answer it. Old habits.

"Hello."

"WILLS! Oh my God! Why are you picking up the phone?" It was Carol, calling from the hospital.

"I picked it up because it was ringing, you nut cake. And you're the one who dialed my number. Is Ms. Bevan okay? You didn't crash her car on the way, did you?"

"No, I did not! Apparently I'm better at driving than I am at basketball. After we got here, they took her right into surgery to get her jaw fixed. Harp broke it in three places and also gave her a concussion!"

"You did good, Carol. I'm so proud of you. My grandparents have been arrested! I can't wait to tell you everything, but I have to get back outside to my mom and the constable. They need to see that old coin."

"You found your mom—and your mom found you!" Carol's voice got a little trembly, but then she started to laugh. "Willa! You finally have a parent who doesn't look eighty-seven years old."

Bev flipped the coin over a few times as she compared it with the flyer photo. It was indeed a flowing hair 1794 silver dollar in perfect condition. As rare as anything. And proof, before any blood tests could be done, that this was the coin involved in the kidnapping of Baby Larkspur.

Bev had walked back to her car to examine the coin. Now she glanced back at Willa and Margaret, who was still plunked on the washtub with her friend rubbing her back, and did her best to not get emotional. She had a lot of calls she needed to make—first and foremost to Randy Tripp—but her mind kept going to how it would feel to tell Margaret the names of her real parents. And what it would be like to break the news to the Larkspurs that they not only had a daughter still alive and well, but had a granddaughter too.

"Oh, screw that Randy Tripp!" Bev swore loudly, startling all three women.

"Excuse me?" Margaret called.

Bev rushed over to them, the coin on her outstretched palm. "This is the coin I was looking for, Margaret! This is the coin your real father gave you—it's the, um—when you were—gosh dang, where do I start?"

Willa and Margaret, Tizzy too, breathlessly waited for her to go on.

Bev gathered herself. "Okay, so after you were born, your real dad stuffed this coin into your diaper—I'll explain that later—and it's been with you and your daughter ever since. Also, do you have any idea what this thing is worth? Depending on who's buying, obviously, you could get tens of thousands of dollars, maybe even fifty or sixty grand for it."

Margaret was reeling. "I don't care how much it's worth! What's this about my real dad? What do you mean?"

Bev took a deep breath and tried to slow right down. "The Bittlemores, the people you thought were your parents, took you from the nursery at Manatukken Hospital twenty-nine years ago. Your kidnapping was famous—it was in all the papers. There was a massive search, with hundreds of people looking for you."

Margaret's face filled with awe. She'd been missed, searched for, wanted.

Bev carried on. "I need to interview those two knuckleheads, but one or both of them went into the hospital the day you were born, pulled the fire alarm and, in the confusion, simply walked out the door with you. And were never caught, until now! Margaret, your mom and dad, your three sisters and their kids—God knows how many nieces and nephews you have— they all live about ninety minutes from here. They've never stopped looking for you. They've never stopped hoping that you were alive."

Willa couldn't keep quiet. "You mean I have *real* grand-parents?"

"Yes, you do. But you guys are going to have to hold tight and not tell anybody about this until I figure a few more things out." She looked around at the mess in the yard, and the peel-ing old farmhouse with its sagging porch roof. "Maybe we can get you into a motel for a few days, or have you stay with a friend—"

Margaret held up a hand, stopping Bev. "We've got the ani-mals to tend to. We need to stay right here."

"Understood. I'll be back in the morning to sort out what's gonna happen next. But I'm going to talk to the Larkspurs tonight. I need to borrow that coin so I can show it to them, but don't worry, I'll take good care of it."

As Bev drove down the lane, she glanced in her rear-view mirror to see two identical-looking women standing shoulder to shoulder in front of the pale-yellow farmhouse, each cud-dling an orange-and-black kitten.

fifty-five

IT TOOK A COUPLE OF DAYS before Mrs. Bittlemore could be interviewed. The buckshot had riddled not only her thigh but one of her ovaries. Doctors operated twice to get it all.

Bev and the other officers talked to Harp and his wife separately. What they got from the two boiled down to a lot of bullshit with tiny fragments of truth speckled in, along with a lot of screaming and crying. But since they blamed each other for everything, it took days to unravel what had gone down.

In the end, Harp was the first to cave, telling Bev that he'd taken the baby from the Manatukken hospital by himself. But he also told her that he only did it because his wife threatened to kill him if he didn't bring home a baby.

Mrs. Bittlemore, in turn, said the whole thing was Harp's idea and she was the one threatened with murder. She told her court-appointed lawyer to communicate the fact that her husband had shot the neighbour's dog right in front of her and told her she'd be next if she didn't go along with his plan.

Two weeks after Margaret and all the cows, pigs and kittens came home to roost, the Bittlemores were both in county lockdown awaiting trial.

⸺

The town of Backhills—more than the town, a hundred miles in every direction—was thrown into a frenzy. Over-the-top tales flew around like a conspiracy of crows. People said that Willa had a twin whom the Bittlemores had thrown down a well somewhere, unable to manage two babies. Dozens of people searched every old well they could find. Even though they came up empty, that rumour still swirled. Townsfolk also claimed the Bittlemores had killed countless hitchhikers and started several barn fires.

None of it was true, of course. The only true things, and they were outrageous enough, were that they had kidnapped Rose Larkspur as a baby and raised her as their own. Then, at fourteen, she'd gotten knocked up and had a baby she gave up so that she could escape from them. No one held that against her. What else could she have done?

The solving of the Baby Larkspur case, and the fact that the kidnappers lived three miles out of town and had been there in plain sight all this time, was the biggest thing ever to happen to Backhills.

⸺

Margaret and Willa and Tizzy paid no attention to the furor in town. The odd vehicle would pull up to the end of the lane, but nobody dared drive down into the yard. Just Nosy Parkers wanting to get a look at whatever they could get a look at. For days, the three of them stayed up into the wee hours, swapping horror stories about the Bittlemores and getting to know each other.

Weirdly, right after he was charged, Harp signed the farm over to Margaret, sending a message through his lawyer that it was hers if she wanted it. In a moment of remorse or regret, or maybe in memory of his beloved mother and father, Harp may have felt like it was the only decent thing to do. The fact that he was deathly afraid of the Devil may also have played heavily into his generosity. Maybe he figured this one "right" thing would keep him from burning in Hell for eternity.

It turned out that Margaret did want the farm, a lot. When she and Willa and Tizzy weren't talking, they were busy clearing out the house, purging it of its sad history.

Every stick of furniture, all the beds, chairs, table lamps, even the curtains. Every mug and plate and fork and knife and ladle and spoon and frying pan and muffin tin. They all went onto a giant pile in the yard, where they burned what they could and carted the rest around back of the barn and buried it. They scrubbed the soup off the floors and counters, and washed the walls and the windows with vinegar and water. When they got tired, they all sat on the floor and drank tea out of Tizzy's giant thermos and feasted on the rest of Margaret's road snacks.

Willa and Margaret were so close in age, they seemed more like sisters than mother and child, and maybe that was a good place to start.

After a day or two, Tizzy pulled her truck farther up the lane and parked by the garden. She told them she was going to stay for a while, if that was okay, at least until they got the farm sorted out. She said the best thing they could do to chase away all the bad memories was to make the whole place into a sort of sanctuary, for the animals and for themselves.

When both Margaret and Willa told her how grateful they were for her help, Tizzy said not to be. "You're family to me, Margo, and I guess that makes you family too, young Mayvale." And Margaret turned away so Tizzy wouldn't see her cry, though these were happy tears.

The three of them would walk out to the field as the sun was setting and bring treats to Dally and Berle and Crilla and the pigs. The cows couldn't believe their good fortune. They had their Margaret back. They still had their Willa. Tizzy soon installed a blow-up pool in the repaired pigsty and the pigs spent their days in the muddy water, happy as Larry. The kittens lived in the house with Orange Cat, doted upon by all. And Orange Cat came and went like the wind.

For the first time since Harp's father had died and his mother was carted off to the asylum, there was peace on the Bittlemore farm.

Soon, lush green grass started poking up around the weary fence posts and over the fields. Willa came in from the yard one morning and said that there seemed to be beets and peas coming up in the garden, which was odd considering Mrs. Bittlemore hadn't even got the garden in before she was hauled off to jail.

Red, blue and yellow wildflowers soon lined the lane out to the road. Daisies and bunches of mint and chives and raspberry bushes found a haven in the sun along the sides of the barn.

The farmland itself knew something big had changed. Things were coming back, living things. Tall grasses and ferns and saskatoon bushes.

It was like the women were literally sweeping thirty years or more of darkness out the front door of the house. Long, warm beams of sunlight threw themselves onto the kitchen floor and crawled up the stairs, bringing light, ease and calm.

There was still an elephant in the room, though.

The Larkspurs, both in their seventies, with those three grown kids and all their grandchildren, had yet to be reunited with their daughter and meet their new granddaughter. It seemed to be faster to get the Bittlemores clapped in jail than to accomplish the most important part of the whole situation.

The police and the social workers insisted that the details needed to be sorted first. Jon Larkspur had to identify the coin, then blood and DNA samples had to be taken and analyzed. Even though the authorities put a rush on it, DNA testing was new, and it was a full three weeks before Bev Oldman came to pick up Margaret and Willa in her patrol car to take them to meet their real family.

~

No one at the Bittlemore farm slept a single wink the night before. Not even the pigs. Connie and Jon were similarly sleepless with excitement.

Bev had picked them up, coffees and muffins in hand—but neither Margaret nor Willa could eat or drink, which was understandable. Even Bev was a nervous Nelly.

They didn't get twenty miles before Margaret wanted them to pull over. "I can't breathe. Can we stop for a little while, please?"

She had that same feeling crawling inside her chest that had tormented her while she and Tizzy were coming to find Willa. When Bev pulled over to the side of the road and parked in the shade of some tall poplars, Margaret looked over her shoulder at Willa in the back seat and said, "Are you okay, Mayvale—I, um, I mean Willa?" After so many years of writing to her little baby girl, Mayvale, she hadn't yet got used to calling her anything else. "I think I'm having an anxiety attack. What if they—"

"Mom, I'm fine. Honestly."

It was the first time Willa had called Margaret "Mom," and it caused her to burst into tears. "Oh my God," she stuttered between sobs. "I *am* a mom."

"Yes, you are, and we're together forever, and we are better than okay."

Margaret swivelled around in her seat and awkwardly threw her arms around Willa, squishing her so hard Willa eventually cried, "Uncle!"

Through her tears, Margaret said, "Ha! I think you might actually be meeting an uncle."

"Nope, just aunts." Willa grinned. "Constable Oldman told me."

"Right! Okay, driver," Margaret joked. "Onward. I think we're as ready as we're ever going to be."

⌒

This time Bev didn't get lost trying to find the place.

As the car rolled up to the end of the long, leafy driveway, they could see a bunch of faces pressed up against the big front window looking out for them. Then the Larkspurs' front door burst open and what seemed to be dozens of bodies came pouring out. Connie and Jon and their daughters and their grandkids, their neighbours and their friends—there must have been fifty people piling out of the modest clapboard house. Margaret and Willa were barely out of the car when Connie threw her arms around them both. Then everyone was hugging like it was a football huddle as a thousand tears ran down every face.

And for the first time in her life, Margaret could recognize herself in her own mother's face—a version that was a few decades older but so familiar. The only thing Margaret was able to croak out was "I'm so sorry."

Connie looked into her daughter's eyes and shook her head gently from side to side. "No, dearest one, you of all people have no reason to be sorry. I never gave up on you. *We* never gave up on you." Connie looked up at Jon, who had come up behind them with outstretched arms.

"And look at us! We're here together now." Jon was clearly trying to keep himself from completely falling apart.

Margaret reached out for Willa and pulled her towards them. "This is my daughter," she said. "Your granddaughter—Willa. Well, Willa Larkspur, I guess."

Willa loved the sound of that. *She* was Willa Mayvale Robert Larkspur and, just as she'd always hoped, there was not an ounce of Bittlemore in her.

Bev had been standing back, watching the happy reunion unfold, all the joy and gratitude pouring out into this unbelievable day. The odds of an ending like this, Bev knew all too well, were rare indeed, much like the coin she'd been holding on to. This was the perfect moment to pull the velvet pouch out of her inside coat pocket and hand it to Jon. "Sir, I believe you also lost this."

Jon opened the purple velvet bag and slid the coin into his hand.

Bev said, "What I've just found out is that your coin is even rarer and more valuable than we thought. A coin exactly like yours just sold at Stack's Bowers Galleries for—and you may want to sit down for this—seven and a half million dollars. So you not only have your daughter back, you're rich."

The Larkspurs were speechless. Jon shook Bev's hand and then pulled her in for a hug. "Thank you, Constable. Thank you for everything. You can't know what you've done for me and Connie and the kids. It's just overwhelming."

"Mr. Larkspur, it has been my absolute pleasure. Now, I'll leave you to it. You guys have a lot of catching up to do."

Bev watched them walk back to their friends and family, smiles on every single face, boundless joy pouring out over everything. Willa and Margaret and Margaret's sisters and nieces—they were a fantastic jumble of arms and legs and hands and fingers entwined around each other, their relieved, excited voices echoing into the trees.

She got into her car and started it up. She noticed Jon waving to get her attention, and then mouthing, "We will take them home later!" She nodded, and he waved again and then turned back into the arms of his family.

Bev closed her eyes for a moment, wanting to burn that picture of all those happy people into her memory. Then she hit the gas, turned on the radio and roared up onto the main road. Olivia Newton-John came on full blast, singing "Hopelessly Devoted to You." The perfect song for a perfect day.

Bev, never much of a singer, couldn't help but sing along at the top of her lungs.

⌒

Hope was hanging from the clouds. Hope was being shot out of all these hearts like a confetti cannon.

Willa stared around at all her new-found family, lingering

on her mother and her grandmother, who hadn't been able to keep her hands off her daughter since their first embrace. And she paused for a moment to remember how truly hopeless her life had seemed not that long ago. But even then the universe had been working to bring them together. The uneasiness in her heart that never went away. The constant feeling that she really didn't belong to the Bittlemores in any way, shape or form. Coming across the photo in the library that looked so much like her "sister." That silly old coin she'd kept for so long, that her real grandfather had tucked into her mother's diaper and that led to this reunion.

Willa vowed then and there that she would never underestimate the small things, not that she ever had. She would never underestimate the unpredictable things, the tiny, insignificant things—because when you tied all those little moments up, they could make something completely fantastical.

And Then What Happened?

An Epilogue

Harp Bittlemore could most always be found in the corner of the prison cafeteria. He never missed breakfast, even though it was terrible, in his opinion. Lukewarm scrambled eggs, cold, unbuttered toast and even colder baked beans. He didn't bother with the coffee, telling the cafeteria worker that it was "undrinkable shit."

His trial took nearly three weeks, but the verdict was unanimous. He was found guilty of kidnapping, unlawful confinement, assault, the attempted murder of Dawn Bevan and animal abuse—both physical cruelty and failing to provide the necessities of life—and other lesser charges that all ran together to make sure Harp Bittlemore would never see the free light of day.

Mrs. Bittlemore did not fare very well during her trial either. She was convicted of being an accessory to kidnapping, of perjury, assault and attempted murder for the poisoned soup she'd tried to feed Willa and her friend Carol, and the unlawful confinement of and vicious assault on Dawn Bevan.

Throughout her trial, Mrs. Bittlemore sat next to her court-appointed lawyer and stared at the wall. When she was given the chance to address the court after her guilty verdict was read, she cleared her throat and said, "I have nothing to say."

Before authorities could transfer her to the Lethbridge Correctional Centre, though, Mrs. Bittlemore collapsed in her holding cell, suffering a massive heart attack. After several attempts to resuscitate her, her heart miraculously began beating again. Ironically, she was taken to the Manatukken hospital to be stabilized and then airlifted to Edmonton for triple bypass surgery. She was eventually moved to the prison in Lethbridge, where she was soon a full member of every support group she could sign up for. She also began teaching bread making and needlepoint to a loyal group of young lady prisoners she fondly referred to as her daughters.

Margaret and Willa thought hard about selling the flowing hair coin, but finally decided they couldn't—that coin was lucky. Jon and Connie Larkspur were happy with that decision, though Jon said he thought it would be a good idea going forward NOT to stick it in any more diapers, which made them all laugh hysterically at one of their many Sunday supper get-togethers.

Tizzy still had her life to live, which meant lots of trucking jobs, but she came back to the farm whenever she could to check in on Margaret and Willa and the animals—whom she had also grown to love more than she ever thought possible. When Tizzy was visiting, she and Dally were inseparable—where Tizzy went, Dally followed. And Tizzy would often marvel, "I swear that little cow understands every word I say." Tizzy had never had so much as a fish growing up, so this was all very new and wonderful for her. And for the cows too. When they saw Tizzy's big eighteen-wheeler come over the hill, they all came running.

And another thing: Tizzy had saved a lot of money over the years. It had been easy to do, she said, because she'd had "nothin' and nobody to spend it on." And soon she insisted that Margo and Willa accept a loan so they could spruce the farm up.

So Margaret and Willa rented a motorhome and moved into it while they bulldozed the house and the barn and every other shack and shed to the ground, not to mention towing Harp's old blue drinking truck to the wrecker's. Then they had another giant bonfire and invited the Starks to come and watch all those bad memories go up in flames.

They built the new barn first, so the animals would have somewhere warm in time for winter. The kittens were happy to nestle back into all the bales of hay stored up in the loft, although they loved being wherever Margaret was, like her own personal cheering section. Orange Cat was happy to lie in the sun and lick her paws. With no one chasing her anymore, or trying to murder her kittens, she felt safe for the first time in her life—and so did Margaret.

Margaret had always dreamed of living in a log house with a big wraparound porch. When she discovered that her father, Jon, had worked in construction for years, she enlisted him to oversee building it. He was too damn old to swing a hammer himself, he said, but he had some sons-in-law who were more than happy to help.

Willa became a bit of a celebrity at school. Everybody within a two-hundred-mile radius had heard about her solving the kidnapping and being reunited with her mother, and about the Bittlemores nearly killing Ms. Bevan. It took some time for things to settle down, but then summer came and went, and they did, eventually.

The big surprise was that Carol actually enjoyed being the assistant coach of the Backhills girls' basketball team. She and Ms. Bevan made a good team, and not just because Carol did all the whistle blowing until Ms. Bevan's jaw recovered. The doctors had had to wire it shut so it didn't heal crooked.

Once the wires came off, Ms. Bevan signed up for karate classes in the basement of the United church. She thought it would be a good idea to learn a few self-defence moves in light of everything that had happened.

Despite the bathroom detention, her broken nose and her come-to-Jesus moment about her home life, Nola was still Nola—mean and sort of nice in equal measure. One big difference? She and her flock made a vow to leave Willa and Carol alone and only pick on other mean people, which seemed to work out quite well for the most part.

Carol's parents started a small fudge business in their garage. Mr. Stark never ate the stuff himself, his health being what it was, but he sure loved to whip up walnut, double-chocolate cherry, Boston cream pie and rum raisin blocks of the *Best Damn Fudge You'll Ever Eat*, which was the slogan he painted on the sign hanging outside their house. They sold out of their fudge every damn weekend, to the welcome surprise of Mrs. Stark, who was thrilled to be making a profit from one of her grandmother's recipes.

Berle and Crilla were happier than they'd ever been. Dally stopped stuttering.

They enjoyed long, lazy days, with more hay than they could eat and more clean, cold water than they could drink. Berle's tail stump didn't hurt anymore either, although she still sometimes felt like her old tail was still there, swishing flies away.

Just for laughs, and maybe to stay in practice, Crilla spelled words out in the dirt every once in a while, things like I LOVE U and SMILE and (one of her favourites) HAPPY COWS. Willa and Margaret knew she was doing it, but they never told another soul. None of them needed a bunch of people flocking to the farm to see a cow that could write in the dirt.

Randy Tripp threw a big party for Constable Oldman, and gave a speech in which he told her, "You've put us on the map, Bev, and everyone here is over-the-moon proud of you."

The constable who had solved a major cold case made all the local papers, and there was even an article in the *Toronto Sun*, one of her hometown newspapers. Bev was happy that her parents saw her redeem herself from the "shooting the thumb off" incident back in her training days. Her dad had wanted her to quit right then and there, but now he was glad she hadn't.

And it turned out that Bev had grown to love Black Diamond and wasn't in a hurry to move on any time soon. Captain Tripp said she was welcome to stay as long as she wanted, joking that "Those city guys will just have to wait their turn." All the other folks at the station had chipped in to buy her a box of red wine and a fancy flashlight that had a pepper spray attachment on the opposite end. She hoped she would never have to use the pepper spray part of it.

Connie and Jon floated on a cloud for months. They had their Rose back, or rather their Margaret. They didn't think they'd ever get used to calling her that, but that didn't matter. Being reunited with their daughter was the most wonderful thing in the whole world. The icing on the cake was their new granddaughter.

Margaret and Willa showed up one afternoon with a special surprise. Willa had a big grin on her face as her mother handed Grandma Larkspur an envelope.

"What's this?" Connie said as she unfolded the stiff paper.

"Well," Margaret said, "I've legally changed my name back to Rose Larkspur. And this young lady here"—Willa grinned even wider—"is now officially Miss Mayvale Larkspur."

Tears filled their eyes as the three women hugged each other tightly. Then they went inside to tell Jon.

You could hear them laughing and talking all the way down the road.

acknowledgements

This story has been living in my head for so long, I can barely separate what is real and what I've imagined anymore. I loved getting to spend the last thirteen or fourteen years with the Bittlemores, even the nasty ones. Now that the novel is done, they feel like relatives I don't get to see much—or in Harp and his missus's case maybe want to see much—anymore.

I started this book all those years ago in a garage in Nashville that had been converted into a guest cottage. I remember the exact hot, humid day, and the beads of condensation dripping down my pop bottle. I didn't know what I was doing. I had never written a novel before, and wasn't so experienced even as a memoir writer back then. I wrote both *Feeding My Mother* and *If I Knew Then* after I started this book.

But I kept coming back to the eighty or ninety pages I had written, picking away at a story that I knew like the inside of my own eyeballs. Finishing it was very emotional. I really don't know if it's good or bad or somewhere in between, but I loved every minute of writing it. *The Bittlemores* carried me past both my parents' deaths, COVID lockdown, a breakup, and finding sobriety; it was like an old friend I kept sitting down with for company and solace.

If I'm honest, I don't have a lot of people to thank. My friends have been asking me how I was doing with this book for over a decade, and none of them doubted I could get it done—so I sincerely thank them all for their cheerleading and their eyerolls when I told them I was still at it. Bev and Lisa and Theresa and Kees and Cynthia and Chris . . . it really did become a running joke.

Allan Reid. I wouldn't be doing any of this had it not been for you.

Bruce Allen, for sending me down a literary path to begin with. You really encouraged me to write, and I don't think I would have without you always saying, "Why the hell not!" Indeed. Thank you.

Nigel Stoneman, I could not have done this at all without your steady hand and your knowledge of the publishing world. The vast amount of experience you shared with me month after month, year after year, was so invaluable. "JUST SEND IT OFF," you said. I remember that phone call like it was this morning. You are more dear to me than you could possibly know. You and Charlie and your mom and Ann and Nelly and Dorset and Daisy and Dolly and Belle and Greta and Midi and Poppy.

And Anne Collins, my steadfast editor and slayer of words, you are just magnificent. How you made sense of everything will always remain a mystery to me. I've never been so scared and excited all at the same time. Your years of poring over good books and bad books and hopeful books and lost books and tangled books and confusing books—all of that culminated in you being able to push me over that hill that writers climb to feel like they just might belong. This is your book as much as it is mine. You're an honorary Bittlemore, Anne, the long-lost cousin who lives in an old house with a lot of cats (not really, but you know what I mean). I am endlessly grateful.

To everyone at Penguin Random House Canada—the incredible art department, the sales team, the publisher, Sue Kuruvilla, and the editorial staff of Random House Canada, the audio group, the publicity and marketing people—and to the bookstores, and to all the fans who have followed me through these many years and supported me every step of the way: Thank you from the bottom of my heart.

JANN ARDEN is a singer, songwriter, actor, author and social media star. The celebrated multi-platinum, award-winning artist was inducted into the Canadian Music Hall of Fame in 2021. She continues to record and tour, and in 2022 released her fifteenth album, *Descendant*. She has written four books, including a memoir of her early life and path to music, *Falling Backwards*, and her two #1 bestsellers, *Feeding My Mother* and *If I Knew Then*. She is the star of her own hit TV sitcom, *Jann*, which debuted in 2019 and recently aired its third season. She also hosts the weekly *Jann Arden Podcast*, exploring what makes humans authentically themselves. *The Bittlemores* is her first novel.